The Cornish *Lady*

NICOLA PRYCE trained as a nurse at St Bartholomew's Hospital in London. She has always loved literature and completed an Open University degree in Humanities. She is a qualified adult literacy support volunteer and lives with her husband in the Blackdown Hills in Somerset. Together they sail the south coast of Cornwall in search of adventure.

The Cornish Lady

NICOLA PRYCE

CORVUS

First published in paperback in Great Britain in 2019 by Corvus,
an imprint of Atlantic Books Ltd.

Copyright © Nicola Pryce, 2019

The moral right of Nicola Pryce to be identified as the author
of this work has been asserted by her in accordance with the
Copyright, Designs and Patents Act of 1988.

1 3 5 7 9 10 8 6 4 2

A CIP catalogue record for this book is available from the British Library.

Paperback ISBN: 978 1 78649 385 9
E-Book ISBN: 978 1 78649 386 6

Printed and bound by CPI Group (UK) Ltd, Croydon, CR0 4YY

Corvus
An imprint of Atlantic Books Ltd
Ormond House
26–27 Boswell Street
London
WC1N 3JZ

www.corvus-books.co.uk

For my Irish mother,
Moyna Snelson

Family Tree

TRURO

PERREN PLACE, PYDAR STREET

Silas Lilly   m.   Jane O'Leary
b.1736   b.1751 d.1789

Angelica   Edgar
b.1774   b.1776

Lady Boswell	*Friend of Silas Lilly*
Sir Jacob Boswell	*Friend of Edgar Lilly*
Molly	*Housekeeper*
Grace	*Maid*
Henry Trevelyan	*Visiting coachman*

TRURO THEATRE

Theodore Gilmore	*Actor / Proprietor of theatre troupe*
Kitty Gilmore	*Actress*
Geryn	*Actor*
Hannah	*Actress*
Flora	*Actress*

TRENWYN HOUSE

Lord William Carew   m.   Lady Clarissa Godolphin
b.1735   b.1740

William	Charles	George	Henry	Frederick	Amelia
b.1760	b.1761	b.1762	b.1764	b.1767	b.1774
m.	m.			m.	
Cordelia	Catherine			Charity	
Polgas	Malory			Cavendish	
b.1770	b.1770			b.1772	

William Henry   Charles   Frederick
b.1790 b.1792   b.1794   b.1795

Admiral Sir Alexander Pendarvis	*Friend of the family*
George Godwin	*Prize agent*
Daniel Maddox	*Plantsman*
Jethro	*Groundsman*
Bethany	*Maid*
Moses	*Gardener*
Capitaine Pierre de la Croix	*French captain on parole*

FALMOUTH

Lord Dexter Entworth	*MP / JP / Local landowner*
Robert Fox	*Ship broker / Importer / US Consul*
Elizabeth Fox	*Philanthropist*
Luke Bohenna	*Physician*
Mary Bohenna	*Friend of Hermia*
Eleanor Penrose	*Concert pianist*
Joseph Emidy	*Ship's fiddler*
Sir Edward Pellew	*Captain of HMS Indefatigable*

PENDENNIS CASTLE

Captain Fenshaw	*Acting Captain of Company of Invalids*
Isaac Evans	*Private*
Patrick Mallory	*Private*
Martha Selwyn	*Prison visitor*

Stay, O sweet and do not rise!
The light that shines comes from thine eyes;
The day breaks not: it is my heart,
Because that you and I must part.

John Donne

Prologue

The Play House, Exeter
Wednesday 27th July 1796

Dearest Angelica,

We leave for Truro tomorrow. The performance next Saturday starts at 7:30 p.m. Come round the back so no one sees you — Theo will be waiting for you at 6:30. Mary Bohenna is also expected.

Yours in anticipation,
Kitty Gilmore

Trenwyn House, Trenwyn
Thursday 28th July 1796

My dearest Angelica,

Think no more of it — don't blame yourself for a moment. We understand you must host your father's dinner on Saturday. One day's delay will make no difference, though we are impatient to have you here.

Until Sunday, Your dearest friend,
Amelia

Dearest Amelia,

And now I hear Father expects us to leave very early on Sunday morning, so I'm afraid you must expect me with the dawn! How can Father think that it is in any way polite? How I hate these last-minute changes.

Your dearest friend,
Angelica

Trenwyn House, Trenwyn
Friday 29th July 1796

Dear Mr Lilly,

I will not hear otherwise — you must allow us to collect Angelica. Your journey to Bristol is quite far enough without adding the distance to Trenwyn. My coach will arrive at ten o'clock.

Yours in friendship,
Clarissa Carew

My planning had gone smoothly — no need to forge signatures or change dates. Lady Clarissa had not written *Sunday* and Father would never think different; Molly would be angry, but she would soon come round.

She Stoops to Conquer lay open in my hands but already I had it by heart; every line on every page, just like my dearest mother.

Enter Stage

Chapter One

Perren Place, Pydar Street, Truro
Saturday 30th July 1796, 10:30 a.m.

Above us, the storm clouds seemed to be lifting. 'Father, perhaps you shouldn't delay any longer. Maybe you should go while there's this break in the rain?'

Father frowned, buttoning up his travelling coat. It was black like all his clothes, well cut and made of the finest quality, but plain and unadorned – almost too severe. He seemed more nervous than usual, all too aware of Lady Boswell's growing displeasure.

'No, no...we must wait and see you safely off.' He reread the letter in his hand. 'Lady Clarissa definitely says the carriage would be here for *ten o'clock*. They must be delayed on account of the rain.'

Lady Boswell shrugged her elegant shoulders. 'Is Angelica's comfort to be considered and not my own? Dear me, perhaps I was mistaken to accept your kind offer...perhaps I'd have been better hiring my own post-chaise?' She smiled and I watched Father melt. She had it to perfection: the coy rise to her eyebrow, the sudden pout accentuating her high cheek bones. 'Your horses are impatient to be off…and we've such a long way to go.'

As if in league, the horses lurched against their harness and Father reopened his fob watch. 'Don't wait, Father. Lady Clarissa's coach can't be much longer – you'll probably pass it on the new bridge.' I caught Lady Boswell's sideways glance, her obvious triumph, and an icy hand clutched my heart.

Silas Lilly was certainly a good catch – in his sixties, he had the energy and enthusiasm of a man twenty years his junior. His greying hair was still abundant, his shoulders straight and strong. He might be a little rough around the edges for the politest society, but that was not going to stop her. Wealth was wealth, and she was clearly prepared to overlook the fact that he had been born the son of a foundry worker. Perhaps she was thinking of teaching him her manners: her ability to walk right past people in need, her inability to think of anyone's comfort except her own.

The luggage was piled high on the roof, secured by a heavy tarpaulin. Almost everyone was going – Father's groom, his valet, his clerk.

'Two months is a long time to be away from home,' I whispered.

He had chosen his strongest mares. The stables were now empty, the grooms taking the remaining horses to our farm on the moors. Molly and Grace were to clean the house from top to bottom and I would spend the rest of the summer with Lady Clarissa and Amelia at Trenwyn House. By the end of two months, Father would have negotiated a new smelting house in South Wales, the horses would be rested, the house sparkling, and Lady Clarissa would have secured my engagement to Lord Entworth.

Only Lady Boswell was beyond my control.

We always attracted onlookers when the carriage left, but today the crowd seemed distant and hostile. They stood watching in silence, hunching together with stooped shoulders. Our house was one of the larger properties on Pydar Street; it had thick cob walls and stone mullion windows, heavy crossbeams and a grand wooden staircase. The thatch had long since been replaced by slates, our five brick chimneys dominating the roofline. Seventy years ago, it was considered the best Truro could offer, but the road was now too busy, our lack of privacy causing Father concern.

A year ago, Father would have left among smiles and waves, small boys chasing after the carriage, but this group stood bedraggled and grey-faced, staring at us from beneath the shelter of an overhanging branch. Their clothes seemed to hang off them, filthy rags wound round their feet in place of shoes.

Molly sighed, shifting her stiff hip.

'Can you find them something to eat?' I asked.

She nodded. 'I'll make them some soup from the leftover mutton.'

Father was helping Lady Boswell into the carriage but at least they were leaving.

'I don't like this one little bit,' I whispered.

'Nor me neither – ye know what they say about two people goin' on a journey…' She shook a crease from her dress. In thirty years, she had never allowed anyone to see her wearing her apron at the front door, always leaving it on a large hook behind the kitchen door. 'They say her first husband was too old to survive the wedding night…an' her second husband gambled away all the money. They say she's not a penny to her name.'

Lady Boswell's eyes were accentuated by the royal blue of her velvet travelling jacket. Her hair was the colour of corn, her mouth reddened with pigmented beeswax. The coy smile was back, a slight flutter to her eyelashes. Her hand with its frill of Belgian lace lingered on Father's and my uneasiness spiralled.

'He's only taking her to her sister – then he's going up to Bristol,' I said with more hope than conviction.

Molly's mouth tightened. 'If ye ask me, she looks like the cat that's got the cream…'

'Oh, don't say that.'

Molly was hiding her dislike of Lady Boswell very well, smiling and nodding to Father as he approached, and I knew to do the same.

Father snapped his watch open and shut. 'I really think we ought to leave, Angelica, though I'd rather see you off first… the roads are awash and I'd like to get through the turnpike before the next shower. But…well…give Lady Clarissa my best regards…and…and, well, I'm sure she'll be successful.' He lowered his voice. 'The man's enamoured of you. You've bewitched him – he'll have no other.' He nodded and bowed, my stiff and formal father, never bending to kiss me, nor chucking me under the chin, nor pinching my cheek, nor showing me any love; my prosperous father, already treating me like I was the next Lady Entworth. 'You've packed my address in Swansea?'

I nodded. 'I'll write and tell you everything – Amelia says Lady Clarissa wants to teach me how to play cricket!'

The hard lines round his mouth softened for the first time in seven years, four months and three days. He even seemed to smile. 'Ah, cricket! It's a long time since I've played cricket.' He seemed embarrassed by his sudden outburst, glancing quickly at the carriage. 'We'll be off then. Take care, Angelica. Goodbye, Molly – two months of no cookin' will do you the world of good. Almost a holiday!'

She curtseyed stiffly. 'Ye think cleaning's a holiday, do ye, Mr Lilly? I'll be thin as a rake when ye return!'

Our smiles were as false as the silk flowers on Lady Boswell's over-large hat. Father and Lady Boswell were in the carriage, the others squeezing next to the driver or balancing among the boxes on the back seat, and with the door firmly shut their sudden intimacy was hard to witness.

'What *do* they say about two people going on a journey?'

Molly's lips tightened. 'They say they come back married.'

'They better not!' I stared at the receding coach. Father had not looked me in the eyes, neither today nor last Sunday when Lady Boswell had taken my place in church, returning the congregation's astonished stares with her particular look of triumph.

Molly slipped her arm through mine. 'We mustn't blame him, my love. Yer father's a full-blooded man, an' she's very beautiful – though no one can ever come close to yer dearest mamma.'

'Father has…' I could barely say the words. 'Father has stopped his payments to *that woman.*'

I knew she would sniff with disapproval. 'Has he now! Well, that's a sure sign – pigs will fly if Lady Boswell don't get her way.' Her voice softened. 'But think on it, my love… if ye're to marry Lord Entworth, ye father will be all alone an' you'd only fret – whether ye like it or not, someone's got to take yer dear mamma's place.'

'No one can take her place.' My desire to cry was almost overwhelming. Father did not know half of what I did – giving alms on his behalf, generous donations to the hospital board. He had no notion I knew all his business and could forge his signature, no idea I knew where to find the keys to his desk. That was how I knew he kept a fancy woman.

In the sun, the houses of Truro would shine like gold, but today the street looked grey, a steady stream of rainwater overflowing the gutter on the other side. The profusion of carts never lessened; the constant tread of mules on their way to and from the mines. If it was not coal or tin weighing them down, it was furze or manure, the mules thinner now, in need of oats. I held my handkerchief to my nose.

Mamma had loved this house, and I loved it too, but Molly was right: the smell from the tannery *was* getting worse. The huge pits where they washed the fleeces and scraped the hides lay overflowing and stagnant, the smell so bad it made grown men vomit. Some said the water was tainted, that the putrid overflow was contaminating the leat running alongside our garden. Some said it was the cause of the sickness.

Maybe our house had seen better days, but it was right

in the centre of town and I loved living so close to St Mary's church. Everything was within walking distance. The assembly rooms were just round the corner, so too, the new library. Best of all, the wharf was so close. I loved the sound of the seagulls, the smell of the ships, the wind blowing salty air up the river. I loved hearing the merchants haggling on the quayside, watching the huge pulleys lift the cargo from out of a hold. I loved the bustle, the smell of pitch and tar and the songs the sailors sang as they scrubbed the decks.

Father's carriage had been blocking the road. Carts were backed up on both sides, the drivers scowling and shouting as they tried to get past. The market would be in full swing; I had watched the boys drive their geese along the street, heard the bleating of the sheep as they passed beneath my window. Pigs were squealing, hens squawking, the market sellers' cries echoing down the street.

Grace stood behind me, all round-eyed and rosy-cheeked. 'Grace, there's obviously been a misunderstanding. Take the luggage back inside. Leave the trunk in the hall but if you wouldn't mind taking the valises and hatboxes back to my room?'

Molly's face turned ashen. 'But, Angelica...Lady Clarissa's carriage will be here any moment...' She knew me too well and her hands flew to her bosom. 'Oh, dear Lord...what have you done?'

'Lady Clarissa isn't sending her coach until tomorrow,' I whispered. '*Kitty Gilmore's* in Truro tonight, but I suspect you already know that. I'm sure that's why Father was so insistent I left today. We're going to the theatre tonight, Molly – both of us. You've got a ticket for the front row, and I'm to meet Theo round the back. I've arranged everything. Nothing can stop us.'

Black clouds were circling the town, letting no light through the small leaded windows. Molly had her hands full, so I lit two candles, quickly returning to the pine table and the well-thumbed script. 'So Tony Lumpkin *tricks* Mr Marlow into believing Mr Hardcastle's an innkeeper and Miss Hardcastle's the *maid*. And she goes along with—'

Molly sniffed. 'I don't like it.' Her voice was clipped, her lips tightly pursed. 'Not one little bit.'

'No, wait…It's good because Mr Marlow finds talking to high-born ladies very difficult.'

'Ye know very well what I mean. I don't like ye lyin' to yer father – nor ye lyin' to Lady Clarissa.' She chopped an onion, thrusting it into the huge pot. Wiping her eyes on the corner of her apron, she shook her head again. 'It's deceitful an' no good will come of it. Ye'll be seen! Honest to God, ye'll be seen, an' ye father will think me part of the plan. Ye know full well Mr Lilly's rules about the theatre. And as fer ye writin' to *Kitty Gilmore* – that was the first thing yer father forbid!' She reached for another onion, giving it less mercy.

I knew Molly would not hold out for long. 'I really *won't* be seen – I'm to go round the back and Theo will let me in. You don't need to come; but I won't abandon Mamma's friends like Father has. They're dead to him – just like Mamma is – dead and dispelled from his thoughts.' I fought the lump in

12

my throat. 'Mrs Bohenna's going to be there, so you must come – Mamma's two best friends – Kitty Gilmore and Mary Bohenna. You haven't seen either since Mamma died…'

'Oh, my love…ye know I want to see them.'

'Well, there you are. Anyway, even if Father *was* here, I'd still go. I'd just climb out of the window.'

Molly placed her palms on the scrubbed table. Her eyes caught mine and she took a deep breath. 'I'm not sayin' I'm not comin'…course I'm comin'…ye don't think I'd give up a chance like this, do you? It's just the shock…an' the worry Lady Clarissa will find out.'

Dearest Molly, always my willing accomplice. 'No one will recognize me and no one will ever know. I've planned everything – I've kept back a charity dress and I've stitched a huge veil on that old bonnet. No one will know it's me – nothing can go wrong.'

Sudden footsteps caught our attention and we turned to see young Grace hurtling down the stairs, almost falling into the kitchen. 'Miss Lilly…quick…it's Mr Lilly. Not *old* Mr Lilly…but Young Mr Lilly…'

Molly's hand flew to her chest and I slammed the script shut, pushing it beneath an empty basket. 'Edgar? He can't be…he's in Oxford.'

'Sir Jacob's come as well. They're just gettin' out…'

'Not Jacob Boswell. Not him as well!' Molly's face mirrored mine. Mother and son – two prongs in the same fork.

Chapter Two

I ran along the hall, pulling open the front door. Edgar had stepped from the carriage and was looking up at the house, his fine cut-away jacket and embroidered silk waistcoat the height of fashion, but he looked thin, his face deathly pale beneath his unruly black curls.

'Edgar! What are you doing here?'

I ran down the steps, flinging myself into his arms, horrified to feel his shoulder blades through his jacket. His breath smelled of tobacco, I felt a fine tremor in his hands.

'Father not here?' He seemed strangely nervous, looking over my shoulder at the empty doorway.

'You've just missed him – he left this morning. He's gone— On business.' I stopped myself just in time; Father's plan to build a smelter in South Wales was to be kept secret at all cost.

'Well, never mind, we did our best.' He kept hold of my hands, turning me round. 'Let me look at you – goodness, Angelica, you're every inch the lady. *Lady Entworth*, if I'm to believe the rumours.'

Perhaps he was ill. Perhaps that was why he had come home from Oxford. Jacob Boswell certainly looked well. He had his mother's extravagant taste in clothes, her thick blonde hair and her aristocratic hauteur. He was laughing, smiling down at me, the Boswell blue eyes meant to be working their magic, yet I would not look at him, acknowledging him only with the briefest of nods.

He shouted to the coachman: 'Take the carriage round the back...' He was so assured, looking up at the house as if his mother had already sold it. 'There's stabling round the back – plenty of room for the coach.'

His assurance startled me. I had not seen him for nearly a year but, at twenty, he had become a commanding figure, a lion where my brother was a mouse. I was two years their senior, this was still my house, and by the way he was behaving he had to understand that. The wheels of the carriage were muddy, the door newly splattered, yet the horses looked lively and there was no sign of luggage. Edgar saw my frown.

He glanced at Jacob. 'We've left our luggage at the inn... it's by the river. We arrived late last night and thought it best not to disturb you. We've been given very fine rooms and we thought we'd stay there...' His laugh had changed. A year ago it would have been a proper laugh but now it was a high-pitched giggle and my heart froze. His cheeks looked gaunt, his heavy black brows too dark for his face. He saw Molly and ran up the steps. 'Molly, lovely to see you. How are you?'

I caught her look of horror. 'Goodness...Edgar Lilly, ye need fattening up. Has Reverend Johns not been feedin' ye? Come here, my love, yer father's not here so we can have a

15

hug.' She clasped him to her bosom. 'What a shame ye missed him…he'll be that sorry. Come, let's see what I can find ye to eat…'

Jacob Boswell was about to follow but I held up my hand and his eyes caught mine. 'Angelica…your anger's misplaced. It's not of my doing.'

His jacket was blue silk, his waistcoat heavily embroidered. His cravat was pinned with a silver brooch, matching silver buttons on the cuffs of his jacket. He looked well fed, staring down at me with a look of insolence, and I tried to keep calm. 'A year ago you joined my brother in his lodgings and his expenses doubled. Father's fondness for your mother persuaded him to increase Edgar's allowance and yet again, his expenses doubled. Six months ago, Edgar writes to tell me of his gambling debts. *His* debts, Sir Jacob, when I know full well he does not gamble, or rather, he never gambled *when he was here*. I paid them, at once, without Father knowing, and then I received another letter. Another twenty pounds needed – on top of the *already* increased monthly allowance.'

A smile curled his lips. 'Oxford's an expensive place…'

'So it seems. And yet, there are no bills for books, just bills for dining out? How much claret does my brother need? No, don't answer.' I looked up. The coachman had turned round and was staring at me. I lowered my voice. 'Now you take rooms in an inn instead of staying here? And who's paying the hire of this carriage? I suppose I must expect both accounts?'

A year ago, I might have smiled back into his handsome face, framed by its golden halo, but not now. Now, his influence over my brother seemed almost sinister; a huge, golden Apollo, overshadowing him with his brilliance. If Edgar had come on his own I might have had a chance to get my brother back, but not now.

The coachman was sitting on his seat, straight-backed, staring ahead, and I called up to him. 'I'm afraid the grooms have all gone to the country so there's no one here to help you. There's plenty of stabling – you've all the choice you need. There's straw to be had but no oats – they've taken the oats with them.'

'Thank you. I'll see what I can find.' His heavily layered coat looked damp, his two hands in their thick leather gloves gripping the harness as the horses shook against their bridles. His face was slender, sunburned, his chin covered in rough stubble. Beneath his wide-brimmed hat his brown hair was cut short, his round-rimmed glasses taking me by surprise. 'Oats are in heavy demand – I'm not surprised they've taken them.'

He was softly spoken, his tone respectful. He was clearly educated, his high cheek bones and round-rimmed glasses giving him the look of a scholar, and I glanced back. 'Let me know if there's anything you need.'

'Thank you, Miss Lilly.' Through his glasses, his eyes held mine – fiercely intelligent eyes, fringed with dark lashes – and my heart jolted. 'Do I know you?'

'No, Miss Lilly. My name's Henry Trevelyan.'

I remembered names and I remembered faces and now I looked more carefully, I could see I was mistaken. 'Don't draw water from the leat, Mr Trevelyan – we think it's tainted. Only use water from the pump at the front.'

17

He touched his hat and I turned to see Jacob Boswell towering over Grace. He was smirking, raising his eyebrows, clearly enjoying her discomfort, and my dislike of him spiralled. Grace's cheeks were crimson and I put my hand on her shoulder, ushering her inside. Behind us, Jacob Boswell's laughter echoed round the hall.

'Oh, Angelica, we could be such friends…if only you didn't think so ill of me.'

We ate at five. Mamma's silver serving dishes glittered in the candlelight; the birds on her Sèvres china placed exactly how she liked them. Her finest crystal glasses glowed red with Father's best claret, the centrepiece of fruit at just the right height. Edgar slumped even lower in his chair. 'I see Father hasn't changed anything…'

'Why should he?'

I bit back my annoyance. This was Mamma's room; Mamma's beautiful green wallpaper with her matching silk stripes on her mahogany chairs. The gold mirror above the mantelpiece had been her pride and joy; her favourite chair still by the window. On good days, sunshine flooded the leaded windows, lighting the faces in the portraits opposite, but today the heavily laden sky filled the room with gloom. If she had lived, Mamma could have had everything ten times over. She could have had her grand house in the country, any number of carriages. She could have boasted a town house bigger than Mansion House.

Jacob Boswell refilled his plate but Edgar had no appetite,

nibbling half-heartedly on a chicken leg and reaching for his wine. Dark curls lay limp against his face, his gaze listless. He seemed reluctant to talk and when he did, he kept deferring to Jacob. I could not eat, but listened in mounting dread. They had not come straight from Oxford; they had been away some time, staying with a friend.

'Did you not think to tell me you were coming?'

Jacob Boswell did not even look up. 'We thought we deserved a spot of fishing and shooting...' He winked at Edgar. 'But we're bored with country pursuits...we've come to town for sport of a different kind.'

I could feel my cheeks redden. That man had to be stopped. They both had to be stopped. 'You're meant to be in Oxford, Edgar – having private tuition. Father went to a lot of trouble to find Reverend John. He's very well considered...many people wanted his expertise. Father's gone to a lot of expense...'

Jacob Boswell must have caught the steel in my voice. He put down his napkin, flicking the lace at his sleeve. 'We've been granted a small *holiday*, Angelica – it's our summer break. We are allowed out *every now and then*. Anyway, we're on our way to Oxford – another week and Reverend John will have Edgar straight back in harness.'

Edgar's cheeks looked sallow in the candlelight; he seemed distracted, restless, a strange nervousness making him fidgety. 'Straight back in harness,' he said sullenly, nothing like the brother I knew and loved.

Jacob Boswell pushed his plate away and reached for a folded newspaper, leafing idly through the pages. 'Lord

Carew's won first prize for his Devonshire bull – that should put him in good humour for your visit.' The next page held an advertisement for Kitty's troupe and my heart began thumping. It immediately caught his attention as I knew it would.

'Here's something of interest...' he said, sitting forward, clasping the newspaper in both hands. *Truro's very own theatre is playing host to Mrs Kitty Gilmore's highly acclaimed production of* She Stoops to Conquer *by Oliver Goldsmith. Mrs Gilmore, a much-loved star of the London stage, has taken this production all over Britain, and we are honoured to welcome her.* Well, that can't be missed, can it?'

Edgar's eyes caught mine. 'Kitty Gilmore?' His mouth hardened; a slight quiver in his voice. 'Mother's friend, *Kitty Gilmore*? No wonder Father left in such a hurry.'

Lady Boswell's eyes were in the room and I knew to be careful. 'You know we're forbidden the theatre.'

Edgar stared at Mamma's empty chair. 'And we mustn't go against Father's wishes, must we?' The lines round his mouth tightened. 'We're to *work...work...work*. We're to be as miserable as sin and take no pleasure...'

The bitterness in his voice sliced my heart. Jacob Boswell was leaning back in his chair, raising his smug eyebrows.

'It's against Father's wishes,' I repeated. 'Anyway, I'm travelling tomorrow so I'm going to have an early night.'

'Oh, come on, Angelica. Where's your spirit?' Jacob Boswell sneered. 'I'll find us a way to get tickets.'

Edgar slammed his hands on the table. 'Christ, I need air...' He stood up, his chair clattering to the ground, his plate crashing into pieces on the flagstones. 'I can't breathe in this place…it's like a bloody tomb. Get the carriage – let's go where there's some life.' He kicked the fallen chair. 'It's nothing but a morgue…a bloody morgue.'

I got up, backing slowly away. Another plate was swept to the floor. Another and another. He seemed consumed by frenzy, his faced screwed tight. He reached the door and I called after him. 'Edgar – you should be in Oxford.'

He swung back, his sunken eyes burning mine. 'Christ, Angelica…what are you – my gaoler or something? Get the carriage, Jake – let's go where we're wanted.'

Through the silence, Grace cleared the table. She was just thirteen and her hands were trembling. My heart was still thumping from the violence of the quarrel but she looked petrified and I tried to reassure her. 'He's just not himself…I'm sorry, Grace, he should never have shouted like that.'

She took a deep breath. 'Wasn't that. I'd forgive Master Lilly anythin'.' She turned and my stomach tightened. 'Miss Lilly…ye know ye always tell us we should speak up? Well, Sir Jacob caught me unawares…he thrust himself against me…really thrust. Said 'twas an accident but he held me… here.' Her young face went scarlet as she pointed to her chest. ''Twas no accident…'twas really horrible…'

I gripped the table, trying to breathe. He was a bully, and bullies must be faced. *Your mother was a whore.* I was back in the school dormitory sitting on the iron bed, forcing back my tears. Mamma was a renowned actress, she was *not* a whore. She was beautiful and intelligent. Never shout back, that made them laugh louder– all of them sneering like Jacob Boswell, disdain dripping from their pedigree noses. Well, they would soon eat their words. When I was Lady Entworth, they would all eat their words.

Jacob Boswell's command rang across the cobbles – 'Coachman – bring the carriage to The Red Lion' – and I glanced out of the window. The coachman was reading beneath the overhang of the stable, quickly tucking a marker between the pages of his book. A frown creased his forehead; he placed the book in his waistcoat and reached for his coat. 'You're due at your sister's tonight, aren't you, Grace?' I said, watching the coachman from behind the green velvet curtain. 'Go at six, just as we arranged. If there are dishes left over you can wash them in the morning.'

'Thank ye, Miss Lilly…I'll try an' get them finished before I go.'

Molly came to my side, a huge tray held sideways against her hip. 'Three plates broke and two glasses.'

The coachman glanced in my direction and I drew quickly back. He was pulling on his gloves in no particular hurry and I bit my lip.

'Edgar didn't even say goodbye. He's changed so much.'

Molly, too, looked distraught. 'I remember the night he was born – the nights *both* of ye were born. I used to rock ye in yer cradles – sometimes long into the night. Yer dear mamma was so proud…wantin' to give ye everythin'.'

'She did give us everything – and she'd be furious at his rudeness.'

'He's young, Angelica, and young men don't like bein'

22

cooped up. I'd say he's over wrought, poor boy – next week he'll be back in Oxford, reclinin' all that Latin.'

Despite my sadness, I burst out laughing. '*Declining*, Molly. It was the Romans who reclined.'

'Declinin', reclinin' – it's all the same. What that boy needs is fresh air an' good food…an' to get away from that leech, Jacob Boswell. He's bad, that man. Like a rotten apple.'

Molly wrapped her cloak around her, pulling the lace on my bonnet to well below my chin. She locked the back door, giggling nervously. 'There, 'tis done…now don't ye go gettin' seen, young lady…' She was wearing her Sunday best, a tinge of rouge on her cheeks.

It was not the first time I had slipped from a house at night and it would not be the last. At school, I would leave the dormitory and run silently down the vast staircase, squeezing out of the small, top window in the laundry room. Through the branches of my favourite tree, I would watch the watery badgers playing in the moonlight, hoping, praying, that Mamma was somehow looking down on me. I would feel her with me, hear her soft Irish accent, and, through my tears, I would promise to fulfil her dearest wish.

My charity gown was drab and ill-fitting. 'No one will recognize me,' I said with absolute certainty. I glanced up. 'There's a patch of blue in the west – this drizzle might clear.' I opened my umbrella. 'We'll go through the back gate and cut along the leat.'

'The road's already blocked.' Molly slipped her arm

through mine, smiling up at me. 'There's not been a crowd like this since Sarah Siddons came fer the theatre's grand openin'.' She glanced into her embroidered bag. 'Honest, Angelica – am I really to sit in the front row?'

Chapter Three

Our land at the back stretched down to the leat. We had an orchard, a large kitchen garden. Geese grazed the grass, hens pecking and clucking amongst the mares in the stable, but with the chickens locked away and the horses at the farm, the yard seemed eerily quiet. 'Come, I've got the key.'

Mamma had once thought to have a fountain built, a rose garden, even a terrace, but I think she loved the simplicity of the garden. A dovecote stood among a jumble of shrubs, an upturned wheelbarrow, a lone blackbird singing from an overgrown hedge. My hem brushed against some lavender and scent filled the air. A huge brick wall skirted the boundary, the back gate stiff on its hinges. The lock was rusty, the key difficult to turn. 'We'll follow the leat and double back so it looks like we've come from the quayside.'

I felt breathless, excitement making me walk too fast. Molly's hip must have been paining her but her smile matched mine. The water in the leat looked murky; the grey drizzle making the path slippery and I held her elbow, ushering her along a back passage where the slops were thrown. I held my breath. 'Mind – lift your skirt. Thank goodness we're wearing stout shoes.' The path widened and we stepped on to the smart new cobbles of King Street.

A long line of carriages stood at a standstill, the coachman shouting and protesting as people pushed against the horses. The line led almost out of town, expensive hats leaning from the windows, feathers fluttering as angry shouts rang down the street. People were disembarking, deciding to walk rather than wait, and the coachmen were despairing. The crowd was growing by the moment, the excitement palpable.

Everyone was laughing, smiling, dressed in their finest, linking arms as they walked up King Street and into High Cross. This was the new Truro: elegant houses with their large sash windows sweeping majestically up to the assembly rooms, curving round to St Mary's church with its new iron railings. The queue to enter the theatre was thickening, everyone looking up at the symmetrical façade and imposing pediment, pointing to the circular reliefs of David Garrick and William Shakespeare. I pulled Molly aside. 'Here, take your ticket. There's a lot of people at the door – take care you don't get crushed.'

She nodded, her eyes wide with excitement. 'I'd no idea there'd be such a crowd.'

St Mary's church was just in front of me, the steeple pointing sharply into the grey sky. The clock struck the half-hour and I knew I must hurry.

I did not need to. Theodore Gilmore was waiting for me,

smoking his pipe by the back door. 'Oh, just wait till Kitty sees you.'

He was just as I remembered him – tall and well built, a slight stoop to his shoulders. He shut the door, ushering me along the crowded corridor, his Irish accent conjuring up a host of memories. 'Mind these steps...careful of this sharp corner – this shouldn't be here but there's no room back-stage. A couple more trunks...squeeze your way past these costumes.'

I dodged the painted sets, brushing against exotic velvets and furs. Rows of hats hung from hooks, swords sticking haphazardly out of boxes. The confined corridor smelled of grease and stale sweat, the heat making me catch my breath. People were calling, rushing from room to room. A young man shot past and nearly sent me flying.

'Hey, steady on.' Theodore shook his head. 'That's Geryn – he plays Tony Lumpkin. Kitty's in here...' He opened the door and stood smiling proudly. 'Here she is...'

Kitty Gilmore was at her dressing table and turned at my entrance. She was dressed as Mrs Hardcastle in a huge grey wig and an elaborately embroidered silk dress. Her face was painted white, her cheeks a livid red. She rose quickly, holding out her hands, and I lifted my veil.

'Angelica, my dearest, let me look at you.' She spun me round, tears in her eyes. 'How you've grown these last years...' Her voice softened. 'Goodness, my dear, you've become the image of your mother.'

I was lost for words, staring back at her. Mamma had loved her so completely. They were from the same small village in Ireland; they had run away together, been home-less together. They would have starved together, had it not been for Theodore Gilmore and his friends in the theatre. Both Mamma and Kitty had auditioned and both of them had been given parts. Kitty had soon married Theo but it was Mamma who had shone the brightest, Mamma who had taken London by storm. Seeing Kitty tore my heart.

'Thank you for sending me the script. I have the play by heart.'

Kitty Gilmore smiled with pleasure. 'Just listen to that diction! You're born for the stage, Angelica – born to recite Shakespeare.'

'I wish I could...' I stammered.

Her dark eyes seemed suddenly wistful. 'We've a full house. Theo's even had to turn people away...' She kept hold of my hands, drawing me back to her dressing table, staring at me from the mirror as she dabbed the perspiration from her top lip. The room was a jumbled mess: bottles and jars littered the table top, a pile of clothes spilled from her chair. It was cramped and crowded, two large vases of flowers in danger of toppling off the small table. The room smelled of lilies and greasepaint, the smoke from the tallow candles making it hard to breathe. 'We've taken this play all round the country...Is Molly round the front?'

I nodded as Theo drew out his watch. 'Forty-five minutes till curtain-up. Just the last stragglers coming in – most have taken their seats. They're enjoying the jugglers.' He was in his late fifties but showed no sign of slowing down. Like Kitty, he wore heavy make-up and a large grey wig. The lines on his forehead cut deep into his greasepaint. 'Flora's late *yet again*. This has to be the last time. I'll not be fooled with — there's plenty can take her role.' He snapped shut his watch, swinging round at the sound of running footsteps. 'Is that you, Flora?'

The footsteps stopped and Theo held the door open to a smiling young woman of about my age. Her dress looked shabby, a slight stain down the front; her hair was lank beneath her bonnet. She hiccoughed and laughed. 'Only ten minutes late...ten tiny...tiny little minutes. I'll be ready in no time.'

Her flushed face and shining eyes were not lost on Kitty. 'You've been drinking, Flora.' She slammed down her brush. 'What are the rules about drinking before a performance?'

The girl rolled her eyes. 'One drink...one *tiny*, *tiny* little drink an' one plate of oysters. I just stepped out for some fresh air and, *purely by chance*, got talking to some gentry who were comin' to the play. They said they'd bring me in their carriage and it was *them* that kept me.' She stood staring at Theo, her full red lips set in a sullen pout. 'I'll get changed right away...'

A bell clanged in the corridor and Theo frowned. 'You've got thirty minutes.' He held the door open, raising his eyes at Kitty. '*Purely by chance*,' he muttered.

Kitty's mouth hardened. 'The girl's a fool. She'll be out at the end of the season.' She added more red to her lips, tweaking a curl in her huge wig and tapped her fingernails on the dressing table. 'There, all set. That will just have to do.'

Theo was fumbling with the buttons on his waistcoat. 'I'll go front of stage and see to the lamps. The wheels are mended on the garden set, so no harm done. Everything's ready.'

Kitty stood to help him, doing up the long line of buttons with nimble fingers. 'Geryn back in good voice?'

'Never better.'

'There you are, then – nothing to worry about. We've worked hard for this.' She patted him affectionately on his chest, reaching up to kiss him on the lips. 'Off you go…we'll be right behind you.' She reached for her fan, stooping to smell the lilies, looking up at me through her heavy lashes. 'For a moment then, I thought you were Hermia. Honest, Angelica, you're her absolute image.' She linked her arm through mine. 'I still miss her, so much.'

'So do I,' I said, my tears welling. 'She would have loved this – Father left this morning.'

'Excellent. Mary Bohenna's coming too…'

'I haven't seen Mary Bohenna since Luke won his bursary and they left for London. I used to see her every day.'

'We were three Irish girls together, all of us as close as sisters. We were as poor as church mice, yet we never gave up hope. Mary was from the village twenty miles away – she had shoes, but your mother and I didn't.' She clasped her chest.

'Kitty, are you all right?'

She took a deep breath. 'Pre-theatre nerves…that's all. I never tell Theo I get nervous…but the truth is it never goes away.' She took another deep breath, exhaling through pursed lips. 'It's passing. Come, it's time to check everyone's in costume.'

Kitty held back the curtain. I was standing where Mamma would have stood, seeing what she would have seen; peeping excitedly round the side of the curtain, gazing at the sea of expectant faces. I never imagined the noise, the heat, the roar of voices. 'They're a rowdy crowd, all right…but they'll quieten once the music starts.'

The assembly room was transformed into a proper theatre. The front floorboards had been lifted and five musicians were settling themselves in the pit. I could see the top of a harp, a cello, two violins and a bugle. The chandeliers had every candle burning and lamps burned in a circle round the stage. People were crowded together in the top corridor, seats crammed into every available space. I could see red uniforms, blue uniforms, rows of ornate silk dresses. There were a host of familiar faces – Father's friends, the ladies from church, several from the hospital board.

Kitty pointed to a row of seats. 'There, those two in the middle. Look how far we've all come.'

I searched the crowd and my heart swelled. Mary Bohenna looked happy and prosperous, elegantly dressed in a blue dress with a fine set of feathers dancing in her hair. Her smile was every bit as lovely as I remembered. 'She looks so well… but…surely…that's Luke? Oh my goodness, you didn't tell me Luke would be here!'

'He's *Dr* Bohenna now, my love. They've left London and he's set up practice in Falmouth.'

I searched the face of my childhood friend. Seven years had changed him from a youth to a man – a serious man, with a furrowed brow and slightly receding hair. He had always looked studious but he had gained gravitas, a slight stoop to his shoulders. He was smartly dressed in dark but not sombre clothes, his white cravat tied in a simple bow. 'Falmouth? Then I might be able to see them. Perhaps I can ask Lady Clarissa to invite them to Trenwyn House?'

Kitty pinched my cheek. 'I'll speak plainly, my dear. Mary and I have had you in mind for Luke from the moment you were born.' She sounded so like Mamma with her lovely Irish lilt. 'It's time you were married – if your dear mother was still alive, she'd have seen to it long ago. But we're here and she's not, so it's time to take matters into our own hands. What is it, my dear?'

I shook my head, smiling, shrugging, feeling strangely like crying. 'I love Luke...I'll always love him, but I can't marry him.' Her face slackened beneath her make-up and I knew I must tell her my good fortune. 'Kitty, promise you won't say anything – promise you'll keep a secret?' She leaned forward and I whispered in her ear, 'It might be that I'm to marry Lord Entworth. He asked Father if he could present his suit.' I know I was blushing. On top of a very hot room, my face was on fire. 'Lady Clarissa is to act as my chaperone. He's to visit me at her house and—'

'Lord Entworth...Lord Entworth? Sweet Jesus!' She was clearly overwhelmed but I could see she was thrilled. 'Your mother's dearest wish was for you to marry gentry, but *Lady Entworth*? Sweet Jesus, Angelica – it's...it's...' She reached for her handkerchief, dabbing her eyes. 'No. No tears...or my make-up will smudge. Just wait till Theo hears of it. I can tell him, can't I?'

Panic filled me. 'No, not yet...not until Lord Entworth has asked me. And...Kitty, can you call me Alice, or something like that?'

She nodded, dabbing her eyes again, 'Of course...Well, *Alice* my dear, we must make tonight count – there'll be no coming backstage when you're married to Lord Entworth!' She pinched my cheek. 'We've ten minutes till curtain-up. You'll not be in the way if you stay here...just keep back to stay out of sight.'

The stage had been transformed into the chamber of an old house. The players were lining up, Theo giving them last-minute instructions. Some had their eyes shut, others were taking long, deep breaths. Miss Hardcastle was to be played by an actress called Hannah Hambley; Miss Neville by the hapless Flora. I could hardly breathe for excitement. This was how Mamma must have felt; how Mamma must have stood. It was in my blood, my bones, my very soul.

Two men had lowered the chandeliers, the candles being slowly extinguished. The expectant hush made my heart thump harder. The musicians had stopped playing; it was growing darker, only grey faces where there had been such colour. Thin plumes of smoke curled from the lanterns, shadows dancing across the closed curtain. Theo nodded to an actor who flung back his head and parted the curtain. He stepped into the lamplight.

'*Excuse me sirs, I pray –*' he boomed.

Chapter Four

I watched in awe, unable to stop my laughter, enjoying the howls of mirth and stomping of feet. Geryn finished singing and the audience started yelling for more.

'I don't get paid to sing it twice,' he shouted back. The stomping grew fiercer, a shower of coins raining down on him. He stooped to pick them up, placing them in a small leather pouch. 'Well...all right then, seeing as it's you...but don't tell Mr Hardcastle – you know what an old skinflint he is...'

The crowd roared their approval and more coins landed by his feet; it was so loud, so boisterous, so completely thrilling. Kitty was smiling broadly; she put her hand on my shoulder. 'He's got a way with them – knows just how to get them going. Once he's got them laughing, they'll laugh the whole way through.'

It was everything I imagined – the heat, the glare of the lamps, the sea of faces. Sweat trickled down my back, my cheeks flushed, my heart racing. The audience was entranced and I laughed with them, squeezing out of the way as painted sets were wheeled back and forth. It was so cramped, yet somehow everyone avoided a collision. The third act was over, the set-change taking place. Behind the curtain, Theo's frown deepened. He shook his head.

'Where is she, for God's sake? She missed several lines… What's wrong with the woman? She looks half-dazed.'

Kitty was also frowning, glancing over her shoulder. 'She needed the privy. Hannah's gone with her.'

Hannah ran from round the back of the stage. 'Flora's got the gripes. She feels sick.' She began pulling off her maid's costume, stepping quickly into the elaborate silk dress Kitty held ready.

'Sweet Jesus.' Kitty tied the ribbons on the bodice, fluffing out the silk petticoats. She beckoned to Theo. 'You'll have to tell the orchestra to play – Flora's sick.'

'Christ, that's all we need. I'll get Geryn to sing again – five minutes…tell her she's got *five* minutes.'

I felt their panic. Where there had been quiet efficiency, there was now definite nervousness. Geryn understood at once and nodded, stepping out through the curtain with an exaggerated smile. He held up his hands, raising his voice. ''Tis my opinion you're rather a *quiet* lot here tonight!' Laughter filled the theatre; there were cheers, rowdy shouts. 'See what I mean…quiet as a mouse…now, how about I get you singing?'

Flora appeared behind me, unsteady on her feet. Her cheeks were scarlet. Kitty rushed to help her, but just one look at her flushed face and Theo shook his head. 'Four lines missed and your words muddled.'

Flora lifted up her chin; her lips were glistening, strands of the heavy blonde wig clinging to her flushed cheeks. 'I've been sick...but I'm better now. I can go on...' Her voice sounded thin, a slight quiver as she spoke. In front of the curtain, the audience were singing. '*Let schoolmasters puzzle their brain, with grammar, and nonsense, and learning...*'

'You look unwell.' Kitty put her hand on Flora's forehead. 'You're feverish...you can't possibly go back on.'

Flora's eyes filled with fear. She wiped a handkerchief across her face. 'I'm better now...I can go back on...honest – I'm better.' She twisted the handkerchief in her hands.

Kitty's urgent look made my heart pound. 'Flora hardly appears in the next scene – not for very long anyway. Perhaps she *should* carry on?'

'And have her vomit on stage?' Theo shook his head, more in exasperation than disagreement. 'This is all we need,' he said again. Beads of perspiration covered his forehead. He must have been burning up under his heavy costume and large grey wig. 'I'll not have you ruin this production. I'll not—'

Flora cut him short. 'Please, Mr Gilmore – I'm fine. Honest, it's already passing...' She looked resolute, knowing her job was at stake.

Theo picked up his cane. 'Just this act, then we'll see. Come, we've wasted enough time – and *no* more missed lines.' He stamped his cane loudly on the stage, his voice booming from behind the curtain. 'Lumpkin?' The orchestra stopped and he shouted again. 'Where's that good-for-nothing, idiot boy? Up to no good, I warrant.'

From the wings, I watched Geryn stop singing and glance

over his shoulder. He lifted his hat, leaning forward to draw the audience into his confidence. 'He calls me idiot, but I'll get the better of him...' He paused. ''Tis Act Four, by the way, in case you've just woken.'

The audience roared their approval, but behind the curtain, I could feel the anxiety growing. The furrow on Theo's brow deepened. He was clearly reluctant but nodded for the curtain to rise. The actor playing Hastings stepped forward, taking Flora's arm.

She took a deep breath. 'I think 'twas the oysters. I've been sick with oysters before.'

She seemed to be doing well, the scene progressing with no mishap; her three lines were soon over, spoken clearly, and I felt myself begin to relax, but once off the stage, she gripped her abdomen, bending over in pain. 'Get a bowl... a bucket...quick.' Her cheeks were even redder, her eyes feverish. 'No...'tis passing. I'll be all right.'

Theo's face was like thunder. Hands on his hips, he shook his head. 'Kitty, someone must take her place.'

'But everyone's twice her size and half her height. Sweet Jesus – what about Elspeth?'

'No, Elspeth's too old and they'll recognize her as the maid. This performance mustn't end in farce – our reputation's at stake. One mishap, just one critic ridiculing our performance...'

Flora grasped her hands as if in prayer. 'I can do it... honest...I can get through this next scene – and I say next to nothin' in the last scene. I can hold out.'

Kitty must have read my mind. 'You said you had this play by heart?'

I nodded, my heart thumping.

'Ye know what I'm thinking, don't ye, my love? Flora has hardly anything left to say. She only comes on at the end – she has, what, three, maybe four lines? It's next to nothing.' I heard the plea in her whisper.

'But, Kitty, what if I'm recognized?'

'In her costume? Under that wig? Angelica, you're her exact shape and size – you'd look just like her. *No-one* will notice because *no-one* will know. Could you remember four short lines?'

I needed to say no. I needed to be sensible and answer firmly. My head knew it to be wrong but my heart…Dear God, my heart wanted it so badly. Kitty put her arm around me, staring up at Theo. 'The audience won't even notice.' Theo shook his head, but he looked undecided and Kitty's voice grew firmer. 'All she needs do is stand in the right place. I'll be right beside her – or just behind the curtain – and I can whisper the lines.'

Flora grimaced, clutching her belly, the pain obviously getting worse. Onstage, the play was in full swing, the audience laughing. Theo cursed, turning at his cue, striding on to the stage at just the right moment. '*I no longer know my own house…*'

Close up, Kitty looked older, the deep lines round her mouth forming cracks in her greasepaint. Her gown was dirty, smelling of sweat, the lace old and torn. She sounded desperate. 'Flora must just get through this scene – then you can switch in the interval. Four short lines – I'll be right next to you.'

She must have sensed my sudden resolve as a smile swept

across her face. She grabbed my elbow. 'Here, start getting changed. There's no time for modesty...get your gown off and put this wrap on.' She beckoned a stagehand over. 'This is Alice – she's an actress. She's going to take Flora's part.'

They began undoing the buttons of my charity gown, lifting the bodice over my head, slipping a silk dressing gown over my naked shoulders. It was not me standing there, but a professional actress, stepping out of her skirts into a change of costume. My bonnet had remained secure and I held the lace to my face, my heart pounding. 'You've seen the way Flora does her make-up – put the beauty patch on your chin and make sure to redden your cheeks. The script's on the table.'

'We did this play at school. I played your role...'

She looked up and smiled. 'I know – that's why I asked you. Tie your hair back ready for the wig. When the play's over we'll ask Dr Luke to check on Flora.'

The actor playing Hastings was called Marcus. He looked far from convinced, holding out his arm, and scowling at Flora. 'Not going to be sick, are you?' She shook her head, and his mouth clamped tight. 'On your head be it.' Their time was up and they stepped laughing on to the stage. '*Ay, you may steal for yourselves next time...*'

'Quick – go and paint your face.' Kitty had hardly time to draw breath. She threw back her head and stepped on to the stage.

'Follow me...' The stagehand grabbed my arm, ushering me down the sweltering corridor. 'Careful ye don't trip – mind them fire buckets.'

Chapter Five

Flora reached for the bucket and I pulled the wig in place, the mass of blonde curls cascading round my shoulders. Footsteps stopped outside the door, Marcus peering through the gap. 'Time's up. You're needed.'

The hot wig gripped my head like a vice; the silk gown, itching me, smelling of sweat but it fitted me perfectly. I was laced to within an inch of my life; I was Miss Neville and I was doing this for Kitty. We stopped in the wings and Marcus grabbed Flora's bonnet from my hands, jamming the pins into my wig. 'There'll be no scene change — we're straight on after *There's morality in his reply...*'

My heart was pounding. I was Hermia's child and I could do this. I had four short lines and I had them by heart. I would copy Flora's walk, the coquettish toss of her hair. But my lines required a change of tone: Miss Neville was resolved *not* to run away and I needed to sound firm, speak with resolution.

Kitty was onstage, pleading with the highwayman amidst howls of laughter. Marcus stood beside me. 'Make sure you speak up…they'll be laughing when Kitty and Theo leave the stage and we must wait until they stop. Face the audience when you speak – it's important they hear every word.' I nodded but I must have looked scared. 'You're an actress, aren't you? Played this role before?'

I nodded again, this time with more conviction. 'I'll not let you down.'

'Ready – now.' Marcus gripped my arm and I took a deep breath. The glare of the lamps was brighter than I expected; the sea of faces suddenly so terrifying. This was not the school hall, the other parents laughing and praising my production – Lady Clarissa, standing up, clapping, enjoying every minute. This was real, and people might recognize me.

The laughter was dying and I stared at Marcus. My chest felt crushed, all breath squeezed from me. Beneath the folds of my voluminous dress, my knees began weakening. *Breathe, Angelica, take your time*. It was as if Mamma was speaking and I caught my breath. Marcus was waiting for my reply.

'*I find it impossible…*'

At once, we were offstage, my hands shaking. I must have done it, and done it well. Everyone was smiling, yet I had no memory – one blink and it was over.

'Perfect, that was *perfect*.' Kitty hugged me to her. 'You've got your mother's instinct. Not a single prompt. Here, my love…' She grabbed the well-worn script, thrusting it in my hands. 'Just one more line – keep next to Marcus. Then we take our bows.'

I never gave them the satisfaction of seeing me searching from the wings – every other parent smiling and clapping their hands, all their brothers, their aunts, their grandparents with their baskets spilling over with treats. They would spread their rugs on the lawn for afternoon tea and praise my acting, but none of them knew I was acting still – laughing and joking, refusing their cakes, far too happy to notice I had no one there for me. Only Mrs Penhaligan sensed my heartbreak, leaving her gift of gingerbread on my pillow the night of the plays.

The candelabras were lit, the pillars of the theatre ablaze with colour. I could see the painted green frieze with its red and gold motives, the rapturous faces as they called for more. Kitty and Theo took another bow and the whistles and cheers grew deafening. A sickening thud almost stopped my heart – Lord Entworth was in the audience.

He was trying to hear what his sister was saying, his face alight with pleasure. He was laughing, clapping his hands, nodding his approval, and I stepped back, trying not to stare. He was so handsome, his blue silk jacket and gold embroidered waistcoat making him stand out from the crowd. His brown hair was tied in a bow behind his neck, a set of curls framing his face. He stood tall and commanding, overshadowing the many men waiting to speak to him.

A movement caught my eyes and panic seized me. Edgar and Jacob were staring at me, trying to catch my attention. One moment they were pushing their way towards the exit, the next they were turning round, pointing to the door. They must have recognized me and I knew to get home. I could hardly breathe, edging slowly off the stage, running as fast as I could down the crowded corridor. A large cloak hung from a hook and I flung it over my head, hiding beneath the soft red velvet. What if Lord Entworth had recognized me as well?

I had planned everything so carefully, hiding my identity, wearing a charity dress. No one except Theo and Kitty even knew my name. The lace had concealed my face and it had been dark in the wings, almost pitch black. Yet, despite the heavy make-up and huge wig, Jacob Boswell must have recognized my voice. He would tell his mother – he would threaten to tell Father.

I dragged back the locks and opened the latch, the night air cooling my burning cheeks, a welcome respite after the smoke-filled theatre. The drizzle had stopped, long black clouds pointing like fingers across the moon. The line of carriages still stretched down the street, the coachmen rolling dice in the glow of the street lamps. I pulled the cloak around me and began to run, my soft shoes making no sound. Molly had the key but the latch on the larder window was easy to undo. I would take the lane round the leat so as not to be seen. I would be in bed and pretend they had woken me.

Boots were racing across the cobbles behind me, a volley of shouted oaths and I ran faster. A hand grabbed me and Jacob Boswell swung me round. 'It's back here.'

Edgar was halfway down the row of carriages, holding open the door. He was not angry but giggling, hanging breathlessly to the handle, doubling up with laughter. 'A promise is a promise,' he seemed to be saying. He sounded drunk, unreasonably excited.

Jacob's grip was painful. He began pulling me towards the coach, forcing me through the door. His hand pressed against my thigh and I tried to pull away, but his grip tightened, thrusting me forward so violently I had to fling out my hands to prevent landing on my face. In the soft glow of the lamplight, they crammed in beside me, Edgar missing his footing, giggling still, heaving himself on to the seat but unable to stay upright.

The door slammed and Jacob lifted his cane to bang on the roof. Now their scolding would start. They would delight in their discovery, make me pay. I had just handed Jacob Boswell the perfect weapon to use against me and I seethed in silent anger, furious at my foolishness.

The coachman called to the horses and the coach jerked forward, the wheels jolting over the cobbles. My departure had been quick and swiftly executed. Edgar was whooping in delight but Jacob remained silent. In the darkness, his hand reached for my ankle, slipping up the inside of my skirts. It burned my knee, moving up my thigh.

His whisper stopped my protest. 'You weren't trying to run away from us, were you, Flora? A promise is a promise.' His voice hardened. 'Stay still, for God's sake...'

Chapter Six

I stared ahead, his fingers fumbling with my garter. Edgar was too far gone with drink to recognize me, he was hardly focusing, but Jacob Boswell was completely sober. One hand was slipping beneath my stocking, the other pulling back my wig, exposing my neck to his hot breath. Disgust tore through me – this was how they behaved, this the sport they craved.

The coach began rattling down the street and across the new bridge. Cobbles gave way to rough stones and I glanced through the window, desperate to follow our direction. The water glinted black in the silver moonlight and I recognized the route we were taking – it was the road to Malpas.

Jacob's deft fingers slipped under my stocking and I knew to sound playful. I must toss my blonde wig and giggle. I must copy Flora's accent, use the words she used. I must purse my painted lips and pout, flutter my false lashes. 'Sir Jacob! Goodness me…don't you think that's just a *tiny*, *tiny* bit naughty? And here's me thinking you were *proper* gentry, inviting me to a fine supper with fine wines!' I reached down, pulling his hand away, giving it a disapproving tap. Smoothing out my petticoats, I managed a pout. 'You've not said a word about my acting. Was I good?' I nudged him in the ribs, giggling, pulling down my hood. 'Just a *tiny*, *tiny* bit good?'

He drew back, his eyes unsmiling. He showed no sign of recognition, reaching instead into his pocket for an enamel snuffbox. 'You were excellent, my dear. You stole the show.' He drew in the snuff, leaning towards me.

'And the singing, Sir Jacob? Did you sing along with Tony Lumpkin?' They must be taking me to their inn. The moment we stopped, I would run, climb a tree, hide all night if necessary.

He slumped back against the leather, drawing in more snuff. 'A fine supper and fine wines.' It sounded more like an accusation, not a question.

'I'm that hungry, Sir Jacob – those oysters were just to get me through the performance.' Another giggle, another shrug of my shoulders.

'Have it your way. I suppose you'll want money, as well.'

In the darkness my heart screamed. Edgar was laughing, colluding, sprawling across the seat in what seemed liked betrayal. His legs were spread wide, his waistcoat unbuttoned; dissolute, unprincipled, everything Mamma would have hated. Neither of them had morals, nor manners, yet Jacob's coldness seemed somehow worse. He took another pinch of snuff.

The river was lost to darkness, the moon obscured by the overhead branches. The carriage lamps lit the trunks of the trees along the riverbank and an owl swooped from the darkness. A streak of white plumage flew alongside us and Edgar whooped in delight, heaving down the window, baying back at the owl like a wolf: my brother, howling like some crazed animal. I wanted to haul him back, shake some sense into him. Lord Entworth must have seen him. Everyone must have seen him.

The coach was slowing, the horses coming to a stop. The smell of brackish water mingled with woodsmoke. Ships lay to anchor on the black water, moonlight bathing the decks in silver light. I recognized the distinctive horseshoe bend and knew we were in Malpas – two miles from home. Jacob grabbed the handle and opened the door, jumping to the ground. He reached up, slipping his hands round my waist. Light was shining through the windows of the nearby inn; men were laughing, a fiddler playing. There was no wind, not a ripple on the water. Ships lay moored against the wooden quay, men roasting fish on the griddle of an open fire. I could hear the splash of oars as men rowed to their ships, their voices carrying across the stillness.

'Wait...' Edgar fell from the coach, trying to regain his balance.

Black curls hung limply across his face, his shoulders slumped: my brother, staggering like a drunk, his shirt untucked, wine stains ruining his silk waistcoat. I wanted to grab him, shake him, tell him exactly what I thought, but Jacob Boswell had my arm in a vice-like grip. He was pushing me towards the inn, his breath short and sharp. The Heron Inn: I had seen it from the river. More a collection of ancient cottages jammed tight to the bend, somehow kept upright by cross-beams and buttresses. A lamp burned by the front door and I turned my face from the glare, pulling my hood lower.

'Not in there, round the back.' Jacob drew me from the door, forcing me down the side entrance where a man lay slumped across some steps. Jacob kicked him to one side, opening the door, forcing me into a dimly lit room. Pungent tobacco fumes caught my throat, the sweet, sickly smell stinging my eyes, and I started to cough.

In the darkness I could make out the shapes of bodies – men and women sprawled on cushions, the women half-dressed, the men lolling to one side. Brass urns lay scattered among the cushions, thin coils of smoke rising from the mouth-pieces. A man was grunting and I recoiled in disgust; the woman was laughing, the man ripping her bodice, exposing her breasts. The door slammed shut and pain shot through my wrist.

Jacob jerked me forward. Through an open door, a man was filling jugs with ale; there were tables, men drinking, a fiddler playing. His grip tightened but I put up no resistance, following him through the door and into the taproom. Lamplight lit the faces of the men round the tables. They looked like sailors – sunburned, rough; sailing up on the high tide, down on the ebb. This was the stopping point, the depth to Truro too shallow for large ships. Here, they unloaded their cargo on to mules, or swapped to boats with shallower keels.

Serving girls swooped like swallows between the seated men, holding large jugs of ale high in the air. They were laughing, calling out, dodging the slaps to their buttocks. Women were sitting on men's knees, everyone playing cards or rolling dice. The heat burned my face, my wig and heavy skirts acting like a furnace. No one seemed to notice I was dressed for the theatre, my face painted, the large patch on my chin. They were all too busy eating and drinking, smoking clay pipes, banging the tables to demand more ale. I turned in horror. Edgar was no longer behind me. The door was shut. He must have stayed in that vile room with the velvet cushions and the stinking smoke.

Jacob's grip was like iron. A large oak staircase swept up the side of the room and his thighs pressed against my skirt, forcing me between the tables and up the staircase. We were halfway to the top, my chances of escape diminishing by the minute. 'Sir Jacob...a fine dinner...you promised me a fine dinner.' Doors led from an upper gallery, a lamp burning against the wall and in the glow of the lamp, I saw his lips clamp into a thin line. Hatred burned his eyes. 'Wait...stop.'

He took no notice, forcing me along the corridor and I knew my time was up. I had to tell him the truth, take the consequences of my action. He would ask for money, accounts would follow. 'Sir Jacob——'

A door burst open and a woman knocked into him. She was clearly drunk, swaying to keep herself from falling. 'For Christ's sake, woman.'

The laces of her bodice were undone, her breasts in danger of springing loose. She was laughing, steadying herself, her tousled hair splaying around her bare shoulders. 'Whoops... sorry, sir...' Her eyes were half closed, her cheeks pale, a

mole prominent above her upper lip. 'Whoops. Sorry, sir…
if ye'll just excuse me, I need some vinegar…' Her goblet
of wine was in danger of spilling, her legs unsteady as she
leaned over the banister. Her voice was hoarse. 'Landlord –
bring vinegar. Did ye hear? Bring vinegar fer a wasp sting…'

Behind us, a voice bellowed through the open door, 'Not
vinegar. Get mud…mud for a poultice.'

Jacob fumbled for his key. 'Sir Jacob, I'm not—' I stopped.
The woman was staggering down the stairs, sipping from her
goblet. Flora had an almost breathless way of speaking and
I knew I must try one last time. Reaching up, I caressed his
neck. 'Maybe I *can* wait for supper…but how about a *tiny*,
tiny glass of wine?' I drew my finger down the buttons on his
waistcoat. 'Why don't I get out of this wig and heavy gown…
and you…go…and get us…some wine?'

A pulse throbbed in his neck. The key turned and he
opened the door, thrusting me forward so violently I stumbled and fell. The door slammed, the key turning once, twice,
locking me in. He knew I was going to run. He knew. To
lock a woman in his room against her will; he was a monster,
turning my brother into a monster. Moonlight flooded the
room, lighting the bed, the dressing table, the wardrobe. A
pile of travelling boxes lay stacked in a corner, a chair by the
window, and I picked myself off the floor, going straight to
the leaded casement. I had squeezed through smaller; it all
depended on the drop.

The window faced away from the river and I leaned out,
desperate at what I saw – too steep a drop. The thatch above
was out of reach, so, too, the porch over the back door. It

must be the kitchen courtyard. Sloping rooves covered several outhouses, a collection of hogsheads collecting rain water. Empty beer barrels lay on their side, a pile of logs stacked in an untidy heap. An arch led through to the stables. I could hear horses, smell the dung, and my panic rose. There was no ledge, no ridge. No foothold – nothing to grab. The best I could expect was a broken leg.

I glanced back at the room. I could wrench the cover from the bed – hang it from the window. I began pulling the heavy brocade, my cumbersome gown tripping me up. It needed all my strength but it was sliding from the bed, lying in a heap by the window. I would use the heavy oak chair to secure it, but I needed a slit big enough for the leg of the chair to fit through.

His razor was on the washstand and I held it tightly, jabbing at the threads until they split and parted. The slash was five inches long – that would have to do. Any minute now, I would hear the key turn in the lock, yet the more I tried to hurry, the more my fingers fumbled. I squeezed the leg through the jagged cut and heaved the cover through the open window. I leaned out, willing the fabric not to tear, yet there it hung, the brocade grey against the limewashed walls.

A movement in the shadows caught my eye. A man was standing in the courtyard staring up at me, the moonlight glinting on his glasses. 'Stay where you are – I'll come and get you.'

I recognized him at once. 'Is the coach ready to leave?'

'Don't use that – I'll come and get you.'

'No – get the coach. Wait for me round the front – if I

don't come, then by all means come and get me. It's the third door on the right.' I reached down, slipping off my satin shoe, throwing it on to the cobbles next to him. 'Please – just get the coach...'

Clasping my skirts, I ran to the door, holding my breath as I heard footsteps on the other side. He would be bending down, putting the wine and glasses on the floor. He would be reaching into his pocket for the key. I was far enough away for the door to be flung open, near enough to run straight through it. The key was turning, the door opening.

'What the hell?' He rushed to the window. 'Jesus Christ!'

He leaned out of the window and I ran through the door, slamming it shut behind me. The key was still in the lock and I turned it once, twice, his volley of oaths making me want to laugh. His fists pounded the door, his shouts growing fainter as I tore down the stairs, running for my life. Hands reached out to grab me, fresh oaths greeting the sharp stab of my elbows, but I did not care. I ran like I had never run, weaving my way through the drunken revellers, reaching the door. I pulled it open to a clatter of hooves.

The coachman gripped my hands, pulling me next to him. He whipped the reins, urging the horses faster. My heart was racing. I had done it. I had outwitted Jacob Boswell. He would never, ever know. No one would ever know. It was thrilling, exhilarating, and I threw back my head, laughing like I had not laughed in a very long time. The key glinted in the moonlight as I held it up.

Part of me wanted to keep it but I stood up, laughing as I hurled it deep into the river. 'Take that, Jacob Boswell.'

The horses' hooves were pounding beneath me, the wind in my face. We were flying, fleeing through the night. It was the most exciting thing I had ever done. A hand reached up and pulled me down. Beneath his heavy hat, the coachman's lips clamped tight. He cracked his whip harder and I wrapped my cloak around me. 'I won't fall,' I shouted. 'I'm perfectly used to sitting on the driver's seat.'

'All the same, I'd be happier with you *in* the coach,' he shouted back.

'I was never going to jump. You don't jump from a window like that – you just make it *look* like you have.' He could think what he liked, it did not matter. All that mattered was for me to get back to Molly. All the same, I did not want him to think me ungrateful. 'It's Mr Trevelyan, isn't it?'

'Henry Trevelyan.'

'Take me back to the theatre please, Mr Trevelyan.'

We must have gone half a mile, no more, and I turned in horror. He was pulling up the reins, slowing the horses to a walk. There were no trees or bushes, the long stretch of road bathed in moonlight, but we were definitely stopping. From the folds of his coat, he drew out a pistol. 'Quick, get in the coach…forgive me if I don't open the door.' He was searching the shadows of the riverbank. 'We're coming to the worst of the ruts. They hide in the dense cover. Be quick – and close the curtains.'

If his pistol frightened me, his words petrified me, and I slipped quickly to the ground. 'Are we in danger?'

He seemed to suppress a laugh. 'Two o'clock in the morning …on the road from Malpas, and you ask if we're in danger?'

This time it was a laugh, a definite shake of the head. 'I'm not sure about you, Miss Lilly, but I consider it very dangerous. Keep the curtains closed — if you hear shots, get as low as you can. *Don't* look out of the window.'

Chapter Seven

I needed to work out what to do. He knew my identity and was going to demand money — no doubt a substantial amount. I would put it under Edgar's expenses. I would be settling this account anyway, so I would add his demands to that. Forging Father's signature was never a problem, but how much would be reasonable?

We were crossing the new bridge and nearly home. There had been no shots, no one intent on robbing us. Henry Trevelyan must have shown me the pistol solely to instil fear. I would not let him intimidate me, nor would I pay him more than twenty guineas. Twenty guineas must be enough.

The courtyard lay in darkness, the empty stables uncannily quiet. He jumped from the driver's seat and opened the door and I ignored his proffered hand, staring across the unlit cobbles. No lamps awaited our arrival, the kitchen was in darkness. Molly must be asleep. Henry Trevelyan secured the horses and drew off his leather gloves.

'Put this journey on to Mr Lilly's account – I presume it's Mr Lilly paying you, not Sir Jacob?'

He took off his hat, running his hand through his short hair. 'I've received no payment, Miss Lilly, though plenty's been promised.' His voice was soft, cynical, but not unkind. His accent was local, educated, his tone gentle. 'In over three weeks, I've not seen a penny.' He had long, tapering fingers, his nails well-cut. He had shaved since the morning, his high cheek bones more prominent without the dark stubble. 'Horses are expensive, they require food and attention, and stabling doesn't come cheap. I may go hungry, but horses can't pull coaches on an empty stomach.'

'Send me your bill in the morning – I'll see it gets paid.'

'Thank you, Miss Lilly. May I see you safely through your door?' He must have seen me glance towards the larder window. He seemed amused, his smile catching me off guard. 'Or are you going to climb through the window, in which case, may I give you a helping hand?'

I did not smile back. 'It depends on whether the back door's locked.'

I heard his soft laughter – if I used the window, I would have it boarded up straight away. He would come back and rob us. No matter how genteel he seemed, when I left, Molly would be in danger. We reached the back door and I tried the handle, relief flooding through me as it turned and opened. Molly was asleep in her rocking chair and jolted awake.

'Oh, dear Lord…Angelica…where've you been?' She struggled up, all elbows and fluster. 'I've been in such a state …not knowin' where ye'd gone…or when ye'd be back…'

56

She looked pale, her mobcap pushed to one side, her frizzy grey hair framing her face. 'Onlookers told me ye'd gone with Edgar but honest to God, what time d'you call this?' Across the darkness, the kitchen clock chimed three.

'We went for a ride in the moonlight. The coach got stuck in a rut and I lost my shoe...we had supper in the inn and now I'm back.'

'Kitty told me everything. Honest to God, did they know 'twas you?' She was struggling with the tinderbox, trying to strike the flint, and I took it from her, the room filling with flickering light.

'No, of course not. They thought I was Flora – the actress. Anyway, it doesn't matter, no harm done.' From the doorway, I heard a cough. The coachman was standing on the mat, his arms folded.

Molly turned even more ashen. 'But he knows ye're not.'

I pulled off the heavy wig, teasing my hair from its vice-like grip. 'He's hungry.' I pointed him to a chair at the table. 'Edgar's late with his account – I believe he needs feeding.'

Molly stared across the kitchen 'Sit ye down...there's plenty fer ye – just give me a minute.'

Henry Trevelyan smiled, drawing out my chair, and I sat stiffly, watching Molly place a plate and mug on the table in front of him. She went to the larder, returning with plates piled high with cold chicken and ham, under her arm, a large loaf of bread. She went back for a knife, cutting thick slices of ham and great chunks of bread, and stood back, putting it safely out of reach.

'There's no point – he's got a pistol under his jacket.'

She sank down in her chair, her eyes wide with fright.

'I may carry a pistol, but I've never shot anyone.' Henry Trevelyan reached inside his jacket, holding it out for Molly to take. 'Here, please...take it. I'd never shoot anyone who makes such fine food, but if I could have it back when I leave?' Molly put the pistol to one side and he started eating, smiling his delight. 'This pickle's really very good.' He sounded wistful, even a little sad, and my fear subsided. He was just a hungry man, praising Molly's pickle. Not frightening at all.

Molly jumped up at the sight of his empty plate. 'There's plenty more – come, eat up.'

Mamma's Sunday baskets lay ready on the sideboard, each brimming with vegetables, eggs and cheese. Mamma never forgot her lowly beginnings or passed a beggar without sending food back, and we carried on taking her baskets to the poorest families in our parish. But we never went inside. Mamma used to. She used to cram into their damp rooms, listening to their heartbreak, trying to do everything she could to alleviate their suffering. Until she caught a fever from the child she had held with such compassion.

Burning up, sweating, covered in huge red blisters; crying out in her agony, her throat so swollen she could not speak. They had kept me from her because I, too, might die. I never saw her again, never heard her laugh, no more to blush at her gentle teasing. Storm clouds had gathered at her funeral, the rain lashing the streets with such ferocity as if furious she had been taken from us. The dull ache was returning. I had to turn away.

A fourteen-year-old girl inconsolable with grief; no flowers to throw into the dripping black hole that would engulf her mamma for ever. No flowers. Father, fighting the wind with his umbrella; Edgar, pale under his huge coat and sodden hat; Molly and I, clinging to each other, hardly able to stand for grief. No flowers. We had forgotten them in our pain at seeing the black horses with their tall feathers pull up outside our house; seeing her coffin placed on to the wagon, the terrible tolling of the church bell.

No flowers to take with her – Mamma, who loved flowers so much, who had always placed flowers in her house. But for the kindness of a woman and a youth sheltering under a tree; a wet hand in a soaking sleeve reaching out to give me his rain-drenched posy. '*Please, take these...*'

I had to keep my face turned away. Molly had picked up one of the baskets and was handing it to Henry. 'Take this basket, Mr Trevelyan...no, honest, I'll soon fill another – there's plenty in there to keep ye goin'.'

Why so sad? Why now? I had seen those baskets every week for seven years and never felt the same pain. Henry handed back the basket, smiling and shaking his head. 'No, thank you, Molly – you've been more than generous...Well, maybe just this jar of pickle?' I wanted to cry, watching his polite manners, the charm with which he spoke to Molly. Mamma would be so ashamed of Edgar.

'Did you watch the play, Molly?' I heard him ask.

'Ooh, I did! I loved it. How I laughed! Honest to God, I never knew 'twere Miss Lilly – I never knew...'

'I did...' He looked up, his blue eyes catching mine

through his glasses. 'It was just at the very end. Am I right, Miss Lilly?'

I did not answer. He was too at ease, his feet firmly under my kitchen table, smiling at Molly who was clearly smitten.

'What were ye readin'? Earlier – out the back? I saw ye had a book. Ye're not like most coachmen, if ye don't mind me sayin'. Ye're a gentleman, Mr Trevelyan – ye've got learnin' written all over ye…'

'Ah, my book…' He reached into his jacket pocket. 'Do you like poetry, Molly?'

'How much does my brother owe you?' I snapped. He needed to go. I knew people like him. One moment they were your friend, the next they were wheedling out your secrets, telling tales to the paper, profiting through your own gullibility. We were two women alone, in a house full of money; there were valuable paintings, silverware, not to mention jewellery. 'I'm sure we can come to some agreement – please add extra for the *inconvenience* of bringing me home and I'll see you're paid promptly.'

He opened his book. 'I've been keeping a daily tally. Three weeks at a guinea a week.' He handed me a bill of expenses. 'The extras are for stabling and food, and I paid a farrier for two new shoes.'

I took a deep breath. 'You need to add tonight's *charge*.'

He stood up, pushing his chair neatly under the table and reached for his pistol. 'There's no charge for tonight.' He stood by the door, throwing the jar of pickle high in the air, catching it expertly. 'I've been more than compensated.

And far better I drove you home than you stole my coach and horses.'

His smile ripped through me and I closed the door behind him, drawing across the locks and turning the heavy key. Yes, I would have stolen his coach, and yes, I would have driven his horses very fast.

'Oh, bless his soul…he's left his book.' Molly eased herself forward, picking up the small leather-bound book. She smiled, handing it to me. 'Go after him, love…take it to him.' I shook my head. He had left it on purpose, no doubt expecting me to follow him. He would make his demands out of Molly's hearing.

I stared down at the worn leather cover, the faded gold lettering *The Love Poems of John Donne*.

'I'm going to bed,' I said. 'Wake me at nine. I'm packed and ready to go. You give it back.'

First thing tomorrow, I would add twenty pounds to his account and send a runner to the inn. Father always left money in his safe so I could pay him promptly. I would arrange for the larder window to be nailed shut, and for nightwatchmen to patrol the house and garden. Molly and Grace must be kept safe.

I stopped on the bend in the stairs, looking up at Mamma's portrait: Hermia, adored by the Prince of Wales, captured by Angelica Kauffman in her most famous role. All my life, I had gazed at this portrait, imagining what it must feel like to pose for such a famous painter. She looked so radiant, her long white gown and abundant black hair cascading under a wreath of flowers; the acclaimed beauty that had lords throwing roses at her feet.

Mamma standing next to me, both of us smiling, her laughter making me giggle. *Of course, you're named after her...* she would whisper. *She's a very fine painter and one day, you're going to be a very fine lady. The fortune teller told me that...* Then her voice would turn wistful. *I have my memories and I have you and Edgar. It's your futures that matter.*

Molly slipped her arm through mine, both of us staring up at Mamma. 'Mary Bohenna was looking the loveliest I've ever seen – quite the lady...And so was Mr Luke – *Doctor* Luke, I should say. London's done them proud. I remember when Mary first came to Truro – if Mary hadn't married Mr Bohenna, yer father would never have met yer mother. Bless her heart. And now, she wants to find Luke a good wife...'

The lump in my throat made it hard to swallow and I forced back my tears. 'They've taken lodgings in Falmouth.'

She squeezed my arm. 'Honest to God, Angelica, I *never* thought 'twas you.'

I wanted to howl with the pain. 'Molly...how did Edgar behave tonight?'

She swallowed, her slight hesitation making me think she would lie. 'Well...seein' as how ye've asked.' Her voice sounded husky. 'He didn't seem himself...not like the boy of old. He was happy, mind, very happy. But it didn't seem natural – like he was with the fairies, or pixilated, or some such thing.'

'Did Lord Entworth see him like that?'

This time there was definite hesitation, a false cheeriness to her voice. 'No, love…not at all. They were in different parts of the theatre – Lord Entworth couldn't possibly have seen him.'

I turned at the top of the stairs. 'Why have you only prepared eight baskets? Why not ten?'

She coughed, bringing out her handkerchief. 'It's what Mr Lilly said.'

'Father?' I could hardly believe it.

'Well, 'twas Lady Boswell – she told me, but yer father didn't stop her. He nodded…so it must be what he wants.'

'What does he want?'

'I'm to cut down to eight baskets this week, then stop at five. Lady Boswell says I've been a deal too generous an' it's costin' Mr Lilly a fortune.'

Anger surged through me – seething anger, flaming my neck, my cheeks, setting fire to my face. The top of my arm still hurt where Jacob Boswell had gripped it, a bruise forming on my wrist.

'Do *twelve* baskets, Molly, and soup by the side door *every* day. Lady Boswell is *not* mistress of this house. Not yet, at least.'

Chapter Eight

On the road to Falmouth
Sunday 31st July 1796, 11:00 a.m.

The sun broke through the clouds, dispelling Molly's fears, and she smiled back at us. My luggage firmly stowed, the two footmen jumped on to the back. Amelia's maid, Bethany, settled herself on the seat beside the driver and Amelia reached for my hand.

'I can't believe I've got you for a whole *two months*.' The dimples on her cheeks deepened. 'Mother's determined *one* of us will marry and as it's not going to be me, I'm afraid it has to be you!'

I loved it when she laughed. This was real laughter, her blue eyes lighting up for the first time in many years. The sun caught her hair: a glimpse of chestnut in the brown curls that swirled beneath her bonnet. She was wearing lemon silk, her hat trimmed with matching ribbons. Molly waved her handkerchief on the front step and though I waved back, I was thrilled to be leaving. 'You're very kind to come and get me.'

Her eyes widened. 'Of course I'd come and get you. I've been longing for your visit.' Her elegantly gloved hand squeezed mine. Her face had perfect symmetry, her eyes framed by long lashes, her mouth generous and full. 'It's a beautiful day after all this rain, but I'm afraid it's come too late. Papa's crops are quite ruined.' She slid up the window. 'Added to which, we've had a stream of visitors and poor Papa's elbow-deep in schedules for the Militia Ballot. Raising the Volunteers is taking its toll – Papa would far rather see to his land. Did you know Titan took first prize in show this week?'

She did not know she was so beautiful, or if she did, she shrugged it off. Her soft voice, her graceful manner, her poise, her grace, the slight tilt to her chin, even her elegant stiff back; these were exactly why Father had sent me to Miss Mitchell's boarding school – at least, that was what he told me. I was to mix with the daughters of genteel families and learn their ways, and you could not get more genteel than Amelia Carew. She was adored by everyone, her innate good breeding and natural beauty outshining us all.

The coachman cracked his whip and we lurched forward. Truro had changed beyond recognition, the rows of smart new houses glowing like gold on either side of us – *the glow of new prosperity*, as Father would say. Two years ago, we would have avoided the stench of Middle Row by taking the crowded back streets to wait our turn at the old bridge, but not now. Now everything seemed to gleam, the filth of the rotting houses carted well away. A new bridge prevented congestion, a spacious new street where once there had been two. Front doors had been turned round, houses completely refurbished to face the new square.

The piles of rubble had been transformed into double-fronted homes with large sash windows and stately front doors. The streets were finely cobbled and lit by oil lamps. Smart iron railings edged the houses, and deep drains ran the length of the streets, channelling the rainwater down to the lock. Water pumps with heavy iron handles lined our route.

Even the wharf smelled fresher, the new sluices bringing much-needed flow to the upper reaches of the river. Huge blocks of tin lay ready to be shipped, mule packs trudging their well-worn path. We stopped to let a line pass – coal for the mines, copper and tin brought back to the dock, the huge piles heaped on to the ore floors to be assayed and transported to Father's smelters. Everywhere was iron. Iron railings, iron handles. Iron hoists, iron pulleys. Iron barges. Everyone needing iron.

'One day, they'll build an iron ship,' I whispered.

I should have known Amelia would take me seriously. 'Will your father commission one, do you think?'

'I hope so. He's planning to enlarge the foundry.'

The vale stretched before us – the rich and fertile valley where the two rivers meet. Usually so plentiful, the trees in the orchards were bare of fruit, yet in the sunshine it still looked beautiful. The river sparkled along the valley floor – the Truro River with its distinctive bend curving round Malpas. My anxiety returned. I had written to Father suggesting he visited Edgar in Oxford. He would not get my letter until he reached Swansea but it was all I could think to do.

In the distance, tall chimneys rose into the cloudless blue sky. 'Those are your father's new works, aren't they?'

I nodded. Everything we saw seemed to be Father's — his smelting works, his half share in the mine, the corn mill he had just bought, but not the carpet manufacturer – not yet, at least. The works would soon be up for sale. Their supply of wool had dwindled through no fault of their own, requisitioned by the militia and navy for uniforms, and they had fallen behind on their payments.

Amelia smiled the same quiet smile she had smiled those seven years ago when she had found me broken-hearted under my bed. Father had no idea how the smoke from his smelter would cling to my silks. The other girls hated me and I hated them back, their snide comments and hateful innuendos only held in check by Amelia. She was the daughter of a lord, the granddaughter of an earl, and though she had stayed at the school for just one term, her friendship acted as a shield, her protective mantle remaining long after she had left. It remained with me still.

Before Amelia came to school, my plea to put on plays had been dismissed as vulgar, yet just one letter from Lady Clarissa and Miss Mitchell jumped to her command. I had permission to put on any play I wanted and every parent came flocking – all of them unpacking their hampers amidst talk of hunting and shooting, of country balls and fêtes. Not one of them knew how the heat from the furnace could burn your cheeks, what molten tin sounded like when it crackled, how you had to watch for exactly the right texture before casting it into ingots. They did not care that iron bridges could span deep ravines: that men had built barges from iron, that ships might one day be made from iron.

The coach slowed, lurching dangerously through a stretch of puddles. Around us, the cornfields lay flattened.

'Frederick's ship is due home soon – Charity's so excited.' Amelia's smile broadened. 'Frederick hasn't seen little Freddie yet and Mother wants us all to go to Falmouth to be there when his ship docks. Mr and Mrs Fox are to host a reception in their new house and Mrs Fox says *you're* to be the guest of honour.'

'Mrs Fox? How very kind of her – I'd love to meet them. I've heard all about them...I've read about their shipping business and Father speaks very highly of Mr Fox, but I've never met them. They belong to the Society of Friends, I believe? Do you know them well?'

'We're getting to know them very well – Mother really likes them. She's on several charity boards with Elizabeth Fox and they definitely see eye to eye.' Her eyebrows rose and I smiled back. 'I believe you'll like Elizabeth Fox as much as we do!'

'I'm sure I will.'

'And, not *entirely* by chance, they've invited Lord Entworth to their reception.' A knot twisted my stomach. To be sought by such a man.

Amelia's smile vanished and she cleared her throat. 'You do know Lord Entworth's duties as Member of Parliament take him to London for long stretches at a time? He's a *very* busy man, he's hardly at home – I only say that because we're such close neighbours and Papa speaks of his affairs.'

'Yes, I do know…'

Her blue eyes stared into mine. 'And he'll most likely want you to stay behind. His two daughters have been motherless for two years.'

I nodded, picturing the two girls running round an empty house, listening for their mother's laughter. Did they stare back at their mother's portrait, trying to remember her? 'I can help them grieve – I know what it's like to lose someone you love. Mel, the difference in our age means nothing – Father was fifteen years older than Mamma and Lord Entworth is only sixteen years my senior. '

'You'll be my closest neighbour and that's every reason to marry him.' She squeezed my hand, her fine calf-leather gloves the ones I had given her for her birthday. 'I hope you don't think I was prying?'

'Of course not, I appreciate everything you do for me.'

The muddy pools in the road were drying. The turnpike from Truro to Falmouth, thundered along by mail coaches, lumbered along by the heavy wagons of the Packet Service. A carriage passed us and I took a deep breath. Henry Trevelyan would have received his payment by now; it must surely buy his silence.

We slowed, turning to the left, jolting uncomfortably through the large gatehouse and into the park. Lord Carew's prize-winning cattle hardly stirred as we hurtled down the long drive beside them. Huge oaks with spreading branches dotted the parkland and my excitement grew. Soon I would see the house with its magnificent gardens sweeping down to the river. I would see the vast sheltered waters of Carrick

Roads with Falmouth in the distance. I pulled down the window, relishing the salty air.

'What about you, Amelia? Will you really never marry?'

Her voice softened. 'I can never love again, nor do I want to. I'm very fortunate – I don't *have* to marry. I've got five brothers and they've all promised to look after me. I can stay at Trenwyn for ever.' Though her words were bravely said, grief etched her face, her beloved fiancé, Midshipman Edmund Melville, lost to her on the other side of the world. 'I'm more than resigned – I'm at peace with the prospect. I never want to leave my garden. You know how much I love my work – can you imagine a husband allowing me to do what I do?'

She had thrown her heart and soul into her physic garden, sending off for plants and seeds, attending to it daily. Though nothing was said, we all knew it to be in his honour. Each plant recorded by exquisite drawings, her love for him in every stroke of her brush.

I leaned out of the window. 'I can't wait to see all the changes. I've not been back since the magnolia and rhodo-dendron were planted...'

'We've a new rhododendron walk and a thatched summer-house overlooking the river.'

The sun warmed my face and I breathed the scent of fresh grass. Two months. A whole two months then I, too, might look forward to the salty breeze blowing through my own window. I would look out over the oaks in my own park. Lord Entworth was in love with me. Even if I pinched myself, I could hardly believe it. Could I love him back? Could I heal his wounds and love his daughters like my own – be the great lady the gypsy had foretold?

'Angelica…you're miles away…Sir Alexander Pendarvis is expected for lunch – have you met him? *Admiral* Sir Alexander, I should say.'

'No. But I know he's your godfather. We've never met…'

'And George Godwin is also expected. You remember George Godwin?'

'Your mother's cousin? Yes, I remember meeting him.'

'He's really mother's second cousin – if that. I'm not sure of the connection. It's all a bit tenuous and very unfortunate. His family have been struggling for a while – bad debt, bad luck or bad judgement, who knows? Poor George. He really is very sweet, but he keeps coming back to seek Papa's advice. Papa secured his job for him – he's a prize agent in Falmouth and he's determined not to let Papa down, but it could be a bit awkward.'

'Why could it be awkward?'

'Because Sir Alex is in charge of all the French prisoners and, out of necessity, he's had to put some of them in Pendennis Castle and George believes they pose a risk. He's told Papa that the castle isn't fit to hold French prisoners and I believe George and Sir Alex have *had words*.' She leaned closer to the window. 'Oh Lord, that's George coming up the drive from the stables…'

'Why do the prisoners pose a risk?'

'It's because the ones Sir Alex has chosen are the ones who dug a tunnel out of Kergilliack Manor – all the way under the yard.'

'They escaped?'

'No, they didn't escape, but it was a very close thing. They were caught because a guard saw dirt in one their hammocks. They were depositing the earth as they exercised. They'd almost reached the outer wall – they'd dug right under the exercise yard.'

'How thrilling…'

'It was, but not for Uncle Alex! He rounded them up and had them taken to Pendennis. Poor George – I think he's out of his depth. He's a prize agent for Lord Falmouth – he says there aren't enough guards and he's probably right. Oh dear, we're going to have to stop.'

A beaming smile brightened George Godwin's pleasant round face. He stepped back, almost crushing Lord Carew's precious magnolia. Amelia waited for him to dust the leaves from his jacket. 'Mr Godwin, take care. Those branches are quite thick. I hope they haven't snagged your jacket.'

His eyes lit with pleasure. 'No…not at all. I saw you coming…I've just arrived…' The footman jumped to the ground and pulled down the steps for him. 'Thank you, such a beautiful day. How was your journey?' He sounded as eager as he looked, his accent not local, more probably from Devon. He had clearly dressed with care, his silk cravat held in place by an enamel pin, a new jacket sitting stiffly across his shoulders. Thick waves of sandy hair framed his boyish face. He was of medium stature, the buttons on his waistcoat straining as he negotiated his seat.

'I believe you've already met Miss Lilly,' Amelia said, leaning back. 'We've had a very good journey, thank you.'

I smiled in greeting but he barely glanced at me. 'I've just ridden from Falmouth – the roads are very muddy. I should have come by boat.' He looked down in sudden embarrassment, glancing back at Amelia, trying not to gaze, and my heart melted. Another lost recruit for her long line of admirers.

Chapter Nine

Trenwyn House
Sunday 31st July 1796, 1:00 p.m.

'Oh, there you are, my dear. Come, let me look at you.' Lady Clarissa put down her basket, holding out both hands and I curtseyed, trying not to look shocked. Her large straw hat was covered in daisy chains, her grey hair loose around her shoulders. Her strong leather gloves were smeared in mud, a large net slung from her shoulder. An apron covered her gown, the hem of which was hitched up to her calf, revealing heavily splattered men's boots.

'Ah, George – Lord Carew and Sir Alex are with Persephone. Sir Alex has a long journey ahead of him, so we'll dine directly.'

She looked round, slipping the net from her shoulder. 'Henry's caught his first seabass. They're just off the jetty – the fish, I mean – not the children. And William caught an eel.' She lifted the cloth of the basket and six glazed eyes stared back at me.

Lady Clarissa was a radical freethinker, a believer in Rousseau, her children raised in nature and given the sort of freedom every child yearns. She smiled broadly, looking back across the newly raked gravel. 'Goodness, where *are* the children?'

A movement in the yew tree caught her attention. 'Oh well, I suppose they don't want their raspberry sorbet after all. Never mind, all the more for us...' She turned amidst squeals and protestations, her two young grandsons leaping from the branches behind her. A groom followed, carrying fishing rods and more nets, and she handed him the basket, straightening her large straw hat. 'All set for tomorrow, Jethro?'

Jethro nodded. 'Yes, m'lady – though we're still four short.'

The carriage pulled away, leaving us standing on the circular drive. 'Do you play cricket?' Lady Clarissa asked George. 'We need to field a full team.'

George Godwin's eager round cheeks fell. 'I'm afraid not. I've never played cricket, but perhaps I could learn?'

'Perhaps.' Lady Clarissa kissed her sodden grandsons in turn. 'Tomorrow, three o'clock sharp. Both of you – ready for cricket practice.' She turned to Amelia. 'What about Charles?'

'Charles is *two*, Mother – I think that's a bit young.' She slipped her arm through mine. 'But Angelica will come – she loves playing cricket.' I caught the mischief in her eyes, both of us remembering Miss Mitchell's unladylike shriek as the hall window smashed.

Lady Clarissa pulled off her leather gloves. She had a distinctive, aristocratic face, her long nose and firm chin softened by her laughing eyes and warm smile. 'We've got just under three weeks to get our team in shape. It's quite wonderful Frederick's coming home – that's three of my five sons who can play, and I count that a blessing. Trelawney must not take the cup again.'

Amelia drew me inside the large front door, almost skipping across the hall. Sunlight flooded through the huge skylight above, lighting the stripes in the gold wallpaper. 'It's the annual cricket match against the neighbouring estate. Oh, mind these buckets,' she said, leading me up the staircase with its mahogany banisters and elaborately decorated cornice. 'The top window's still leaking – that last storm did a huge amount of damage.'

She opened the door to my room and I rushed to the window. The river stretched below us, the water so blue, the sun's reflection glinting like pieces of broken glass. 'I'd forgotten how beautiful it is,' I said, gazing across the lawn to the orchard beyond. Two rowing boats lay moored against a small jetty, a ship bobbing at anchor in the bend of the river. It was so peaceful, so breathtakingly beautiful, and I breathed in the salty air, watching the river birds wading across the muddy banks.

'On days like this you can almost see the rooftops of Falmouth – that's Pendennis Castle.'

'You know George Godwin's in love with you, don't you?' I whispered.

Amelia's cheeks flushed. 'I know – I don't want him to be and I certainly don't encourage him.' The scent of roses filled the room and her voice lifted. 'Mother's got plans to build an orangery but for the moment those hothouses are where Mr Maddox propagates his plants.'

'Is he still with you?'

'Daniel Maddox? Yes, but his work's finished really — everything he's planted has taken root. The shrubbery's complete and the saplings are thriving.' She pointed across the park to a group of young oaks protected by a heavy fence. 'He's planted the bigger trees but he can't plant the saplings for at least three years — he's got fifty growing in tubs in the walled garden. The more precious plants he tends in his hothouse. See...down there?'

A jumble of roofs huddled against the walled garden. 'He's growing pineapples and melons...and extremely rare orchids. I believe he's moved his bed in with them.'

'He sleeps in the *hothouse*?'

She nodded, trying to suppress a smile. 'He has rooms in the gardener's cottage, but he won't leave his plants. His prime possession is a night-blooming cereus and he's convinced it's about to flower. The poor man does nothing but stare at it — willing it to open.'

'How exciting. Will it bloom while I'm here?'

'It might. He's installed a bell to ring so we can come the moment the flower opens. I've promised to draw it — I've everything ready.' There were new smile lines by her eyes, a definite lifting of her chin, even laughter in her whisper: 'What with Papa waiting for Persephone and Mr Maddox with his night-flowering cereus, we can hardly sleep at night.'

Footmen carried in my luggage, and the young maid who had accompanied us was holding a steaming pitcher. Amelia smiled. 'Mother won't take too long to change. Ask Bethany if there's anything more you need.'

Our rooms had an adjoining door and I looked round, taking in the Chinese wallpaper, the delicately engraved animal paws on the legs of the table and chairs, the embroidered silk birds with long tail feathers hanging round the bed. A desk was neatly laid with paper and quills, a huge vase of roses sitting on the table. Removing my bonnet, I washed my face and hands, smiling at Bethany as she unpacked my valises. There was a knock on the door and Charity Carew stood in the doorway.

'Is that you, Miss Lilly? We've been so looking forward to your visit.' Blinded by a childhood illness, Charity Carew tapped her lacquered stick in front of her. She had the looks of an angel and the intelligence of the sharpest attorney. She seemed to remember everything. Her blonde hair fell in soft curls round her face. 'I hope you like the roses – after so much rain we thought they might spoil.'

Amelia came to her side, leading her across the room to join me at the window. 'Some of Charity's China roses are very rare – they've come all the way from Bengal.'

Charity smiled. 'We're expecting two more plants any day now – from Kew Gardens…some of Mr Slater's new *Crimson Roses*. There's been a real scramble for them but I believe they've put two aside for us.' She had a beautiful voice, as cut-glass and chiselled as Amelia's. She, too, was an earl's granddaughter, every inch of her refined and elegant. She had captured Frederick's heart with her beauty and quiet humour, but it was her knowledge of animal husbandry that I most admired. She could remember every detail – the pedi-gree lines for each of Lord Carew's cattle, the exact yield each of the milkers gave.

'Who's Persephone?' I asked.

'She's our large black sow – she's farrowing. She has the sweetest nature and we all adore her. I'm surprised Lord Carew hasn't ordered her inside.'

Amelia smiled. 'There's plenty of room in the scullery – how is she?'

'Definitely nesting – she's rearranging her bedding and banking up the straw so the signs are all there. We usually reckon on three months, three weeks and three days which takes her to tomorrow but that might not be the case with a China cross-breed.'

'She's Papa's beloved black sow from China – he crossed her with Solomon,' Amelia explained.

A bell sounded and Lady Clarissa's laughter rang up the stairs. Amelia squeezed Charity's arm 'The sea's so blue, Itty – and Frederick's out there – just beyond the horizon. He's probably gazing across the ocean this very minute, counting down the hours until he sees you.'

Charity clasped her silver locket to her heart. 'Eighteen months is a very long time.'

'But he's coming home…'

At the foot of the stairs, I glimpsed the elaborate table with its huge silver tureens and my heart sank. Two footmen were standing by the door, others waiting behind the chairs. Amelia saw me stiffen.

'Don't be frightened, Angelica. Sir Alex's reputation may

be a bit gruff but under that stern exterior, he's as soft as butter.'

Sir Alexander Pendarvis, stern faced yet smiling, knighted for exceptional gallantry, stood by the French window, his travelling clothes immaculate. He bowed at our approach. 'Ah, my dears – the Three Graces could not look more lovely.'

Chapter Ten

I was sitting on Lord Carew's right, an honour not lost on me. George Godwin was on my other side, the light luncheon turning out to be a huge rump of beef, piles of roasted potatoes, and asparagus grown and cut by Lady Clarissa. The plates were cleared, the raspberry sorbet tasting as delicious as it looked.

'So, you're to go to Bodmin first, then up the North Road? Good Heavens, you'll be away for months.' Lord Carew leaned back in his chair. He was strong for sixty-one, his ruddy cheeks aglow with good health. His red felt cap was pulled low over his bald head, his white side whiskers almost meeting under his chin. Bushy white eyebrows joined forces across his brow. 'Why up there?'

Sir Alex looked up from his sorbet. 'Norman Cross is the site we've chosen. It has the clearest advantage – a good water supply and good road access. More importantly, it's sufficiently far from the sea to deter escape.' He was a slight man, wearing a simple grey wig tied in a black bow at his neck. Though he was clearly dressed for travel, his well-cut jacket was of exceptional quality. I tried to smile but his eyes seemed to pin me as he spoke. It was as if he was not looking at me, but into me. 'We've four thousand prisoners expected from the West Indies, Miss Lilly, and nowhere to put them. As it is, our prisons are crammed to over-capacity. If this prison isn't built by December, disease will spread and many will die.'

'What about the new prison on the moor? Is that to go ahead, Sir Alex?' asked Charity.

'Indeed, it has to — but it's to be built of stone and that will take too long. The prison at Norman Cross will be built of wood. Five hundred carpenters are lined up, ready to start.'

Lord Carew swirled his claret. 'Falmouth certainly can't take any more.'

Lady Clarissa had changed into a green silk dress; her shoulder-length grey hair was swept back in a large coil and held in place by an emerald clasp. She had pearls at her neck, an emerald ring glinting on one finger. Behind one ear was a pink rose, a hermit shell wound around one of her fingers. Pinned to her bodice was a small bunch of lavender. 'What bothers me is that so many of the prisoners are merchant seamen. They have their wives and families with them — they're good seafaring men, devoted to traditional values. Their ships don't stand a chance against our cannons.'

'Very few shots are fired, my dear. No one's going to risk losing either the cargo or the ship. Merchant ships are expected to surrender — the victor takes the ship and impounds the cargo. It's the rules of warfare.' The affection in Lord Carew's voice was obvious. He smiled lovingly at his wife. 'They take our supplies and we take theirs. Blockades only work if supply ships are prevented from getting through. How else did we seize the French colonies?'

Sir Alex shook his head. 'You're right, though – families shouldn't be held as prisoners. We've a clear list of who to send back – chaplains, priests, surgeons, pursers, school masters...*all* women and children. But wives simply won't leave their husbands – whether from Spain or from the Indies, from Norway, Sweden, France, it's always the same – merchant seamen's families live on board and they've nowhere else to go.'

'I hear the number of prisoners is nearing eleven thousand.'

'And rising daily, Charity. The Transport Board can barely keep abreast of the lists. Many prisoners remain unaccounted for – held offshore in stinking hulks.' He took an appreciative sip of his claret. 'We need the new prisons *today*, let alone by Christmas.'

I had been following the conversation in growing alarm. 'But won't it be over by Christmas, Sir Alex?'

'We'd all like to believe that, Miss Lilly – but not to build the prisons on that premise would be reprehensible. Towns like Falmouth can barely cope. Provisions are in short supply and the sheer numbers of French prisoners makes for fierce discontent. Yet the rules of warfare must be adhered to – *every* French prisoner has the right to receive full rations.'

'My friend, Elizabeth Fox, says it's getting worse...but it's hardly surprising. Amidst such starvation there's real anger.

Men see provisions pouring into the prisons while their own families starve.'

Lord Carew nodded. 'And she's right, Amelia. Mrs Fox must have been referring to the ship that arrived five weeks ago. Stuffed to the gunwales, it was, with American wheat – like manna from heaven – yet they had to anchor in the Sound while Captain Fenshaw made the quayside safe. Even as it lay to anchor, he had to post guards to protect it. Some brandy, Alexander?' Sir Alexander Pendarvis shook his head. 'That cargo was subsidized by the importer at four pounds three shillings. That's *last year's* price. Yet even as the women held out their bowls, there were profiteers haggling on the quayside, determined to seize the cargo.'

'You've lost another harvest, William?'

'One scorched summer followed by two rain-lashed harvests. The conditions for sowing were bad from the start – the crops never stood a chance. Now we've lost what there was – all of us, not just my land. There's nothing to salvage – no oats, no wheat. My turnips and potato fields never stood a chance.' He drained his glass, wiping his mouth with his napkin. 'I've got land under water and fields too heavy to harrow.'

Charity nodded. 'Our fattening stock has been commandeered by the navy. It's right our men get good food but it's no wonder there's severe discontent. Women need to feed their families. Their children are weak, yet they hear the French prisoners carve intricate trinkets from their meat bones and sell them at a high price.'

Sir Alex refused more claret, thanking the footman with a gracious smile. The more I saw of him, the more I warmed to him. He treated Amelia and Charity with such respect, even talking to me as if he was talking to an important member of the Admiralty. His eyes were piercing because he was interested in what I was saying, not looking over my shoulder wanting to talk to someone more important. His reputation was legendary – knighted for valour, for actions over and above the call of duty. He had swum to a sinking ship with a lifeline, saving the lives of everyone on board.

He spoke softly, answering Charity's question. 'Indeed. We must ask why the French are in no hurry to get their men back: putting ever increasing obstacles in my way, blocking every attempt I make to instigate an exchange. *Every* prisoner swop I have tried to negotiate has ended in failure.'

'It's as if they *want* them to remain here.'

'I believe they do – and why not? Six days a week on a quart of beer, one and a half pounds of bread, three-quarters of a pound of fresh beef and, let's not forget, half a pint of dried peas on four days? Not to mention four ounces of butter and six ounces of cheese on Fridays! It's a crippling food bill. I believe it's most certainly in their interest to keep as many prisoners as they can on British soil.'

'You believe it's a tactic to weaken our already weakened economy – to instigate unrest, even riots, to force us to make peace?'

'You have it in a nutshell, Charity. And it's working. Without question we should give the prisoners their full rations – absolutely – it's our duty as a civilized nation, yet we have bread riots and the cost of food is rising by the day. Britain cannot afford this war.'

'Are they doing the same for our prisoners?' Amelia's voice rang with pain.

Sir Alex's face fell. 'In truth, Amelia, I cannot reassure you. I've clear evidence their treatment falls well short of our expectations.'

Three large windows opened on to the vast terrace with its intricately sculptured urns spilling over with flowers. A soft breeze blew through the open doors, filling the room with the scent of the garden. The room felt homely for all its grandeur, the portraits of the family looking lovingly down on us. The biggest painting was my favourite: Lord Carew had his arm round Lady Clarissa, both of them sporting large straw hats. Their five sons were so alike; the eldest four standing either side of their parents, smiling and holding up fishing rods, while Frederick and Amelia knelt on the ground, playing with a puppy. Lord Carew had a shotgun slung over his shoulder; there was a brace of pheasants in the foreground, the house in the distance, and I felt a pang of emptiness – a terrible longing I found hard to control.

Love oozed from every object in the room – Amelia's paintings, a bird mosaic crafted from shells picked up from the beach. Pebbles with holes in them, displayed as proudly as the best family silver. Lord Carew's huge leather trumpet which he used to bellow orders, his marching grandsons kept in line, his plantsmen and gardeners directed to position trees from the house. No wonder Amelia had only stayed at the school for one term. I, too, would never want to leave this place.

George Godwin glanced at Amelia and my heart burned;

both of us were outsiders, the mantle of this extraordinary family warming our souls. I could understand his desperate desire to belong, how empty he would feel on the long ride home. Lord Carew smiled at his wife. 'You're staying very quiet, Mr Godwin.'

George Godwin almost gulped his wine, a slight sheen on his forehead as he cleared his throat. 'I believe the prisoners have settled in very well. They've access to fresh air—'

'And the attention of a barber. No razors?'

'No razors, no twine, no knives. Their hammocks are hung from hooks.'

Lord Carew seemed pleased. 'Splendid. So all is resolved in Pendennis?'

A slight tremor made George's crystal glass sparkle. He seemed undecided whether to speak. 'It's...it's still not to my satisfaction...the situation worsens by the day. Captain Fenshaw is doing all he can but the truth is I've drafted a three-page letter of protest to Lord Falmouth.'

'A letter of protest! Good God, man!'

George Godwin could barely keep his hands steady. 'I haven't sent it...I'd very much appreciate it if you'd read it, Lord Carew. I'd value your opinion.'

Chapter Eleven

Lord Carew looked distinctly annoyed. 'There's nothing you can tell Lord Falmouth that we don't already know.'

George Godwin's mouth twitched. He took a gulp of wine and squared his shoulders. 'If I may...Sir, Pendennis Castle is a complete shambles. There's woeful lack of supervision – if any. Our fortifications are nothing but crumbling batteries housing ineffective cannons. The biggest natural harbour in the south coast – the first port of call for ships crossing the oceans – and every ship that seeks shelter is exposed to danger.'

Sir Alex Pendarvis stared back across the table. 'We are all too well aware of this, Mr Godwin.'

Beads of sweat dotted George Godwin's brow. 'I have to speak plainly – to speak the truth. I have prize money arriving weekly, the vaults are filled to capacity, and every wagon I send to London requires guards to march alongside it. The wagons are slow and need guarding day and night – each guard needs to be armed. Captain Fenshaw gives me his best men for the wagons, but each time that depletes our numbers back at the castle. Those that are left are, well, they're none of them fit – they're either too ill or too old.'

Lord Carew's bushy white eyebrows contracted. His voice softened. 'There's no need for your letter, George – Lord Falmouth's fully aware of the situation. Captain Fenshaw's doing his utmost under very difficult circumstances. We've made a splendid appointment – Captain Melvill is to take position as Lieutenant Governor very shortly. He's a well-respected, *thoroughly* experienced Army officer and his priority will be to raise a volunteer artillery. I can guarantee he'll tighten up the garrison and these concerns you quite rightly raise will be addressed. Not long now, George. Lord Falmouth appreciates how hard this is for you.'

George glanced at the open door, lowering his voice. 'A Company of Invalids has *no* place defending Pendennis Castle. You must understand, I can't stand by without voicing my concern.' He cast an agonizing look at Amelia. 'Habitual drunkenness…a long absent captain…command devolved to a man of uncertain health. I wish it was otherwise but Captain Fenshaw commands little respect – his orders are often disregarded by the men.' He mopped his brow with his handkerchief. 'The state of the Company is not just lapse, it's defective. An attack on Falmouth would meet no resistance – those cannons are too heavy to be manned by men *invalided* out of service. Most are too drunk or disabled to follow orders. They're old…they have little or no strength…'

Sir Alex folded his napkin, placing it on the table. 'We're well aware of the picture you paint. I'm also well aware that my prisoners have added to your workload. Nothing is how we want it to be. The strain on everyone is telling and you have every right to voice your concern. Indeed, I applaud you. It takes a brave man to speak up like you have, but everyone's hands are tied. There are no rabbits to pull from hats. Mustering volunteers takes time. The agent I have appointed in my absence will take care of everything to do with the prisoners. He'll take full responsibility for their welfare and security. They are under his jurisdiction – his total command.'

George nodded. 'Thank you, Sir Alex.'

Lord Carew got to his feet as Sir Alex rose. 'Captain Philip Melvill will soon have the garrison swept clean and the batteries rebuilt. In a few months, Pendennis Castle will be *impenetrable*, but in the meantime, your job must be to hold the fort.'

George Godwin rose, pulling back Lady Clarissa's chair. 'I hope that goes without saying. I'll defend Pendennis if I'm the last man standing – but can I expect Captain Melvill soon?'

A look passed between Sir Alex and Lord Carew. 'Four weeks, maybe more. By the first week of September, if all goes well.'

'*Four* weeks! Sir, I beg you to advance his arrival.'

Lord Carew stood stony-faced. 'He's coming as fast as his business commitments will allow. He's a very busy man – highly sought after – and we're lucky he's chosen us at all. He could have the pick of commands. You must hold the fort, Mr Godwin, and there will be adequate recompense for your troubles. By all means send your letter, but my advice is that the less this gets out, the better for us all.'

Amelia grabbed my elbow, pulling me through a rose-covered arch. Behind us, Sir Alex was taking his leave, promising to send Lady Clarissa's best wishes to his wife. 'Quick, Angelica – down here.' She led me into the newly planted rhododendron walk. 'Poor George – that was very brave of him.' She glanced back. 'But it will have done him no favours with Sir Alex.'

In the dappled shade, the path seemed to glitter. 'The path's sparkling.'

'Mother's mirror splinters – she had them sprinkled in with the crushed shells to make the path sparkle.' We descended the twisting path, the scent of yew trees mingling with drying seaweed. Amelia opened the iron gate that led into the walled garden. 'This way...through here...mind you don't trip over Mr Maddox's rabbit traps. He's put wires everywhere – they're attached to bells. It's made all the difference.'

Long rows of plants lay baking in the hot sun, their names written on slates beside them. Amelia smiled, thrilled by my sudden gasp. 'We've got twice as many plants now – and there's the same amount again under glass. Most are doing well. We've planted them alphabetically – that was Charity's idea. That's why you can still see spaces...' She started leading me through the herbs, stooping to snap off a shoot, rubbing it between her fingers, holding it out for me to smell. 'That's willow bark – it's taken very well. They use it mainly for fevers and pain.'

Potting sheds lay huddled against the wall and I saw the familiar thatched outhouse with the painted green door. 'Does Moses still live there?'

'Yes, I couldn't manage without him. He does all the propagating – he grows all the plants we send away so, really, I should call it *his* garden. I come down in the morning to see what he's been doing. Samuel worked by night and Moses continues the same. He picks up the snails – that's another reason why our stock's so healthy.' She held a bunch of herbs in each hand.

'He gardens at night?'

'More and more – it's getting to the point I hardly see him. I understand it but I don't like it. I wish he'd mix more with the other servants but…well, he's different, that's all.' The blue ribbons on her bonnet matched her dress; her stout shoes an important requisite for the stony path. The sadness in her face returned. 'He's becoming more and more of a recluse – he sleeps by day and gardens by night. He looks frightening but really he isn't. He's as gentle as a lamb – I just wish people would understand that.'

'Poor Moses. Not being able to speak or hear.'

She nodded. 'He's not stupid in any way. He can shake his right hand to say yes and his left hand to say no. And just the other day, he took a stick and I'm sure he was trying to draw in the dirt. It was very jerky, but I think he was drawing two bee-keeper's hats. Wasn't that clever? He was clearly asking for a new hat.'

A deaf mute child, the same age as the heir to Trenwyn House, washed on to their beach in a laundry basket, Lady Clarissa scooping him out of the water without a second thought, giving him to her childless head gardener to nurture and love. The child's mother must have known just when and

92

where to float that basket, but she could never have guessed her imbecile child would end up growing herbs for every apothecary and physician in Cornwall.

Amelia pointed to the hothouse on the other side of the wall. 'We won't bother Mr Maddox...not today...it's Sunday and he's probably very busy.' The hesitation in her voice was unusual. She seemed guarded, a momentary crease to her brow. 'He's just received a new seed catalogue so we better leave him in peace. He can show you his pineapples tomorrow.'

From the other side of the wall came the sound of a loud splash, followed by a peel of laughter, and Amelia picked up her skirts and ran. I followed hard on her heels, hurtling through the gate and on to the shingle beach. A dog was splashing noisily, making its way towards us from the middle of the river. Lady Clarissa was in a rowing boat, peering over her raised oar, a small child wobbling precariously by her side. Amelia stopped running, waving her herbs in delight. 'It's all right. It's only Mother teaching Freddie to row.'

The rowing boat was bobbing violently and I stared in disbelief. 'But Freddie's only fourteen months old...'

'I know – isn't he clever? Just look how he's grasping that oar.' She put down her herbs and clapped her hands. 'He's really getting the idea.' The tiny child beamed back, letting go of his oar, clapping back at his aunt with complete adoration, and I looked down in horror. A huge black dog was shaking salty water over my new silk gown.

'Don't mind Horace,' Amelia said, stooping to pet the huge brute. 'He looks fierce but he's nothing but a furry bundle – he's Charity's and goes everywhere with Freddie. Did you like your swim, you gorgeous, gorgeous boy?'

She stopped, suddenly pointing to my feet. 'Look, Angelica …a lucky pebble – see the hole right through it? It's yours – pick it up.'

'Shouldn't it be *finders keepers*?'

'No, it's yours if you pick it up. Come…let's see if these raspberry leaves help Persephone to farrow.'

I woke with a hammering heart. Babies were in the water, French prisoners running riot through the house. I was at a grand reception, Miss Mitchell staring up at her broken window, demanding my parole. Henry Trevelyan had hold of my hand – I was in a coach, thundering through the night.

The night before, Lady Clarissa had prescribed buttered eggs and warm milk, smiling when she saw I could hardly keep my eyes open. 'A bit more fresh air and we'll soon have your bloom back,' she had said, marching me up the stairs and opening the wardrobe door. 'I've taken the liberty of putting some rather less formal gowns in here – I hope you find something to your taste.' She had settled herself on my bed. 'I can be as formal as the best of them *when* I need to be, but I believe our spirit should remain free. Do you agree, my dear?'

'Yes…I do…' I had replied.

'Truth, not artifice,' she had whispered. 'Truth and beauty go hand in hand. Without truth, beauty is only skin deep, yet we live in a world of great artifice. Nature has no artifice, Miss Lilly – we see her brutality as well as her beauty.'

I had nodded, fighting an unexpected rush of tears. It was lovely having her sit on my bed. No one had sat on my bed for seven years, not even Molly. She reached over to kiss my forehead. 'You're very welcome here, my dear,' she had whispered.

My nightmare was abating and I threw back my covers, dashing to the window, pulling up the casement. Moonlight glistened on the river, its silver light almost as bright as day. I could see the bricks in the wall, the glasshouse glinting between the branches of the tulip tree. The scent of herbs and roses was intoxicating, the smell of salt in the fresh sea breeze. Owls were hooting across the river, the rowing boats lying idle against the jetty, and I breathed in the beauty of the night. The tide was high, the sheep grazing the orchard, the cattle ruminating in the pasture beyond.

I leaned further out. A man was tending the bees in the orchard, moving slowly between each group of beehives, and I knew it to be Moses enjoying the serenity of his night-scented garden. I turned to listen. A muffled sound caught my attention, heart-wrenching sobs drifting through the adjoining door, and I put my ear against the polished wood, pushing it gently open. Amelia was sitting by her window, a letter in her hand. She was staring at the moon, more letters piled on her lap. Her cheeks glistened as she turned.

'It's all this talk of prisoners…and the fact everyone else is coming home. Some nights I hardly sleep. I just stare at the moon…hoping he might be looking at it too, wondering if—' She stopped, lost in another sob.

'Wondering if you're still waiting for him...that you haven't given up hope?'

She nodded, her lace nightcap pinning her ringlets in place. 'We were going to get married when he returned but I wish we hadn't waited. I wish I'd had his child – like Charity and little Freddie. That way he'd always be part of me. It's so hard, Angelica.' She wiped her eyes with her lace handkerchief. 'It's hard because some days I almost forget him. Whole days go past and I realize I've had a lovely day – like today. Then the moon shines so brightly and I feel guilty... like I've abandoned him.'

The letter trembled in her hand and I took it from her, placing it with the others, tying the blue silk ribbon carefully around them. 'Come back to bed, Mel.' A shaft of moonlight lit the brocade and I lifted the cover, slipping between the silk sheets next to her. 'Will you show me your paintings in the morning?'

Her voice grew stronger. 'I'm compiling my own compendium of herbs – their uses as well as their propagation. I've done twenty so far – I'm very pleased with them.'

I could barely speak the words I knew I must say. 'It was a dangerous undertaking. There were very few survivors.'

'I know...but two men were taken prisoner – that's enough to keep hope alive.'

'*Two* men, Mel...not *three*,' I whispered. 'Seven men were buried...they were all accounted for.'

Chapter Twelve

I cannot remember ever being so happy. My borrowed gown was particularly pretty. It had a blue satin frill round the scooped neckline and lace at the elbow, and was perfect for leaning over Persephone's sty, perfect also for playing cricket with the boys, and walking along the beach. My bonnet was tied with lilac ribbons and a parasol completed my outfit. Already I was competent at deadheading China roses.

Charity held Freddie in her arms. 'Here, smell this one – it's my *Portland* Rose.'

She cradled the delicate bloom in her hands, lifting it for me to smell. Flowers cascaded from the surrounding arbours, butterflies resting on the brass dial of the central plinth, and Amelia continued her explanation of the morning routine. 'Mother likes to attend to her correspondence and household arrangements in her boudoir until eleven, and I try to spend the mornings painting or drawing – *when I can*.' She pursed her lips, pinching Freddie's fat pink cheek, smiling back at his delighted giggle. 'And Charity likes to spend an hour or so with Papa discussing the livestock.'

'I help him to remember who we bred with who – cross-breeding's one thing, inter-breeding quite another. I just remind him of their bloodlines and suggest future matches.'

Amelia cut another stem, placing it in her basket. 'We hardly ever see my brothers, William and Charles. William's organizing the Volunteer muster and as busy as Papa with the estate and Charles' duties as rector keep him tied up in the parish.' She handed me a pink rose to smell, snipping the stem short, tucking it above my ear. 'When we've done our morning's work we come out and cut fresh flowers for the house and then we await the invasion.'

'The invasion?'

'Not the French – the children! Young William and Henry spend the morning watching for the flag to go up. See the flagpole?' She looked up at the huge yellow flag fluttering from the roof. 'It's Mother's way of communicating to both houses.' She pointed across the bay. 'The Old Rectory's just over there...and Manor Farm is next to that group of trees. Cordelia's seven months with child so she's resting...but the boys come whenever they can.'

'What does a yellow flag mean?'

'A yellow flag means the grandsons are welcome – a blue flag means compulsory attendance. No flag means she's busy and a red flag means she's making gingerbread.'

A line of twine linked Freddie to Charity's wrist. She put him down to totter among the roses. 'Which means, of course, that *everyone* comes!'

A tall, thin, man with stooping shoulders and tousled black hair entered the rose garden; his tweed jacket was patched at the elbow and slightly too big for him, his boots well-worn and scuffed. His leather apron was tied twice around his waist, his hat at an angle. He put down the large earthenware pot he was carrying and took off his cap; his face was sunburned, fresh earth on his hands as he smoothed his hair.

'Good afternoon, Mr Maddox...'

'Good afternoon, Miss Carew, Mrs Carew.' He clutched his hat, staring at the mud on his boots.

'May I introduce Miss Lilly to you? Miss Lilly, this is Mr Maddox, Papa's plantsman.'

I had seen him before from afar, but I had never met him. He smiled shyly, still trying to restore order to his tousled hair. He looked round at the profusion of roses. 'I hope you like Mrs Carew's rose garden, Miss Lilly?'

'I do, very much – and I'm looking forward to seeing round your hothouse.'

He wrung his hat like a cloth, stealing a glance at Amelia. 'You're very welcome – it would be a pleasure to show you round.'

We turned at the sound of running footsteps.

'Ahoy there...' Two small pirates were hurtling through the gate, cutlasses held aloft, their chubby legs exposed to the air. 'Grandma says to tell you that your brother Edgar's expected. You're to come with us...'

The ground spun beneath me. 'Edgar! He can't be—'

'Will you give us your parole, or shall we bind you?'

'No...you have my word...' My sudden dizziness was making it hard to breathe. Edgar and Jacob should be on their way back to Oxford – what if they told Lady Clarissa they had seen me, and not Father? Lady Clarissa would realize I had lied. I felt sick with fear. 'When's he expected?' I managed to ask.

William scratched his charcoal beard. 'Think Grandma said two o'clock.' He smiled as his cousin tottered towards him and held out his arms. 'Do you mind if we take Freddie prisoner instead, Miss Lilly?'

'No...go ahead...I don't mind at all.' What if they discussed the play? Panic filled me, yet I must look pleased. I must skip a bit, look excited. 'Goodness...they can't find me dressed like this – I must go and change. Perhaps I'll go and meet them.'

My eagerness taken for excitement, Lady Clarissa suggested I walk down the drive to greet them. I was as far as I could reasonably go, having promised to remain within sight of the house, and I waited in the shade of the magnolia bush, trying not to pace about. The cows no longer saw me as interesting, the sheep long deciding I was not a threat. Bees buzzed loudly on the honeysuckle behind me, labourers mending a fence in the pasture beyond, but I barely saw them. All I could do was stare at the gatehouse.

A trail of dust followed the coach as it drew nearer and I stepped on to the drive, holding up my hand. Henry Trevelyan slowed the horses and stopped, jumping unsmiling to the ground. I had not meant to look at him, but caught his eye. 'You received your payment?'

His mouth set hard as he opened the carriage door. 'I did.'

Edgar's face held a look of mischief. 'Good. We weren't sure if Lady Clarissa would get my note in time. We didn't want to risk your displeasure *again*.' He smiled. 'I need to apologize, Angelica – no hard feelings about the plates?' He looked almost handsome, his unruly black curls freshly washed, his clothes impeccable. But for his sunken eyes and the pallor in his cheeks, he looked like my brother of old. 'We're not staying – just passing really, and thought we'd say hello.'

Jacob Boswell leaned forward. 'Won't you get in?'

I smiled with relief. 'No…thank you. Now you've apologized, you can carry on. There's no need to stop—'

'And risk Lady Clarissa's displeasure?' Edgar's high-pitched giggle was back. 'No, we're committed. How's the old bird?'

'Rather busy – I can send her your regards and tell her you were in a hurry…'

'Busy sea-bathing from her jetty? Get in, Angelica.' The edge to Jacob's voice made my heart thump.

'I must say, I'm looking forward to meeting the old bird – I gather she's a hoot. Perhaps she'll have us running naked round the shrubbery?' Edgar leaned out of the window. 'The house isn't as grand as I'd expected – more like a large country villa.'

'Edgar – don't speak like that. It's disrespectful.'

A conspiratorial look passed between them. Edgar waved

my rebuke aside. 'Get in, Angelica. You must know why we've come.'

Henry Trevelyan held out his un-gloved hand and I took it to stop my sudden giddiness. They knew. They were going to make me pay. Jacob Boswell leaned back against the leather seat, indicating for me to sit next to him, and I took the seat opposite, staring back at him as he flicked the lace at his sleeve. 'I believe you're quite familiar with this carriage?'

Excitement lit Edgar's eyes. 'The thing is, Angelica, we wheedled it out of Molly. Now...you know how these things work. You *don't* tell Father I'm not in Oxford and we *don't* tell Lady Clarissa you lied to her and went to the theatre. It's as simple as that.' He must have seen me flinch. 'You haven't already written to Father, have you?'

I kept my gaze straight. 'No, of course not. He still thinks you're in Oxford.'

'Splendid, then we're agreed.' The hatred in Jacob's eyes might once have unnerved me. Now I was ready for it. It was Edgar who upset me.

'You have my silence,' I said.

Edgar's hand began tapping his knee, again the high-pitched giggle. 'We'll tell the old bird we've come straight from Falmouth. Actually, that's the truth. We've been staying at Jake's. We've been visiting his sisters in his mother's absence – that's a good brotherly thing to do, don't you think? That should gain him favour.'

Brotherly thing. I fought my rush of fury. 'To get to Jacob's house, you'd have to pass through Truro. Yet you didn't stop to see us?'

'Honest, Angelica, you look just like Father when you frown. Don't worry – I'll be all politeness and manners.' He giggled, glancing at Jacob. 'The thing is…well, the truth is we've run out of money and Father *did* say we're forbidden the theatre.'

Jacob Boswell remained staring out of the window, a smirk lifting the corner of his mouth. I could still feel the tightness of his grip, yet his grip on my brother was far more sinister. 'I can't do anything about that. I'm here for two months and I've no access to Father's money.' It was hard to breathe, hard to remain calm – to make a man blackmail his own sister. Jacob Boswell was a monster.

Edgar opened his ebony snuffbox. 'I can wait two months, Angelica. Just give us what you've got…then a monthly rise would be appreciated. You can put it down to one of your charities…'

Jacob took the proffered snuffbox, pinching some snuff between his thumb and forefinger. 'It might not be news to you, but the actress playing Miss Neville was taken ill before the end of the play – *someone else* took her place. Flora told us all about it.'

Seething anger stung my eyes. 'I've got twenty guineas in coins. That's all.'

Edgar's breath reeked of tobacco and alcohol. He leaned to kiss my cheek. 'I'm sure you've got more than that – it's lovely to see you, by the way.'

I fought back my tears. Never let bullies see you cry. I had learned that long ago. I wanted to beg him, plead with him, shake him, yell at him. I wanted to tell him how sad Mamma would be, how disappointed Father would be, but I bit my tongue, watching the gravel widen as we passed the coach house. The carriage slowed to a halt and he looked up at the house with its large sash windows and parapet framing the top.

His high-pitched laugh squeaked like a mouse. 'Thought for a moment you were going to say how Father would be *ashamed* of me – how Mother would think me a *disgrace*.'

Chapter Thirteen

'No, thank you, no more frangipane.' I could barely swallow. They would leave after tea and my ordeal would be over. Lady Clarissa smiled and put down her cup. Her greatest pleasure was to take tea in the shade of the large spreading oak.

'Lord Carew must have been detained – his duties as Lord Lieutenant of Cornwall take an enormous toll on his time. My eldest son, William, is Lieutenant of Division and between them they collect the returns. They're organizing the muster but raising these Volunteer companies is taking time – funds must be sought, uniforms bought. It's not something they can rush.'

Though we nodded in reply, all eyes were on the cricket practice taking place on the lawn. A handful of men had gathered round Jethro who was showing them how to hold the bat. The two eldest grandsons were engrossed, the two youngest running circles round their nurse, but it was not them that caught my eye. Henry Trevelyan was marking out the pitch in long straight strides. He knocked the second wicket into place and Lady Clarissa smiled. 'Do you play cricket, Mr Lilly?'

Edgar must have expected her question. 'Not as well as I should, Lady Clarissa.'

'And you, Sir Jacob?'

The golden halo shook. 'I'm not one for cricket.'

Wickets in place, Henry Trevelyan rolled up his sleeves and took the bat from William, repositioning it in the boy's hands as Jethro directed the men where to stand. Lady Clarissa's smile broadened. 'Who is that man?' she said, as Henry Trevelyan leapt up to catch the ball.

Edgar shrugged. 'He's our coachman.'

Henry bowled the ball to Young William who hit it straight towards the glasshouse and Lady Clarissa stood up, clapping her hands. 'Excellent, well hit! He's your coachman and you don't know his name?'

I gripped my hands under the table. Names were important to Lady Clarissa and I was petrified she would think my brother rude. 'Didn't you say his name was Henry Trevelyan, Edgar?' Lady Clarissa turned and my cheeks flamed. 'I think ...that's what you told me...wasn't it, Edgar?'

The sun was catching Henry Trevelyan's white shirt, his top button was undone. He looked strong, wholesome, his shoulders broad, his bare arms browned by the sun. He bowled again, and this time William sent the ball swinging towards the beach.

Clouds were forming in the west, the sea breeze rustling the leaves in the branches above us. The tide was high, skylarks singing in the sky. It was so perfect I thought my heart would break – Young William and Henry, throwing back their heads, laughing, hitting the ball, running, shouting, the smell of herbs and seaweed adding to the sound of leather against willow. A perfect day, in a perfect setting, laughter echoing across the lawns as more and more people put down their spades and hoes to come and watch. Mr Maddox sat hugging his knees on the grass, others taking off their jackets, spreading them on the lawn. The sort of day I dreamed of – the sort of day I never had.

Lady Clarissa frowned at the gathering clouds. 'It looks like that front's setting in. Why don't you two gentlemen stay the night? There's plenty of room in the guest suite – and Lord Carew will be very disappointed to miss you.'

I stared at Edgar, willing him to refuse. He should be playing cricket, rolling up his sleeves, throwing back his head in laughter. I wanted him to look wholesome, handsome, run and catch the ball. I wanted to be proud of him, not sit dreading his sudden laughter, the restless tapping of his hand against his knee.

Applause drifted across the lawn. Henry Trevelyan had just bowled Jethro out. There was back slapping, smiles, arms round each other's shoulder, and I gripped my hands tightly.

Edgar reached for his snuffbox, looking quickly at Jacob. 'That's very kind of you, Lady Clarissa – we'd be delighted.'

'Did you say it looks like rain?' asked Charity.

Amelia glanced at the lonely figure of Mr Maddox. 'I do hope not. Mr Maddox is convinced his cereus will bloom tonight. He'll be devastated if there's no moon – but it does look like it might cloud over.'

Jacob Boswell was all smiles and charm. 'A cereus? Then that settles it – we must stay, we couldn't possibly miss such an opportunity. It would be an honour, Lady Clarissa, thank you.' He caught my eye. 'Edgar would love to have Miss Lilly's company a little longer – they must have so much to catch up on.'

The lemon syllabub had long turned to dust in my mouth. I sat watching the footman refill Edgar's glass while Jacob Boswell smiled his refusal, hardly drinking at all. He had been charming and witty throughout dinner, his amusing stories about Oxford making everyone laugh. He looked so at home, his easy manners and pleasantries second nature to him. He charmed Amelia by praising her garden, impressed Charity with his knowledge of botany. He knew all Frederick's tutors and spoke highly of them. 'Josiah Temple-Thwaite is a very fine teacher. He may be lost in his own thoughts for most of the time, but he knows his stuff.'

'Frederick said he was one of his favourites. We have his book – Amelia's read it from cover to cover, haven't you, Amelia?'

Amelia looked up. 'I read so many – I've read them all.'

Charity smiled. 'Frederick said he admires William Wandsbough very much. He's the most senior in the faculty for botany – he's Dean and very influential. I believe he comes from Cornwall. You must have come across him?'

'Indeed, I know Mr William Wandsbough very well. He's very learned but rather terrifying.'

'Oh!' Charity giggled, wiping her mouth with her napkin. 'Then you won't want to give him Frederick's regards, but I know Frederick would like to be remembered to him.'

Jacob smiled. 'Mrs Carew, consider it done. I shall gird my loins and enter the lion's den. Perhaps, knowing Lieutenant Carew might work in my favour — a little star-dust goes a long way.' His laughter and elegance dominated the room. By comparison, Edgar seemed to sink lower in his chair, hardly saying a word. His eyes looked glazed, like the fish in the basket.

'If you've come from Falmouth, then you'll have heard about the robberies.' Lord Carew put down his spoon. 'Dreadful business all round. Coaches just aren't safe any more — there's been jewels taken…watches…money.'

The emeralds on Lady Clarissa's turban glinted. She was dressed in elegant silk, no sign of daisy chains. 'I suppose we must expect this to happen more and more. Starving men will risk anything to feed their families…'

'They're saying…' Lord Carew leaned forward, carefully choosing two ripe pears from the fruit bowl, 'that the man — or highwayman, as people are calling him — has a French accent. They say he swears in French.'

'French?' Jacob Boswell seemed to find it amusing. 'Surely they've rounded up all the prisoners?'

Lord Carew swilled the pears in the crystal water-bowl. 'From what I hear, that might not be the case. Rumour has it that a number of French prisoners have made their way to

Falmouth and are stealing anything they can get their hands on – to fund a ship to take them to France.'

'Surely not? Stealing from coaches will get them hanged – Lord Falmouth will have no scruples but to see them swing.' Lady Clarissa handed me a silver filigree bowl filled with marzipan-coated cherries and I took one, passing the small bowl to Amelia.

'Who can they trust to get a ship? They'll have to commission one from here. But who's going to help French prisoners escape?'

Lord Carew reached for a clean napkin, drying the pears carefully. 'Many might well be tempted. Don't forget, Amelia, my dear, that prisoners are mouths to feed and most round here would be glad to see the back of them. Men will risk a lot to feed their families – I believe many may well be tempted.' He was less cheerful tonight, his formal wig and embroidered waistcoat seeming to restrict his enjoyment of the meal. Shadows under his eyes dimmed his usually ruddy complexion. 'I believe Lord Falmouth has set a watch in place. Now, if you'll excuse me…I'm not one for cards.'

He stood up, smiling at Jacob, bowing politely to Edgar. 'Make free with my port and brandy. Make yourselves at home – I'm going to check on Persephone, then my bed beckons.' He bent to kiss Lady Clarissa's proffered cheek. 'Splendid duck, my dear. Splendid evening all round.'

Jacob stood in response and I could hardly bear to watch Edgar's clumsy attempt to bow. He gripped the back of his chair, a slight slur to his words. 'Delighted…lovely evening, Lord Carew.'

The clock struck ten as we stepped on to the terrace. The breeze had freshened, a band of thick black clouds stretching across the night sky. 'Oh dear, poor Mr Maddox,' whispered Amelia. 'There's no moon at all.'

Lady Clarissa's gown rustled. She drew her Indian silk shawl around her, her rings glittering, and I forced back my tears. She had gone to so much trouble, dressing with such elegance, ordering such a fine meal, yet Edgar had hardly spoken one word to her.

'Goodnight, Mr Lilly, Sir Jacob. When you're ready to go to bed, Jethro will see you to your rooms. Please feel free to enjoy the terrace.' A slight break in the clouds made her look up. 'It might just clear – if the wind picks up it might blow away the clouds. Either way, rest assured Mr Maddox will ring his bell if anything happens!' She smiled, linking her arm through Charity's. 'We've had rather too many late nights waiting for this flower to open, but do join him by all means. He'd be glad of your company.'

A look passed between Edgar and Jacob and a shiver ran down my spine. Jacob Boswell smiled his most dazzling smile. 'I think we must, Lady Clarissa. We can't miss this for the world. Thank you for the delicious dinner – and perhaps we *will* have a glass of port. It would be a terrible shame if the moon came out and we missed the flowering.'

Edgar's tobacco smoke drifted from the terrace; I could hear them talking, see them leaning against the balustrade, brandy glasses in their hands. Lord Carew did not like Edgar, none of them did – they were far too polite to say anything but I could see it in their eyes. All of them smiling politely but thinking him so rude – an uncouth boy with no charm or manners. My emptiness felt like pain.

A jug of water stood on my washstand, and I splashed the tears from my cheeks, holding the soft towel against my face. Amelia must not hear me cry. The silver clock chimed one; it was so late, yet I would not undress until Jethro took them to their rooms. Edgar might become unruly and I would need to go to him. He must not disgrace us, not here, not with Lady Clarissa being so good to us. Yet that look between them both had held such mischief.

The night sky seemed lighter, the moon just visible behind the thinning clouds; silver streaks lit the lawn and I returned to the window to resume my vigil. There were no voices, no tobacco smoke, and I leaned out in sudden panic. The clouds had parted and moonlight flooded the garden. The terrace was empty, a shadow passed along the path in the direction of the shrubbery and I grabbed my cloak.

Chapter Fourteen

The dining room had been cleared, a single candle burning on the table, and I ran to the open French window, slipping silently across the terrace. The tiny pieces of mirror glinted in the moonshine, the path as clear as day. It felt bewitching, enchanted, and I breathed the magic of the night as if running through the midnight garden in Mamma's portrait. Oberon could be watching, Titania and Puck, any number of fairies weaving their spells.

'Edgar?' I called. An owl hooted in reply. They were further ahead than I thought.

The old brick path lay to my right and I followed it through the arch, skirting the wall of the walled garden. The glass hothouse lay bathed in moonlight and I opened the door, the air hot and humid, the pungent smell of damp earth and strong perfume exotic and exciting. It seemed like some faraway paradise, orchids hanging from their silver branches, the air heavy with the scent of lilies. Mr Maddox's dark hair was bending over a potting table at the far end. He turned quickly, his obvious surprise turning to sudden pleasure.

I cleared my throat. 'Hello…is my brother here? Only I thought I was following them, but I seem to have lost them?'

He seemed distracted, looking over my shoulder, searching the space behind me. 'Are you alone? Is it just you?'

The impropriety of my visit must have struck us at the same time. 'I'm sorry…it was a mistake…goodnight, Mr Maddox…only, I thought my brother was here. I'm sorry to have disturbed you.'

He clasped his hands together. He seemed to be struggling, hiding his obvious disappointment. 'Not to worry… perhaps another night. The moon's just come out…so… well.' He smiled bravely. An open bottle of wine stood on the table behind him and he must have seen me glance at it. 'Please don't judge me, Miss Lilly.'

'Judge you?'

'Drinking alone. Only…well…it gets very lonely when you're always by yourself. I don't suppose you can join me, to wish me well on my next venture?'

I shook my head, reluctant to go further from the door, but his words held such pain, the loneliness in his voice tearing my heart. 'Why must you leave?'

Across the silver plants, I saw his mouth tremble. He ran his hands through his hair. 'I have to go.' He glanced up. 'Miss Lilly – you have tears in your eyes.'

'I hate to see unhappiness.'

'You're very kind. Forgive me.' He hid his face with his hands. 'But your kindness does me no favour – you better go, Miss Lilly.'

'But Mr Maddox, what is it? What's happened? Is it the cereus? Has it died?'

'No, not that.' His shoulders slumped, tears pooling in his eyes. He bit his bottom lip. 'Miss Lilly, do you know what it is to love so deeply it stops you sleeping and eating...even wanting to live? I must walk away from here and *never* come back. I'm destroying myself by staying. I must leave.'

I had never seen a man so distraught. Pain crumpled his face, his hands trembled. I had seen the way he looked at Amelia, how they all looked at her. 'Oh, Mr Maddox...I understand, I really do.'

He sniffed, bringing out a soiled handkerchief. 'Please, Miss Lilly – forget this conversation. It's the wine – and the sudden, tremendous hope she was with you.' He blew his nose, his voice breaking. 'Every full moon...*every* full moon, I pray the cereus will bloom. I sit willing it, cajoling it, desperate to see the first sign of it opening. I picture her absolute delight...how she would smile at me...how happy I would make her. How we would sit in the moonlight, marvelling at the sheer beauty of the delicate bloom. But instead I sit alone, waiting and hoping, knowing I must leave before I say something, or *do* something, to give myself away.'

He blew his nose again, his tousled hair in disarray. The patches at his elbow looked black in the moonlight, earth staining the cuffs of his sleeves. 'Forgive me. Please let this stay between us. I'm sorry for my outburst. I've written to Kew and hope to hear from them soon. In time, this will all pass.' He glanced at the tightly closed bud, shrugging his shoulders. 'I apologize I can't see you safely back to the house but I must maintain my vigil – just in case.'

His smile broke my heart; George Godwin, Daniel Maddox, and every other man who met her, all enthralled by Amelia's beauty and kindness. 'My brother and his friend must have gone to bed,' I said across the silent orchids. 'Goodnight, Mr Maddox. I promise I won't breathe a word.'

At the arch, I looked back through the gate to the walled garden. Moses was stooping between the herbs, placing what must be snails in a bucket. He stood up, his arms and head wobbling. Wisps of lank hair fell across his eyes. He looked thinner, older, smiling shyly when he saw it was me, and I knew I must wait while he picked me some lavender. He shuffled towards me with his sideways gait, his face pale and gaunt in the moonlight, a dribble of spit glistening on his chin. He looked frightened, as if trying to gauge how far he could approach before I ran away. He held out the small bunch of lavender, his hands jerking back to his chest, resting against his heart.

'Thank you,' I said, smelling the heady fragrance. I rested the bunch against my heart, imitating his action. 'I shouldn't really be here but I love your garden…and you're very clever. Miss Carew says it's *your* garden really.' I knew he could not hear but he seemed delighted, smiling and nodding back at me.

I turned in fright. A man was standing on the path behind me, his white shirt glowing in the moonlight. He had washed his hair, his chin closely shaven. He straightened his glasses.

'I didn't mean to startle you, Miss Lilly. May I see you safely back to the house – or is the night still too young?'

He pulled a watch from his pocket. 'I suppose it *is* only two o'clock.'

I took a step back. 'Thank you, Mr Trevelyan, but I'm perfectly capable of walking back by myself.' He was after more money; the whole lot of them after more money.

He stayed by my side. 'Most people would have run – from Moses, I mean.'

'Well, I'm not most people.'

'Indeed you're not. And before you think ill of me, I'm not after more money.' His voice was soft, caring, no hint of threat, and an ache filled my heart. For some terrible, unknown reason, I felt like crying. Yet I had to explain.

'I thought Mr Lilly and Sir Jacob had gone to the hothouse – but I was wrong.'

'Jethro took them to their rooms. I saw you run across the terrace and into the shrubbery so I came to see you safely back.'

'I'm in no danger, thank you, Mr Trevelyan.'

'What about the danger of enchantment, Miss Lilly? Puck might be watching, Oberon and Titania fighting over you this very minute – the interference of woodland sprites can cause great mischief.'

I wrestled his joyous laughter from my mind, his sunburned arms, Freddie on his shoulders as he bowled to William. 'No danger of enchantment,' I replied firmly.

Black clouds once again obscured the moon, plunging us into sudden darkness, and I stood breathing in the scent of roses; it seemed wrong to feel so sad amongst such beauty.

He stood beside me in the darkness. 'The cruellest of their

tricks is their passion for unrequited love – making you fall so deeply in love with someone who does not love you back, or even know you're there.' He spoke softly, an echoing sadness in his voice. 'The pain of enchantment lingers for ever. Mr Maddox knows he must leave, just as I must leave.'

I tried to laugh. 'Not you as well? Please, Mr Trevelyan!'

He held out his arm and in the half-light I hesitated, not knowing whether to take it. 'I will only ever love one woman – I'll survive without her love, I may even grow prosperous, but she has my heart and I'll not marry anyone else. Not even for companionship. My nephews and nieces will have my full attention and any fortune I accrue they can spend as they like.'

I took his arm. 'Why won't she marry you? You seem a perfectly pleasant man – and you're very good at cricket. Has she seen you play?'

His laughter caught me off guard. 'You think that should do the trick?'

I smiled back. 'Well, it's a good start. I think she's being rather fussy and really rather silly, so you're probably better off without her.'

The path glinted ahead of us, his voice a whisper. 'She's neither silly nor fussy. And she doesn't know I love her.'

I swung round. 'Well, then it's you that's being silly, Mr Trevelyan. How can you expect her to know how much you love her if you haven't told her? You can't rely on woodland sprites and fairies – a woman can't just guess. You need to give her *some* clue at least. Perhaps she does love you but is just too shy to make her feelings known?'

I had spoken sharply and glanced up. He smiled, but not before I saw pain deep in his eyes. 'I'm too late, Miss Lilly – she's to marry another.' He let go of my arm. 'And I must accept it.'

We walked on in silence; George Godwin, Daniel Maddox, Henry Trevelyan, even Amelia. Love was meant to turn you giddy with joy, not rip you apart. He had a kind, compassionate face and read love poems; a woman should not torment such a gentle man with intelligent eyes and strangely attractive glasses. It was wrong, cruel. In the distance, a dog barked, an owl hooted, and I looked across the lawn to the house.

'Mr Trevelyan, how long has my brother been in Falmouth?'

'About a month.' His abrupt tone startled me.

'*About* a month? How come you don't know for certain? You brought him from Oxford.'

He shook his head, his mouth tight with disapproval. 'They engaged me in Falmouth, Miss Lilly, and that's where we're to return tomorrow. Where they've been before that I cannot say.'

An icy hand squeezed my heart. 'Goodnight, Mr Trevelyan. I can see my way across the terrace.' I would wait for the next band of clouds to give me cover. If the moon was too bright I might be seen.

He was watching me, seeming to read my mind. 'Too dark and you might stumble, too light and you're in danger of being seen.' He smiled. 'But I imagine you already know that. Perhaps you should go now – under the cover of this shadow.'

I watched the terrace through the half-light. 'Where did you learn to play cricket?'

'In the back alleys of Truro – not with real bats, of course, just planks of wood and a rag ball wound tightly in leather.'

The band of cloud passed, the moon lighting the terrace as bright as day. 'You're not really a coachman, are you, Mr Trevelyan? Coachmen don't tend to read poetry – least not the ones I know. Molly thinks you've hit hard times.' His silence made me turn and I caught my breath. There was pain in his eyes. 'I'm sorry. That was very insensitive of me...you don't have to answer.'

His voice was a whisper. 'I'm not a coachman. I barely like horses and they certainly don't like me. I work for Admiral Pendarvis. He's my patron and a man I greatly admire. He's asked for my help and I've given it willingly. Coaches are being robbed by men speaking French. We believe thieves are posing as escaped French prisoners, and being a coachman puts me right in the thick of things.'

'Why would they *pose* as French prisoners?'

'We don't know; to engender a climate of mistrust, perhaps? Many resent the rations the prisoners are given – and people are easily swayed by false information. Falmouth's a tinderbox at the moment. Just one spark could lead to anger and disorder. Sir Alex needs to get to the crux of the matter and he's asked for my help – but I must ask for your silence, Miss Lilly. My motives are honourable, even if my disguise is not.'

'Your disguise lets you down rather badly – your hands, for a start; and those love poems will have to go. You need a bushy beard, Henry, and—'

His smile ripped through me. 'I can't be parted from the

poetry. I hate wearing a beard and I'd rather not have dirty fingernails, but I like the way you called me Henry. Can we be friends, Miss Lilly?'

A scattering of clouds gave the perfect cover, yet the sheer beauty of the night made me reluctant to leave. 'Goodnight, Mr Trevelyan,' I said less sharply than I intended.

The house was in darkness, no candles burning in any of the rooms, and I rushed up the steps, tiptoeing across the terrace. The first window was locked, the second, the third, and panic filled me. None of them would open.

'We'll try the kitchen door.' He was behind me. 'We need to go round the back. Jethro may still be up.'

I drew a deep breath. 'The servants will talk...'

'They may have gone to bed.' A lamp burned against the coach house, lighting the gravel on the circular drive. 'We can cut across the gravel and use that gate – mind these poles and ladders.' I could barely see him but followed his voice, almost bumping into him as he held out his hand. 'Careful, there's a pile of tiles here.'

A glow of light beckoned, more lamps burning against the side of the house; we were in a cobbled courtyard surrounded by red-brick buildings. Shadows flickered across a row of closed doors. 'I'll try the kitchen.' In the half darkness, I saw him smile. 'In the absence of an open window – that is.'

Across the stillness the dog began barking again and I searched the shadows. Anyone seeing me would think me wanton, visiting Mr Maddox, alone with Henry Trevelyan. The clouds broke and a shaft of moonlight lit the ladders leading to the roof. I studied the planks which formed the scaffold.

'Here you are—' In the moonlight, Henry Trevelyan's frown deepened. 'Miss Lilly – please reassure me you're not thinking of *climbing* back to your room?'

I put my foot on the ladder. 'The hall window's open and it's only a series of ladders. The men have been working up there all day and if it takes their weight, it'll take mine. I'm not scared of heights, but I am scared of my reputation. Women aren't silly weak creatures, you know – we're perfectly capable of climbing ladders. It won't be slippery and I'll hold very tight.'

He ran his hand through his hair, shaking his head. 'I'm not questioning your ability, just questioning the *necessity*. Some like to use doors, others like to use windows. But if you *did* want to use a door, the kitchen's unlocked.' He bowed formally. 'It's your choice, Miss Lilly.'

'No one's in the kitchen?'

'No. The night porter's doing his rounds. I reckon you've got about five minutes.'

I took a step down. Another time, another place, and I would have relished the challenge. 'The door it is then,' I whispered.

His laughter sent a wave of warmth surging through me. 'A good decision but I can understand those ladders must look very temping. Goodnight, Miss Lilly.'

Chapter Fifteen

Bethany pinned the last curl in place. 'Miss Lilly, ye have the loveliest, thickest hair – there, all done. Do ye want both ribbons or just the one?'

I stared back at my reflection. I had hardly slept and a bit more colour would not go amiss. 'Both ribbons.'

'There's no one else up – ye're an early bird, all right! There – looks lovely. Shall I bring ye up a tray?'

'No. I'll come down. I'll get a breath of air. Are you sure my brother isn't up? Only, I thought they wanted to leave early.'

'No sign as yet.' Her eyes plummeted to the floor. 'Ye wouldn't know this, Miss Lilly, least I don't expect ye to remember...but ye once helped a lady back to her home. She'd fallen through sickness and ye took her in yer carriage... ye called the doctor an' ye paid his bill.' She looked up, tears stinging her eyes. 'Only, that woman were my mamm, an' we can never thank ye enough...'

'I do remember,' I replied. There was love in her eyes and I looked away. 'I'm glad I helped her, is she well now?'

'Yes, she's a maid at Mansion House,' her voice faltered. 'We'll never forget what ye did.'

Unease was making me restless, and staying in bed when the sun was shining seemed a waste of a beautiful morning. Grabbing my cloak and bonnet I raced down the stairs, crossing the hall to the dining room. A French window was open and I stood on the terrace breathing in the smell of early dew. The tide was out, wading birds picking their way through the stranded seaweed.

I crossed the terrace, taking the path to the cobbled courtyard. A groom was filling a bucket from the pump and smiled as he saw me. 'For Persephone,' he said, glancing at the gate leading down to the sty.

I walked beside him, lifting my skirt though the path was well brushed, almost as clean as the house. My heart jumped. Henry Trevelyan was leaning over the sty, scratching Persephone's floppy black ears. He looked up and I caught my breath.

'Miss Lilly, what a lovely surprise.'

I would have to leave. The involuntary jolt was disturbing, my sudden pleasure making me blush. 'I didn't mean to disturb you.' My voice was clipped, my gaze fixed on the enormous black pig with the most endearing eyes I had ever seen.

'Don't go.' His waistcoat hung on a post behind him, the sleeves of his white shirt rolled to the elbow. Round his neck he wore a checked cravat and I hesitated, watching him lean over to scratch Persephone with a forked stick. She grunted in pleasure. 'You can take over if you like…'

The groom swilled the fresh water into the trough. 'It can't be much longer now.'

'Do use my stick.' Henry Trevelyan glanced up and my stomach contracted. I could not speak, a terrible confusion swallowing my words. I had seen a glimpse of us both as clear as day. It was so real, so joyous, making me blush and I stared at the ground. I had seen us leaning over the sty, his arms encircling me, his face against mine. We were laughing, reaching over to tickle Persephone. It was as if I had willed it, wanting it to happen.

'No, thank you. I'll dirty my gown.'

'You won't,' he reached for his jacket, 'you can lean against this.'

The groom was walking away and I knew I must follow. 'No, I must go.'

'Wait.' His voice sharpened. 'I'm glad I've had this opportunity to see you alone.' He reached into the pocket and drew out a leather purse. 'You don't need to buy my silence, Miss Lilly.' His eyes scorched mine and shame shot through me. He could not be bought, yet my brother would buy my silence; Jacob Boswell would take everything he could.

He must have seen my hesitation. 'I'll only accept the money I'm owed, nothing more.' He counted out twenty pounds, handing them back. 'Please do me the kindness of believing not everything's done for profit. Some things are done for—' He stopped.

I clasped the notes in my hand, unable to look up. His words had been said kindly but they held censure, even ridicule. He thought me shallow. He thought me immoral. He thought I was like Edgar and Jacob – more money than sense.

I kissed Edgar goodbye with both relief and anger, turning before the carriage had left. He had most of the money I had brought with me and I would pay the rest when I returned to Truro. I could not settle but passed from room to room, a terrible emptiness taking hold. I was *not* shallow. Not immoral. Henry Trevelyan had judged me too harshly.

The door of the library was ajar and I pushed it open, the smell of leather and polish meeting me in equal measure. Three large windows faced the front drive, the grooms raking over the disturbed gravel outside. Long bookshelves dominated both ends of the room, a table set with sturdy leather chairs positioned in the centre. A large fireplace stood behind me, paintings of prize-winning cattle and horses staring down at me as I ran my finger along the rows of books. The library in Carrick Hall would be bigger than this – and grander.

I had only seen Carrick Hall from the river but knew it to be the largest mansion on the Fal estuary with its long elm tree drive and statues by the riverside. I could organize fêtes and concerts to raise money for the new hospital. We could make our own theatre and put on plays. French prisoners on parole were giving dancing lessons and I would hire one for all of us – even the servants. I would fill the house with laughter. We would give balls. We would have gala evenings with lanterns stretching all the way down the drive and along the river.

Father was not a reading man but I loved books and read what I could. I began searching the shelves, finding no order. The books seemed haphazardly placed, French philosophy side by side with agriculture, military lists stacked rigidly against rows of poetry. I was half-hoping I would not find what I was looking for but there it lay next to a book of botanical prints – *Poetry by John Donne*.

I turned round. Hushed whispering filtered from behind the half-open door, someone was crying. 'No never. Course not – but she wants no more said.'

'But surely she must think…'

'No – she's sayin' nothin and nor must we. She'll hear no more of it. She says we've to put it down as lost, an' that's the end to it.'

''Tis not the end.'

Sudden silence followed; a scuttling of feet. Charity pushed open the door, her beautiful lacquered stick tapping the ground in front of her. 'Are you in here, Angelica?'

'Yes, I'm here.' She seemed troubled and I rushed to take her arm. 'Is anything the matter?'

'No, nothing. I just wondered if you'd like some company – only with your brother leaving, I thought you might feel a little lonely?'

Something about her smile looked forced. 'Charity, I believe there *is* something the matter – please tell me. I've heard all sorts of whispering.'

She felt the book in my hand. 'You've chosen something to read – what is it?'

'It's the poetry of John Donne. We did his religious poems at school but I've never read his love poems. Do you know them?'

This time her smile was genuine, bordering on laughter. 'His love poems are very passionate, Angelica – they're about

127

the physical love between a man and woman. School mistresses don't let their girls anywhere near them! But I do know the poems and I'd love to hear them again.' She drew me towards the large table. 'Will you read them to me?'

I helped her into a chair and opened the book. 'Something's gone missing, Charity. I heard the maids talking about it. Something's lost – do you know what it is?'

She covered my hand in hers. 'Oh dear, I thought you might have heard.' She drew a deep breath. 'It's the little silver dish – the one we used last night.'

'The one with the marzipan cherries in it?'

'Yes, that's the one. The maids have searched everywhere but these things happen…bits and pieces can get swept up and thrown away. Lady Clarissa wants nothing more said. She won't search the servants' rooms and as far as she's concerned, the episode's over. The piece has gone and no one's to blame.'

Blood rushed to my face, a furious pounding in my chest. Had it been Jacob Boswell or my brother? Heaven knows they had had long enough to take their pick. To steal from such dear people – to walk away with a silver dish as if by right? Lady Carew would not search the house because she would never think to blame her devoted servants. She knew the dish was not to be found; she knew it was halfway down the drive, soon to finance vice and debauchery.

'Lady Clarissa must…' Shame and disappointment burned my cheeks. 'Charity…is my brother or Sir Jacob under suspicion? Am I under suspicion?'

Charity's hand gripped mine. 'No, of course not, Angelica! Put that straight from your mind.'

'But Lady Clarissa must have her suspicions…' My voice trembled, tears filling my eyes.

'Neither you nor your brother are in any way implicated. You know, Angelica, being blind is not always such a disadvantage – it makes you develop other senses – such as the way you hear voices.'

'Voices?'

'I judge people by their voices; well, I don't *judge* them so much as get a *feel* for them by the way they speak. It can be more helpful than you think – no outward appearance to dazzle or intimidate you, just the integrity of their voice. Your voice, in case you're wondering, is full of exceptional kindness.'

I gripped the book harder. 'And my brother's?'

'Is full of exceptional sadness.'

That left one other person. 'And Sir Jacob's?'

She drew her hand away. 'Full of self-importance and deceit. Now, be a dear and read those poems before anyone comes.' She giggled like a naughty schoolgirl. 'My sister used to read them to me and I was terrified we'd be heard – either that, or we'd set fire to the bedsheets. I didn't understand them then, but I do now. They're so romantic – so exactly how it is.'

My cheeks began to flame, burning fiercer with every poem. They spoke of lovers entwined on crumpled sheets, the dawn peeping through the curtains, the sun rising on a night of passion.

'That's the bit that's so real,' Charity whispered. 'The terrible pain of knowing you have to part.'

Torrential rain lashed the windows, a battalion of black clouds darkening the sky. Blown sideways in the ferocious wind, the huge red flag somehow clung to the flagpole, the ringing of the kitchen bell and the smell of gingerbread drawing us all into the kitchen. Everyone was there: Lady Clarissa in a huge white apron, Young William and Young Henry standing on chairs against the scrubbed table. Charles and Freddie were sitting on it, their mouths smeared with raw mixture. Lord Carew stood in delighted expectation.

'This one's yours, Grandpa.' William handed him the figure of a huge bull.

'Well, well. If it isn't Titan,' he said, tickling Freddie's knees amidst squeals of laughter.

William handed Charity a rose with iced petals, Amelia a large paintbrush. The servants had figures with caps and bonnets, the grooms had horses. Jethro had a cricket bat, Horace had a bone. Young Henry smiled, keeping mine for last. 'We've made you Fersefony,' he said, beaming from ear to ear.

I took the huge fat pig, my heart swelling. 'I can't eat her. I'll keep her for ever.'

Last Christmas, the smell from a gingerbread stall in the market had prompted a pang of remorse. I had never properly thanked Mrs Penhaligan for the gifts left on my pillow. She had been so kind to me, encouraging my theatricals, suggesting plays to Miss Mitchell, never missing a single performance. Reverend Penhaligan was a school governor and their visits became my greatest pleasure. The stall next to the gingerbread seller was piled high with silk shawls from India and I had bought one on impulse, sending it to Mrs

Penhaligan with a letter telling her everything I was doing. Her reply had brought me such happiness – she adored the shawl, Reverend Penhaligan was well, and they still visited the school whenever they could.

'You've got to eat her.'

'No...I can't. She's too lovely to eat.'

Lady Clarissa wiped the flour from her cheek. She turned quickly. 'Ah, Mr Maddox, you've come just in time. The boys have made you a gingerbread pot with a sapling growing in it.' She held out the plate. 'Goodness, are you all right? Is there something the matter?'

He had clearly been running and it was hard to tell if his grimace was pain or pleasure. His cheeks were flushed, his chest heaving. He held out a letter. 'If I may...I need to speak with Lord Carew.'

Lord Carew peered from under the table, his two young grandsons looking up beside him. 'Good news, I hope?'

Tears stung Daniel Maddox's eyes; it was as if he did not know whether to laugh or cry. In the end, he did both. 'Wonderful news...I can hardly believe it – yet to leave here...My joy is tinged with sadness.'

Lord Carew got to his feet and took the letter in his large hands. 'Course not. A young man like you should spread his wings...'

'It's from John Fraser. Look, he's signed it. He's offering me *assistant gardener* in his Charlestown nursery. That's Charlestown of the *Eastern States*...' He reached for his handkerchief, his soiled hands shaking. 'Look – read this. *The plants remain in good health and are worth five guineas a piece...they're to be shipped as live plants.* I'm to organize the shipping. But first, we're to sail to St Petersburg to collect some Tartarian cherry plants. He wants me to prepare the collecting boxes – he's sent the design.'

The second page of the letter showed details of a wooden box with a raised glass lid. Lord Carew studied it carefully. 'Well, well, yes, very sturdy. There are plenty of good carpenters around here who can help you with this.'

'They need to be deep enough for a decent amount of soil yet airy enough to afford adequate light – like a portable glasshouse. I'm to join him when his ship docks in Falmouth.'

'Splendid. Does he say when that'll be?'

Daniel Maddox peered at the letter again and shook his head. 'No. But he does say once the cherries are established, we're to collect further plants – from the Allegheny Mountains. I'm sorry – I can't stop shaking. You must think me so feeble only…it's long been my ambition to become a collector. And now it's happening, it's almost overwhelming.'

Lady Clarissa poured a glass of brandy from a crystal decanter. 'Nonsense, Mr Maddox, it's quite the best news we've had. We must celebrate. Here, my dear, steady yourself with this. Of course, your gain is our loss, but we've always known we must lose you one day. The *Eastern States of the Americas* – my congratulations, indeed.'

Daniel Maddox downed the proffered drink in one large gulp. He stood straighter, his shoulders back. 'I owe this all to you, Lord Carew. To be singled out like this – it can only be because of your recommendation. Without your patronage—'

'Nothing that you don't thoroughly deserve.' Lord Carew smiled at Lady Clarissa. 'But we expect you back one day, don't we, my love? And whatever you're shipping – we expect the pick of the crop! Indeed, I rather like the sound of those cherries. Persephone's partial to a bowl of cherries.'

'These ones are *white*.' He glanced at Amelia. 'Mr Fraser's a commissioned collector for the Tsar of Russia.'

'Tsar *Catherine*? Good grief, man, you'll be mixing with very exulted company.'

'The cherry trees belong to her…but I'll send you one, I promise – whatever it takes, I'll make sure you get your own tree.'

Amelia clapped her hands. 'How splendid. Yes, please. How long do you expect to be away?'

'I don't know, Miss Carew. Three years – maybe four. I'll leave thorough instructions for the gardeners. The saplings must be left in their tubs for at least another two years. I'll make a detailed list of all my requirements – the care needed every month for the next two years so the gardeners know exactly what to do. Everything's well established – I wouldn't leave if my work was in any jeopardy. I love this garden too much to endanger its success.' He turned awkwardly, almost stumbling from the room.

Amelia stuffed the last piece of her paintbrush into her mouth. She seemed suddenly carefree, almost girlish, tickling her nephews to make them squeal. 'I'm still hungry. I know, let's eat William…or Freddie…or Charles.'

The boys screamed in terror, screeching round the kitchen, the dog barking happily, joining the chase – the smell of the baking, the smiles on every face; the cook shielding the boys under her voluminous white apron. Lord Carew's voice boomed across the kitchen. 'Retreat…retreat. Company regroup.' He gathered the boys together, diving back under the table. 'Heads below the parapet – wait for the enemy to disperse.'

The rain lashed against the glass, the wind rattling the windowpanes. I drew the curtains closed, putting down my candle as I climbed into bed. I hardly heard Lady Clarissa's tentative knock.

'You're not asleep, are you?' she whispered, peeping round the door.

'No – I've been watching the storm.'

Her silk nightcap was fringed with lace, an exquisitely embroidered shawl covering her nightgown. 'Well, move over, young lady – let me in.' I pulled back the bedsheets with a rush of pleasure. She smelled of rosewater, my delight increasing as she squeezed next to me. She drew the cover over us. 'Are you enjoying your visit?' she asked.

'Yes, very much. You're so kind to have me.'

She drew the candle nearer and unfolded a letter. 'Mr Maddox was not the only one to get post today. My very good friends, Robert and Elizabeth Fox, are hosting a reception in Falmouth next week and they have invited Lord Entworth to come…and this, my dear, is his letter, inviting you to be his *escort*.' She held up a sheet of high-quality paper, beautifully written, with an embossed gold crest shining at the top. 'How well do you know Lord Entworth, Angelica?'

'Not very well – I've only met him three times and each time was very brief. We haven't really spoken – not so I can say I know him.'

'That is what I suspected. I have to tell you, that this *soirée* has been long anticipated and will be eagerly attended.' The sudden beating of my heart made it hard to answer; so public an appearance, everyone speculating, watching my every move. Lady Clarissa must have felt me stiffen. 'I'm sure you understand that by singling you out for such an honour, he's leaving society in no doubt of his intentions. It's a very clear message.'

'Should I accept? It seems very formal.'

'It is formal   very formal, but we must go. I'd not miss it for the world and nor would Charity and Amelia. We'll ask Elizabeth to arrange a private introduction *prior* to the soirée – a small group of no more than eight or ten so you can exchange a few words. I know she'll be more than agreeable to do that.'

An eagle with a pointed beak perched on the top of the crest. I could hear the excitement in Mamma's voice: *It's your destiny, my love…a great lady…the gypsy's quite adamant. Just think, my grandson will be a lord!*

'But, so far, you like what you see? Lord Entworth is someone you would *like* to marry?' Her voice softened. 'Has he, *could* he, win your affection, my dear?' She smiled at my confusion, raising her eyebrows. 'The truth please, Angelica. I'm not pursuing anything if it isn't what you want.'

The heat in my face was unbearable; the letter looked so

formal, yet what else did I expect? I hardly knew the truth – my brave face put on every morning like a Greek mask. Truth meant recognizing the look in people's eyes, the constant judgement – too rich for some, too tainted as *trade* by others. Truth was eyes weighing up how much they could overcharge me, or how generous I would be if they invited me on to their charity board. Truth was pinches, innuendoes, vile lies about my mother.

'He has won my admiration,' I said slowly. 'He's everything I look for in a man. He's kind and courteous…very attentive, and very—' I stopped, unable to go on.

'Handsome?'

'Yes – very.' I looked away. Here I went again, I hardly recognized myself any more, the slightest kindness bringing tears to my eyes. I was the glittering jewel of Truro merchant society, fewer than three men at my side and mothers would push their sons forward. It was never *if* but *who* I would marry. 'Sometimes…well, sometimes I think I shouldn't marry at all. It's like walking on a tightrope – have you seen them? They balance with an umbrella or cane and everyone watches, waiting to see if they fall off.'

She sighed softly. 'Is that how you feel, Angelica? That you might fall off? Or is it that you worry people *want* you to fall off?'

I knew Lady Clarissa would understand. 'It sounds churlish, doesn't it? Like I'm a spoilt, ungrateful child, wanting more than's good for me.' I had never spoken like this before, not to Amelia, never to Molly, certainly never to Father or Edgar. The thought of Edgar made my stomach tighten. 'I don't know where I belong any more. Father doesn't see it but I catch the envy in people's eyes. They expect me to marry well, yet they remember my mother came from nothing. It's like they can't forget it and they don't want me to forget it — like I'm reaching too high and they want me to fall.'

In the glow of the candle she looked younger, the fine lines around her eyes less visible. Shadows flickered across her straight, aristocratic nose. 'Nothing's too good for you. You must believe that. But, take it from one who knows — you must shut your ears to malicious gossip.'

'It's hard to shut your ears when they're pinching you as they say it.'

Her arm slipped round my shoulder. 'That malice was a little while ago now – it's time you put those thoughts aside. Try not to bear grievances. Rise above them. Holding a grudge will eat away at you like a canker.'

'There was no need for their cruelty. I'd no idea girls could be so vicious…Father sent me to learn their ways, but believe me, if he knew! If he knew how close I came to scratching them back – like a cat with my claws out. I could have called them far worse – my foundry language would have stopped them in their tracks.'

'*Foundry* language?' She laughed. 'Have you taught Amelia *foundry* language?'

Her soft laughter made me laugh with her. 'No…and I never will. It was only because of Amelia I held back. She was like an angel, sent to protect me. Without her, I'd have scratched and kicked and sworn every oath I knew.'

'People follow by example. Don't you think those girls

might have been just as lonely – just as lost? That they were jealous of you? After all, there are only a limited number of titled men out there. Your beauty,' she lifted my chin, 'your *extreme* beauty, coupled with the fact that you're a very rich woman, poses serious competition. And I mean *serious*.'

'We weren't so very rich then – Father's real wealth came after Mamma died. I never saw him, Lady Clarissa. He was always away – brokering deals, amassing a great fortune. He abandoned Edgar just like he abandoned me…he never came to my plays and never went to see Edgar.' The ache burned my heart. 'I used to sneak out of the dormitory at night. There was a tree I used to climb – I'd sit amongst the branches where no one could see me. Sometimes, I cried so hard my chest would feel bruised the next day. I'd just lost my mother, yet still they called her names.'

Her voice was warm, loving. 'Let it go, my dear. Don't hold grudges. You've performed Shakespeare – you know how the pursuit of vengeance leads down a lonely path.' She handed me her handkerchief and I wiped my eyes, avoiding the lumpy rose, the work of a child. 'The power of grievance, old wounds suppurating, feuds between families in the name of revenge? Those plays tell us everything we need to know and we must learn from them. Did I tell you I once had the very great pleasure of seeing your mother onstage?'

'You did? Oh my goodness – I never knew…'

'In London. It was one of her earlier plays; she was Hermia, the part that made her famous. Everyone was spellbound – it wasn't just me. I honestly couldn't take my eyes off her and nor could the critics. We all knew we were witnessing something very special – that she would go on to make her name. You must always be proud of her.'

I could not speak, the ache burning my heart. Like Daniel Maddox, I would have to leave this extraordinary family and face the world beyond their gates; Moses in his sanctuary, George Godwin, desperate to belong, all of us seeking shelter in the house and garden with its ringing laughter and running feet, its mantle of love enfolding us all.

'Well, my dearest, Lord Entworth knows your background and it hasn't stopped him coming forward.' She pinched my cheek. 'Those girls at school were right to see you as a threat – give them credit for that, at least!'

I smiled. 'I think that's why I like him. It's as if he understands and he's offering me a safety net…telling me not to worry – that if I fall, he'll be there to catch me.' The gingerbread pig lay propped against my dressing-table mirror. 'Lady Clarissa, please be honest. Would I pass as gentry?'

A tear rolled down my cheek. It was not pain I was feeling but relief. I was talking candidly for the very first time, as if I had lanced a boil and expelled the poison. 'I was mortified by Edgar's behaviour tonight. Compared to Sir Jacob, he was boorish and vulgar. I can't tell you how ashamed I felt. Mamma would have been horrified because he wasn't brought up like that…but since he's been in Oxford he's become very ill-mannered. It was horrible to watch – really, really horrible and it makes me nervous. I'm scared he's going to show us up and Lord Entworth won't want him as a brother-in-law.'

She slid her arm from around me, tapping her fingers together, resting her forefingers against her mouth. The harshness in her voice was unmistakeable. 'How well do you know Sir Jacob Boswell?'

'He's more my brother's friend than mine. He's at Oxford with him. He's in the same lodgings. And through him, Lady Boswell has become...' I fought to say the words, 'a *particular* friend of Father's.'

'How particular?'

'*Very* particular.'

She sniffed, shaking her head. 'I won't hide my disquiet, Angelica. I've known the Boswells all my life. Jacob Boswell's father was an unprincipled gambler. On his death, he left his estate mortgaged and his family in penury, yet by the way they live no one would guess. A good many businesses were ruined because of them and very few merchants extend the Boswells credit any more. I only tell you this, so you know.'

Two prongs of the same fork, tearing into my family. Her eyes held anger, the fine lines hardening around her mouth. 'Those names Charity mentioned – the names of Frederick's tutors? They were fabricated, my dear. Both of them made up, and yet both of them known very well to Jacob Boswell. You heard him tell her he would pass on Frederick's good wishes?'

She pulled back the covers, stepping gracefully to the floor. 'Charity heard something in his voice. Looks are deceiving. Without truth, there is no beauty. Best to be warned, don't you think?'

Centre Stage

Chapter Sixteen

4 Dunstanville Terrace, Falmouth
Sunday 7th August 1796, 4:00 p.m.

I stood by the sash window, gazing across the forest of masts to the seaport beyond. The house was the fourth in a row of a newly built terrace leading up from the town square. Two large windows stood either side of a painted blue door, another three windows on each of the two floors above. The kitchen and scullery were in the basement, the maids' rooms in the attic.

Lady Clarissa pulled off her gloves. 'Most of the other houses have been commissioned by packet captains – I believe the terrace is to stretch right out of town.'

'It's such a lovely view. I can see why everyone wants to live here.'

'We bought it for Frederick and George – somewhere for them to use when they're in Falmouth. It's proving very useful – and very comfortable.'

The drawing room had windows at both ends, a huge pianoforte in one corner and a group of delicate mahogany chairs upholstered in yellow stripes by the marble fireplace.

A display cabinet held china vases; paintings of ships in full sail adorned the walls. It was bright and airy, despite the grim weather. Amelia came to my side, pointing across the grey water. 'That's Flushing and Penryn's down river – you can just about see the top of the church...and that big building is the Greenbank Hotel. And that's Fish Strand Quay.'

The journey down river had not been pleasant. *Lumpy*, Lady Clarissa had called it. *A bit too fresh to be pleasurable*, but I was already feeling better. Taking the coach had been out of the question: the roads had been impassable. Better to face a bumpy sail than be stuck in a quagmire.

'Wait till you see it in good weather. The sun sets right over those fields and we catch the last rays through these windows.' Amelia pressed her face against the glass. 'Oh, goodness, they're here already. That was quick.'

Lady Clarissa looked up from sifting through a pile of calling cards. 'Splendid. Dear me, is everyone in town?' She put the cards back on the silver tray, smiling broadly as Charity and an elegant lady entered the room. 'Ah, Mrs Penrose, how lovely you look.'

'Thank you, and how lovely *you* look, Lady Clarissa.' She was tall and slim, dressed in a ruby gown with a cream underskirt, her bonnet trimmed with velvet ribbons. Her thick brown hair was neatly coiled behind each ear, a series of small curls framing her face. She must have been about forty, her complexion flawless, her brown eyes alight with pleasure. 'You weren't too blown around on your journey, I hope? Charity tells me it was rather rough.'

'A good blow never does anyone any harm. It seems every-one's here. I hope you've found good lodgings?'

They embraced and my nervousness left me. Mrs Penrose had been Charity's governess and I was dreading she might dismiss me as unaccomplished. I had never mastered the piano, I could not sing and I hated Latin – everything Amelia said Mrs Penrose excelled in. Yet just one glance and I saw kindness in her face. 'I've taken a house in Market Street for the last three weeks and thank goodness I did come early – there's a real scramble for lodgings. I gather people are doubling up on rooms.'

Charity had never looked lovelier, her cheeks aglow with happiness. Her blonde hair curled in soft ringlets beneath her blue bonnet, her travelling coat still buttoned against the rain. She hugged Freddie to her. 'Your papa's coming – he's nearly here. Oh, Freddie, you're going to love him so much. You'll adore him.' She looked up, smiling shyly. 'Like we all adore him.'

'When are they expected? I recognize some of the ships in the fleet.' Amelia stopped. 'What manners, I'm so sorry. Miss Lilly, may I introduce Mrs Eleanor Penrose. Mrs Penrose, this is my dear friend, Angelica Lilly.'

We both curtseyed, her smile holding such warmth. She had a timid way of holding her head. 'I'm delighted to meet you. I've heard so much about you – all good, I hasten to add.'

She was poised, but not arrogant. I had expected her to be more commanding. I had heard about her, too: the concerts she gave, her virtuoso performances raising vast sums for the new hospital.

145

Charity squeezed Freddie tighter and Horace wagged his tail at the ensuing squeal. 'They're only days away – the storm was in danger of blowing them too far south so they took shelter in Ireland. The fastest ships are here but *Circe* can't sail very fast.'

Amelia blanched. 'Is she damaged?'

'No, the ship's perfect. The delay's because they're bringing in a French prize – she's slowing them down.'

Lady Clarissa must have seen Mrs Penrose's quickly hidden frown. 'Well, thank heaven it was our gain and not our loss. Sir Alex won't like the thought of more prisoners but I'm sure they've been treated with every respect and afforded every consideration.' She glanced at the large frigate anchored off the quay. 'I see Captain Pellew's here.'

Mrs Penrose nodded. 'He's been here for two weeks.'

'Splendid. And are we to see him at the reception tonight? You have Mrs Fox's invitation to dine?'

'Yes, everything's arranged.' Their voices held a note of tension, some silent communication that was lost on the rest of us. Amelia lifted Freddie to the window, pointing out the ships in the harbour, while Charity took Horace by the collar, pulling him reluctantly towards a waiting footman. I joined them at the window, but I could hear Mrs Penrose lower her voice. 'My husband's not bringing any prisoners, Lady Clarissa,' she said in almost a whisper.

'*None at all* – are you sure? Sir Alex will be grateful, but it seems a little strange.'

Eleanor Penrose shrugged. 'Mouths clam tightly shut every time I ask – no one's saying anything. All I can glean is that there are no prisoners left to bring. I cannot believe Admiral Penrose acted cruelly in any way, but there are whispers. They say men change in the heat of battle.'

A footman stood at the door, waiting with a heavy marble vase in his arms, the large arrangement of flowers obscuring his view. He staggered towards the table and we watched in amazement as forty orchids clung doggedly to their single stems. Another footman carried a small velvet cushion and though he bowed to Lady Clarissa, he came towards me. On the cushion, more orchids lay threaded together with tiny pearls, next to them a small leather case with a silver clasp.

Lady Clarissa nodded. 'Open the case, my dear.'

My fingers fumbled as I undid the clasp. A beautiful pearl necklace lay coiled against blue velvet and my stomach twisted, the room suddenly so hot I thought I might faint. I had never seen such exquisite pearls, each pearl of equal size, each glowing with an iridescence that made them almost luminous. The posy of orchids had been threaded with further, smaller pearls and wound round a silver hair pin. My heart thumped. 'Am I to wear these tonight?' I managed to whisper.

'Why, certainly, my dear. It would be most appropriate to wear Lord Entworth's corsage – indeed it would be most impolite not to do so.'

My mouth was as dry as dust. Lord Entworth was showing me such consideration yet I felt suddenly so frightened. 'And the pearl necklace?'

Lady Clarissa raised her eyebrows. 'He clearly intends you to wear it.'

He was offering me everything – position, wealth, high standing in society. One word from me and people would jump to my command. Plays would be permitted, broken windows shrugged off with a laugh, yet as I stared at the exquisite pearls, I wanted to cry.

Lady Clarissa's sharp tone cut through my thoughts. 'But you will *not* wear them. Wearing them would immediately signify acceptance of his hand. This gift is a sign of control, my dear. He may not like it, but you must start as you mean to go on. He cannot *assume* you'll wear them, just like he cannot assume you'll marry him.'

My heart leapt with relief. 'But won't he be angry?'

'My dear girl, what a lot you have to learn. Whether you accept him or not, it will do Lord Entworth no harm to enter a state of nervous expectancy – you of all people, my dearest, can stand your ground. We are not racehorses to be bought. Women should not fall at the first hurdle – because those who do never properly pick themselves up – the damage is done and they never have free rein.' Her tone lightened. 'Now, I suggest we hurry. The water won't take long to boil – we've got just over three hours to transform ourselves from drowned rats into elegant society.'

Lord Entworth sent us his carriage, a courtesy not lost on Lady Clarissa. Grove Hill House was on higher ground, reached only by a steep lane; in good weather it would have been a pleasant walk but with the rain still persisting we were more than grateful for Lord Entworth's kind offer. Charity stroked the new leather seat. 'Are we driving, or flying? This carriage has awfully good suspension.'

The lane narrowed, a pair of fine gates marking the beginning of the drive. Amelia peered through the rain-spattered window. 'It looks like the Luscombe oaks have taken – and look, they've planted a row of elms.' The spindly trees were blowing in the wind, most of them surrounded by stout wooden frames. 'I hope it's not too wet – Mr Maddox avoids summer planting. He insists on late autumn, before the frosts but after the threat of scorching.' She glanced up at the grey clouds. 'But, quite honestly, a bit of scorching might not go amiss. I've almost forgotten what the sun looks like.'

They were being so kind, their smiles designed to encourage, yet the knot in my stomach was getting tighter. I had dreamed of this, planned for it, lay awake imagining it, yet now it was happening, I felt sick with anxiety. I knew I looked my best, my cream silk gown could not be faulted, Lord Entworth's orchids entwined among my ringlets, yet I felt I was about to go onstage.

A crest was carved in stone above the front door – not an eagle, but a fox with a bushy tale, his paw resting on a fleur-de-lis. A footman came quickly forward holding an open umbrella while another pulled down the steps. The house was newly built, the grand entrance leading us into a spacious hall. 'This way, if ye please, Mrs Fox is expecting ye in her private sitting room.'

Our cloaks dispensed with, the footman led us up the wide staircase. Below us, maids were scurrying backwards and forwards across the hall, their dishes held high to avoid collision. Footmen were carrying chairs; candles were being lit. Through an open door, I glimpsed a table set with glasses, a huge punch bowl taking pride of place. At the top of the stairs Lady Clarissa lifted my chin with her fan.

'Now then...it's just them and us – and Lord Entworth – nothing frightening at all. I believe George Godwin's coming later. Are we ready, girls?' She paused, tweaking a feather here, straightening a crease there. Finally she was satisfied. 'Straight back, Angelica – chin a bit higher. He's a man – not a lion.'

Chapter Seventeen

Elizabeth Fox stepped forward, welcoming us with gracious kindness. She was so much younger than I expected. Her gown was unadorned, a very plain grey, only a simple arrangement of lace at her throat. She looked demure, yet not severe, her tightly drawn-back hair held in place by a simple white cap. Her eyes were intelligent, kind, her nose rather snubbed, her mouth heart-shaped even when she smiled. 'How lovely you could come, Miss Lilly. I've long wished to meet you.'

'And I you, Mrs Fox.'

Her plain clothes seemed to suit her. Her smile was mesmerizing, her eyes shining with a light of their own. 'I believe you have met Lord Entworth?'

My nerves had got the better of me, no chance to hide the sudden fire burning my cheeks. He was so commanding, so elegant, standing head and shoulders above the other men in the room. He had watched me enter and had come straight over. His bow was formal, even stiff, his first glance

151

of pleasure turning to a slight frown. I even caught a glimmer of uncertainty cross his eyes.

'Miss Lilly, this is an honour. Lady Clarissa, Mrs Carew, Miss Carew.' He bowed again, a slight bite to his bottom lip. 'Lord Carew is well, I hope?'

'Very well, thank you, Lord Entworth – but unable to be prised away from Trenwyn.' She turned and shook her head. 'Elizabeth, my dear, Lord Carew sends his apologies but, well, I hope you don't mind. His pig is to farrow...'

Elizabeth Fox laughed. 'Of course we don't mind. We never mind what Lord Carew does – he wouldn't be Lord Carew if he put a soirée before his animals. He must be very fond of this pig. Is it part of his new breeding programme?'

Charity nodded. 'Yes, on both accounts – she's the last of those black pigs from China. Lord Carew's convinced she'd make the perfect cottage pig. We're trying to breed ones that are docile yet yield good meat – and Persephone's certainly very docile. We all adore her.'

Lord Entworth smiled. He was standing so close to me, his blue silk jacket cut to perfection, his cream waistcoat heavily embroidered with gold thread, buttoned with pearls. 'If the rumours are true, I believe it is *you* who are behind these stock improvements, Mrs Carew. Lord Carew's clean sweep of prizes has left us all reeling – best in show for everything, if I'm correct?'

'Yes, I'm afraid you are.'

He glanced down and our eyes caught. 'The rest of us must sharpen our game – we can't possibly let this continue.'

A man was walking towards us, smiling as he took his wife's

arm. 'How kind of you to come, Miss Lilly – I'm delighted to meet you.' Robert Fox was short in stature, dressed as soberly as his wife. His black breeches and jacket were of fine quality but held no embellishments. He wore no gold buckles, no tiepin, just a simple gold chain stretching into his waistcoat pocket. His hair was dark, curving into arches as his hair receded. But for the difference in age, I could have been looking at Father. 'You braved the sea, rather than the roads, I gather? A good decision – surely this must be the last of the storms?'

Lord Entworth nodded. 'I sincerely hope so. The roads are a quagmire.' He turned, addressing only me. 'I often ride across my fields to Falmouth. It's an easy journey to the water's edge, and once in Flushing, I take the ferry. Do you ride, Miss Lilly?' His voice held an echo of shyness, his eyes glancing down as he spoke.

The others were drawing slowly away: Lady Clarissa making her way to the chaises longues by the marble fireplace; Elizabeth Fox linking arms with Charity and Amelia, taking them to the window to point out where she had planted Lord Carew's saplings. We were suddenly alone, just the two of us. 'I don't ride very well at all...I wasn't brought up with horses. In town, I either walk or take the carriage.' I was talking too quickly; I would have to slow down.

There was power in his face, a cleft in his square chin; fine lines radiated from his eyes, a crease between his eyebrows. The lines down each side of his mouth made him look stern, even uncompromising; his chin was freshly shaven, a black bow holding back his brown hair. Grey hairs flecked his temples, a set of curls framing his forehead. Not yet forty, he was a man in command – a man in his prime and the heat returned to my cheeks.

'Thank you for the beautiful orchids…' I managed to say. 'And thank you for the pearls – I've never seen such beautiful pearls. I hope you don't mind that…I'm…not…wearing them.'

He glanced up at Lady Clarissa's sudden laughter. She resumed her conversation by the fireplace and his voice dropped. 'Not at all, Miss Lilly. You must only wear those pearls *if* and *when* you want to – in fact, you need never wear them.' The kindness in his voice was laced with uncertainty. He grasped his hands together. 'I'm sorry, Miss Lilly. I believe I acted wrongly in sending them. I should have waited.'

His nervousness surprised me. I had expected him to be self-assured, even arrogant, but his eyes held such sincerity.

'They are a very generous gift – but not unwelcome.' I looked up and smiled.

He held my gaze. 'Dear Miss Lilly, please be patient with me. It was wrong to send those pearls – I should have held back but instead I rush at you like a racehorse bolting from my stable. Please forgive me.'

'Not at all, Lord Entworth…there's nothing to forgive.' A racehorse falling at the first hurdle, Lady Clarissa was right; I had a lot to learn.

His anxiety seemed to deepen, the emotion in his voice painful and raw. 'Miss Lilly…we've precious time to talk …I'm sixteen years your senior, I have two young daughters and I spend more time than I like away from home – but that

I intend to change. I'm still young at heart and I'm young in body – I believe I'm in good health…'

Good health, good shape. I could hardly control my blushes. The gold in his embroidered waistcoat glinted in the candlelight. His eyes were blue, full of hurt. 'Miss Lilly, I'd like to tell you something that I'd prefer you not to repeat – please keep it to yourself.'

He was not petrifying at all. He was kind, courteous, his manners impeccable. He was treating me with such consideration, not trying to possess me but paving the way for honesty. The pain in his eyes was almost unbearable.

I nodded. 'I promise. I'll never speak of it to anyone.'

He drew a sharp breath, glancing to see how much longer we might be left alone. 'My first marriage was arranged and I accepted the situation. I truly believed love would follow – but I was young and I was naive. Lady Entworth was polite to me in public but we barely spoke in private.' Talking of such things was clearly distressing him. He breathed deeply, wiping his hand across his mouth. 'Carrick Hall is a very large house and it can be very lonely – I don't mean now, I mean if you're caught in a loveless marriage…Miss Lilly, the moment I saw you, I was drawn to you. It kindled in me such an ache…I have been lonely for a very long time. I want to hold in my arms a woman that I adore and who loves me back, not one who derides me, who barely tolerates me, who locks her door so firmly against me.'

'Lord Entworth…I—'

'Please, Miss Lilly, let me finish. I know I shouldn't speak so plainly and I don't mean to frighten you…but you must understand I'm a target for ambitious mothers and as such, I'm wearied by it – yet when you entered the room you didn't even look at me. You were like a breath of fresh air, completely unaware of your beauty – no calculating greed in your eyes, no assumed coyness, no trying to catch my attention. I couldn't stop looking at you and I still can't. I'm drawn to you so completely – so utterly, hopelessly, drawn to your joy, your beauty, the kindness in your eyes…'

He swallowed, his Adam's apple catching the lace at his neck. A flush covered his cheeks. 'Miss Lilly, all I'm asking is that my second marriage is based on love. My feelings for you will never change, but I can turn and leave – I'll not pester you and I'll never beg.'

A rush of tenderness filled my heart. This was so different from what I had imagined. He was asking for my love, not demanding it, not expecting it. I felt almost dizzy. His smile was tentative, definite shyness in his eyes. His voice dropped. 'Do you believe in love at first sight – that one, piercing moment when one soul recognizes another? Or do you think that too romantic?'

I could not answer. A footman had just conveyed a message to Mrs Fox and she clapped her hands, glancing quickly at the painted dial of the long-case clock. 'Goodness, that went very quickly. Our guests have all arrived – shall we go down? Mr Fox, if you escort Lady Clarissa…Lord Entworth, if you'd be kind enough to take Miss Lilly.' She put her hand through Charity's arm, holding out the other to Amelia. 'Can you hear a fiddle?'

The door to the drawing room was open, the room full, necks trying not to crane as we swept down the stairs. I caught the surprise in their eyes, recognizing three girls at once from school; they looked older, plumper, all of them sweeping their fans across their faces in sudden panic. The fiddler continued playing and the chatter resumed. Lady Clarissa smiled. 'That's a very lively jig, how jolly – are we expected to do the hornpipe, Mr Fox?' She glanced over her shoulder. 'Do you dance the hornpipe, Lord Entworth?'

'Not if I can help it, but I believe Captain Pellew dances it very well – perhaps he's proposing to teach us.'

Forty people at least were holding glasses, well into their conversations; some were dressed in plain clothes, others in fine silk, but the predominant colour was blue. A dozen officers in his majesty's navy stood resplendent in their white sashes and fine gold braid. Others must have been packet captains, or merchants, most of them wearing their prosperity more flamboyantly than their hosts.

Robert Fox's progression through his guests was slow, each person greeted with the same warmth and humour. We were just behind him, Mr Fox turning to induce us. Voices were rising and I hardly caught their names but most seemed to know Father and sent him their regards. At last, I found a chance to escape – Amelia was alone by the window.

'It's very crowded…I feel a bit hot. I'm going to join Miss Carew if you don't mind?'

Lord Entworth's brow creased. 'Not at all – shall I get you a drink? There's lemonade.'

'No – I'm fine. I'll join Amelia by the window.'

Two men were blocking my way, one a naval captain in resplendent uniform, the gold glinting on his epaulettes, the other Mr George Godwin, and I managed to squeeze past without disturbing them. 'An excess of *twenty thousand* – I only know because I'm prize agent for Lord Falmouth. I believe the navy has taken *Virginie* on.'

'Indeed.' Captain Pellew's sunburned face looked over George Godwin's shoulder.

George Godwin's plump cheeks flushed, he wiped his forehead. '*Two* ships and not one member of your crew injured.' Dog-like devotion shone in his eyes. 'My prize agency is here in Falmouth and I can assure you of the highest efficiency. I've many names on my books—' His face fell. Captain Pellew was walking away, people parting to allow him through.

'Poor George,' whispered Amelia. 'I told him to approach newly commissioned lieutenants, not hardened prize-takers like Captain Pellew.' She drew me to the other side of the window. 'Don't let's be caught again. George has just spent a quarter of an hour discussing his new jacket. It's very fine, but that can be said in four words. You see the man playing the fiddle?' I stifled my surprise; the fiddler was a black man. Another man stood next to him, both wearing naval uniforms. 'He's from HMS *Indefatigable* – Captain Pellew's ship.'

'He must have been a slave,' I whispered.

Mrs Penrose joined us, standing elegantly between us, her voice matching my whisper. 'He was enslaved from the Gulf of Guinea but he's more recently from Lisbon. Captain Pellew believes his playing raises his men's morale.'

'I'm sure it does – he's very good. Did Captain Pellew free him?'

'Not exactly. HMS *Indefatigable* was in Tagus for repairs and after Captain Pellew heard him playing, he had him pressed into service.'

The fiddler was a young man with wiry black hair, his face etched with pain. 'Is that so terrible? At least he's free. There are no slaves in our navy.'

'I should hope not! But it's taken a lot of contrivance to convince Captain Pellew to bring him here tonight. The poor man's virtually a prisoner. He takes solitary meals because he's the only black man among the crew – they won't eat with him, yet they dance to his music. He's never let off the ship...tonight's quite an acceptation.'

I was appalled, immediately saddened. 'But that's so horrible – how come he's here tonight?'

'Lord Entworth asked especially...and as Captain Pellew is no fool he agreed – he knows who to please.'

'Lord Entworth asked?' Unease churned my stomach. It felt so wrong. 'But it's really horrible – it's like they're exhibiting the poor man.'

Mrs Penrose drew a deep breath. 'Yes, Miss Lilly. They might as well be parading him in chains. Come, turn away, we mustn't be seen staring.' She linked her arms through ours. 'A lot of people have heard about the fiddler, but what isn't common knowledge – and which is the most appalling part of this sorry story – is that his name is Mr Joseph Emidy and he's a virtuoso violinist. He's one of the finest players in Lisbon – in fact, the *leading* violinist in the Lisbon opera. Here, sit down. I thought that might shock you.'

She handed me a glass of lemonade. 'But…a man of such talent – forced to play jigs? It's unthinkable. Captain Pellew must be told…'

Mrs Penrose smiled. 'It was after a performance at the Lisbon opera. Captain Pellew watched him playing in the orchestra pit and ordered the poor man's kidnap. His thugs were waiting for Mr Emidy at the stage door. They dragged him aboard *Indefatigable* and kept him hidden. Once out at sea, he was shown to the crew.'

'Like a trophy,' whispered Amelia.

Nausea gripped me. 'But that's terrible. We must do something – that poor man, he must think us barbarians. A man of such talent—'

'Hush, my dear. Smile. Keep your outrage hidden. Mrs Fox is bringing us company.'

At the sight of the two familiar figures, my heart leapt with pleasure. Lady Polcarrow smiled broadly, stepping forward to greet me. 'Miss Lilly, what a lovely surprise.' The feathers in her turban fluttered. 'We weren't expecting to see you here – I'm sorry your father isn't with you.'

Five weeks ago we had celebrated the opening of Sir James' new lock. I had been their guest of honour, sitting under a decorated bower while the children danced and gave me flowers. 'Father's away on business.' I could say no more. They must not know the smelter in Sir James' new harbour was to be the last one Father planned to build in Cornwall.

They were a striking couple: Sir James with his dark, stern looks; Lady Polcarrow with her exquisite beauty, her ruby-red gown reflecting her chestnut hair. 'Do send my regards to your father,' she said. 'I did so enjoy your visit.'

Sir James nodded. 'Yes, indeed. Please do. A very enjoyable day. My attorney's prepared most of the contract – he's at the harbour now, ironing out the finer details. Another week and I'll have it signed.' He bowed to Mrs Penrose, smiling ruefully. 'Mrs Penrose, delightful though it is to see you – I've been sent on an errand. Lord Entworth is hoping – indeed, I believe everyone in this room is hoping – that I might be able to persuade you to play? Having a member of the Truro Philharmonic amongst us raises such high hopes and it's fallen on me to request such an honour.'

A number of guests must have heard his request, their soft murmurs growing into excited chatter. Elizabeth Fox smiled back at her guests. 'I wasn't going to ask and I certainly wasn't going to presume – but, well, now Sir James *has* asked… would you mind, Mrs Penrose? The pianoforte's been pushed into the corner but it would be no bother to bring it forward. There are plenty of chairs…'

An excited buzz accompanied the scraping of chairs. Mr Fox nodded to the servants – an impromptu concert was about to take place. The piano stool was positioned correctly, Mrs Penrose smoothed her skirts. 'Goodness, what shall I play?' Suggestions rained down on her, the ladies now seated in a neat row round the piano, the men standing behind their chairs. Mozart was the clear favourite, though some were calling for Beethoven. 'You choose, Sir James. What would you like to hear?'

Sir James stood tall, his stern face impassive. He leafed

through a pile of music. 'I'm not sure – this – yes, play this. Do you know "Melodie" by Mr Gluck, Mrs Penrose?'

'I know it very well.' Eleanor Penrose took the proffered sheet, pinning it behind the music clips, linking her fingers together before stretching them out. 'But I'm not sure it's the best choice – it's written for a violin. The piano's merely the accompaniment.' Shocked silence greeted her words and she turned quickly round.

Sir James was no longer by her side. He had taken Mr Emidy by the arm, leading him forward, encouraging him with smiles and nods. The poor man looked petrified, glancing round to seek out Captain Pellew. He was right to be scared: Captain Pellew's furious eyes glared back at him but Sir James took no notice, guiding Mr Emidy carefully towards the piano. He bowed respectfully. 'Mr Emidy, would you do us the very great honour of letting us hear you play?'

Tears pooled in the poor man's eyes, his lips began quivering. Mrs Penrose played some notes and he nodded gratefully, readjusting the strings as he tuned his violin. Everyone was staring at him, some believing it to be for their entertainment, but others looked uncomfortable, frowning at their hands, disliking the thought of the poor fiddler's impending ridicule. His nod indicated he was ready, and he placed his violin under his chin, at once lifting his chin higher. His eyes shut tightly and I knew he must be imagining himself back in the opera house.

The first swing of his bow and I thought my heart would break; the plaintive notes soared round us, the pain almost too much to bear. The intense longing seared our hearts; a man held against his will, setting his notes free, willing them to wing their way across seas. No walls, no irons, no chains – the sheer beauty of his music soaring across vast oceans, unlocking shackles, bringing hope to anyone who would listen. Tears rolled from his shut eyes. He had the score by heart – no longer playing in his head, but stretching out his taut bow, melting the hardest of hearts.

A breeze blew through the open window, moonlight flooding the decks of the anchored ships. Silhouetted masts bobbed in the outgoing tide, the clinking of the rigging carrying across the silent water. Amelia drew her shawl tighter. 'Not one single cloud. Look, the stars are so bright.'

Neither of us wanted to sleep, both of us hugging our knees, flushed with success. Thirty people had signed Sir James Polcarrow's anti-slavery petition and more had pledged their support. 'I knew Sir James was a staunch abolitionist – I've admired his work for a very long time and I've heard him speak but I never knew…'

'Robert and Elizabeth Fox are members of the Society of Friends – most of their acquaintances are abolitionists.'

I was not thinking of everyone else. I was thinking of Lord Entworth – without his intervention, the concert would never have gone ahead. 'I admire Elizabeth Fox so much – she's very forthright in her views. I had a long talk with her on women's education and the condition of prisoners – she believes the prison system is outdated and inhumane.'

'I hope it stays nice for your walk tomorrow – she wants

to show you round...you better wear stout shoes because she walks very fast. Angelica, are you ever going to stop smiling? Look at you, see – there you go again.'

'I can't help it...' I was smiling; smiling and smiling. Hugging my knees and hugging my heart. 'If Lord Entworth hadn't persuaded Captain Pellew to bring Mr Emidy, Sir James' plan would never have worked.' It was hard to describe how I felt; perhaps it was pride, or respect, but it made me so happy. 'I've got so much to learn about Lord Entworth.'

Amelia reached up to close the sash window. Her face was in darkness, her voice soft and loving. 'Yes, you have – but don't worry, you've plenty of time. Mamma's told him he's to wait until her birthday to propose. There's always a big party after the cricket match because it heralds the harvest – not that there's going to be much to harvest this year.'

A shaft of moonlight caught the gingerbread pig on the dressing table and my smile vanished. 'I can't think why I brought Fersefony,' I whispered.

She laughed, pulling the soft eiderdown round us. 'Poor Fersefony – don't throw her away. Keep her as a keepsake.'

I did not return her laugh but stared into the darkness. There must be no keepsake, the moon was keepsake enough; one moonlit walk and one brief conversation did not make you love a man. 'Does Lord Entworth play cricket?' I asked.

She giggled. 'Lord Entworth play cricket? Goodnight, Angelica. We really better get some sleep.'

Chapter Eighteen

Falmouth
Monday 8th August 1796, 11:00 a.m.

We were to meet Elizabeth Fox at the corner of Market Strand; I was to spend the morning with her while Amelia and Charity took up Mrs Penrose's offer of a bracing hilltop walk in the hope of seeing distant white sails.

She smiled and waved at us as we crossed the road. 'Well, here's a change in the weather – today, we need parasols yet yesterday it was umbrellas! How do you like our town, Miss Lilly?' Her white bonnet glowed in the sun, her rosebud lips parting in a conspiratorial smile. 'I thought we'd walk down to the quay and visit the warehouse. I can show you my desk.'

Amelia and Charity wore mufflers despite the warm sun. 'And we're going to the top of the hill to look out for Frederick's ship,' said Amelia. 'Mother's busy answering her correspondence and doesn't mind what time we get back. She says we're to seize this glorious day and make the most of the sunshine.'

We walked together as far as the High Street before parting company. Falmouth seemed a very pretty town, certainly very busy. It consisted of one long street with a series of narrow alleys leading down to the waterfront on one side, and a wooded hill rising steeply to the fields on the other. It looked strangely prosperous, the new houses every bit as grand as Truro. The shops looked well-stocked and the market place was teeming: pie sellers shouting, chickens in crates, squawking geese. I had expected the streets to be full of potholes but the cobbles were sound, the sewers flowing freely. But for the sudden envy gnawing my stomach, everything would have been perfect. 'You have a desk, Mrs Fox?'

She laughed gaily, linking her arm through mine. 'Yes, in our office – but please, do me the honour of calling me Elizabeth. And may I call you Angelica?' She did not wait for my reply. 'I thought you might like to see where we run our business but we can walk through the elm park if you prefer. Wood Lane leads up to a flower meadow and there's a rope walk, or we could go to the windmill – or visit the pyramid, or walk to Swan Pool...'

'No, I'd love to see your office. Is your warehouse on the new quay?'

'We've several warehouses. One's upriver in Penryn next to our timber mill, one's on New Quay where we keep the goods for the insurance claims, and we've several more along the river that we rent out – some for grain, some for rice, occasionally it's salt, but usually it's stocked with barrels of pilchards. The trade in pilchards is thriving – but to the Indies not the Mediterranean – hence the need for so much salt.'

The tall warehouses crowded above us, numerous fish

cellars and boat builders vying for space along the water-front. We crossed Custom House Quay and the Quayside Inn, skirting the fish crates and lobster pots, the fishing nets drying in the sun. Men were rolling barrels along the cobbles, dogs barking, seagulls screeching as they dived to catch the discarded guts. It was noisy, vibrant, the sun's reflection making me blink. 'We're just over there – past Bank House. Are you all right? I'm not walking too fast?'

Our stout shoes echoed along the quay, our skirts clutched in both hands. She was six years my senior and had two small sons, yet she strode along the wharf as sturdily as any man. Nods and raised caps greeted her at every turn, each smile reciprocated, each nod returned with the same quiet dignity. Fishing ships crowded the quay, cranes lifting huge sacks from the hold of a lugger. 'This is the inner harbour – it's mainly for the fishing boats. The Packet Service moors against the quay of the Greenbank Hotel – see that ship over there?' She smiled, pointing to a brigantine bobbing at anchor in the sunshine. 'She's ready to leave – the moment the mail arrives the postmaster rows out the sacks and the captain weighs anchor. No time's wasted.'

A row of very fine double-fronted houses fringed the road. 'This is Bank Street – and that's Bank House.' She stopped, looking up at a large red-brick building. 'And this is our warehouse. I hope you don't mind stairs – the office is on the second floor. The ground floor's a warehouse, the first floor we let out to a delivery company, and the top floor's used by sailmakers. They run a repair business – we supply their canvas.'

That first flicker of envy was burning like fire.

Why keep me from the foundry? I knew everything about Father's business – the price of refined tin, block tin, the escalating cost of coal. I knew the wages he paid, the overheads, the wastage. I knew the names of the ships that brought his coal, the ones that took his ore. I knew the harbour dues, the escalating costs of late shipment, the charge of keeping ore on the quayside. Yet his office was forbidden me, my place to remain decoratively at home, or accompany him to fine dinners; every attempt to become involved denied by a frown or a curt shake of his head.

I stopped, but not through exertion. Smoke from the smelter did not cling to my clothes because Father forbade it, but why? Why keep his children from what had made them? Elizabeth Fox saw me rest my hand on the banister.

'Are you all right, Angelica? Only you look a bit pale – these stairs are a bit steep, here, come in and sit down.' She opened the glazed door and a clerk rushed forward to hold it for us. Robert Fox looked up from his desk, pushing back his chair as we entered. He hurried across the room with obvious concern. 'Miss Lilly, are you unwell?'

I drew a deep breath. 'No…I'm very well, thank you. Please, don't be concerned.'

The room was orderly, the desks neat and uncluttered. Leather-bound ledgers lay stacked on the shelves and I fought the jealousy ripping through me. Commerce fascinated me, and here was Elizabeth Fox with her very own desk. It was respect I wanted to see in people's eyes. Not envy. Not dislike. But respect. Respect earned through my own merit.

'My goodness – you can see everything from here.'

Huge windows gave sweeping views of the town and surrounds: the bustling quays, the vast expanse of Carrick Roads, the sparkling waters of the seaport of Flushing. To the north, rocks spilled into the sea beneath the jagged promontory, the crenellated tower of Pendennis Castle dominating the skyline. The clerks resumed their writing and Elizabeth opened a ledger.

'Angelica, you said you wanted to sign the petition?' She handed me a pen and I sat in the proffered chair signing it in a clear hand. 'Another four pages and the ledger will be full – Sir James is to take it with him to London. He'll put it directly into the committee's hands. Slavery will end – it's just a matter of perseverance.'

Her clipped smile stopped me from smiling back. She was clearly uncomfortable and I glanced back through the entries; there must have been a hundred signatures, the last thirty in the same coloured ink.. I searched the names. 'I don't see Lord Entworth's name. Has he signed it previously?'

Elizabeth was not by my side but by the door, opening it for an elderly woman who was struggling under the weight of two heavily laden baskets. She was dressed identically to Elizabeth in a dark grey dress and a white shawl around her shoulders, the same stiff white bonnet over her tightly drawn back hair. 'Susan, let me take these. You shouldn't have come all the way up with them.' The baskets looked like Mamma's and my heart swelled. Elizabeth took them, smiling back at me. 'I divide my day between playing with my sons, helping in the office and doing charity work – these are for the women in the town gaol.'

Robert Fox spread his hands wide. 'This is our office. We've several aspects to our business but from here we run our ship brokering company. I'm Consul for the States of America and as such I broker all trade with the Americas. Most ships entering Falmouth register with us one way or another – very few ships arrive without some sort of damage.' He pointed to a brig entering the harbour. 'Either storm damage or enemy fire.' He went to the telescope. 'That ship, for example, is from Boston and I suspect there's damage of some sort.'

Elizabeth looked round. '*Fortitude*? She's made very good time.'

Her husband nodded. 'I'm afraid I must leave you, Miss Lilly. It's unfortunate timing, but that's the grain we've been expecting – and grain can't wait.'

Elizabeth beckoned me to the telescope and the ship came clearly into focus: a three-masted brig with a British flag fluttering at her stern. 'From Boston?'

'All the way from Boston. My husband needs to assess the cargo *before* it's unloaded. Wheat fouls very easily, even in the strongest of sacks. A damp ship or long delays can prove detrimental and the longer corn or wheat stays on board, the more likely it is to ruin.' She took her turn at the telescope. 'And *we* pay the loss, but…that ship looks sound…there's no outward sign of damage.'

Robert Fox grabbed his hat and cane. 'We impound all spoilt cargo in our warehouse and sift through it for salvage – we can usually sell a small proportion of the stock. What we can't have is the ship's owner claiming the grain's ruined and selling it on *after* we've paid the insurance! You'd be surprised what they try – though that's never the case with the *Tregellan Line* but other shippers aren't so honourable.' His hat in place, he bent to kiss his wife. 'We'll run through those timber accounts tomorrow.'

A movement caught his attention and he rushed to the window. 'Goodness, what's going on?' A crowd in ragged clothes was surging down Dunstanville Terrace. They were running, gathering momentum, soon to reach the High Street; no shouts, no sticks, just a mass of people heading purposefully towards the docks. 'Oh no – not again. We'll need to send someone out to *Fortitude* to tell the master not to dock. He'll have to anchor in the Sound again. They've recognized the flag – they know it's grain.'

Elizabeth pressed against the window to get a better view. 'There's more of them this time. We must hold them back – it can't be like last time.'

'I'll try to reason with them…Elizabeth, go home…now. Please, you mustn't get hurt. If this turns nasty you could get knocked over like last time. Go home, please – get everyone together and lock the doors. Lock the outer gate.' The clerks joined us at the window. 'Please take Mrs Fox home…escort Miss Lilly back, if you would, and I'll go down and reason with them. We must prevent another riot.'

Elizabeth nodded. 'They've come because they're starving, Robert – they just want to feed their families. They know a tenth of that grain is set aside for charity – they just want their fair share.'

'I know, but hunger leads to violence. Last time, they smashed the windows and rammed the doors. I can't risk you being here.'

'That's because they thought the warehouse was full and we were keeping it from them.'

Robert Fox ushered us towards the door. 'This time I'll make sure the doors are wide open so they can see it's empty. I promise, I'll do everything I can.' He reached for his keys, locking the door behind us. 'There's so much corruption they believe us part of it. Miss Lilly, your safety's paramount. Go with Benjamin – Lady Clarissa must know you're safe. Cut up Quay Hill – avoid Market Street. You better hurry.'

We rushed down the stairs, my heart pounding. I had seen riots in Truro – ugly brutal riots, with tinners carrying picks and shovels. A skirmish had taken place below my window: one of the tinners knocked to the ground, his skull smashed and bleeding.

Once past Bank House, Elizabeth stopped, her chest rising and falling as she caught her breath.

'We believe these riots are orchestrated. We think men *dressed* as vagrants push their way to the front of the crowd. It's them that cause the panic – they're the ones who use violence – they throw the first stones.'

A group of dock workers were hauling an empty cart next to the warehouse and we watched Robert Fox stand on the cart to shout instructions. Men started rolling barrels across the quay entrance, a makeshift barrier beginning to take shape. The open doors of the warehouse showed the empty interior and the clerk called Benjamin pointed me forward. He was in his late fifties, soberly dressed in a dark jacket and breeches, his long beard and soft strands of hair matching his immaculate white necktie. 'Allow me, Miss Lilly...I'll get you home. Follow me. No need to be alarmed.'

A steep alley rose sharply from the main street and I followed quickly behind, cutting up another small lane before he slowed our pace. Breathing heavily, he shook his head. 'Mr Fox doesn't deserve this. He's scrupulous in his dealings. Once the grain's in the warehouse he'll divide it fairly – there's plenty for everyone. Some of the grain's destined for the navy but most is to be kept in Cornwall. If only they'd wait. Just one day – two at the most.'

The shouts on the quayside were getting louder. They sounded angry, menacing. Drawn to their doors by the sound of running feet, women stood staring wide-eyed in fear. Men were rushing past, shouting over their shoulders. 'Vagrants – another bloody riot. Get the Fencibles – the bastards will burn the docks.'

The stately sweep of Dunstanville Terrace rose gently before us and we started walking more slowly. A middle-aged woman walked a few steps ahead of us, her hat held in place with one hand, a basket clasped in the other. She was smartly dressed and obviously in a hurry but she stopped suddenly and we almost bumped into her. Benjamin doffed his hat. 'Oh, 'tis you, Mrs Bohenna – I thought 'twas you we were following.'

'Mrs Bohenna – how wonderful. It's me...Angelica Lilly.'

Close up, I could see the last seven years had been kind to

her: new lines softened her face, her blonde hair now a beautiful white. She had the same half-moon eyes, the dimples when she smiled. She was elegantly dressed in a dark blue skirt and matching jacket, her straw bonnet tied with a silk bow beneath her chin.

'Well, bless my soul. Will you look at you? Of course, you're Angelica — and very beautiful you are too.' She took hold of my hand, pressing my fingers to her lips. 'And very lovely to see you.'

I felt suddenly shy, blinking in the bright sun. I could hardly hold back my tears. 'Did you get my note? I didn't know where to send it — I just wrote *Dr Bohenna, Falmouth*. You look really well...it's so lovely to see you.'

But something seemed wrong, a look in her eye, her voice rather strained. 'And you, my dear. You look the picture of health. I was thrilled to get your note — and quite by chance, I'm on my way to Lady Clarissa with a letter of my own.' She smiled at Benjamin. 'But, seeing as how we've had the good fortune to bump into each other, perhaps we can continue together? I'd call that a fortunate coincidence, wouldn't you?' A group of men rushed past. 'Goodness me! Do you know what's going on? I've been nearly knocked flying several times.'

Benjamin frowned, shaking his head. 'There's likely to be another riot, Mrs Bohenna. More grain's arrived from Boston and it may turn ugly. I suggest you stay indoors.' He looked up at the rise of the hill. 'It may prove a false alarm, but best to stay safe. How's the good Dr Bohenna?'

'Very well, thank you, Mr Troon. And your good self?'

'Doing nicely, thank you – now that Dr Bohenna's medicine's working so well.'

I had forgotten her beautiful dimples, her soft Irish accent. The way she remembered names, concentrating on people's concerns, making them think they were the most important person in the world. 'Well now, there's no need for you to brave that hill, Mr Troon, though we'd welcome your company – we can carry on from here. I'll see Miss Lilly safely back.'

We stood smiling at his retreating figure, waving as he turned from sight. At once, her smile vanished and her voice became urgent. 'Angelica…is Lady Clarissa expecting you soon?'

'No – I wasn't given a specific time. I was invited for the whole morning and told to take my time…the others have gone to the top of the hill with Mrs Penrose – Lady Clarissa had a few visits to do. She may not even be home.'

'That's perfect and *very* fortunate. Come, my dear…' She slipped her arm through mine, drawing me quickly down the hill and along the High Street. 'I'll explain everything when we're home. I live just here.' A brass plaque shone on the door, the proud words *Dr Luke Bohenna, Physician* glinting in the sun. 'Come, in here – where no one can see or hear us.' She ushered me along the hall into a beautiful drawing room. 'Angelica, sit down, my dear. I was on my way to Lady Clarissa to deliver you *this*.'

I took the letter she held out, the urgency in her voice making my heart race. It had been hastily written on poor quality paper.

Dear Miss Lilly,

Your brother is accused of highway robbery and is held prisoner in Pendennis Castle.

Please come at your earliest convenience.

Henry Trevelyan

The room began to spin, I wanted to vomit. Mrs Bohenna knelt by my feet, flapping her fan.

'Breathe deep, my dear, have some air. I know what it says because I have my own letter. Luke's with him now. It must be a mistake...I'm sure it can be easily rectified.'

'Highway robbery? That's ridiculous...Edgar has no need to—' The words caught in my throat.

'I know – the idea's preposterous. It must be some idea of a prank, only it's not funny at all. But this disturbance on the dock is a stroke of luck – for us, anyway. If you're not expected home, we'll go there now.'

'Henry Trevelyan wrote to you as well?' The sight and sound of his name had made my heart burn, the thought of him with Edgar strangely reassuring.

'No, my letter's from Luke – your letter was enclosed. Edgar's been held under the name of Tom Ellis – and it must stay that way. No one must know.' She reached for my hands, they were soft like Mamma's, her eyes every bit as loving, her voice as tender. 'Luke recognized him at once. He attends the prisoners at the castle and saw Edgar being brought in...Perhaps you should cover that beautiful dress of yours – if we're to keep Edgar's identity a secret, you

176

mustn't be recognized. Perhaps, wear my cloak and one of my bonnets?'

The shock was passing, terrible fear making me shiver. 'Thank goodness Henry Trevelyan's with him. He'll know how to help us.'

'We mustn't delay. It's a good mile to the castle and mainly uphill, but you're wearing strong shoes so that's a start.'

Chapter Nineteen

The sun was fierce against my cloak, the sky intensely blue, almost cloudless. Most of the path had dried but some rainwater still pooled in the deeper ruts. We had stared up at the imposing tower of Pendennis Castle for most of our walk but now it had disappeared from sight, the well-worn path growing steeper by the minute.

We stopped to catch our breath, looking down to the quay-side. Shouts had followed us as we climbed the hill and were growing louder. A ring of men in red uniforms were closing round the protestors, each entrance to the dock blocked by mounted soldiers, and my heart sickened; it looked like the rioters were receiving a heavy beating. *Fortitude* lay at anchor on the shimmering sea, a swarm of red-coated soldiers guarding her decks.

'They've called the Dragoons. Oh dear, not again – surely there's no need for that. Last time Mr Fox said the protesters had agreed to wait, yet in charged the Dragoons and everything turned violent. It's a terrible business. Luke saw to a man trampled by one of the horses. The man's leg won't heal and he'll never work again. Luke says the riots are instigated. Why would you instigate a riot?'

'Profit – or expedience, there's always a scramble – procurers for the navy want all the grain shipped to Plymouth and local merchants want it shipped to Truro. Give a town a reputation for rioting and the ships will divert elsewhere.'

She seemed surprised. 'You're very knowledgeable, Angelica. I suppose your father discusses everything with you. You must be such a comfort to each other.'

The town had been sheltered from the wind but on the cliffs a fresh breeze blew against our cheeks, the scent of gorse carrying with the salt. The lace on Mrs Bohenna's bonnet fluttered and she tucked her straying hair in place. I turned, trying to hide the sudden emptiness her words had brought. The gulf between Father and I would never allow for intimacy. Neither was a comfort for the other.

'Shall we go on?' she said, lifting the hem of her skirt with both hands. 'There's another steep rise then it flattens and we'll see the gatehouse. There's been dysentery at the castle, some of the men have been very ill.' She paused and my stomach tightened. I knew what she was going to ask. I had been waiting for this.

'Who is Henry Trevelyan, Angelica?'

I had thought never to see him again, yet the thought of seeing him now brought a rush of pleasure. 'He was Edgar's coachman. We met briefly at Trenwyn House – he taught everyone how to play cricket.'

She was certainly surprised. 'A coachman? Well, I didn't expect you to say that!'

'He's not a real coachman…he was at the time, but it was only temporary. He's very upright…and dependable.'

She smiled. 'Men who play cricket usually are. Well, let's just hope he can vouch for Edgar and get him freed.'

The path broadened to solid cobbles; ahead of us, the gatehouse stood flanked on both sides by large grassy banks – the outer bastions of Henry VIII's castle. The deep moat held little water, the gatehouse rising austere and formidable. A covered passageway led from under a stone arch with an intricately moulded pediment. 'You can understand how the royalists managed to withstand a siege for so long,' I said, fighting my fear.

We crossed the bridge to the gatehouse entrance. Two soldiers were leaning against the stone walls with rifles slung across their shoulders, and stood to attention, barring our way. Mrs Bohenna smiled, the ribbons on her bonnet fluttering. 'We're here to meet Mr Henry Trevelyan…or Dr Bohenna. It's about the new prisoner.'

'Well, there's joy for an old man. Look at you – with your bonny ribbons and lace and your pretty Irish accent.' The soldier smiled broadly, wiping his hand across his grey beard. ''Tis a long time since I've seen the Old Country… but there's nothin' lovelier than an Irish maid. Nothing at all. Baskets for the prisoners, is it? You just leave them with me and I'll see they come to no harm.'

Their muskets resting on the stones beside them, Mrs Bohenna smiled back at the two elderly men. 'We've not brought baskets – we're here to visit a prisoner. We need help to find Dr Bohenna or a man called Henry Trevelyan. I believe both are still in the castle. It's them we've come to find…'

'Oh, sorry my dear, my hearing's not what it was. You'll need a pass an' you'll need an escort.' He shuffled us through a side door to a desk in the gatehouse and began rummaging through the drawers, searching a carved box to find a stamp. Finally he picked up a quill and dipped it in the ink. 'I'm Private Mallory and no one goes anywhere without me giving them a pass. Your names, if you please?'

I bit my lip but Mrs Bohenna spoke loudly and clearly. 'I'm Mrs Bohenna – Dr Bohenna's mother, and this is *Miss Ellis* – the prisoner's sister.'

'Well, well, the pleasure's all mine – Dr Bohenna's mother, indeed. You must be so proud – your son's both a gentleman and a saint – an' that's God's honest truth. Here we are, all stamped and correct.'

The entry book duly signed, Private Mallory stood under the arch of the gatehouse and blew a shrill whistle. The courtyard looked deserted and ramshackle, a limping soldier making his way towards us. One red-brick building looked serviceable but everywhere else seemed in a state of disrepair: windows were broken, doors hanging from their hinges. Tattered signs hung crookedly over unpainted doors, the words *Stores* and *Munitions* barely readable. Untidy piles lay covered by large tarpaulins, empty barrels lying on their sides. Crates were stacked under a makeshift wooden roof, bales of straw left haphazardly under the shelter of the over-hanging buttress. Horse dung carpeted the cobbles, weeds blooming between the uneven stones, poppies blowing against an upturned cart.

The soldier was making his way slowly; his gait looked painful, his uniform in the same state of disarray. Stains streaked his jacket, his buttons dull, his boots scuffed. 'Private Evans will take you from here.' Private Mallory's smile lit his face. 'He's Welsh, mind, and no one in their right mind like the Welsh – but he's one of the good ones. He's got six kittens in that guardhouse of his – daft old bugger.'

An open field lay between us and the castle's keep. Sheep were grazing the tufts of grass, chickens scratching the dirt by the outer walls. Cows were chewing the cud, three horses at grass behind a stout ring-fence. The wind was fiercer, the smell of salt stronger. We were on the highest point of the rocky promontory, surrounded by sea. Huge cannons stood evenly spaced along the battery, pairs of guards standing at ease alongside them. Ahead of us, the castle looked foreboding; long slits sinking deep into the thick granite walls, the tiniest of windows, a flag flying from the battlements.

Private Evans stopped to draw breath, his toothless smile designed to bring comfort. His jacket was undone, the inside pocket bulging and squirming. 'Not all six are in the box,' he wheezed. 'This one likes my pocket.' He lifted out a tiny grey kitten and held it by the neck, kissing it softly. 'I've called her Lily – ye can take yer pick of the rest, but this one's staying with me.'

Two tiny blue eyes stared back at me. 'Lily?'

'After my mother – she was a real beauty, just like this

little mite.' I smiled, but hardly heard him. A shield of the Tudor Arms was carved above the gate, hideous gargoyles staring down at me. A heavily studded oak door stood shut in front of us, the wooden portcullis doing its job to strike terror. It had to be a mistake – a terrible prank. I stepped forward, thinking to climb the staircase, but Private Evans stopped me. 'No, not the living quarters, my dear – the prison's down here.' I followed, swallowing my fear as a separate door took us spiralling down a set of stone steps. We were going deeper and deeper, leaving the light behind us.

Two guards stood with their shoulders slumped, easing themselves to attention as they saw us approach. In the flicker of the rush light, a thick oak door with a small grille and large iron bolts blocked our way. 'These gentlemen will take ye from here. A good day to ye, ladies. And all the more pleasant for your company.'

Our pass duly studied, the new guards opened the door to a dimly lit corridor with worn flagstones and smooth granite walls, the air so rancid it was barely breathable. The musty dampness stung my nostrils, the fat from the candles making me want to retch. Two shut doors led from the right, two more rush lights burning against the wall, and I caught my breath, my fear doubling. Light permeated the darkness at the end of the corridor and we walked slowly towards it, the corridor ending in a large room with a huge stone fireplace and an arched brick ceiling. Light was filtering through a small mullion window, the panes dirty, smothered with cobwebs, and I caught the outline of a carved Tudor rose.

'We have to get him out of here,' I whispered as Mary held her handkerchief against her nose.

Benches were stacked on top of each other, pushed to one side; a long trestle table lay in the centre and arched alcoves bit deep into the granite walls. A group of guards were playing dice in the corner and shook their heads. 'He's next door,' and we returned to the dim corridors and stood outside the first shut door. The guard knocked, opening it slowly. 'There's visitors fer ye, Mr Trevelyan. Not prison visitors – they want ye personally.'

The reply came instantly: 'Allow them in.' His voice made my heart thump. He sounded so authoritative, ready to take command.

'Henry Trevelyan will help get him out of here – he's a good man, I know he is,' I whispered.

The guard stood to one side and we stepped into the small room, the high, pointed window grilled and barred. A desk stood in the corner, a table and chair. In a deep recess, I caught the outline of a bed, a wooden chest, and a washstand with a jug and basin – a prison cell, but no sign of Edgar. Henry looked up, no trace of a smile.

'Oh, thank goodness – Mr Trevelyan. You've got him released? Edgar's gone?'

Henry Trevelyan bowed stiffly, formally, remaining behind the desk as he took our permit from the guard. He nodded in dismissal. 'Thank you. You may leave us. I'll vouch for their presence.' A ring of keys lay on the desk in front of him, heavy keys full of malice, and my heart ripped. Treachery screamed from the hostility of his stiff shoulders, the damp walls of the prison beginning to close round me.

His dark jacket and breeches were barely visible against the blackness. His silk cravat was neatly folded, his white shirt well laundered, his chin closely shaven. His short hair looked newly washed, his glasses catching the light from the single candle burning on the desk. 'You've made very good time – I'm glad you got my message.' His voice was firm, no trace of the man who had laughed at me in the moonlight. He pointed to an open grille and I gripped my skirt. 'Your brother's in there. Mrs Bohenna, may I introduce myself? I'm Henry Trevelyan—' He stopped, his eyes boring into mine. 'Dr Bohenna is with him – go through, the grille's not locked.'

Edgar lay slumped on the floor, his dishevelled hair falling over his face, and I thought I would scream. His eyes flashed with fright. He was shaking, his hands trembling. I burst into tears and he began to wail, high-pitched howling echoing round the cell, and my fear turned to fury. I rushed towards him. 'He's petrified…he's ill – we have to get him out of here – get him out – now.'

Mrs Bohenna flung off her bonnet and rushed to Edgar. 'Dear Lord, would you just look at the poor boy. Has he a fever? Those shakes are so violent – why look at him, he's just skin and bones!'

Her voice must have soothed him; he stopped howling, holding out his arms to sob against her shoulder, and she held him to her, pulling back his hair, kissing his forehead. 'Hush now, Edgar, my love. Hush now. We'll get you out of here.'

Luke Bohenna drew me away, leaving his mother cradling Edgar in her arms, and we watched from the open grille. Edgar seemed calmer, his shaking subsiding, his eyes glazing over. Luke cleared his throat.

'Miss Lilly, I'm sorry we meet again under such circumstances.'

I looked deep into the eyes of my dearest childhood friend – Luke Bohenna, always dependable, always correct; keeping us all from mischief, catching me when I jumped from the trees he told me not to climb. I wanted him to hold me now, not stand so stiff and formal.

'I'm Angelica, Luke – I'm not *Miss Lilly*.' He put his arm around my shoulder and I leaned against him, forcing back my tears. He had changed, but only slightly. His brow was furrowed, his hair receding. He had put on a little weight and was no longer the thin waif we teased for quickly outgrowing his clothes. 'Luke, I'm so glad you're here. Edgar's drinking too much. He's very thin…and he's changed so much…I'm worried about him…'

Henry Trevelyan was watching us from the desk and I walked quickly towards him. 'Henry, who should we ask to release him? Is it Captain Fenshaw? Has he been sent for? Whoever arrested him was clearly mistaken – Edgar may be a drunk, but he's not a thief. Where's Sir Jacob? Is he here, too?'

Luke came to my side, his voice soft but firm. That was what had changed most about him – he sounded authoritative, a man whose words were listened to. 'Edgar's not under Captain Fenshaw's jurisdiction, Angelica. If he was,

186

he'd be in the cells of the guardhouse. These cellars are the old kitchens – they've only been made into prisons from necessity. They may be guarded by the soldiers but they're under the jurisdiction of the Transport Board. Sir Alexander Pendarvis commissioned them and he takes full command.'

'But Sir Alex may be away for a month! We can't wait for him – we have to get Edgar released. I can pay *any* amount of surety – *whatever's* necessary. Henry, can you help? They seem to trust you. Who do I pay to get my brother released? The man who arrested him clearly wants money, so he can have money – we'll give him everything he wants.'

Luke held Henry Trevelyan's eye. 'This isn't about money, Angelica – if it was, I would have already paid.'

Henry was looking down, staring at the papers on the desk, and I fought to breathe. 'Surely, it's no different than bail? Who arrested him? Which idiot thinks my brother's a highway robber?'

Henry Trevelyan's stony face was answer enough. 'I arrested him, Miss Lilly.'

The sternness in his voice, his absolute authority... 'You did?' I needed to steady my voice, show no sign of the pain. 'On whose authority did you arrest my brother?'

Luke drew up a chair but I shook my head. I would stand face to face with this man who masqueraded as a coachman, spying on innocent people.

'On *my* authority, Miss Lilly. Sir Alex has appointed me agent in his absence. I represent the Transport Board and take full responsibility for the French prisoners in the castle – and any other business pertaining to prisoners brought here under the Conventions of War.' His eyes scorched mine yet I would not look away.

'My brother has nothing whatsoever to do with the *Conventions of War* – and well you know, Mr Trevelyan,' I snapped.

He readjusted his glasses. 'I wish that was the case, Miss Lilly, but I'm afraid it isn't. For nearly three weeks, I've been investigating the reports of robberies from coaches and inns. In each case, they point to a man with a French accent.'

'My brother is not French, Mr Trevelyan.' Anger spurred me, yet my fear was spiralling.

'Rumours are spreading that escaped French prisoners have made their way to Falmouth and are stealing anything they can to fund a ship to take them home. That includes robbing coaches – so, in the early hours of this morning, I set a trap.'

'You set a trap?' I could not believe it. He was so barefaced, so underhand.

'Very few coaches left Falmouth last week but once the rain stopped, many thought to start their journeys. I knew with all the muddy ruts any highwayman could expect to have easy pickings and it took hardly any time at all for him to fall into my lap.'

'Your lap?' The worn flagstones spun beneath me. 'I'm sorry, Mr Trevelyan – you set a *trap* and an innocent man falls into your lap?' Furious tears blurred my eyes. I never knew I could feel this angry.

'Not an innocent man, Miss Lilly. Your brother was masked and had a scarf covering his chin; he was on a horse and he was brandishing a pistol. Not only that, he was shouting in a French accent, telling everyone in the coach he would kill them if they didn't hand over their valuables.' His voice had been matter-of-fact and detached, yet now it softened. 'I'm very sorry, Miss Lilly, I know how awful this is for you, but it's the truth.'

'How can it be the truth? Who else was there?'

'That's where we're very fortunate. No one else saw the incident so I was able to bring him straight here – otherwise, he'd be in the town prison. He was drunk, acting like a madman, his shouting alone enough to get him arrested. It was sheer chance he chose my carriage first – if he'd chosen any other he'd be on his way to the gallows.'

I kept my voice icy calm, though my heart was hammering. 'You arrested him with no one else present, Mr Trevelyan?'

'I did.'

'Then you can just unarrest him.'

His look did not waver; those eyes that had once held such laughter, now hard and unyielding. 'No, I can't.'

'Yes, you can. It's in your power. You can just say you made a mistake.'

'I didn't make a mistake, Miss Lilly.'

'But it's your word against his. Edgar was drunk and you set a trap – he probably just staggered towards your coach and, suddenly, he's arrested and you've got your French highwayman.'

Henry Trevelyan shook his head, pointing to an oak chest. 'No, Miss Lilly. I can show you the mask, the scarf and the pistol. They're under lock and key. His horse is in the paddock.'

'But it's just your word against his. There's no evidence the pistol or the scarf and mask *belong* to my brother. You could have had them with you, when you *set your trap*.'

'Along with the small silver dish and necklace I found in his pocket? That alone would get your brother hanged. Your brother is short of money, Miss Lilly. I believe two or three items have gone missing from houses we've visited.'

I took Luke's proffered chair, the room spinning round me. Mrs Bohenna stood behind me, her hands on my shoulders. But for the comfort of her open palms, I would have put my head between my knees to stop my dizziness. Luke was speaking, his voice tender.

'Angelica, there's something you need to know. Edgar shows all the signs of being drunk but if I'm right – and I have every reason to believe I am – what we're facing is more serious. From what Henry's told me and the signs I see – his emaciation, his tremors, his high excitability coupled with nervous agitation, his terrors and disinhibited howling – all lead me to believe Edgar is in the clutches of opium.'

I covered my face with my hands – the foul sickly smoke, the fumes rising from the mouthpieces of the brass urns; women sprawling with their bodices gaping, men with their mouths wide open. The pain was so fierce, I wanted to scream.

Luke took my hands. 'Angelica, I can help – we can all help.' His voice was loving. 'Henry's ordered a better bed and twice-daily hot water. We'll get a basket of fresh fruit delivered every day and I'll visit twice a day.'

Tears pooled in Mrs Bohenna's eyes. 'Oh, the poor, dear, motherless boy. I'll come too, Luke – we'll not leave him alone. I'll come every morning and nurse the poor boy back to health. I'll bring the basket and I'll bring fresh broth. We'll get him strong again — just you see if we don't.'

Henry Trevelyan was staring at my hands held so tightly by Luke. He shut his eyes, drawing a deep breath. When he opened them I saw a glimmer of the man whose smile had very nearly stolen my heart.

'Henry, please let us take him home,' I whispered. 'Please say you made a mistake. Please don't file the report. Please, Henry, let him go. He's not a bad person — it's just the alcohol and opium muddling his mind. He can't have been acting maliciously. He's innocent — you must know he's innocent?'

The glimpse of tenderness vanished. Henry Trevelyan's face grew stony. 'I'm sorry, Miss Lilly. Your brother was brandishing a pistol and threatening me in French.'

Tears rolled down my cheeks. 'Please, Henry. Please release him. Please let us take him away.'

His mouth clamped tighter. 'I'm sorry, Miss Lilly. Your brother must remain my prisoner until Sir Alex returns.'

Deepest anger welled through me, ferocious fire burning my cheeks. How dare he speak to me like that — his previous charm, his smiles and laughter merely a ploy to gain information? I hated him; hated his duplicity, his so-called morality. 'Mr Trevelyan, you've chosen the wrong man to imprison. I'm not without influence. I have powerful friends and they will ensure my brother's release.'

His voice dropped, his eyes piercing me through his glasses. 'Miss Lilly, I did not choose your brother, he chose me. And though Lady Clarissa may well turn a blind eye to the theft of her silver dish, Mrs Cornelius has already issued a reward for the recovery of her necklace. If any of your powerful friends think that by threatening me I will keep silent, they will find themselves mistaken. The moment anyone asks me why I arrested your brother, I will furnish them with the full account, together with the details of the stolen goods found in his pocket – and the pistol, scarf and mask.'

Mrs Bohenna squeezed my shoulders. 'I'll return this evening with fresh clothes and new linen.' She turned to Luke. 'It looks like there might be trouble on the wharf – another grain ship's arrived and you might be needed. Now, if you could see us out, please, Mr Trevelyan, we'd best be getting back.'

Chapter Twenty

'Why couldn't he release him?' I gulped the salty air as if drowning. How could I have begged like that, demeaned myself for his enjoyment? I was as furious with myself as I was with Henry Trevelyan. 'Edgar might have behaved badly…in fact, I've seen him behave very badly. I know he can be wild and unprincipled, but he has nothing whatsoever to do with the French. If Edgar was dressed as a highwayman, then it can only have been for some stupid prank and anyone in their right mind would recognize it for that – just a terrible, misguided stupid prank – nothing more.'

'Angelica, how well do you know Henry Trevelyan?' Mary's voice was calm, her mouth held tight.

'It's obvious I don't know him at all!' I breathed deeply. I had never, ever begged before and I would never do so again. 'I had him down as a gentleman but he clearly isn't. We need to find someone in authority – someone who can override his unlawful arrest.'

Private Evans ambled towards us, slipping the kitten back into his pocket as we followed him across the rough grass. At the gatehouse, Private Mallory was waiting to sign us out. 'Will you come again and grace us with that lovely smile of yours, Mrs Bohenna?'

'Indeed I will, Private Mallory. And I'll bake you some potato bread – to remind you of home.'

Once over the drawbridge, she put her hand on my shoulder, drawing me back. 'If you mean Lord Entworth, I'd advise you against it. And it's no good looking so shocked, Kitty told me.'

I stared back at her. 'She wasn't meant to tell anyone.'

'Well, I'm not anyone, am I? I'm her best friend – of course she's going to tell me. And you were very good in the play, by the way – very good. Just like your dear mamma... Now, about Henry Trevelyan – the truth, please, Angelica.'

We picked our way down the path, my burden lifting with every step. She said nothing, grateful for my hand when the path was slippery, resting on a boulder as I finished. 'And that's the truth.' Well, half the truth; she did not need to know about the moonlit walk in the gardens of Trenwyn House.

'So, Henry Trevelyan was commissioned by Sir Alex Pendarvis to investigate the robberies and he thought to pose as a coachman to be in the very thick of things. I'd say that's clever, wouldn't you? And your brother and Sir Jacob hired him – so he knows your brother frequents opium dens. He refused your offer of a bribe to keep quiet about both the play and being kidnapped and he clearly disliked you offering to pay for Edgar's release. I'd say *not* a dishonourable man, then, wouldn't you?'

'He clearly is — don't you see he was threatening us? If I go to anyone in authority, he'll hand them the dish and the necklace and Edgar will be arrested again.'

'Well, yes, I agree he has us over a barrel, yet keeping Edgar's name secret is in itself a puzzle. Why's he done that? He knew Edgar's identity the moment he saw him, yet he chose to file the arrest under Mr Ellis?' Her soft blue eyes looked remarkably sharp. 'You've told me absolutely *everything*, have you, my dear? There's no reason why Mr Trevelyan might be protecting Edgar — or someone close to Edgar?'

'No, no reason at all.'

My answer had been quickly said and she raised her eyebrows. 'Well, we'll just have to wait for Edgar's head to clear so he can tell us his side of the event. Come, we must hurry. But let me assure you, my dear, I'm going to get that boy back to health if it's the last thing I do.' She drew a deep breath, wiping away a tear. 'I was wrong not to come back. I should've come back the moment your poor mamma died — what kind of woman abandons her best friend's children? You poor bairns — you were left motherless to face the world and I should've taken no notice of your father.'

'I always thought you two had quarrelled...'

She stopped to catch her breath, staring down at *Fortitude* now moored alongside the quay. A line of soldiers guarded the empty dock, the cranes straining under the weight of huge sacks. 'We did, my love, and it saddens me greatly.' The hurt in her voice wrenched my heart. 'I wrote to tell your father that as Luke was well settled in St Bartholomew's Hospital, I'd be more than happy to come back to look after the pair of you...I told him, plain and simple, that I didn't like the idea of you going to that fortress of a boarding school so soon after your poor mamma left you...and that I'd be happy to come back to Truro to be with you both. But he was adamant. He wrote back – in no uncertain terms, mind – saying that you were very well cared for and that I was to stay in London with Luke. He said you were getting on as well as could be expected without your dear mother.'

'That's because they censored our letters. I used to write each letter at least four times. In the end, I just gave up and wrote what they wanted me to write.'

She pulled me to her, holding me tightly. 'Oh, you poor wee child. You weren't happy there, were you? And there I was believing you didn't write because you'd settled in so well and had such smart new friends – like Miss Carew and Lord Entworth!'

'We could only write to close family. Anyway, you changed your lodgings – when I did write, my letter was returned. You didn't leave a forwarding address...'

Her hand flew to her mouth. 'Oh, my dear love, how can you say that?' She retrieved her handkerchief, wiping her sudden tears. 'I sent my new address straight away. You must believe me – it was the very first thing I did.'

Seagulls were screeching across the rocks, their haunted cries tearing my heart; both of us so wounded, both trying to hold back our tears. 'Yes, well. Father probably didn't want you to come back to Truro because he was too busy with his fancy woman. He didn't love Mamma. He was carrying on with a woman before Mamma died.'

I knew it would shock her but I could not stop myself. She had asked for the truth and after years of hiding behind my mask and not showing my true feelings, I was telling her every last grain of it. All the people I loved – her, Luke, Edgar, even Kitty and Theo Gilmore – swept conveniently far away so Father could pursue his wealth and keep his fancy woman.

She blew her nose. 'Well, they should marry – seven years is quite long enough. And it's time you called me Mary, my dear.'

The breeze blew against my cheeks, the sun sparkling on the vast blue waters of Carrick Roads. In the distance, I could see the curve of the river and the bay below Trenwyn House. 'It's all over – he finished with her three months ago.'

'How do you know that? I hope it's not servant gossip.'

'No, it's not. It's all neatly entered in Father's accounts. Did you know if you press a key into warm wax, they can cast you another? A friend of mine in the smelting house did it for me. Of course, I said it was *my* key, not one for Father's desk!'

'Angelica!'

'Well, I like to know what's going on – and I noticed the payments stopped three months ago but that's hardly surprising. It had to end because Lady Boswell has now got her beautifully manicured nails into Father. They left together – the two of them alone in the carriage all the way to her sister's house – *if* that was where they were going. Molly's convinced they're going to come back married. Are you all right, Mary, only you don't look very well? Is it the heat? Let's get you to some shade.'

The pain left her face, in its place, steely resolution. 'Angelica, you and I are going to go straight back, and you, my dearest child, are going to write a very long and detailed letter to your father.' Her lips pursed. 'You're to tell him everything – about Edgar but *most especially* about Jacob Boswell's atrocious behaviour. If Lady Clarissa has expressed her doubts about the Boswell family, then we must act on them. Make sure you tell him about Kitty Gilmore and that you were excellent in the play. No more lies.'

She looked distraught, fighting back her tears, and a lump caught my throat. 'No more lies. I'll tell him everything.'

She blew her nose. 'I don't believe Henry Trevelyan's a wicked man, Angelica – I think he's just doing what he believes is right. It can't have been easy having you plead with him like that – a weaker man might well have given in.'

'It would have shown great strength, not weakness.'

'Well, whether we like it or not, he speaks the truth – if Edgar had been arrested by anyone else he'd be facing the gallows by now.'

An icy hand gripped my heart. 'But it's only his word against Edgar's – what if his precious Transport Board just wants to stop the rumours about escaped French prisoners? Henry Trevelyan would need to arrest an Englishman, wouldn't he? He'd need to bait a trap to catch some poor, misguided man with an opium addiction who can't answer back. That's what we're facing. He set a trap and he caught his man.'

The town was uncannily quiet, groups of people huddling together with anxious frowns. The market had been cleared, the children playing hopscotch, their mothers looking over their shoulders with furtive glances. Mary opened her front door and picked up a beautifully written invitation from the silver dish on the table.

'Well, this is very kind – I'm honoured, to be sure. And so will Luke be – look, Angelica, Lady Clarissa has invited us to her musical evening tomorrow. How very kind of her.'

My bonnet changed, my shoes rubbed free of mud, and I stood on the doorstep ready to leave. I turned with a jolt. Horace was crouching at my feet, looking up at me with cocked ears and wagging tail, and I turned in delight. 'Amelia, Charity, what perfect timing! This is my friend Mrs Bohenna. We bumped into each other and I lost all sense of time. Mrs Bohenna, may I introduce my very good friend, Miss Amelia Carew and her sister-in-law Mrs Charity Carew?'

They curtseyed, their open parasols shielding them from the sun. 'Elizabeth told us Benjamin had said you'd met each other so we knew you were safe. What a terrible to-do. It's all quiet now but it sounds like there was a terrible free-for-all. Major Basset called in the Dragoons. Apparently there was such a crowd he read the riot act...and we've heard he's had four people arrested. Mamma's furious and so is Elizabeth. She said the whole affair was heavy-handed and conducted in very bad spirit.'

Mary stooped to stroke Horace's head. 'A terrible business indeed – poor starving men...Well, we can only hope and pray they show some mercy and set them free. But, seeing as you're here, Miss Carew, I'm thrilled to accept your very kind invitation. Dr Bohenna and I will be honoured to attend your mother's musical evening – it's very kind indeed of Lady Clarissa to invite us. I'll write to her, of course, but just while you're here.' She smiled. 'You have a very fine dog, Mrs Carew. A wolfhound of some sort?'

'A wolfhound of *all sorts*, Mrs Bohenna, but he has a very endearing character and is highly intelligent. He adores my son and never leaves my side. My husband brought him home after a walk. Apparently the dog was starving and just got up from the ditch and walked by his side. That was that. He hasn't left mine or my son's side since.'

Mary Bohenna straightened. 'What a dear dog. I wonder, would it be possible for me to see Angelica again tomorrow? I know we've spoken all morning – but we've still so much to catch up with. I was a great friend of her dear mother. We lived in Truro before we moved to London.'

Amelia slipped her arm through mine. 'Of course it would. Would eleven o'clock suit you, Mrs Bohenna? We can drop Angelica off on our walk with Freddie.'

Sunbeams streamed into the room, lighting the whirls on the carpet, glinting on the silver ink pot on the desk in front of me; Charity and Amelia were singing, Mrs Penrose accompanying them on the piano. Lady Clarissa and Freddie were rolling oranges to each other across the floor and I had nearly finished my letter. I reread the last paragraph.

Jacob Boswell's conduct towards me in the coach confirms he is both dishonourable and a bad influence on Edgar, yet my concerns go deeper than that. Jacob Boswell neither drinks nor takes opium. He remains in control of his actions, never stepping out of line, yet I witnessed him lead Edgar straight into an opium den when he should have been seeing him safely to bed. I believe he encourages Edgar to take the substance. The more Edgar loses control of his senses, the more money Jacob can squeeze out of him. Lady Clarissa speaks of severe debt, a history of gambling, and I truly believe it was Jacob Boswell who stole Lady Clarissa's silver dish.

I had never spoken so freely to Father, nor ever admitted to myself how much I wanted to. But Mary was right. From now on, everything would be different. No more lies, no more play-acting. No pretending to be someone I was not — *truth, not artifice*, as Lady Clarissa had put it.

Amelia drew her cloak around her, gazing up at the starlit sky. There was no wind, just the fresh smell of salt and the sound of a lonely fiddle. 'The town's very quiet — and you're very quiet, too. You've hardly spoken all evening. No one expects you to sing, Angelica. Why don't you read a poem — or say one of those long soliloquys you were made to learn as a punishment? *Circe* isn't expected in tomorrow. We've another day to wait — poor Charity can hardly bear it.'

Moonlight danced on the black water; my best friend, yet I knew I must keep silent. I could not tell her Edgar lay shaking

201

in a prison cell, watched over by a man I had once thought honourable. 'This must be so hard for you,' I whispered.

She swallowed, shrugging her shoulders, clasping her hands together. 'I don't know – I thought it would be. I was dreading it yet…' She hesitated, as if not wanting to say the words she was about to say. 'I saw his mother today and her grief is still so raw, yet mine…my grief's still there – it will always be lodged deep inside me – but I was talking to her and I suddenly realized I had no memory of his face. I can't see him in my mind any more – I'm losing his memory and that saddens me almost more.'

I reached for her hand. 'He wouldn't want you to be sad. He'd want you to be happy.'

'That's what Mother says.' She forced a smile. 'Mrs Bohenna seems a very pleasant lady. Her bonnet was particularly pretty and she has such a warm smile. She's Irish, like your mother?'

'She's so like Mamma, I didn't realize how much I missed her until I saw her today. Mary and Mamma were friends in London – Mary married an apothecary and came to Truro and Father used to visit their shop. Mary thought Father would be perfect for Mamma so she asked him to deliver a parcel to Mamma when he next went to London.'

'She brought your parents together?'

I nodded. 'I've known Luke all my life and I'm so happy for him. He's where he should be, doing what he always wanted to do. I used to goad him into misbehaving but he never did! He was too upright – he always wanted to be a doctor and now he is one.' I reached for my handkerchief, the tears I had been trying to hold back flooding my cheeks. Luke was there for Edgar, he would get him better. 'I've always adored Luke. Wait until you meet him – I know you'll like him.'

She reached for my hand. 'Angelica – don't cry.' I could not answer, the kindness in her voice making it worse. 'Is it seeing Luke again? You love him, is that it?' She lifted my chin, forcing me to look at her. 'Is that what this is all about? You don't *have* to marry Lord Entworth, you know.'

I shook my head, pulling the lace on my handkerchief. 'I don't know what I feel about Lord Entworth. He has such a powerful presence...when I stand next to him my heart races, but I think it's fear, not love. He's utterly charming but I keep thinking I might say or do the wrong thing.'

She squeezed my hand. 'You silly goose – you never say or do the wrong thing. But fear's not a good start to a marriage – especially you who are so fearless. Tell him you'd want to race gigs down that long drive of his – that you're passionate about plays and reading – that you'd want all your servants to learn to read and write. Let him know of your generous gifts to the library and hospital.'

'Anonymous gifts are meant to remain anonymous, Amelia!' I looked up. 'And what do you mean...fearless?'

She smiled, smoothing a tear-soaked curl from my cheek. 'Standing up to Miss Mitchell? Leaving her in no doubt about how she should be *educating* us, not just teaching us how to embroider or get in and out of barouches? Angelica, we won't leave you alone with Lord Entworth if it's making you uncomfortable. If you feel the need to be rescued, just swap your fan into your left hand and we'll come running. That's the signal I always use.' She closed the shutters. 'Come, we really do need to get some sleep.'

You who are so fearless. The gingerbread pig lay flung in the waste bin, the pain of Henry Trevelyan's betrayal still cutting like a knife. I had been too free with him, both times completely myself: no mask, no biting back my words, the real Angelica Lilly standing so defiantly, the horses' hooves thundering beneath her. Laughing at the danger, flinging away the key; the real Angelica Lilly slipping from the house by moonlight, glancing up at the ladders she knew would take her back to her room.

I had exposed myself so completely. Well, let him know the real me, let him take heed. Let him understand just how fearless I would be in my brother's defence.

Chapter Twenty-one

Charity and Amelia turned to wave goodbye. 'What a lovely little boy – as blond and bonny as his mother.' Mary turned, picking up a basket, handing me another. 'This one's for Edgar, the other's for the men at the gate – poor souls, so far from home and most of them unwell.'

We followed the well-worn path, the seagulls calling from their wide circle above us. 'I left Edgar as comfortable as I could. The dear boy's just skin and bones, and I've learned words I never knew possible – dreadful they were.'

I grimaced, raising my eyebrows. 'Mamma called it *foundry language*. Luke never let us teach it to him.'

'I should hope not! I've brought a rabbit pie and plenty of oranges – Henry needs feeding just the same as Edgar.'

Private Mallory was waiting for us, his coat tightly buttoned, the last wisps of his grey hair oiled neatly across his forehead. 'And a very good morning it is, Mrs Bohenna. Well, now then, you shouldn't.' He beamed broadly as Mary reached into her basket. 'Cherry jam – would you believe that, Private Evans? And a wee drop of whiskey? You're too good to us, Mrs Bohenna. I'll sign you in. Just you follow young Evans – no need for paperwork.'

'And how is Lily today, Private Evans?'

'Purring like a tiger, Mrs Bohenna.' We crossed the grass, the sheep bleating loudly as a group of choughs strode angrily among them. The sea was calm, a ship with white sails entering the harbour. Private Evans shielded his eyes from the sun, wheezing as he smiled. 'I'll be waiting for you, ladies. Just you take your time.'

Once again, we spiralled down the ill-lit stone steps. Today, I was prepared. No more begging. I would inform Mr Trevelyan I had written to Father and would engage Matthew Reith, the best attorney in Truro. It was not exactly true, but it would scare him.

The door was half open, thin light filtering through the window, but the room smelled fresher, a proper bed and table in Edgar's cell, a vase of flowers on Henry's desk. He stood up as we entered but I walked past him, pushing open the heavy grille to Edgar's cell. He was sitting on his bed, freshly washed and shaved, and looked up when I entered, a haunted plea in his eyes. I ran to him, throwing my arms around him.

'I don't remember anything – nothing. I just woke up in here and that's the honest truth.'

I drew him down to the bed, sitting next to him on the horse-hair mattress. 'Try to remember – try hard. And don't pretend. I want the truth.' Mary and Henry were standing by the grille and I glared up at Henry Trevelyan. 'Has Jacob Boswell come yet?'

He shook his head. He looked tired, dark circles under his eyes, his hair ruffled. 'I had men out looking for him. He was seen this morning boarding the stagecoach to Truro.'

I bit back my anger. 'Your *so-called* friend has deserted you, Edgar. There's no one else to speak for you. It's just you – so I need you to tell me everything. Let's start with your *exact* movements on Sunday evening.'

'I don't remember. Christ Almighty – if I could remember, d'you think I wouldn't say? I'm in for coach robbery—'

'Right, listen, Edgar – no swearing. No more licentious behaviour. No laudanum of any kind. No drink. No lying. No feeling sorry for yourself. Have you got that?'

'Christ, Angelica—'

'*No* swearing. Now, tell me, what did you do on Sunday evening– where did you go? Think, Edgar. Which den did you go to? Was it one like the Heron Inn but somewhere in Falmouth? You must remember how you started the evening?'

His bony fingers trembled against his pale face, his lank hair falling across his forehead. He began shaking, sweating, tears streaming down his face. 'I don't know its name. It's down by the wharf – behind the brewery. There's a place you get to from the old sewer – it's no more than a room.'

Mary brought him a tankard of freshly squeezed lemons. 'Here, my love – it's sweetened with honey and will do you the power of good. Well done remembering – that's got us started. Now what else can you remember? Who was there? Who were you talking to? Can you remember faces, or names, or what you talked about?'

Edgar threw back his head, laughing through his tears.

'Mrs Bohenna, we don't talk – there's no discussing politics or the state of the war. We just—' He clasped his hands over his face again, crying piteously. 'You sound just like Mother. I remember her voice.'

'Well now, she wouldn't want you crying like that, would she? Think, my love. You were in this den. Now what was going on? Who was there?'

He went rigid, staring with open eyes, like a statue, frozen, unable to move, and I willed him to breathe. He gasped for breath. 'There was a woman. I can remember a woman. She was – she was dancing, undoing her bodice…'

'We don't want to know that, Edgar.'

'No Angelica, I remember now. She was goading us – all of us. She held up a necklace telling us how easy it was – how the coaches were leaving, how the first one who brought her back a necklace could…'

Henry unlocked a drawer. 'Was this the necklace, Mr Lilly?'

'I've no idea. I hardly saw it. Christ, I remember now. I remember searching my bag for money and I found a silver dish. I had no idea it was in my bag.'

'You didn't steal it from Trenwyn House?' My voice was like iron.

'No, of course not. Never. I'd never seen it before.'

'You had. You were just too drunk to notice.'

Mary squeezed between us. 'Now, now, no quarrelling – we're family and we help each other. We don't judge. Go on, my love. What happened with the lady? Think hard, try to remember.'

He clutched his stomach, wincing in pain. 'I remember reaching out to her. She was holding up the necklace, laughing, saying it was easy – the coaches always slowed at a certain point and all you had to do was take their money.' He shook his head at Mary's proffered tankard, pushing it away.

'No, drink it, my love. It will do you the power of good. Now, what else did this brazen harlot say – or do?'

Edgar smiled, the boy in him shining through his gaunt cheeks. 'She said to shout in French – and I remember now – she said she had a pistol for anyone *man enough* amongst us.'

Mary clamped her hand across her mouth. I wanted to scream, shake him, howl at him. I wanted to be sick. In the stunned silence, Edgar slipped slowly to the floor, curling up like a small child, his hands over his head. Mary clutched my hand. 'So you took her challenge?'

He lay on the cold flagstones, clasping his head tighter. 'No. No. Believe me, I wasn't man enough for her. I didn't take the pistol. I didn't. I gave someone the silver dish and I…I just bought what I needed.'

'You didn't need it.' I sounded angry but fear twisted my gut. What if he was guilty? Dear God, what if he was guilty?

Henry stood at the grille, his voice firm. 'He did need it, Miss Lilly. Once in the grip of opium, the body's cravings take over all rational thought. It's the only thing that drives them. Edgar's illness will take time to conquer – these cravings will continue for a long while yet.'

I slid to the cold stone floor, taking Edgar into my arms. 'Why, Edgar?' I could barely speak, my words a whisper.

'Why when you have so much, when you lack for nothing? When you have—'

'Such a promising future?' His voice was hard, bitter. 'A lost, grieving boy sent away at twelve to make a man of him? Ordered to Oxford to make the sort of friends I needed – for what? For some glittering political career...or, let's get to the crux of the matter, to marry a title to fulfil Mother's dreams? "Come this way, lords and ladies...line up, line up...we'll supply the fortune; all you need do is supply the title...here, join the queue. Have your pedigree ready...my desperate father will pay anything you ask."'

I held my clenched fist against my mouth. 'Edgar, stop. Please, stop.'

'Oh, I stopped, all right. Well, they stopped it for me. The truth is, Angelica, I was sent down two months ago – but I'm glad it's over and done with. I couldn't take it any more. Everyone sneering at me, detesting me, laughing at my stupidity – but what did I expect? I'm not clever – I should never have gone there. Every day my shortcomings exposed to ridicule, never learning quickly enough, never writing cleverly enough. My place at Oxford was *bought*, not earned – every day bringing the same terrible panic.' He looked up, pain deep in those haunted eyes.

'I thought a Sunday-evening exercise would be a stroll along the river. Imagine their laughter when I was handed an off-hand translation from the little-known work of Grotius on the *Evidence of Christianity*. Christ, Angelica, I could hardly understand it in English, let alone Latin. I started copying work, pleading with Jacob to write my essays. When they found out, I was publicly shamed, given warning after warning, but Father never failed. Oh no, Father *never* failed. There was always another bursary, or the offer of a new set of dining chairs – or money to refurbish the Dean's sitting room. *Old Smelter Boy's father trying to buy him some class.* We're from the gutter, Angelica. Our mother was a—'

'No she wasn't.' Mary's voice was firm but calm. 'You can say what you like about Oxford. I never thought you should have been sent there – nor to Harrow. You can be sent down a hundred times and I wouldn't give a fig, but don't ever say that about your dear mother. She was a good honest woman. She may not have been a saint, but you mind your tongue. You should be proud of her, not listen to gossip.'

Sobs wracked Edgar's chest, his eyes and nose streaming. 'That was my daily taunt – *Hey, Smelter Boy – I hear your mother was the Prince's favourite.*'

'Well, so she was. She was everyone's favourite.'

He took my handkerchief, slowly blowing his nose. 'One evening Jake got us tickets to the opera but my toothache was unbearable. He gave me laudanum and suddenly, miraculously, my fear left me. The music was sublime, lifting me to heights I had no idea existed; the peace was exquisite – like being cradled in velvet arms, carried above the hurtful taunts. They all take laudanum. They take it for pleasure, to enhance the music, but I took it to get back to this heaven on earth. A few drops and I became brave, witty and charming – full of clever retorts and answers that made everyone laugh.'

Mary wiped her eyes. 'Well, now. You've no need to be anyone but yourself.'

I fought my anger, the thought of Jacob Boswell, taking the first coach to Truro. 'I presume Jacob Boswell kept up a ready supply. Did he take any?'

The haunted look returned. 'I thought he did. I thought we were taking it together. He led me to believe I was hardly touching the stuff. Then I began needing more and more – quickly, and in larger doses. The penny that first bought happiness turned to shillings and then guineas.'

'And Jacob Boswell always found a plentiful supply!'

Edgar nodded. 'Stronger drops and different ways to ingest it – or smoke it. Jake always knew where to find the nearest den. Turkish opium is my favourite, but that's eight guineas a pound. Do you know they make it into cakes? Cakes like Lady Clarissa served us.' His laugh was hollow, his bony fingers clasped over his face. 'My cravings just get worse and worse – my nightmares more and more terrifying: I go to hell and back, yet I can't stop. I can't stop and I hate it. I hate it, hate it.'

His voice dropped. 'Jake moved into my lodgings and started asking for money. He threatened to tell Father.' His hands began to shake, his movements increasingly violent. He started crying and I held him tightly, my anger making it hard to breathe. I should have visited him when the accounts doubled. I should have alerted Father.

Henry Trevelyan coughed. 'Mr Lilly, may I suggest you and I sit down to this rather delicious rabbit pie? Then may I suggest another sleep, followed by some exercise round the keep? We can go and see to your horse.'

Our eyes caught. We did not need his false pity, nor was I

fooled by his friendly politeness. 'I'm not ready to leave, Mr Trevelyan. If you don't mind, I've some questions I'd like to ask my brother.' I turned my back, keeping my voice steady. 'Edgar, the night you were arrested – was Mr Trevelyan still in your employ? Did he take you to this den and was he waiting for you outside?'

Edgar stopped crying, wiping his hand across his nose. 'My coachman turned gentleman gaoler? No, we'd dispensed with his services – we'd no money and Jacob said he was getting on his nerves.'

'Was Jacob with you?'

'Of course he was. He's my trusted procurer. I don't know Falmouth but he knows it like the back of his hand. He knew just where to go.'

'This woman had the necklace so she must be the thief – or at least *know* the thief. Describe her, Edgar.'

'What I saw? You really want to know?' His laugh was cynical, chilling my heart.

'I want to know her hair colour, her eye colour – and what she was wearing.'

He laughed again, his voice mocking. 'It was dark, Angelica. And she was in a state of undress – a man doesn't look to see the colour of a woman's eyes when he can feast his own elsewhere.'

The chill turned to ice. 'You disgust me, Edgar.'

'I disgust myself.'

'Come now. Angelica, time is getting on and we really must go…Mr Trevelyan's right: Edgar, you must eat everything you're given and you must try to sleep all you can. And if Mr

Trevelyan's kind enough to take you out for some fresh air, then so much the better.' She put her hand under my elbow, helping me to my feet. 'But put your mind to it – we need a better description of this woman.'

Henry Trevelyan reached down to his desk, picking up a small, leather-bound notebook. 'I spent last night in the den, Mrs Bohenna. The woman's name is Lottie Lorrelli. She hasn't been noticed there before but she was seen leaving with Edgar. People remember her being of medium height with brown hair. Eye colour unknown.' He handed me a notebook. 'I wrote this down in front of the witnesses – here, you can see they've signed it, or made their mark.'

A chill took hold of my heart and I shivered. His evidence would hang Edgar. Those words, on that paper, signed by four people – exactly one scrawl, two signatures and one mark – would be enough to get Edgar hanged. I could hardly breathe, fierce, icy fingers gripping my heart. Henry Trevelyan was watching me, his eyes softening. I glared back. 'The woman's name is clearly fabricated and these could be, too. I need full names, occupations and addresses.'

The pity left his eyes, in its place, stark authority. 'I have their names and addresses on the next page. Here, Miss Lilly – all clearly listed. And I've instigated a search for the woman – the horse, however, is registered to a nearby inn. I have the time, and the name of the person who hired it.'

'Good. That's something, at least. Who was it?'

'The horse was hired by your brother, Miss Lilly.' Henry Trevelyan reached for a chair. 'Please sit down...I understand how distressing this is for you. May I get you something?'

I clutched Mary's arm. 'You're not sorry at all – why should you be? But that can't possibly be the case. My brother would have been in no fit state to hire a horse.'

He turned the page in his notebook. 'Mr Lilly signed the ledger and I agree he was in no fit state to either hire or ride a horse. His signature is illegible but his name is clearly printed beside it. And before you suggest it wasn't your brother, I'm afraid the innkeeper gave me a very detailed description.' He held the page open. 'Please read it – halfway down the page – the description fits your brother exactly.'

Black untidy hair, green silk jacket and breeches, embroidered cream waistcoat, silver buckles on his boots, each incriminating word written in Henry Trevelyan's neat, cramped handwriting.

Somehow, I managed to make my way across the swaying flagstones and out of the door. The ground was spinning, all breath squeezed from me. The door shut behind us and I doubled over, certain I would be sick. Mary leaned against the damp wall, clutching her hands across her mouth. 'Dear God, the foolish, foolish boy.'

We fought to regain our senses as a voice echoed along the dimly lit corridor. A man was giving commands from the other side of the door, the guards sliding back the heavy bolts. The man's instructions were growing increasingly anxious and as the door swung open, my heart nearly stopped. A familiar figure stood in the glow of the rush light.

'Oh no!' I whispered. 'It's George Godwin.' I pulled Mary back against the wall. 'He's a friend of Lady Clarissa – a cousin of some sorts. He'll recognize me.'

Four soldiers were dragging two wooden chests along the

flagstones and as George Godwin stopped to wipe his brow, a tall man in uniform took charge. 'No less than three on the door. Stand to. Once these two are in, there's another two to follow.'

'That's Captain Fenshaw,' Mary whispered. 'I've seen him in town.'

Panic filled me. 'If George Godwin sees me, he'll link me with Edgar. I've told them I'm the prisoner's sister and we look so alike.'

'We'll say we're visiting the French prisoners – for Mrs Fox.' Mary slid her hand along the wall. 'Better still – here's an alcove, some sort of recess. Come, squeeze in here…it's so dark, they may not see us.'

There were only two doors leading from the dim corridor, the one we had come out of and a similar door ten yards further towards the outer door. George Godwin was making for that door, a set of heavy keys rattling in his hands. The lock scraped open and I caught a glimpse of the inside of the room. It was clearly another cellar but much brighter and larger, the heavily grilled window admitting long shafts of light. A desk sat under the window, next to it, a bookcase stacked full of heavy ledgers. Brass candlesticks dotted the room, a chair in one corner, the beginnings of a stone fireplace.

George Godwin's voice rose in panic. 'There's only room for two more in the vault – but there's another four chests coming and I've *nowhere* to put them. I have to get this lot to London…now…this delay is unacceptable. Your men are very slow, Captain Fenshaw. If they aren't back by Monday,

I'll have to go above your head and request assistance from Major Basset.'

'My men can only go as fast as the horses, Mr Godwin – four and a half days there, four and a half days back. You've already commandeered my best men, and I've none left to spare.' He watched the soldiers drag the heavy chests along the flagstones, the light catching the brass buttons on his uniform, his florid face and bushy moustache, picking out his stiff, painful movements. He was tall, dark-haired, probably late forties. 'That's it – keep them coming. That's the last for the vault. Double the guard outside this door and I want three more men on the outer door.'

George Godwin ran his hands through his already dishevelled hair. 'I'll have to cancel my commitments…I'll need someone in here with me – at *all* times. I'll need food and water. I'll need a bed. I'll need to wash. And I'll need a firearm.'

Captain Fenshaw winced as he straightened. 'Very well, Mr Godwin, I'll see to all that. I, myself, will be part of your guard and I can assure you my men are only days away – a week, no more. We'll get your prize money safely to London – we always do. Now, if we can just get those papers signed and lock this vault, we'll secure the other chests behind the grilles with padlocks and chains.'

The men heaved the chests into the room and the door banged shut, plunging the corridor, once again, in half-light. 'Quick, Mary – before they come back out.'

We ran swiftly down the corridor and through the outer door, nodding to the remaining guard before hurrying up the stairs. Private Evans was waiting for us in the shade of the portcullis. 'Are you all right, Mrs Bohenna...Miss Ellis... only you don't look very well?'

Far, far from well: I was shaking, gulping down the air. Father may not even get my letter, the only address I had for him was in Wales and even by express that could take a week. Henry Trevelyan was tightening the noose and I had to do something. My legs felt weak and I almost stumbled.

Private Evans turned. 'Come, my dear,' he said, his kind eyes searching mine. 'Take my arm. I may be old and unsteady, but between us, we can manage.'

At the gatehouse, Private Mallory drew me towards the bench. 'You're as pale as a ghost. Here, Miss Ellis, have a wee drop.' He handed me his hip flask. 'A wee drop of Mrs Bohenna's medicine and you'll soon be fighting fit.'

The fiery whiskey burned my lips, the heat of the sun beginning to take the chill from my heart. I took another sip, garnering all the strength I could muster. A woman was standing beneath the gatehouse arch, her demure dress and severe bonnet silhouetted against the sun. She had a basket on each arm, both brimming with fruit and vegetables, the necks of two wine bottles protruding from each basket, and she stopped, nodding as she passed.

'Good day,' she said, reaching for one of the bottles and handing it with a smile to Private Mallory. She had a pretty face, large eyes, a mole above her upper lip.

'Probably one of Mrs Fox's visiting ladies,' whispered Mary. But I was lost in thought and hardly spoke the whole way down.

We stopped to let a group of men pass and I whispered, 'We have to find Lottie Lorrelli. Do you know a man you can trust, Mary? He won't need to know about Edgar or his whereabouts...but just someone who can ask a few questions? We need to trace Lottie Lorrelli — someone must know her. Offer whatever it takes.'

Fear filled me, but it was anger driving me now. 'Edgar may have left with that woman...and he may have hired the horse, but it doesn't make him a highway robber. No one has seen that woman before, and if your man can't find her, then she doesn't exist. She's part of the trap — Henry Trevelyan's trap.'

Chapter Twenty-two

Lady Clarissa held up her letter. 'Ten healthy piglets and Persephone's thriving. That's splendid.' Her silk gown shimmered in the light, her hair adorned with jewels and fine feathers. 'Lord Carew apologizes for his absence, Mrs Penrose, but I'm afraid we all play second fiddle to his beloved animals.'

Eleanor Penrose looked up from arranging her sheet music. 'There'll be plenty more musical evenings for poor Lord Carew to sit through.'

Lady Clarissa's eyebrows shot up. 'Fidget through – I believe you mean.' She held up another letter. 'And George Godwin regrets that *circumstances beyond his control* must lead him to cancel his attendance this evening.'

Her quick glance was not lost on Amelia who pursed her lips. 'Poor George – he was so looking forward to coming, but we must be grateful that he's busy. I believe his business is beginning to do very well.'

The evening sun was streaming through the windows,

lighting the vase of orchids and the backs of the chairs grouped neatly round the piano; twenty guests were expected, the concert was to last an hour and there would be refreshments afterwards. Our careful preparations were now in place and everything was ready. Amelia was looking her loveliest in a cream silk gown with matching roses in her hair, Charity in soft peach with two diamond pins holding back her ringlets and I had chosen my lemon damask with its cream outer skirt and matching lace at my elbows.

The footman coughed politely. 'Mrs Bohenna and Dr Luke Bohenna.'

Mary curtseyed, and as Luke bowed I felt a rush of pride. They were both so smartly dressed, their clothes fashionable, Luke's well-cut jacket and dark breeches both dignified and professional. As a child he had been bookish, even a little awkward, yet now his presence seemed to fill the room; he looked upright and honest, a man to trust, his slightly receding hairline and furrowed brow marking him out as approachable and kind. His smile was shy, almost deferential, lingering on Amelia before returning to Lady Clarissa.

'I'm delighted to meet you both,' she said, beckoning them to the small group of chairs by the fireplace. 'Do sit. I invited you early so we could talk.' The introductions completed, she smiled at Mary. 'Have you settled well in Falmouth? Angelica tells me you're newly arrived from London. I believe you trained as a physician at St Bartholomew's Hospital, Dr Bohenna?'

I sat stiff-backed and smiling, for all the world as happy as Charity, yet Edgar's sadness was tearing me apart. The afternoon of forced jollity had given me a headache and I could not rid myself of the terrible anxiety wrenching my stomach. I felt like a spring stretched too taut, wanting only to curl up on my bed and cry. We were the advantaged children of a prosperous man, living a life of plenty. We lacked for nothing, everything given to us the moment we asked. To outsiders, I must seem so confident, driving around town in Father's carriage, escorting him to fine houses, always laughing and smiling. I gave my opinions on charity committees, told everyone my strong desire to see all women taught to read and write, yet the truth was we did not have the one thing that would bring us happiness – Father's affection. Since Mamma's death we had both been floundering. Now Edgar was drowning.

The talk turned to laughter and I tried to smile. Mary and Lady Clarissa were deep in conversation. 'My husband was an apothecary in Truro. I met him when he was training in London and returned with him to take over his father's shop in Truro. We lived above the shop in Boscawen Street until he died. He was always so proud of Luke and wanted him to be a doctor…but, well, I only wish he could see him now.' Mary shrugged her delicately embroidered silk shawl. 'You must forgive a mother's pride, Lady Clarissa, but after my dear husband died I thought all hope of Luke entering the medical profession had died alongside him.' She glanced across at Luke and smiled. 'Yet we were to be so very fortunate.'

'You deserve to be proud, and with good reason. Angelica tells me Dr Bohenna won a bursary from the Worshipful Company of Apothecaries.'

'Well, yes – but no, as it happens. Certainly we were led to believe the bursary was awarded from the guild, but when Luke wrote to thank them, they denied all knowledge. That's when we realized his good fortune rested on the goodness of my husband's sister.'

'Well, I'm sure she's delighted. Money very well spent, I would say. Does she live in Truro?'

Mary shook her head. 'No, in Kent and we hardly ever see her. But she won't hear of us thanking her. She denies the gift and the only reason we can think is because she's several other nephews and nieces and hasn't the same funds for them all. To this day she'll accept no thanks. And there it must remain – our attorney is adamant Luke's benefactor shall remain anonymous.'

Luke and Amelia were deep in conversation and it was becoming more and more apparent that he was finding it difficult to look Amelia in the eye. He continued to address his hands. 'Miss Carew, a physic garden is exactly what the new hospital will need – indeed, it's what we all need.'

A faint blush coloured Amelia's cheeks. 'I hope to be in full production for the opening…but for the moment, I supply both dried and living plants to a number of physicians. I send supplies to apothecaries all over Cornwall.' She smiled at his creased brow. 'I could supply you, too, if you have the need.'

Mary and Lady Clarissa's conversation was pleasant and joyful, but the more Amelia and Luke talked, the more animated they became. Amelia's knowledge of herbs was clearly delighting Luke.

He glanced up at her, obviously taking the chance. 'Oh,

I do have great need, Miss Carew. A number of the French prisoners are suffering from purulent gum disease – some of them quite severely – and a mouthwash of vervain would be highly beneficial. I could certainly do with some of your willow bark, and do you have horseradish? I use it as a stimulant.'

I watched the growing happiness on the faces of my two dearest friends and my heart lurched. Dear God, I had been so blind. A wave of dizziness swept over me, my chest tightening as I tried to breathe. It had been staring me in the face all this time and yet I never thought to question it.

Lady Clarissa rose to discuss last-minute arrangements and I managed to whisper, 'Mary, Father told me Luke's bursary was from the Worshipful Company of Apothecaries – he was absolutely adamant. He kept repeating it – he still does sometimes.'

She looked puzzled. 'No, my dear, he knew as soon as we knew...' The colour drained from her face. 'Oh, my dear, what are you saying...?' She put her hand to her mouth. 'My dear girl...what do you mean...?'

How could I have been so blind? I had wronged Father so completely, jumping to the worst possible conclusion, judging him unfairly. Mary was struggling to hide her own shock. 'You don't think? You don't think...?'

'Twenty pounds a month for seven years? Mary, I took you for his fancy woman.'

She went as white as a sheet. 'Oh Angelica, I'd no idea – none whatsoever. I never thought it was from your father. He was always so very stern – I thought he disapproved of me, yet that dear, kind man, giving us everything. That's true charity and goodness. Not wanting me to know…if I knew… Oh, Angelica, if I knew I'd have come straight back to Truro to be with you – yet he refused to make me choose between my own son and his children.' She wiped her eyes, her hands trembling. 'I must write to him…but how can I thank him? Oh, my dearest, what a day this is turning out to be.'

The room was filling; Mr and Mrs Fox were next to arrive and my heart leapt in pleasure as Elizabeth signalled me out. 'Miss Carew, Mrs Bohenna, what a beautiful evening. I'm sorry our walk was cut short yesterday, Miss Lilly.' She lowered her voice. 'There was nothing Mr Fox could do. He says it wasn't a riot…he's adamant there *weren't* as many as fifty and they *weren't* rioting. Yet five men were arrested and taken away without warning. It was heavy handed and unjust—' She stopped.

Lord Entworth had just entered the room and was standing by the door. He handed his cane to the footman and stood watching us.

Her voice hardened. 'They were poor and they were starving – they'd heard there was grain and their only thought was for a fair share.' Her heart-shaped lips tightened. 'We can only hope Lord Entworth will show mercy – hopefully once in possession of the facts humanity might, for once, prevail.' She stopped again. 'I'm sorry, I'm forgetting myself.'

Lord Entworth's attention was commandeered by two men in naval uniform but though he answered their questions, he kept looking across the room at me: not boldly, but rather shyly, his timid glances asking for encouragement.

Yet all I wanted to do was to run from the room and bury my head in my hands. I felt like doubling up with the pain of my stupidity, all those years of thinking ill of Father; the gulf between us all my own making.

Mary had regained her composure; she and Elizabeth Fox were enjoying a lively conversation but Edgar's heart-wrung words still rang in my ears. *We'll supply the fortune; all you need do is supply the title.* I wanted to scream with mortification; my dowry dangled for the best taker, as if I was up for sale. Edgar had felt ridiculed and the more I thought about it, the more I understood – both of us being moulded and shaped to follow Mamma's dreams – Mamma's dreams. Not our own.

Lord Entworth was making his way towards me and I wanted to run. *Smelter Girl's father trying to buy her some class*, I felt belittled, like chattel. Elizabeth Fox watched his approach and slipped from my side.

'I'll leave you, now. We'll talk again later,' she whispered.

He towered above Mrs Bohenna, bowing politely. His smile was warm, his conversation pleasant, and I tried to quell my rising panic. He put his hand in his jacket pocket and pulled out a small satin sampler which he carefully unrolled. The worked stitches were charming and simple, obviously sewn by very young hands.

'Miss Lilly, if I may give you this.' He smiled shyly, almost blushing, a slight stammer as he continued, 'It's a present from my daughters to you – it's their very best work, though I understand you might think it childish.' He reached into his waistcoat pocket. 'And they also insisted I show you their miniatures…but perhaps, you might not want to see them?'

Mrs Bohenna was immediately charmed by the two pale-faced girls looking out from their gold frames. 'Oh, well now, they are very beautiful. What lovely girls you have, Lord Entworth!'

A lump lodged in my throat; I could barely look at them. The two girls had dark curly hair, pinched faces with long noses and large, mournful eyes. Their tightly fitted dresses looked distressingly formal and my heart wrenched; two sad, motherless girls, desperately wanting their father to find someone who would love them. Lord Entworth stared down at the miniatures, hardly glancing at me. 'You must forgive a fond father – they are my pride and joy, Mrs Bohenna. And, one day, I hope to have a son to continue the family line. My house is too quiet – the rooms should be ringing with children's laughter, yet, I fear the girls' governess is too strict.'

I held the tiny sampler, my heart breaking. There were six tiny flowers each threaded with different coloured petals. 'Thank you. It's beautiful. Tell them I'll always treasure it.'

Lady Clarissa clapped her hands and waited for the room to quieten. 'Thank you,' she called above the last rumbles. 'Could I ask you to take your seats? I believe we are ready to start.'

I handed back the portraits, rolling up the satin embroidery, putting it carefully in my own embroidered purse. An iron clasp had me in its grasp, squeezing all breath from me.

'Will I have the honour of hearing you play, or are you singing tonight, Miss Lilly?'

I could hardly breathe. 'I'm very bad at the pianoforte, Lord Entworth. My playing's not up to such an occasion and neither's my singing.' Mamma's dreams, not mine – Mamma sitting on my bed at night, laughing her gentle laugh, telling me how proud she would be if her grandson was a lord; Mamma making me believe I wanted it too, moulding my dreams and aspirations, making me think it was my destiny, that I had no choice. That being a great lady meant marrying a great lord.

I did not love him. I could never love him. I was just like all the other girls, pinching and scratching, elbowing away the competition to secure a good future. All of us led to believe our happiness rested on rank and fortune. 'Mother was a famous actress,' I managed to say, 'and I take after her. Lady Clarissa has asked me to start the evening with a sonnet.'

'How very charming! I'm sure that will give us all such pleasure.' People were taking their seats and he put his arm out to escort me to the piano. Everyone in the room was watching us and I held my chin higher. Had he come to Father, or had Father gone to him? 'I'm sure my daughters would like their own theatre when they're older. It would be no trouble to convert one of the larger rooms into a theatre. What are you reciting tonight? One of Shakespeare's love sonnets, I hope?'

'Yes, indeed.'

I had practised the eighteenth sonnet all afternoon and could only guess he had seen it on one of the programmes we had put on every seat. He left me standing by the piano, bowing politely, the gold embroidery on his waistcoat dazzling me in the evening sun. Mary and Luke were in the front row and I stood waiting for the last guests to take their seats. The room was growing quieter, the sea of expectant faces looking quizzical, yet friendly. He may say the right words, give me every indication of his affection, but he did not look at me the way Luke looked at Amelia, or Robert Fox looked at Elizabeth. He may want to marry me, but he did not love me.

Lady Clarissa smiled, settling herself comfortably next to Mr Fox, yet now I was about to start, I did not want to speak of love. I wanted to speak of mercy. I had wronged Father so completely, Edgar lay shut behind bars on the whim of a man who was underhand and cunning, and men whose only crime was hunger were imprisoned and facing the gallows. A soliloquy of twenty-two lines lay etched in my mind and never had the words held such meaning. One glance at Elizabeth Fox and my courage soared.

'I'd like to make an alteration to the programme,' I said, steadying my voice. 'The speech I would like to recite is from *The Merchant of Venice* and I hope it speaks for us all.'

The last time I had said these words had been in Mrs Mitchell's study, her furious eyes following every last syllable, hoping to catch me out. The words had meant nothing then, but now I understood them. From now on, I would be myself. I would be like Elizabeth and speak up for what I believed. Not living Mamma's dreams but living my own.

> *The quality of mercy is not strained,*
> *It droppeth as the gentle rain from heaven...*

I finished and the room erupted in applause, everyone smiling, some nodding: Lord Entworth stepped forward, standing next to me, clapping his hands. The applause abated and he offered me his arm, leading me back to my chair. He sat down, flipping back the coat-tails of his jacket, and leaned towards me. 'That was enchanting, Miss Lilly, absolutely enchanting.'

Charity and Amelia started enthralling us with their singing and I breathed deeply. Smoke from the smelter *did* cling to my clothes because it clung to my heart. I did not want my freedom exchanged for a title and a huge mansion with imposing gates, my future pinned to a man's side, held in place by stiff protocol and expectations. I wanted to be like Elizabeth Fox; I wanted to see the respect she saw reflected in people's eyes. I wanted to visit prisons and campaign for reform – for the abolition of slavery, for women to be educated. That stab of envy at seeing her desk had been my heart warning me I was hurtling too fast into a marriage I did not want.

Mrs Penrose stood, bowing to rapturous applause, agreeing again and again to yet another encore. This was to be the very last piece and Amelia and Charity stood to join her. Lord Entworth leaned closer, reaching slowly for my hand.

I had watched him during my speech, seen the tightening of his jaw, the sideways glance he gave Elizabeth. He was clearly angry, his smile too late to hide his obvious displeasure. The racing of my heart was fear, not excitement; he was too powerful, too controlling, the present and paintings of his children designed to coerce me. I was angry now, ready to set myself free.

'I'm…I'm sorry…it's rather hot in here.' I pulled my hand away and began fanning myself with my left hand. Across the room, Amelia smiled and I saw genuine pleasure in her eyes. She linked arms with Lady Clarissa and they made their way quickly towards me.

Chapter Twenty-three

They slipped their arms through mine. 'My apologies, Lord Entworth, but several people are requesting to meet Miss Lilly and time is running short. Did you enjoy the concert?'

He bowed, smiling back. 'Very much, Lady Clarissa. As always, the music and singing were sublime. Indeed, Miss Carew, I haven't heard better in London.'

Lady Clarissa held his gaze. 'Thank you. Are you to return to London soon?'

'At the end of summer – I return in September.'

'Splendid.'

I curtseyed, and found myself propelled by the two of them across the room. 'You don't like Lord Entworth, do you?' I whispered.

'It is not for us to like him, my dear – it is *you* who are the object of his desire. We merely promised an introduction so you could get to know him. If what you learn is not to your liking, then you have no reason to marry him.'

'He asked Father — and Father's so honoured...so very thrilled.'

Lady Clarissa squeezed my arm. 'I know, my dear. But perhaps we can persuade your father towards someone of your own choice...?' She began leading me to Luke Bohenna.

He had his back to us, helping himself to an asparagus tart from the table. His mouth was full when he turned, his cheeks reddening when he saw the three of us smiling back at him. He held up the plate and we each took a tart, standing like naughty conspirators until the last bite was swallowed. 'That was delicious,' he said, wiping the crumbs from his mouth.

I thought they would stay but Amelia and Lady Clarissa backed slowly away, leaving us alone by the table. Luke watched Amelia's retreating figure and I knew he had joined the long rank of lost men.

'She's very clever,' I whispered. 'She's as knowledgeable as any apothecary. She's studied all Frederick's botanical books from Oxford — there's nothing she doesn't know about herbs.'

Across the room, Lord Entworth was watching me, his jaw clamping tighter by the minute. 'She's my best friend,' I continued. 'But you need to know she's suffering from a broken heart. Three years ago her fiancé was lost at sea and she's haunted by the thought of him lying in some filthy gaol. She's certain he'll come back to her one day...and she's waiting for him. She acts happy but there's deep sadness beneath all those smiles.'

'I sensed that. I can see it in her face and hear it in her

laughter.' His voice dropped. 'I would wait all my life for her, Angelica. I'd be content just to be her friend – and if her fiancé comes back, then her happiness would make me happy.'

'No it wouldn't. It would break your heart.' Amelia was clearly trying not to look at us. 'Look at you – with your smart clothes and beautiful manners – I'm so proud of you, Luke. In fact, I'm a little in awe of you.' I put my hand on his arm, reaching up to whisper, 'But we can't marry now, can we? Not now you're so obviously smitten with Amelia.'

He smiled his shy smile. 'You're more beautiful than ever, Angelica. And as for awe – well, just look at you! You dazzle the room…you've got such grace and intelligence.'

'You used to tell me I was too wild and impulsive – that I'd break every bone in my body.'

'I still think that may be true.'

'I used to love your bookish ways…you were always so serious. Half the time I did things just to shock you!'

He reached for my hands. 'I know – like insisting on teaching me *foundry language*. I loved you for that. I think I was even a little envious – I couldn't bring myself to be so abandoned.'

'So, the fact that I've waited patiently for you for all these years doesn't count?'

He smiled, patting my hand as he held it on his arm. 'We're brother and sister, Angelica – a marriage between us would never work. I know you too well – I'd tell you not to do something and you'd go straight off and do it…then I'd go to a lot of trouble to rescue you and you'd be furious and shout at me. I don't mind how impulsive you are as a sister but as a wife…?' He smiled, shaking his head. 'I wouldn't know whether to bring you a ladder or just leave you where you were. Do you still climb trees?'

'Sometimes.'

'And climb out of windows – and go clandestinely to the theatre and perform in plays? You were very good, by the way.' The lines by his eyes crinkled; he had such kind eyes, full of compassion and humility. 'If we were to marry I'd never sleep at night for worrying what you were up to.' He turned round, gazing back across the room. 'I don't have any other brothers or sisters – just you and Edgar. '

'What you're *really* saying is that you've fallen hopelessly in love with Amelia, and why shouldn't you? But I warn you – you've joined ranks with several others and it won't be easy.'

'I understand that.'

A group of naval officers were crowding round Amelia and his brow furrowed along its accustomed crease.

'Evenings like this are very hard for her. That's why she loves her garden so much. Thank you for being here, Luke – for Edgar…for me. I don't know what I'd do without you and Mary. I hate Henry Trevelyan. Should I write to Mr Reith, do you think? He's the best attorney in Truro?'

A group of people were making their way towards us and Luke led me away from the table. 'You may hate Henry Trevelyan, Angelica, but I consider him a very fine man. The difficult truth is that someone should have locked Edgar up a while back – I don't mean in gaol, I mean at home. If he were free, his cravings would take him straight back to that opium den. Locking him up has probably saved his life.'

'But not there! Not that terrible place. It's damp and airless. He needs a soft bed and fresh air and exercise – we have to get him out of there.'

'But where can he go? To a house with doors and windows that open? The opium Edgar consumes is foul – it's dangerous. What we use is purer, but even so we boil it to make a tincture. Our doses are correct to the very last drop but the opium he gets hold of is unrefined and unpredictable.' His voice turned firm. 'Staying behind bars is almost a blessing. It gives Edgar a chance to clear the drug from his system. It takes time and that's exactly what Henry's giving him.'

'Henry is not acting in Edgar's interest. He's acting out of self-interest.'

'Maybe – but if Henry hadn't arrested him Edgar could have fallen and broken his neck. Leave Edgar to his own devices and it's just a matter of time before he stumbles into the river and drowns like all the others. Angelica, my dearest sister – I can't over-emphasize the gravity of Edgar's ill-health. Men waste away and die with this illness because no one has the ability to keep them from what they crave.'

I stared at him, fighting my tears. 'Henry Trevelyan wants Sir Alex to come back and heap him with praise – at the sacrifice to my brother's life.'

'I've watched Henry Trevelyan and I've talked to him. He's not after glory and he doesn't seek praise. He's an honest man who cares about your brother, and he cares about—'

The group of people passed in front of us, each with a plate piled high with tarts.

'If he cares about my brother he'd drop all charges.'

'That's another reason why I can't marry you. You don't really listen.'

'Yes I do – but you must allow me my own opinion.'

'Of course I allow you your own opinion – I always have and always will – but in this case, I believe you're wrong. Henry Trevelyan wants to find this woman as much as we do.' His voice was soft and loving, his eyes full of compassion. 'I understand why you feel this way, but I believe we must work *with* Henry, not against him.' He looked up. Mary was making her way across the crowded room towards us.

'What a wonderful evening this has turned out to be. Lady Clarissa has invited us to visit her beautiful house and garden. She believes you may be interested in seeing Miss Carew's physic garden, Luke.'

Luke's cheeks flooded with colour. He glanced towards Amelia. 'That's very kind of her.'

I raised my eyebrows. 'Mary, you need to know – Luke's fallen hopelessly in love with Amelia—'

'Angelica!' Luke searched the room, running his finger under his stiff white cravat.

I slipped my arm through Mary's. 'I'm absolutely heartbroken – he says he won't marry me. He says I don't listen and he'd not sleep at night because I'm wild and uncontrollable.'

Luke's blush doubled as he shook his head. Mary raised her eyebrows. 'Perhaps he's right, my love.' She smelled of lilac water and rose soap. She was ten years older than Mother and every bit as beautiful, her soft white hair pinned gently beneath her velvet cap, her cheeks slightly tinged with rouge. She glanced at the table. 'Look, there are just a few tarts left. Luke, be a dear and secure me a small plate.'

We watched him make his way to the table, reaching it at the same time as Amelia. They laughed and Mary's smile broadened. 'I always wanted you two to marry...but, well,... it seems it's not to be. You're both destined for others.'

Lord Entworth was watching us, tucking his watch back into his embroidered gold waistcoat. 'I don't love him,' I whispered.

She smiled her soft smile. 'You do...and I didn't mean Lord Entworth.'

Amelia pulled up the eiderdown and I blew out the candle. She puffed up her pillow, her curls held tight beneath her lace bedcap. Neither of us were tired, the excitement of the evening still buzzing in our heads.

'You didn't tell me Elizabeth hates Lord Entworth. I thought they were friends. I thought she often invited him to their house.'

'No, never. He only came to Elizabeth's soirée because Mother said that was where he could meet you. Elizabeth saw her chance and asked him to persuade Captain Pellew to bring his fiddler – he had no idea Mr Emidy was a highly proficient violinist. The truth is Lord Entworth won't sign Elizabeth's petition because he owns half his brother's plantation in Virginia. We thought you knew that.'

Nausea churned my stomach. 'I had no idea.'

She was fidgeting with the lace on her sleeve. 'The truth is…neither of us like him and Papa absolutely detests him. I'm delighted because now Mother says we can all go home. She doesn't want us to be here when Frederick arrives – she wants Charity to have him all to herself. She wants us to leave tomorrow on the early tide…and I can't say I'm sorry because I'm missing my garden. This sun will have done the plants a world of good.'

'It's very kind of Lady Clarissa to invite Mary and Luke to Trenwyn. Luke's really looking forward to seeing your garden.'

I waited and was not disappointed. There was stoicism in her voice, a sense of forced jollity. 'He seems a very kind man. Honestly, Angelica, you're such a silly goose. I can't think why you even contemplated marrying Lord Entworth when Luke Bohenna loves you so much.'

'We haven't seen each other for seven years but it felt just like yesterday. He was always so protective – always standing up for me when I was in trouble. I love him and I can't be more proud of him.'

'I'm so happy for you. I think you'll be very happy together.'

'I love him…but like a brother – nothing more. And he loves me like a sister, but anyway, it's just as well I don't want to marry him because he's married to his work. It's the only thing that matters to him. He hasn't time for marrying or love. He thinks of nothing but treatment and cures.'

She caught her breath, her voice lifting. 'He asked me for

some willow bark and digitalis and as much vervain as I can spare – you probably know it as wild hyssop but it's in the books as *verbena officinalis*. I've got plenty of them all.'

I snuggled next to her, hiding my smile. 'I don't know it as anything, Mel.'

She remained silent, no doubt walking between her rows of herbs, deciding which to show Luke and which to harvest for him. For my part, I was running up that rocky promontory, spiralling down the stone steps, watching Edgar from the grille of his damp cellar. Amelia's breathing grew rhythmical but I could not sleep, going over the evening – Lord Entworth with the miniatures of his daughters, Elizabeth Fox with her pretty white cap and glass of lemonade. I could not rid my mind of my brother sprawled on the floor of a den with a half-naked woman.

My heart thudded, my eyes opened – the woman who had passed us at the gate had smiled at us. I had been blinded by the sun but I had seen that smile before – seen that exact mole somewhere very recently. Not dressed soberly but half-naked, a wine goblet swilling in her hand. She had been tottering towards the banisters – she was the woman in the Heron Inn who had bumped into Jacob Boswell.

I needed to breathe, stop the pounding in my heart. She might have been wearing demure clothes and a severe white bonnet but it was the same woman. She fitted the exact description: Lottie Lorrelli – half-dressed and drunk, brown hair and medium height.

I slipped from the bed, my hands trembling. I struck a flint and the candle glowed – they would expect me to write a farewell letter to Mary and deliver it safely. I reached for some paper.

Dearest Mary,

Do you remember when we left the castle this morning a woman passed us carrying two baskets? She is not what she seems. I last saw her burst from a room in the Heron Inn that night of the play. On that occasion she was scantily dressed and very drunk. She has brown hair and is of medium build with a mole above her lip. It was that which caught my attention.

I believe she is Lottie Lorrelli. She bumped into Jacob Boswell that night and she would have seen Edgar taking opium. She knew just how to trap him.

Please tell Luke and please have your man find her.

Written in haste,

I remain, your dearest friend,
Angelica

Chapter Twenty-four

Trenwyn House
Friday 12th August 1796, 8:00 a.m.

We watched the boat inch towards us with her mainsail lowered, the wind on her stern. 'They've got wind and tide,' Amelia shouted to Young William as he ran down the jetty. 'Make sure you catch the rope first time and secure it tightly. The wind's stronger than you think.' She glanced at me and I caught her excitement.

Daniel Maddox frowned. 'Best if I catch the rope. She must have a steady landing or the glass might break.'

He followed William down the jetty, frowning as the wind threatened the safety of the first four plant boxes that had been especially built to John Fraser's exact requirements — the wooden troughs deep enough for a substantial amount of soil, the glass domes tall enough to give sufficient light and air.

I waved at Mary and Luke, my concern mounting. I had not heard anything for three days and I was desperate for news. Mary was wrapped up against the cold grey sky, but Luke wore no overcoat, standing squarely on the deck to throw the rope. The glass domes lay half-covered in canvas and Daniel Maddox's frown deepened. He ran his hands through his unruly hair. 'Steady now – there mustn't be any damage.'

The ropes secured, Luke jumped from the deck and held out his hand to help Mary down the gangplank. He smiled shyly, looking up at the vast sweep of lawns to the house above. 'What a beautiful house, Miss Carew. I'm surprised you ever want to leave. Is that your garden behind the wall?'

'Yes,' Amelia replied, smiling back at him. 'It's sheltered from the wind, which makes it ideal. The walls retain the heat and give protection but I have hothouses as well.' She had opted to wear her green gardening-gown; after all, this was a visit to her garden. She looked relaxed and informal, her bonnet blowing in the wind. Glancing over her shoulder, she saw Moses peering from behind the door. 'Moses does all the propagating. He's the real gardener – he separates the plants and pots them on. I just dry the herbs and measure them out.' She turned to Daniel Maddox. 'May I introduce Daniel Maddox, Mrs Bohenna, Dr Bohenna? He's the professional plantsman among us. He's responsible for all the newly planted trees and Mother's new shrubberies. His help has been invaluable, but we're soon to lose him – more's the pity.'

Amelia had always been guarded in his company, but now he was going she seemed more at ease. She was clearly pleased to see Luke and Mary, talking rather quickly and smiling broadly. A flash of sorrow crossed Daniel Maddox's sunburned face and he bowed, turning to give instructions to the boatmen.

'And this is William, my nephew,' Amelia said, holding William firmly by the shoulders. 'I think we'll keep him well away from that glass.' She waved up to the terrace. 'Mother's watching from the house – breakfast is ready.'

Mary pulled her cloak tightly round her. 'I'm sorry our visit is so early, Miss Carew – you really shouldn't have come down to wait for us. It's very kind of you, of course, but I wouldn't have you catch a chill on our behalf.'

Taking Young William's hand, Amelia led them across the shingle towards the steps. The wind whipped her cloak, her curls escaping their hold and framing her face. Colour tinged her cheeks, real joy in her smile. 'The tide's the tide, Mrs Bohenna. It's so strong at this point it's virtually impossible to sail against it. And I always get up early as the garden's so beautiful in the morning. Sometimes it's shrouded in mist – sometimes it's wet with dew. I like watching the sun rise and the birds feeding on the shore. Do you get up early, Dr Bohenna?'

'Yes, always, but then sometimes I don't go to bed. I'm at my patients' disposal, Miss Carew. Whole days can pass and I forget to eat. Mother has to drag me to the table.'

Mary stooped to pick up a shell and we heard Amelia laugh. 'Goodness, then we are honoured, Dr Bohenna.'

'We must catch the tide back – we've four hours, I believe. That will make a very pleasant break.'

With the others a little way ahead, Mary reached into her bag. 'I've a letter for you from Edgar. He's doing very well and I believe his dear soul is coming back to us. The day you left was the worst, honest to God, he did nothing but shake

– shake and shake, and swear like you'd never believe – but since then he's been as quiet as a lamb. He cries a lot, my love, and it breaks my heart to hear him. There's so much sadness there – such pain and hurt and anger. He's very bitter towards your father, though the truth is I believe your father was just doing what he thought was right. Or rather – doing what your dear mamma would have wanted him to do.'

I put Edgar's letter quickly down my bodice, helping Mary up the steps and on to the path. 'Mamma always spoke of Edgar going to Oxford, but she would never have wanted me to go to that dreadful boarding school. She'd have hated the idea.'

A puzzled frown creased Mary's brow. 'No, my love, your mother always intended you to go to that school. She often spoke of it. She wanted you to mix with the daughters of the gentry and learn their ways. You were to gain polish and be taken for a lady…she wanted you to make friends with girls like Miss Amelia Carew and be invited back to their grand houses.' She looked up at the graceful façade of Trenwyn House and smiled. 'Your dear father was just following her wishes.'

A knife sliced my heart, the pain so severe, I wanted to scream. All these years, I had been so angry with Father. 'Why didn't he come to my plays, Mary? That would have made all the difference.'

'Oh my dearest…Look at you, my love. Look in the mirror and who do you see? You've grown so like your dear mamma…and putting on your plays like you did?' She slipped her arm through mine, her voice softening. 'Angelica, the truth is your mother never wanted you to follow in her footsteps. She wanted better for you. Her life wasn't easy – some would think the life of a stage actress is exciting and glamorous but the truth is your mother was ready to leave the stage. She was tired...she was...Well, she wanted stability, and your father offered her so much.'

I could not speak, a gaping black void opening before me. I was tottering on the edge, about to lose my footing. 'She was what? Mary...were you about to say she was with child?'

'Good Lord, no! Whatever gave you that idea? I think perhaps it was because I told her how happy I was in Truro and how settled I'd become...and how parts of Cornwall reminded me of the cliffs back at home in Ireland. Your father visited our shop just before he left for London and I asked him to take a present and letter from me to Hermia. We told him to take the chance to visit the theatre and he stayed a month just to court her! Love can strike like that. He wouldn't come home until she agreed to marry him.'

'I know – she once told me Father had commissioned the painting just so he could talk to her while she posed for it.'

'I think the reason your father didn't go to your plays was because he *couldn't* go, because he was too scared to go. He'd be in far too great a danger of letting down his guard – his sternness is his protection, Angelica. I think we both see that now.'

'What about that woman – Lottie Lorrelli? Has she been found?'

She paused, shaking her head. 'Luke thought he saw her

cross Market Square and tried to follow but I'm afraid he lost her. Henry's keeping a watch for her at the castle.'

I could hardly believe my ears. I felt suddenly furious. 'You told Henry Trevelyan? Mary, he'll warn her – he probably already has. We'll never find her now – she'll be long gone. Our only chance of freeing Edgar, and you told Henry Trevelyan?'

She swung round, holding me back. 'Why are you so against him, my love? Is it because he doesn't do your bidding – or because he hasn't fallen at your feet like every other man?'

Her words were kindly said but fierce, none the less. I had been chastised like a child, a spoilt child. 'No! Of course not. Anyway, he wouldn't – he's in love with a woman who won't give him the time of day. And she's right – he clearly can't be trusted.'

Little Charles hurtled down the lawn far faster than was safe and Amelia swept him up, handing him straight to Luke. I watched Luke swing him round and emptiness swamped me. I was among the people I loved the most, yet I felt strangely lonely, my whole world turned upside down. Mary pursed her lips, her voice clipped. 'Well, that's a pity. A man like Henry Trevelyan should be snapped up. Let's hope this woman sees some sense.'

Lady Clarissa had also chosen to wear one of her least formal gowns. Having been away from her grandsons for five days, their many gifts still dangled on ribbons round her neck

– apart from the hermit crab that had been put back in the water. The conversation was flowing, the time passing so quickly that Lord Carew remained at the table long after the food had been cleared. His face as ruddy as his felt cap, he beamed at Luke.

'Persephone shows no signs of ill-health – but perhaps a medical opinion might not go amiss? Know anything about pigs, Dr Bohenna?'

'Nothing you don't already know,' laughed Luke, pulling back Amelia's chair to begin the tour of the garden. 'I'm rather afraid of pigs – but I believe they're highly intelligent animals that can be very loving.'

The bushy white eyebrows rose. 'Ah, well, there you have it. These black pigs from China are said to be particularly docile. We have it on good authority that they don't like to roam and we're confident they'll make the perfect cottage pig. A man must be sure of his pig – for the safety of his children...and visiting doctors.'

I was desperate to read Edgar's letter, and with everyone leaning over the sty admiring Persephone's healthy fat piglets, I seized the chance, remaining behind in the doorway of the nearby stable unable to wait any longer. I slipped the seal.

Dearest Angelica,

I need you to understand the remorse and loathing I feel for myself. That I have inflicted this pain on you and Father is unforgivable. I deserve your censure, yet at the depths of my sorrow, I cannot help but be grateful that for the first time in seven long years I am surrounded by the love and kind administrations of people whose goodness I can only hope to repay. Luke and Mary have brought such light to my darkness. They give me the will to conquer my demons; for let me assure you, they are indeed demons.

I lack for nothing. Some days my head feels clear, other days my mind is filled with such torment. I dislike myself and I dislike what I am putting you and Father through, but believe me when I say I will do everything in my power to clear my name — no, not merely my name, our name. The name we should be proud to bear.

I am not a thief. I am simply a misguided and foolish man. I should have had the courage to stand up to Father, but all that will change. I have written to him and explained everything and I await the consequences of his great anger.

In the meantime, Henry remains a fair and just gaoler. His walks are doing me the power of good and our interesting discussions stretch long into the night. Oxford taught me nothing, yet Henry's philosophizing and poetry speak deeply to my soul.

Please believe me when I say I have every intention of fighting this evil. When I stand on that witness stand and take my oath, I will be upright and sober. I owe that to you, to Father, and to the memory of our beloved mother.

I remain, your affectionate, if troubled, brother,
Edgar

I folded the letter, a slight tremor in my hands. The hatred he felt for himself was so visceral I had to force the tears from my eyes. I should have been there for him, understood him better. I was his older sister yet I had been too self-seeking, too full of my own resentments to pay heed to his. I should have taken more responsibility, stopped my headstrong ways: always doing what I liked, when I liked. Molly loved me, just as she had adored Mamma, but she would never think to stop me. Between Molly and Father I had been indulged more than was good for me.

Mary came to my side and I blinked back my tears. 'So Henry Trevelyan's a bit of a philosopher, is he? And Edgar's discovered poetry?' I sounded harsh, but I could not help it. My heart was breaking.

She nodded and we walked in step, following Amelia across the terrace to the conservatory where she was to show us her paintings. 'Henry Trevelyan is a highly intelligent man. We've had some very lively discussions over supper – in fact, some very pleasant evenings.'

My flash of envy turned to fury. 'He did that to me – making friends, showing consideration and warmth, playing cricket and running around with the boys on his shoulder. He whirled Charles around, just like Luke – only it was sunny and he was in his shirtsleeves.'

'You sound very bitter, Angelica.'

'Lulling everyone into believing he has our good intentions at heart.'

Amelia was laying her paintings carefully on the table, each one as intricate and exquisite as the others. She seemed shy at first but as their speechless admiration turned to loud praise she pulled open another drawer and brought out some more. Luke shook his head in wonder.

'Miss Carew, the detail is quite extraordinary – they are so lifelike I want to pick them from the page.'

'I've another seven to paint then I'll have completed our twenty-seven most used herbs. I'm painting them in every stage of their growth. Here are the seeds…and here are the flowers. I come back to the paintings and add each stage during the growing season.' She blushed, suddenly aware of how close they were leaning.

Luke straightened and smiled, opening the leather bag that was slung across his shoulders. 'I've brought you a book, Miss Carew. Please keep it for as long as you like – that is if it's of any use to you. It's my father's *Compendium of Herbs*. It's rather old now and very well thumbed…some of the pages are coming loose but I wondered if it might be of interest?' He sounded hesitant, holding it shyly. 'Of course you must have plenty of other books but his notes are interspersed among the pages – they're his remedies and tinctures, which you might find interesting. This, for instance, is the mouth rinse I'm going to prepare with your vervain.'

Amelia took the book, smiling down at a black-and-white etching with the cramped writing down one side. 'It's lovely, thank you, Dr Bohenna. I'll certainly enjoy reading this.'

The stable-yard clock struck twelve and Lady Clarissa looked up in surprise. 'Goodness, this morning has gone very quickly and we still have so much to show you.'

Smiling as she named each plant, we followed her slowly through the shrubbery and down to the walled garden, the gravel sparkling despite the dull day. Young William walked proudly by Luke's side, telling him he was going to be a doctor when he grew up. Yet despite the warmth and love surrounding me, I felt strangely chilled. I had lost all sense of joy, my stomach churning with constant nerves, my listlessness hard to contain.

Moses had left a small wooden box of eggs and three jars of honey on the seat outside his hut. The stone jars had pieces of garden twine tied in a bow around them and Amelia whispered, 'They're a present for you from Moses, Mrs Bohenna. I hope he comes out but he's very reclusive. He'll be watching, so you must take them or he'll be very upset.'

Mary was thrilled. 'Well of course, I will. It's very kind of him. It's a lovely present, and I must thank him for going to so much trouble – tying such pretty bows and making them look so lovely.' She stepped forward, knocking gently on his door, opening it a tiny bit. Moses stood blinking in the light. 'I'm thrilled and honoured to have such a present,' she said, more with gestures than with speech. She pointed to the garden. 'Will you not show us round, Mr Moses? My son's a doctor and very grateful for the herbs you've wrapped so nicely for him.'

She stepped away, Moses smiling and twisting his hat in his hands. He began shuffling towards the plants with his sideways gait, Mary talking happily, smiling back, asking him questions he could neither hear nor answer. At the end of the last row he stooped to cut her some lavender, holding it out for her with his lopsided smile.

'Thank you, Moses. They smell wonderful. I'll dry the flowers and make lavender bags to hang among my clothes.'

Luke frowned and stepped forward, miming a sore back.

'Are you in pain, Moses — perhaps a touch of rheumatism? Would it be helpful if I took a look at you?'

Moses glanced round, his face filling with panic. He started jerking violently, his head wobbling and he hurried back to the safety of his closed door. Luke looked stricken. 'Oh, dear, I'm so sorry, Miss Carew. The last thing I wanted to do was to frighten him — but he looked in pain. It was thoughtless of me.'

Amelia shook her head. 'It's not your fault. He's very shy and runs at the slightest fear. But I think you're right — perhaps you should see him professionally. Give me a little time and I'll try to persuade him.'

The plants, eggs and honey stowed in the waiting boat, Mary stood with her arms full of flowers, watching the sky darken beneath a band of black clouds. The garden had weaved its magic and they were clearly not ready to leave. Luke bowed from the deck, waving as he repeated his heart-felt thanks. The boatman pulled the ropes and the boat drifted slowly on the outgoing tide. I wanted to go with them but waved goodbye, Lady Clarissa shouting from the jetty that they must come back as often as they liked.

The sails unfurled, catching the wind, and she drew out a letter. 'Mrs Bohenna was kind enough to bring me this letter from Frederick. They've had quite enough of Falmouth and are coming home. They arrive tomorrow.' The boys danced round in pleasure and she handed the letter to Amelia. 'But that's not all. They are bringing with them Capitaine Pierre de La Croix — the captain of the ship they took as prize. He's given Frederick his parole.'

'Real parole?'

'Yes, boys. Real parole. He's an officer so he's sworn an oath not to escape or aid the enemy in any way. He's not to be imprisoned but will be housed in Bodmin under the strictest conditions. Until he goes to Bodmin, he's to remain with Frederick. Imagine – we're to have our very own French *capitaine en parole*.'

Young William beamed. 'Will he play cricket with us?'

Lady Clarissa took the letter back from Amelia. 'Indeed he must. If he doesn't already know the rules, we will take it upon ourselves to teach him. If the French played cricket, there would have been no need for their revolution. A duke can be bowled out by his servant, an earl caught by his footman. There is no rank on the cricket pitch – always remember that. *Liberté, égalité et fraternité* is the very essence of cricket.'

The unseasonal bite to the wind blighted Lord Carew's happiness at Frederick's homecoming; he stood watching the heavy clouds in mounting dismay. 'Another week of sun and the fields might have had a chance to dry – we might even have saved a remnant of the wheat…but if these clouds persist there'll be flooding. And sodden fields mean no sowing of the turnips or potatoes. Everything we plant will wither.' He paced the room like a caged bear. 'The last thing we need is sodden fields. We need to get the ground prepared and the winter wheat established.'

Lady Clarissa handed him his brandy but turned abruptly.

'Goodness, who can that be?' Someone was banging loudly on the front door, footsteps rushing across the hall. Almost immediately the footman opened the door. 'An express, my lady.'

Lady Clarissa clutched the back of the chair. 'From the Admiralty?' she whispered.

'No, my lady. Looks like it's from Truro.'

She took the letter, her face flooding with relief. 'It's not even for us – it's for you, Angelica. I am sorry, my dears, but every time an express is delivered I think the worst. Frederick may be safely home, but his brother is still at sea.'

It was my turn to stare at the letter. I did not recognize the writing and tore the seal, surprised when a sample of material fell to the floor. I picked it up. It was heavily spun silk, emblazoned with pink flowers that were really quite hideous. In horror, I read the hastily scribbled letter.

Dear Miss Lilly,

I'm writing this letter on behalf of Molly. She hopes your well, but begs your asistance. Tomorrow, at ten o'clock, Mr Sewell of Sewell and Sons is to come to mesure for new drapes. He says Lady Boswell has choosen this very fine material and has requested he starts before her return. He is to mesure all the downstairs rooms and Molly is besides herself with despair. He won't hear no for an answer. She has no way to refuse his request, yet believes you will not approve and will be very angry. Please advise her as to what she must do.

Yours in haste,
Mrs Edison

Beside it, written in her best writing:

Please come,
Molly

Fury blazed in my cheeks, my anger so great I could hardly read the words.

'How dare she? Poor Molly's distraught.' I handed the letter to Lady Clarissa, holding up the hideous material as if it was a rag infected with plague. 'She's right about me being angry. It's bad enough her having the affront to change the curtains, but with this? It's…it's like the material for some *boudoir*…some scurrilous bawdy house.'

Amelia and Lady Clarissa read the letter, their eyes wide with shock. 'Oh my dearest love, though it pains me greatly we may have to consider the possibility that Lady Boswell is now married to your father.'

'Oh, dear God.' They led me to the chair, kneeling by my side, and I fought the dizziness sweeping through me. Father had not received my letter, or if he had, it had arrived too late. Lady Boswell was strengthening her hold, declaring war with her terrible effrontery. 'How dare she show so little regard for my feelings?' I took the letter, rereading it with pursed lips. 'The letter says Lady Boswell, not Mrs Lilly – that at least is something! If his instructions come from Lady Boswell, then I've every right to delay the measurements. I need to see them – but what if they're signed by *Mrs Lilly*?'

Lady Clarissa searched my face. 'Who is Mrs Edison?'

'She's Molly's best friend from church. Molly reads better

than she writes and I usually write her letters for her but I told her to ask Mrs Edison if she needed anything – they're very good friends and I know she'll keep this private. Look – Molly's written "please come", did you see?'

'I did, my dear, and I believe you should go. This is not a burden a servant should have to bear alone – indeed, it speaks volumes for the nature of the woman that she could even consider such an action. Apart from the choice of such distasteful material, her action is totally reprehensible and I agree you must stop this at all cost.'

'But can I go?'

'Indeed, you must. Molly needs you. It is unfortunate timing – in that we are to welcome Frederick and Charity home tomorrow and therefore we cannot go with you – but, on the other hand, the carriage will be free and at your disposal. Bethany can accompany you. She can see her mother and you can return when you have told Mr Sewell that, *despite his instructions*, he must wait until your father returns.'

Her kindness was overwhelming and I wiped the tears from my eyes. 'I'll come straight back.'

'Of course you will.' She handed me the brandy she was about to drink. 'Have this. Perhaps you do need to go home, my dear. I am not alone in thinking a look of sadness has crept into your eyes and I do not like it. Are you no longer happy here, Angelica? Are you very homesick?'

I shook my head. 'No…no, not at all, I love being here. I want to be here more than anything. I'll sort things out with Molly and come straight back.'

It was always worse when people showed such consideration. My emotions were so brittle; another kind look and I knew I would cry. I wanted to tell them everything, that the sadness was panic; that men were not what they seemed. That my brother had been caught in a trap and falsely accused. That Henry Trevelyan had made it abundantly clear he would hand over the necklace and silver dish if I asked anyone to interfere. That even if Lady Carew believed in Edgar's innocence, the owner of the necklace would pursue him to the gallows.

I looked away, preparing my mask. I must bite my lip, smile and maintain the artifice until Henry Trevelyan was made to see reason.

Chapter Twenty-five

The outskirts of Truro
Saturday 13th August 1796, 9:00 a.m.

The horses slowed and Bethany put her round cheek against the window. She had filled the carriage with her excited chatter the whole journey, but I was glad of her company. 'Course I don't mind comin'. I'll take them vegetables to the Town House an' go an' see if Mamm's free. They're bound to give her a moment or two. Then I'll collect what's on Lady Clarissa's list an' I'll come straight back fer ye' She smiled shyly. 'It's been that lovely ridin' in the carriage – it's very kind of ye. I'd have been proper soaked by now.'

The market crowds were slowing us down, the journey taking longer than expected. 'I can't imagine I'll be very long. I'll send word once my business is finished then we can head straight back – once you've seen your mother, of course.'

Men were pushing their market trolleys in front of us, geese herded by young boys, maids carrying milk churns on their shoulders. The bustle I knew so well – the sights and smells of my childhood. We turned the bend, finally drawing alongside the house, pulling round the back to the large courtyard. Grace came running from the stable and by her smile I knew she must have been willing me to come.

'Ah, Miss Lilly, thank goodness.' She pulled down the steps, looking over her shoulder to the kitchen door. 'Molly will be that pleased to see you. She's in a terrible state.'

'Well, I'm here now, so she has nothing to fear.'

She ran the back of her hand over her mouth. 'Well, yes – but 'tis very unfortunate. Molly's worried now on account of tellin' ye the wrong day. Mr Sewell's gone out of town – he's changed the day. Says he's comin' tomorrow now. Goin' to come at twelve tomorrow. Ah, here's Molly now.'

Molly almost tumbled from the door, flinging her arms wide before remembering to curtsy. The coachman gripped the reins, steadying the horses as she came hurtling towards us. 'Oh, Miss Lilly – he's not to come today. Look…'tis such a rude note – 'tis almost unreadable – ten o'clock tomorrow he'll come – or twelve. Honest to God, it's either ten or twelve …he thinks nothin' better than to have me wait his pleasure.'

Her cheeks were flushed, her brow furrowed. She shook her head. 'I had it just this minute an' here ye are – an' he isn't. Honest to God…to put ye through that journey fer nothin'. What am I to do? Must I admit him or do I show him the door? He's that fierce – 'tis like I'm dirt under his feet, and yet I knew his mother – and her mother before her.' She rested her hand on her hip, wincing in pain.

'Molly, don't worry. I'll stay.' The coachman had been following every word. 'Is it possible? Could you send a message to Lady Clarissa? Explain I need to stay – until twelve tomorrow?'

260

The coachman nodded. The capes of his driving coat still glistened with rain, the large brim of his hat pulled low over his face. 'I'll leave the coach at the Town House an' ride a pony back. I'll tell her ye're not like to get anythin' resolved till noon tomorrow. I reckon she'll tell us to stay the night at the Town House.'

'Tell her I'm sorry. Please collect me only at *her* convenience.'

He nodded. 'I'll explain everythin' fer ye – an' all bein' well, I'll be back fer ye just after twelve tomorrow.'

'Thank you.' The footmen's red capes looked equally soaked. 'I'm sorry to inconvenience you. Please go and get dry.' Bethany smiled from the window and I followed Molly to the kitchen door.

The back of the house seemed somehow smaller, even shabby, the paintwork on the back door scuffed, a pipe ending short of a drain. Compared to the beautiful brickwork and stone sills of Trenwyn House, the crooked beams and sloping roof looked tired and lopsided and I felt suddenly ashamed. Father must be persuaded to leave.

Molly peered round the kitchen door, her eyes sparkling. 'Well,' she beamed, 'did I do well?'

A voice boomed from the corner of the kitchen. 'Quite the professional actress, Molly, my dear. You did so well, I might even think of employing you.'

I swung round. 'Kitty? What are you doing here?' She was sitting on a chair out of sight from the window, a bundle in a woven shawl on the table in front of her. She looked younger without her stage make-up, her thick black hair tied simply

261

behind a lace cap, her red velvet gown trimmed with black embroidery.

She stood up, holding out her arms. 'A little subterfuge, my dear, but how else could we get you here? We have very little time. Henry will be here any minute. Put these on. I've collected up what I can – they're the best I could find and they fit his description perfectly…'

My stomach tightened. 'Henry who?'

'Henry Trevelyan.' She was busy untying the bundle in front of her, pulling out a carefully folded plain grey dress. Under the dress was a white shawl. 'He's here now – just crossing the courtyard. That's good timing.'

Henry was greeting Grace, nodding and smiling as she pointed to the door. His umbrella was dripping, his boots wet, a large hat pulled low over his face. Grace ran ahead and opened the door and Henry Trevelyan stood smiling on the threshold, turning to shake his umbrella, handing it to Grace along with his hat. He glanced quickly at me, bowing to Molly and Kitty who stood smiling back at him. Adoration shone in their eyes and I gripped my chair.

My surprise turned to anger. He had them eating out of his hand, Molly scurrying to get him a drink, Grace taking his coat, shaking it on the doorstep before hanging it by the stove. They hardly looked at me, all round eyed and purring as Henry sat at the table. 'That's perfect, Kitty. Have you got the wig?'

Kitty held up two boxes. 'You've several to choose from.' She opened the first box, bringing out a hideous pile of hair, laying another wig on the table in front of her. 'Which do you think, Henry?'

I had never been so furious. 'Perhaps *one* of you might have the courtesy to tell me what's going on – *in my own home?*'

Kitty unfolded the gown, shaking out the creases. 'You're to go with Henry – you've very little time.' She pointed to the Chinese screen folded in the corner of the room. 'Grace, be a love and pull the screen out. I meant to do it but haven't had the time. Angelica, get behind it and Henry can explain everything as you get changed.'

I caught Henry's gaze and my heart jolted. 'I'm not going *anywhere* with Mr Trevelyan. How can you trick me like this? It's despicable. Mr Trevelyan cannot be trusted – you think nothing of sending me off with a man you don't know?'

The smile left his eyes. 'I need you to identify the woman you accuse of being Lottie Lorrelli, Miss Lilly. Your brother has no recollection of her face but you do. We saw her on one of our walks – she was scurrying round the battlements and she fitted the description Luke gave me. I arrested her but I've no reason to hold her – other than on your suspicion.'

I held his gaze. 'I won't go with you alone. Someone must come with us.'

Molly looked thunderstruck but Kitty shook her head. 'You have to, my love. You must do it for Edgar. Henry's given us his word you'll come to no harm. We can't go – we must remain here if anyone comes. The coachman may come back and we'll need to tell him you're tired…that you're in bed and don't want to be disturbed. Now, hurry. What time does the ship leave, Henry?'

Henry reached for his fob watch. 'We've just over half an hour – she sails at ten thirty. The clothes are so no one recognizes you, Miss Lilly – you'll look like every other prison visitor.'

I made no move, standing defiantly though Kitty was directing me behind the screen. Henry Trevelyan stared back at me, matching my defiance. Where there had been laughter there was challenge, a firmness round his mouth. He looked tired, black circles shadowing his eyes, slight stubble on his chin. He was wearing sober clothes to match the dress Kitty held out.

'Thirty minutes,' scolded Kitty, 'to turn you from such a beauty to dull old dishwater.' She reached over, dragging her bag across the floor.

They seemed so sure of him and my anger rose, all three of them casting smiling glances, seeking his approval: Molly packing his leather bag with food for the journey; my brother's gaoler, summoning them as bold as brass, telling them about Edgar when I had not breathed a word.

'You may trust him,' I said, standing my ground, 'but I don't. It's only his word against Edgar's – no one saw the incident. He's duping you, just like he dupes everyone else.'

Molly shook her head, smiling fondly back at me. 'Honest, my love! We wouldn't send ye off with a man we didn't know. He's not dupin' us – he's *Henry* – ye wouldn't know him, but he's *Henry* – from number twenty-two Tannery Lane, or was it twenty-three?'

Chapter Twenty-six

The River Truro: on board ship
Saturday 13th August 1796, 12:00 p.m.

The wind bit deeper and he must have seen me shiver. He took off his coat, holding it up for me, refusing to take no for an answer, and I let him slip it over my shoulders, clasping it against my chest. It was made of fine cloth and beautifully tailored. We had hardly spoken; his hand gently on my back as he shepherded me across the quayside and up the gangplank of the awaiting lugger. Despite his asking, I had shaken my head firmly; I did not want to go below. I wanted to remain on deck and watch the river.

The tide had turned and was taking us with it, the flow as fast as anyone could row. The tips of branches dipped beneath the water, swept sideways by the current; a raft of flotsam formed our escort – planks, old crates, ropes and up-turned barrels bobbing in the water beside us. Several ships had slipped their moorings before us and were pulling ahead, others following, the wind steering us down the top reaches of the river towards the large bend that curved around Malpas.

'Are you quite sure you're not cold?' he said, smiling down at me.

I chose to ignore his misplaced pleasantries, staring instead at the riverbank.

'Can we at least call a truce, Miss Lilly? It'll be a good four hours to Falmouth with this headwind – and that's a long time to go without talking.' He was leaning against the bulwark, amusement in his voice. 'I thought you'd relish the prospect of helping your brother – and it was only *the tiniest little lie*, as I believe Molly says you call it. She says you do it all the time – write letters from people who may or may not exist. *Arranging things*, I believe she said.'

It was number 23; I remembered it now, 23 Tannery Lane – down to the end of Middle Row, then the squalid turning to the right.

The wind whistled through the rigging as it funnelled down the river. There must have been ten of us wrapped up against its force. The ship was heavy with lime, the sails arching, the timbers creaking. Crates of apples were stacked high on the deck, the Master shouting instructions at the crew as they navigated the river. The Heron Inn stood deserted behind its empty quay and I knew we must be thinking the same thought. Then, I had been blonde, my dress frilly and cumbersome; today I was brunette, my gown plain and severe.

I must have been frowning as the furrow on his brow deepened but still I would not speak. He shrugged, leaning closer so those behind us could not hear. 'She says her name is Martha Selwyn. She says she takes the baskets for the members of her church who are too elderly or infirm to walk to the castle. It's a case of simple compassion – they send the baskets because they're concerned for the welfare of the French prisoners – as are many. She fell to the floor in a faint when I suggested she might be Lottie Lorrelli, frequenter of an opium den by night.'

At some stage, I would have to speak so it might as well be now. 'That's the first thing to learn – how to fall in a faint when you're accused of doing something wrong. I hope you didn't believe her, Mr Trevelyan?'

He smiled. 'I didn't, but I had to go through the motions of getting her to a chair and bringing her some ale. The truth is I'm on very thin ice – her arrest has no authority. My action will be construed as unlawful but I took the chance. If you identify her as the woman in the inn, then I have every right to hold her. If, on the other hand, she's the innocent, and the rather charming young chapel-goer who she's claiming to be…then I'll be facing a mound of trouble when I get back.'

Woodsmoke drifted on the wind, blowing above the trees. I was still seething at their deception. It was not the plan; it was the way Henry Trevelyan had gone behind my back, eliciting the help of my friends and servants. It was underhand, like everything else he did.

'Never go behind my back again, Mr Trevelyan. '

'I had to act quickly…I needed your help and I needed to extricate you from Lady Clarissa without you having to lie. Kitty wrote the letter and chose the fabric – they'd used it in a boudoir scene, I believe. Was it really appalling?'

The wind ruffled his collar. He looked somehow out of

place on the deck of the ship – if not standing over a desk with heavy keys, he would be better placed in a library or a study with some weighty tome open in front of him. His high cheek bones made him look refined, his glasses bookish and intelligent. He had the same air as Luke – compassion for humanity etched across his brow. He suited his sober clothes; it lent him gravity, but not severity.

Number 23 had been the last in the row. The last house before the filth of the pits flooded the dirt track. I could see the child in his eyes. I remembered his pinched face and haunted gaze staring at me from the window as I waited in the carriage. He had never smiled but had stood staring out through the filthy glass, his house forbidden to me through dirt and disease.

'You used to watch me through the window,' I said, more curtly than I intended.

He turned away, his voice gruff. 'I apologize for my rudeness, Miss Lilly.' He kept his eyes on the riverbank, watching the smoke from the charcoal burners, the children running along the riverside, the donkey struggling to pull a cart piled high with driftwood. He seemed to want to look everywhere except at me.

The last house next to the tannery; the smell so awful, I wanted to vomit. Yet Mamma had insisted I must not hold my handkerchief against my nose. 'You never came out. The other children used to come out and stroke the horses but you never did. Why didn't you come and say hello?'

He swallowed, his gruffness turning to hoarseness. 'Because I had no shoes, Miss Lilly.'

'Molly recognized you – that first night when you were in our kitchen, she recognized you, didn't she?'

'I didn't intend her to recognize me – nor did I intend you to.'

The veiled threat in his answer made my stomach tighten. 'You were spying on us, Mr Trevelyan, hoping to hide your identity?'

'Not spying. And I didn't reveal my identity because there was no need – but Molly saw something and remembered. A habit can be a dangerous thing…'

'What habit?'

He shrugged his shoulders, his voice softening. 'The habit of diving into a basket to reach for the chutney – then throwing it in the air and catching it like a cricket ball.' His chin rose. 'I always used to throw the chutney in the air to frighten Molly. She'd shake her head and raise her eyebrows and your mother used to laugh. She used to say, *One day, you'll miss that, Henry, and it'll fall and break*. It was pure bravado on my part but if I didn't make a joke of it, I thought I might cry.' His voice dropped. 'I'll never forget the taste of Molly's chutney. I used to pretend I wasn't hungry but my mother knew differently. One spoonful of chutney can last a long time.'

The crew began hauling in the sails. 'Mind ye heads – take a step back…steady as she goes.' They held the ropes tightly, letting the sails out on the other side of the ship, and we watched them fill, feeling the sudden pull as the power of the wind took hold.

'Without your mother we'd have been destitute. I'll

never forget her kindness. My mother took in sewing and we scraped by.' There was no seeking pity in his voice. No reproach. No sense of injustice or anger, just stating the facts like Mamma used to state them.

'Mother had no shoes when she was young. She stole a pair so she could stowaway and leave Ireland.' I had never said those words before, yet they slipped from my tongue before I could stop them. 'She risked getting hung but she was determined to escape the beatings.' I stopped. I was telling him too much. Like the night in the shrubbery when I had talked to him as a friend.

'I'm glad she got away. Unlike your mother, my childhood had been happy. My father was a clerk as my grandfather was before him and I believe we would have prospered, but unaccounted losses were found in the company where my grandfather kept the books. Large sums had gone missing and the blame was placed squarely on my grandfather's shoulders.'

'That's terrible – I assume he was innocent.'

'That's very kind of you, Miss Lilly – others presumed him guilty. He was charged with fraud and false accounting and they demanded he repay the missing sum. It was a substantial amount of money and he obviously couldn't pay so he was imprisoned for debt. My father then spent every hour God sent him working to repay the losses.'

'But he didn't succeed?'

'He did succeed – finally. In time for my grandfather to come home to die.'

'I'm so sorry.'

'Thank you, it was a bitter loss. Gaol fever had my grand-father in its grip but we got him home and that pleased my mother. My father's heart was never sound and the very next morning he failed to rise from his bed.'

'I'm so sorry.'

'He'd used up all his strength to clear our name. My mother had just given birth to my second sister and all Father's earnings had been used to pay the debt. We'd moved from a comfortable home to the rooms by the tannery. We had nothing. My mother was still weak from childbirth and found herself alone with three small children to feed and clothe. But for your mother's goodness we'd have been on the streets.'

I was grateful he stayed staring ahead and did not look at me. The smell from the tannery had been so foul: I had sat fighting my nausea, counting down the minutes, impatient to leave. Yet that was the home of Henry Trevelyan – a boy too proud to cry at the sight of a basket, too ashamed to let me see he was wearing no shoes.

The river was widening, narrow strips of mud glistening down either side of the wooded banks. Herons stood silently at the water's edge, cormorants stretching out their wings to dry. There was salt in the air and I breathed deeply, freeing myself from the smell of the tannery. Soon we would cross to the right side of the river and navigate the tight bend below Trenwyn House. Henry's jacket was warm around my shoulders.

'You think me profligate, don't you? You think Edgar and I are spoilt.'

He did not answer, then his voice hardened. 'On the contrary; I became your brother's coachman because I owed it to your mother to see Edgar came to no harm.'

A shiver ran down my spine. He had known Mamma – he held her memory in his heart and I stifled my tears. I wanted to tell him I was glad he had made good, that Mamma would have been thrilled that the family had risen from their misfortune, but I could not. He was my brother's gaoler. 'If you really mean that, you'd free Edgar…'

His mouth tightened. 'I can protect his identity but I can't set him free. The robberies must be accounted for – I owe that to Sir Alexander Pendarvis.'

'Please, Henry. For Mother's kindness – for Molly…'

He stared ahead. 'Your mother's generosity kept us alive but I owe everything else to Sir Alexander. I was one of his Foundation Boys. From the age of eleven he fed and clothed me and spared no expense on my education. My debt to Sir Alexander knows no limit and neither does my admiration for him. The prisoners in Kergilliack could only dig that tunnel because files had been smuggled into the gaol. The same prisoners are in my care and we have a series of reported robberies. I have no idea who is out there or what their plan is but your brother is the only link.'

The captain bellowed from the tiller: 'Slowly does it…keep watching…shout when we're clear.' A notorious mudbank reached far below the waterline, grounding unwary ships who failed to give it a wide berth. Silence fell among the passengers as we watched the ship edging closer to the right-hand bank; the crew were running along the deck, peering over the side, shouting back to their captain. 'Two feet star-board....starboard. That does it…the pole's passin' to port.'

The wind was lost behind the trees, the sails jolting on their slack ropes, but for the fast-flowing current, we would have been in irons. The ship kept its course, inching slowly round the bend, and we caught the wind again, the sails filling, sweeping us towards the wide waters of Carrick Sound.

On the rise of the hill, Trenwyn House came slowly into sight. Rowing boats were moored against the jetty, laughter ringing across the sweeping lawns. They could not see me, but I saw them – a tall blond man in naval uniform, three small boys running rings around him. Charity was clapping her hands, Amelia clutching a cricket bat, Lady Clarissa poised to bowl. A second man in naval uniform stood awkwardly by the wicket, Jethro showing him how to hold the bat, and from the deck of the ship we saw bemusement in the shrug of the Frenchman's shoulders.

Henry's smile turned to sudden laughter. 'Eighteen months at sea and straight out to play cricket. The poor man – he can't possibly have bargained for that.' Our eyes caught, and a visceral pain seemed to tear me apart.

'That's Captain Pierre de la Croix – he's given his parole to Frederick but I expect you already know that. You probably had to give your permission.'

His shoulders stiffened as he lifted his chin. 'Yes, as a matter of fact, I did give my permission.' A new harshness entered his tone. 'Miss Lilly, I understand how difficult this is for you. I know you may want to elicit the help of your influential friends—'

'*May* want to? Of course I want to – but you threatened me, if you remember, Mr Trevelyan – the necklace and the silver dish that you'll hand over at the first sign of interference? I've only agreed to come with you because I want to help my brother – please don't think I trust you. The first sign of *any* danger to Edgar's life and I'm going to elicit the help of—'

'Lord Entworth? Yes, Miss Lilly, I'm fully aware of your situation – Molly made it quite clear how proud she is of your imminent rise to the highest echelons of society.'

I felt crushed by the bitterness in his voice. 'Molly had no business telling you.' I was going to say Matthew Reith, the foremost barrister in Cornwall, but if he thought I was to marry Lord Entworth then so much the better. Let him believe Lord Entworth would throw his weight behind me: let him understand I would do anything in my power to save my brother from the gallows.

'Edgar and Sir Jacob Boswell often spoke of your engagement – I think there are very few who *haven't* heard, but I must warn you, I know Lord Entworth and I know his methods – he and Sir Alex have locked horns on many occasions. Lord Entworth may be all powerful, but in your brother's case, we have the law on our side.'

My heart froze. 'Is that another threat, Mr Trevelyan?'

His voice was like iron. 'Merely stating the truth, Miss Lilly.'

Chapter Twenty-seven

Awkwardness fell between us. He held his shoulders stiffly, firmer lines forming around his mouth, and I took off his coat, no longer wanting it around my shoulders. He took it back, protesting I must not get cold. There was tension in his voice, formality in his movements, and we stood watching the deepening waves in frosty silence.

'Would ye like an apple, sir?' Dirt smudged the pale face of the boy holding up his basket; the sleeves of his jacket were turned at the cuffs, a rope keeping his trousers in place. Henry nodded, choosing two of the reddest apples and handed him a coin. The boy stared as if turned to stone. 'I've...I've no change.'

Henry shook his head, turning round, throwing one of the apples in the air and catching it with a smile. The boy's mouth gaped, his eyes filled with tears. 'Thank ye, sir...thank ye... thank ye.' He almost tripped over his feet as he ran to his mother.

Henry swung his leather bag from his shoulders, opening

the buckles to put the apples inside. The chequered cloth must have caught his attention and he glanced at me. 'Shall we eat, Miss Lilly? Molly's packed us a very fine meal.'

'I'm not hungry. You may eat if you like.' It had been a sovereign – a gold sovereign.

'Are you sure? This all looks very appetizing.' He laid the cloth out on a wooden crate, arranging the food carefully. 'Let me at least give you a slice of Molly's home-cured ham…oh, look…how wonderful – she's given us some of her home-made cheese. And look, some rather lovely apple tart – this is a real feast.'

He sounded like an excited child and I had to turn away. He had known Mamma. He had loved her. Any other time, any other situation, and I would have warmed to this man who took such delight in simple fare – a man who recognized hunger in a young boy's eyes. I took his proffered plate, staring at the ships that were pulling away from us.

'I wonder where those ships are going? When a ship slips her moorings, my curiosity is always aroused.' The corn bread was freshly baked, the cheese unlike any other; the jar of chutney lay untasted in the bag.

'So's mine,' he replied, smiling but not looking at me. He was eating his meal carefully, savouring every bite. 'I believe your father has a fleet of ships – I believe he imports coal from South Wales and uses the same ships to export his ore. Useful to have his own wharf.'

'He doesn't have his own wharf. He wishes he does – competition for space is fierce. He has constant rows with the harbourmaster. He gets fined for blocking the quayside…yet delays happen all the time and where else is the coal meant to go once it's unloaded? The penalties for blocking a wharf have become very costly.'

'And rightly so.'

'Yes, rightly so – but the quays are too crowded. There's insufficient space for the demand and the increased mooring fees add greatly to the cost of the cargo. The low tide delays too many ships...too many vessels have deep drafts and those who time the tide wrongly risk getting grounded. Many have to stop in Malpas – then they miss their place on the quayside and that also attracts a fine. Father uses the wharf further up, but the costs are crippling.'

'Surely it's good for the town to have a busy port?'

'But it's not good for businesses that have to pay the spiralling harbour dues. Some ships aren't insured against blocking the quayside. There's a very fine line between profit and loss. Father's decided to build his next smelter in Sir James Polcarrow's new harbour. The sea lock will ensure a quick turnover and there's plenty of space for his ore.'

Henry uncorked the ale, pouring it into two pewter cups. 'Sir James is very far-sighted. But tariffs and taxes change by the week – it's not always the fault of the harbourmaster.'

'I know – it's because we're at war. Truro's problems are nothing compared to ports like Falmouth or Plymouth.'

His eyes pierced mine. 'You take a great interest in ships, Miss Lilly.'

'Women don't just like to sew and read novels, Mr Trevelyan – we're just as interested in newspapers. We're an island nation – ships are in our blood. This war is about protecting our shipping interests as much as anything. Our trade routes need to be maintained.'

He handed me a pewter cup. 'Those who control the trade routes hold the greater power. Crush your enemy's prosperity and you crush your enemy's ability to fund wars.'

'Exactly. Trade brings prosperity and prosperity funds hospitals and schools as well as war. We need all the prosperity we can get.'

'Yet France has *opened* her ports to neutral trade.'

'France can do what she likes. I believe Britain must look to her own interests. We must protect our trade routes – allow unrestricted trade like the French and we'll lose our advantage. If ships are allowed to trade with countries prohibited to them before the war, then Britain's trade will suffer, and probably very badly.'

'I see you're a protectionist, Miss Lilly. You believe Britain must protect her interests at all costs?'

'Why not? Would you have us hand everything over to the French?'

'No. But those forbidden to trade with British colonies think very differently. Many view your protectionist policies as discriminating against countries who are struggling to make their way – imposing shackles on the weak. What about the countries striving to trade without the benefit of colonies?'

'The French have colonies – the Spanish – the Portuguese – the Dutch. Britain's not alone in owning colonies – nor in wanting to protect her home markets.'

'Yet the new regime in France thinks differently. Their

278

Republican idealism fuels a desire to embrace free trade. Allow a country to trade with whom it wants and you liberate it from tyranny and oppression. And many would argue they have a point.' He took off his glasses, cleaning them with a freshly laundered handkerchief. 'Take America, for example; she's no longer protected by Britain — she fought hard for her independence only to find her ships barred from every British port — *every* port in *every* British colony is now lost to her. Her prosperity is threatened.'

'Some may argue that those terms were made very clear when they fought for independence.'

'Indeed they were. Yet it was a risk they were willing to take. They had hoped for better terms — they view Britain's imposed trade restrictions as gross discrimination.'

'I understand that, Mr Trevelyan. The states of America are calling for reciprocity — what we might call an equal playing field. Britain's hampering their prosperity and they're demanding we improve our treatment of their ships in their home market. The spiralling tariffs and high import duties are crippling their new government and in order for them to flourish they need to establish new trade routes or negotiate better deals with the British colonies — trade routes they've previously used, but now find themselves barred from. Of course they're fighting for free trade.'

'Indeed, Miss Lilly. You have it in a nutshell.'

The approbation in his smile jolted me into smiling back. I had never talked so freely — certainly never with Father. If only he would not smile at me like that: if only he would shout, or argue, not speak so eloquently. I turned away, biting my bottom lip. There was so much more I wanted to discuss. I felt suddenly envious, imagining Luke and Mary and Edgar sitting round the table, having thrilling conversations about commerce and philosophy. Was this how he talked with Edgar long into the night? Reading poetry as the dawn broke?

'If the ship's neutral then aren't the goods neutral? Only, I've heard neutral vessels are being seized.'

He looked up, obviously delighted I wanted to continue our discussion. 'Neutral ships should be safe, Miss Lilly, but the truth is they're not. We're at war – no ships are safe.' He smiled again and I knew to look away. 'To sail French waters you need a signed piece of paper – a *rôle d'équipage* – or the cargo will be confiscated. Yet how to obtain a French-issued pass without entering French waters eludes most people!' He laughed and I tried not to laugh with him. My heart was ripping in two. For the first time in my life a man was speaking to me as an equal, as if he valued my opinion. He looked down at the last piece of apple pie. 'Miss Lilly, may I tempt you with another piece of pie?'

He smiled again and I hated the way his eyes held such brilliance; intelligent, laughing eyes – the eyes of my brother's gaoler.

'Molly will have put it in for you,' I said sharply. 'She always expects men to have second helpings.' I stared at the riverbank, watching the ship's wake disturb the ducks swimming among the reeds.

He frowned, shaking his head. 'That hardly seems fair. May I suggest we go half and half? Here…' He cut the remaining piece in two, quickly handing it to me to stop it breaking into pieces. He licked his finger and the icy grip resumed its clutch.

'I presume Sir Alex secured you your job with the Transport Board? What do you do? Supply the prisons – organize their food and clothes? They must need boots and hammocks and you must have to keep everyone updated in London.'

'*Should* I be employed by the Transport Board then yes, that would be my job.' He wiped his mouth with one of the napkins and started returning everything to his bag. 'As it happens, I didn't take up Sir Alex's offers of employment – it was against his advice but I was too restless.' The tension in his jaw returned. 'My mother had remarried and my family were well cared for…a ship was leaving for New York and I boarded it.'

'You went to America?' I had to hide my sudden envy.

'I was twenty-one.' He did up the buckles on his leather bag, replacing the strap over his shoulder. 'I needed to be out in the world.' He stood up, staring stonily across the river-bank across the vast gardens of Carrick Hall and I knew I, too, must glance along the line of Greek statues.

I must let my eyes linger on the rills and fountains. He must see me smile, as if remembering some whispered inti-macies in the folly. I must incline my neck, gaze across the splendid gardens to the imposing façade of the Palladian mansion. He would be watching from the corner of his eye and I would not disappoint. First a shallow intake of breath, then the slightest flicker of my eyelids – I knew exactly what to do; I had it to perfection.

His face grew severe. He turned, staring at the distant turrets of Pendennis Castle standing stark against the Falmouth coastline. 'There's a rowing boat waiting for us when we dock. We'll row round to the side of the castle – the climb will be steep but you're less likely to be seen. When we get to the prison, I don't want you to speak to Edgar.'

I caught my breath. 'Not speak to Edgar? You must allow me that!'

'No, Miss Lilly. If Edgar knows you're there, he'll tell Luke and Mary.'

The icy grip tightened its hold. I could hardly breathe. 'Mr Trevelyan, I am *not* your prisoner – you cannot deny me my brother or my friends.'

He drew me forward, staring down at the foam frothing against the bow. His voice was terse, for my ears only. 'Miss Lilly, I haven't been entirely honest with you. If you confirm the woman *is* the woman you saw in the Heron Inn, then I'm within my rights to detain her, but detaining her will lead us nowhere. Her associates will melt away – they'll hardly come and claim her – and my arrest will be pointless. I'll still have no idea where she lives, where she goes, or who she associates with.'

My heart was thudding; I knew exactly what he was saying. Henry had sent Kitty his exact requirements – the same grey gown, the same brown wig. I was not dressed for my own disguise; I was dressed to be her. Those intelligent eyes held challenge, a look of conspiracy. 'Molly and Kitty have no notion of my plan or they'd never have agreed to help – and if Edgar sees you he'll tell Luke and Mary, who'd never permit it.' He held my stare. 'I'll be right behind you but I'll remain out of sight.'

'Who is she, Henry?'

'Martha Selwyn's certainly not her real name. She buckled under pressure when I told her I'd seen her in the Heron Inn that night. I told her I was dressed as a coachman and saw her go upstairs with a man and she admitted being there – but she denies everything about the necklace and the Falmouth den. She says she's never seen Edgar – certainly never goaded him into robbing coaches as a Frenchman.'

'Lying toad.'

'I said I didn't believe her sudden conversion to Methodism and she broke down. I left her crying piteously, pleading for me to understand how hunger leaves people with very little choice. I'm not judging her, Miss Lilly, but I do need the truth.'

My heart was hammering, leaping in my chest. 'Where does she get the baskets?'

'I don't know. I had to leave to catch the tide.' He was standing so close, his jacket brushing my shawl. His voice dropped. 'I'm not forcing you into doing this, Miss Lilly. It's entirely your choice but I need a good actress – someone who's fearless and…and there aren't very many of you about.'

'I'll need a mole above my lip and I'll need to observe her movements – and listen to her speech. She mustn't see me watch her.'

'She's in the cell next to Edgar's. You can remain in the shadows – she won't see you but you'll see her.'

There was something in the way he had laid out the food, something in his movements. The hairs on my arms rose, a shiver ran down my spine. 'How do you know I'm a good actress – four very short lines at the very end of a play is hardly enough for you to judge.'

I thought he would not answer. It was as if he was struggling to find the words. He stared ahead, the wind blowing the crests of the waves into a fine spray. 'I saw all your plays, Miss Lilly – every single one of them.'

I could not speak, a cold shiver taking hold. That first day, I had thought him familiar but I remembered him now; standing over a hamper, rubbing his hands in expectant pleasure. 'You saw all my plays? How come you were at the school?'

He tugged his collar against the wind. 'My mother married one of the school governors – Reverend Penhaligan. They live in the rectory next to the school. We sat on the lawn with our hamper along with everyone else.'

I could almost taste the gingerbread she had left on my pillow; a lonely child sitting on the branch of a tree in the moonlight, savouring every bite. Never once did I think it was one mother repaying the kindness of another.

'And as for fearless...' I heard him say. 'How many times did you run away? Is it true you stood in the middle of the road when you saw Lord Falmouth's coach and demand he take you home?'

I could hardly breathe for the pain. 'Three times,' I managed to whisper. 'And it wasn't Lord Falmouth. It was Lord North.'

Chapter Twenty-eight

The wig felt too hot, too tight, my dreary bonnet pulled so low down my forehead I could hardly see. The wind was lessening but even so, I tied the heavy ribbons tighter. The gangplank had no rail and Henry held out his hand, holding my elbow to stop me slipping on the wet wood. A long line of men with barrows began pushing towards us and we squeezed our way through the gaps. 'The boat's down the next alley. I'll row us round.'

I kept my eyes down, nodding in agreement. The alley was dark and stank of urine and I lifted the hem of my skirt to keep it from the filth. A set of worn steps led down to the water, three rowing boats pulling softly against their ropes. A boy sat on the top step with a fishing line and jumped up as Henry whistled. He opened a door behind him and held up two oars, adoration in his eyes as he staggered back. 'Safe as anythin'.'

'Thank you, Seth – you're a good boy.' He put a coin in the boy's hand and helped me down the steps, waiting until I was safely settled before sitting on the seat. The boy handed him the rope and helped push us away and we glided through the tangle of entwined ropes, weaving between the anchored hulls and out of the harbour. Henry's rowing was fast, his arms heaving against the growing swell as we approached open water.

'We'll skirt these rocks then cut back in. At least there's no rain – and the wind's dropping.'

He had stripped off his jacket and rolled up his sleeves and I looked away, staring along the jagged rocks of the peninsula. People were walking up to the castle and I turned to watch the seagulls swooping round a fishing boat, the ships taking down their sails, anywhere but at Henry Trevelyan. His clasped wrists were almost touching my knees. Mrs Penhaligan's son; the pain was almost unbearable.

I remembered him now. He had been thinner, lankier, a youth not a man. We had bumped into each other. He was carrying a hamper and stood back to let me pass. He had looked down but I glanced back to thank him and our eyes had caught. I had thought how kind he looked, his shy smile making me smile back. He was rowing fast, hauling us through the water with obvious ease. The wind was ruffling his hair and I forced myself to look away. He was watching me. 'You're my eyes – let me know if I get too close to the rocks.'

The sea smelled so salty, the air so fresh, and I stared at the waves frothing around the jagged outcrop. 'I can't see why people row backwards. What's the point? It's ridiculous not being able to see where you're going.'

There was no joy in his smile, a catch to his voice. 'A lot

of people can't see where they're going.' The cliffs towered above us, dark and foreboding. Guillemots called from the crevices, seagulls circling above us. Waves splashed the bow, the spray stinging my lips, but we were making progress, pulling along the headland in the heavy swell. A small beach was just visible beneath the jagged cliff and he glanced over his shoulder.

'We're here,' he said, swinging the boat round, and we drifted silently into the sheltered water. In the shadow of the cliff, I could just make out a set of roughly hewn steps.

He took off his boots, leaving them behind as he slipped from the side. The water reached to his thighs and he grimaced from the cold, pulling the boat quickly towards the beach. The hull scraped soft sand and he stopped. 'I think that's as far as I can pull you.' He held up his arms to lift me to dry land.

He had stared at me from his filthy window. He had loved Mamma. He had watched every one of my plays and his mother had shown me such kindness. He spoke to me as an equal, treated me as intelligent, yet he was my brother's gaoler. 'I can jump from here.'

He pursed his lips, shaking his head. 'You could but your shoes will stay wet until you return to Truro – I have a change of clothes. You'll stay wet. Let me help you, Miss Lilly.'

He was staring up at me, stubble shadowing his chin. His glasses were covered with spray and he slipped them off, wiping them on his shirt. His eyes were blue like the sea, his brows brown like his hair. He was no longer sunburned but looked paler, freckles dusting his nose and forehead. He gripped the side of the boat. 'Please, Miss Lilly – you mustn't get your shoes wet.'

I put my hands on his shoulders, letting him hold me, and he swung me round. His arms were stronger than I had imagined, swinging me effortlessly in the air, holding me against him, and I put my arms around his neck, allowing myself to be carried.

He put me down on dry ground. 'I'll hide the oars – the steps are steep, take great care.'

The way was overgrown, Henry turning round, helping me over the boulders when the path disappeared. It was clearly never used, the spreading thorns catching my hem, the gnarled roots nearly tripping me up. The clouds were thinning, watery sun shimmering across the sea, but we were deep in shade, climbing steeply to the battlements above. A turret stood proud of the fortifications, the path cutting deeper into an overhanging crevice.

'Are you all right?' he asked and I nodded, following him through a narrow gap hidden behind a rock. Through the darkness, I saw a grilled gate.

'It's a tunnel to the inner gatehouse.' He reached into his jacket for a set of heavy keys. 'They dug this during the siege – and they nearly succeeded.'

'To bring provisions in?'

'No, it was the Parliamentary forces trying to dig their way in.' The lock was stiff and took some turning and he ushered me forward, picking up the lantern that hung by the grille. He reached into his pocket, striking his tinderbox and the candle caught, the light reflecting in his glasses.

'It's very steep and it's wet and slippery. Will you be all right?'

I nodded, our shadows dancing against the glistening wall. The cave smelled dank and sudden cold penetrated my clothes. He saw me shiver and stripped off his jacket, but I shook my head. 'You'll get dripped on from above.'

'I don't mind. My cloak is thick enough.'

The passage was roughly hewn, narrowing considerably as we climbed the steep steps. Henry held the lantern high. Water was oozing from the rock face, the steps black, uneven, and I lifted my hem. At a sharp turn he stopped and took my elbow, helping me across a jagged rock as sharp as a knife.

'The bats might stir in this next bit,' he whispered. 'You're not afraid of bats, are you, Miss Lilly?'

'Not at all – I love bats,' I lied.

A heavily grilled gate loomed ahead of us and Henry handed me the lantern, reaching once more for his keys. His gaoler's keys. 'There are only two sets of keys to this tunnel. I have one and Captain Fenshaw has the other. We'll come out at the turret we saw from below. This last bit was only dug recently but it's going to be sealed. The whole tunnel's going to be filled.'

He locked the heavy grille, ushering me up narrow spiral steps to another thickly grilled gate. He unlocked it, blew out the candle and left the lantern on a hook. 'We'll make it look like we've come along the walls.' The stone corridor ended in an arch and I could see the battlements above. Henry took my arm, opening a heavy wooden door, and I saw the entrance to the turret. Two soldiers were sitting on benches and eased themselves upright, nodding and smiling as Henry addressed them.

'Good day, gentlemen. All quiet, I hope?'

I pulled my hood low over my bonnet. The soldiers were smiling at me with obvious pleasure. 'All quiet, Mr Trevelyan. Miss Martha, what brings you this way? No baskets with ye, tonight?'

I smiled but looked down, struggling to remember how the woman had spoken but Henry ushered me forward.

'I'm just showing Miss Selwyn the fortifications. As you were.'

The turret door opened to glorious sunshine. We were in the inner field, soldiers sitting on the grass by their cannons, the sheep watching us, and I breathed deep for courage. The heavy portcullis and intricate Tudor crest loomed in front of me, the two guards standing to attention. I did not look up: the rancid smell had set my heart racing.

'Does anyone know she's already here?' I whispered.

'No. The inner guards were helping George Godwin and the outside guards were unloading the straw. It was a lucky coincidence. I managed to bring her in without anyone thinking it was an arrest. Only Captain Fenshaw knows she's been arrested. I left him in charge of them both – no one else goes into my rooms, except George now and then.'

I kept my hood pulled over my bonnet, smiling at the guards, shrugging my shoulders at their obvious disappointment. George Godwin's door was shut, and more guards struggled to their feet as we passed. Each guard had hoped for something.

At the door of his gaol, Henry paused. 'You can change your mind, Miss Lilly. You can walk away from this.'

'I'm not afraid – I'm prepared to do anything to prove my brother's innocence. I'm here for *him*. Only him.'

He heard the iron in my voice and his mouth hardened. 'Once inside, slip to the left. There's a screen you can hide behind. I'll cause a diversion.'

He unlocked the door. 'Is everything as it should be?' He left the door ajar, walking into the room, and I saw Edgar's cell was unlocked. Captain Fenshaw and Edgar were playing cards at a table, the soft glow of the candle lighting their faces. My brother looked relaxed, even happy, smiling up at Henry as he stood by the open grille.

'You've come at just the right time, Henry. My winnings have turned to losses. I'm down to five almonds where once I was the proud owner of three oranges and two lemons. Luke will scold me and tell me I'll come down with *scrofula!*'

Captain Fenshaw laughed, easing himself upright. 'Well, you're in luck – I'll swap them back for the almonds. Dr Bohenna has me on ginger and turmeric and says lemons and oranges make my joints worse. We've spent a very pleasant day, Henry. Have you been successful?'

'Not as successful as I would have liked – oh. . .' He tripped on the rug, bumping into the table leg, knocking the candle to the ground and I slipped quickly through the door behind the wooden screen and held my breath. They had not heard me.

'No harm done. Here, let me relight it.' Defuse light shone through the barred window, and I peered from behind the thin join in the screen watching Captain Fenshaw strike the tinderbox. His actions were stiff, his fingers clumsy.

'I'll catch a breath of air and have something to eat – I've promised to stand guard with Mr Godwin tonight.'

'You work too hard, Andrew.'

Captain Fenshaw did up his top button with the same painful movements. 'Needs must, I'm afraid. We've sickness among the men and Mr Godwin's wagon's not yet back. Everyone's pressed, though I do agree, some work harder than others.' He smiled and bowed. 'Goodnight, Mr Ellis. I've enjoyed our day together.'

Edgar stood up and tears sprung to my eyes. He looked taller, more upright, no longer shaking, no high-pitched laughter. He bowed back, and I caught a glimpse of my brother of old.

Captain Fenshaw stopped at the grille of the other cell. 'Goodnight, Miss Selwyn,' he said with the same polite bow.

'Goodnight, Captain Fenshaw,' came the soft reply. My heart jumped. I did not recognize her voice.

Chapter Twenty-nine

Henry pulled his chair against Martha's locked grille. 'Come forward please, Miss Selwyn. Bring your chair nearer so we can speak without shouting.' His voice was kind. 'I'm not judging you. I believe you've done nothing wrong – I think you're being used by someone and I need your help.'

Martha remained lying on her bed, her silence filling the cellar.

Henry reached for his notebook. 'For the last three weeks you've brought two baskets full of provisions – every Tuesday afternoon and every Saturday evening, to be precise. You carry these baskets up the hill for an undisclosed benefactor and you give the contents to the French prisoners. I believe you're to bring two more baskets again tonight – is that correct?'

The silence continued and Henry's pen remained poised above the pages of his notebook. 'I need to know *who* gives you these baskets, and *why*? If you give me their names and

293

addresses I'll be able to let you go. Without those names and addresses, you'll stay and face the direst of consequence. The charge against you is serious. You've been arrested for aiding and abetting a known criminal.'

'I didn't…I told ye…I don't know what yer talkin' about.'

'I need the facts, that's all. Who gives you the baskets, Miss Selwyn? We know they're not from members of the chapel as you first told me. I need to know *who* these people are and *why* you bring their baskets?' He looked down at his notebook. 'You can expect very little mercy if you remain so resolutely quiet. Silence condemns a prisoner as surely as lies. The truth, please, Miss Selwyn. Bring your chair to the grille and tell me the truth.'

I peered through the tiny gap, listening to her chair scrape across the flagstones. The candle caught her face and my heart thudded. It was her. Not just her dark eyes and wide mouth and the jut of her chin, the mole above her lip, but the way she tossed her head. Her voice was trembling, full of resentment; a deep voice I would have to catch exactly.

'I don't know who sends the baskets, and that's God's honest truth. I've nothin'…nothin' at all. I'm dirt poor…I was given these clothes an' told to take the baskets an' I get a shillin' fer my trouble. That might be nothin' to ye, but it's life an' death to me. It's an honest job.'

'Who hands you the baskets? I need a full description.'

'I can't tell ye. It's a different boy each time.'

'A boy?'

'A different one. I wait by the chapel door an' a boy brings the baskets. Different one each time.'

'The chapel in Killigrew Street?'

She nodded. 'I have to get there for eight, an' I'm always on time, though the boy sometimes keeps me waitin'.'

She spoke differently to the guards: more refined and less aggressive. I must capture the toss of her hair, the slight slope to her shoulders, the way she leans to one side when she walks. I was trying to remember her silhouette against the sun, the way she carried the baskets on each arm. She had stopped and nodded, her 'Good day' sounding sweet and sincere. I remembered her smile as she reached into the basket for the bottle. She had bitten her bottom lip. Yes, bitten her lip and not looked up – as if she were hiding her true identity. And she had a soft veil over her bonnet, I would need that too.

'Where do you take the baskets back – to another boy waiting by the chapel? The prisoners put their work into your basket. Who takes these pieces?'

'I believe they get sold an' the money pays fer more food.'

'They're worth a lot more than the food they buy. Who sells them? I need to know the name of this unknown bene-factor. Who wields you like a puppet, Miss Selwyn?'

She clasped her hands against her face, her voice heart-wrenching. 'I don't know, an' that's the honest truth. I collect the baskets from the boy just like I told ye...but I take the baskets back across the river. I go to the Ferry Inn in Flushin'...I sit at the back next to the door and sometimes I can wait fer hours. But it's dry and warm, an' no one bothers me. There's always a drink waitin' fer me an' a pie...I just sit tight an' enjoy my meal an' I wait.'

'Who collects the baskets?'

'I don't know his name. He comes through the door besides me an' just takes the baskets.' She was crying now, wiping her eyes with the back of her hands. 'He's nice to me. He don't touch me or ask nothing more of me. He just takes the baskets an' sees that I'm paid an' I'm fed. What harm can that do? That don't make me a criminal.'

'It doesn't, Miss Selwyn. Many would take the work and be grateful for it. I need a description of this man – his age, what he wears…how he speaks.'

'He don't ever speak. He slips the shillin' on the table as he takes the baskets.'

'Go on.'

'He's not young, not old. It's dark that end of the inn an' I hardly see him – he wears black clothes and covers his mouth with a scarf. But he's bushy eyebrows, I can tell ye that fer certain, an' he's got a scar low on his forehead – above his eye.'

'Anything else?'

She shook her head, tears streaming down her face. 'I'm innocent, honest I am…like I said – he leaves the shillin' on the table and just sweeps away the baskets. He don't speak or look at me. He's there one minute, gone as quick.'

Henry handed her his clean white handkerchief. 'That's the only time you see him, Miss Selwyn?'

She blew her nose, nodding vigorously. 'Ye don't know hunger, do ye? Ye don't know what ye have to do to survive. I do a lot of things I don't like doin'…but takin' baskets an' eatin' a good meal an' getting a shillin' fer my trouble seems an honest way of stayin' alive. Ye judge too harsh...everyone judges too harsh.'

Henry shut his notebook and reached for his pocket watch. 'I never judge and you're wrong. I do know what hunger feels like.' He walked to his bag, reaching for the two apples, handing one to Edgar who stood wide-eyed by his grille, the other to Martha Selwyn who was still crying into his handkerchief. 'I believe you, Martha. For the first time, I believe you're telling the truth.'

He lit two more candles, grabbed his coat and bag and walked to the door. He was just the other side of the screen and I knew to slip quickly out behind him. Martha's voice rang from her cell. 'Thought ye said I could go – thought ye said ye believed me.'

'One more night,' he called, unlocking the outer door. He reached for her cloak and bonnet. 'I'll be back.'

He locked the door behind him, pulling me quickly into the same recess where I had stood with Mary. Two guards sat either side of George Godwin's locked door, two others guarding the heavy outer door. We could hear them laughing, rolling their dice. In the dim glow of the stinking rush light, he handed me the bonnet.

'Here, swap bonnets. This one's bigger and the veil will cover your face.' He leaned a little closer. 'Hold still, I've a stick of charcoal – let me draw her mole.' I lifted my face and his hand cupped my chin, his face so close, I could feel his breath against my cheek. 'It's just gone seven, we've very little time.'

'I can go on my own – there's no need for you to come. I'll

collect the baskets and come straight back. Everything must remain as usual. I know where the chapel is and I know to wait for a boy. It won't look right if you follow me – they'll see you. You know she gives the bottles to the guards?'

'Prisoners aren't allowed alcohol…everyone knows their gifts to the prisoners are shared by the guards – food for the prisoners, the odd glass of whiskey or wine to smooth the passage in. That way, everyone's happy. I can't stop it. No one stops it. It's part of the arrangement. I don't like the thought of you going alone.'

'I'm perfectly capable of collecting the baskets.'

'It's your safety I'm concerned for. Take this.' He pulled a silver whistle from his pocket, negotiating my huge bonnet to place the chain round my neck. His hands brushed against my cheek. 'Use this at the slightest scare. It's very loud – I'll probably hear you from here.' He smiled. 'Here's her cloak. Pull the hood over your bonnet and use this muffler – best act like you've a sore throat.'

The guards pulled back the heavy lock and I turned from the lamplight. 'Will we see ye again tonight, Miss Martha?'

I nodded, smiling, but caught my breath as George Godwin rushed quickly past me. He raised his hat, half bowing, half nodding, slipping quickly through the gate to the door of his room. I turned with relief as the gate slammed behind me, the lock scraping, and I walked swiftly up the spiral stairs, breathing in the fresh evening air. Martha Selwyn was lying. She was in that room in the inn and she was the woman who had framed Edgar.

The courtyard of the gatehouse looked even more

ramshackle. A new delivery of straw was piled untidily against the storehouse and a couple of soldiers were trying to unravel a dirty tarpaulin. Private Mallory waved me forward, shaking his head as the tarpaulin ripped in two. I walked swiftly through the gate and across the stone bridge and stood staring down at the ships in the harbour. It was so beautiful it took my breath away. The sea was red, blood red, and I stared in awed wonder. It was as if the sky was on fire – huge bands of orange and pink blazing across the evening sky.

Chapter Thirty

The church clock struck eight and I looked around. I was in Killigrew Street, standing outside the chapel, arranging my skirts, trying to look like I did this all the time. Shouts were ringing from the taverns, a few carts clattering along the cobbles. After a week of rain the streets smelled fresh, everyone out enjoying the warmth of the evening sun. Children played hopscotch on the flagstones beside me, a group of girls chanting rhymes as they skipped.

My stomach tightened. Three men were looking at me; one coming towards me.

I smiled at his greeting. 'Good evening, Sister.'

He had bushy eyebrows but no scar. He was young, his clothes sober but not dark, and I looked down, not knowing what to say. At once, I saw a young boy struggling down the road with two baskets and I turned from the man to greet him. The boy was thin, pale, poorly dressed, with sores around his mouth and a runny nose. He put the baskets by my feet and ran quickly away and my fear rose. The man was still by my side.

He picked up the baskets, handing them to me. 'Are you sure you can manage?' His smile seemed genuine but I could hardly tell. 'These baskets are very heavy. I'd be happy to carry them for you.' He smiled again, his face flushing scarlet, and I shook my head.

'That's very kind of ye but...I've someone waitin' to help me. I'm betrothed, sir...I thank ye for yer kindness but he's waiting fer me just round the corner.'

My heart hammered. Had I sounded like her? I leaned slightly to one side, taking the baskets from him. Perhaps he had just plucked up the courage to come and speak, perhaps he was not a thief, or the man behind the baskets, either way, once round the corner, I put the whistle to my lips, walking as fast as I could, my ears straining for the sound of his footsteps. None came, and I began to relax, the last streaks of setting sun lingering on my back as I laboured up the path.

The baskets were indeed heavy, the bottles protruding from beneath the cloths, I was used to wearing gloves and the rough handles chaffed my palms. No wonder she carried them on her arms. I stopped where I had stopped with Mary, the clear view of the path reassuring me that I was not being followed. The air was still, not a breath of wind; goats were bleating behind their fence, a blackbird singing from the branches of a hawthorn, and I lifted the cloth to see what I was carrying.

There was hard cheese, soft cheese, a whole side of ham; four pottery jars, sealed with wax. There were carrots, apples, walnuts and small cakes squeezing between the bottles, almost spilling over they were crammed so full. One basket had a notebook, a quill and some ink; in the other, a small prayer book. I replaced the cloths, lifting the baskets back on to my arms. I was halfway there; the sky was darkening, the air growing cooler.

Private Mallory held out his hands and ushered me forward. 'My dear Miss Martha, 'tis a heavy load, so it is. We thought you'd not be back again tonight. Bless my soul, what an angel you are. An angel, sent from God above to comfort the sick and lonely.' He glanced into the basket and I stood in the shadow, biting my lip, hoping the veil on the ugly hat was doing its job. I handed him a bottle and he stroked it appreciatively. 'From Portugal, I see – like the last one. Well, there's a treat for an old man. 'Tis a lovely evening, so it is, but mind there's a chill in the air – you wrap up, lass, lest you catch cold.' He smiled again. 'No need for paperwork – I'll see you get signed in.'

I had no idea my heart could beat so fast. The sky had darkened to deep mauve, the sea still lit with streaks of fire. At the castle gate Private Evans smiled, anticipating my pleasure, holding Lily aloft, and I put down the baskets, taking her from him. I held her to my lips, kissing her soft head and she mewed in my hands. 'How's my lovely Lily?' I whispered, looking down at my baskets. 'Will you have something against the chill of the night, Private Evans?'

He laughed his wheezy laugh, shaking his head, a secret tap directing me to the flask in his pocket. 'I've still a drop or two left – whiskey eases my joints better than wine. Give it to them downstairs – they do all the hard work, I just get to sit and admire the sunset.' He stared across the sea to the ships just visible in the fading light. His voice turned wistful. 'And a beautiful sunset it's been. It's not home, but it'll do very well.'

Once more down the spiralling stone staircase, the stench of confined air growing stronger with every step. It was not fear making my heart race, but excitement, anticipation: the thrill I felt when I slipped from the window to climb the tree; when I watched the badgers playing in the moonlight; when I went to the theatre; when I stood in the moonlit garden, talking to Henry Trevelyan. I would find this man. I would find this man and save my brother.

The guards straightened when they saw me; each of them with white hair and stiff joints, or amputated legs or fingers. Each invalided out of service and retained on low pay – a Company of Invalids guarding the only fortress capable of defending Falmouth against enemy invasion. My liking for them all had long turned to fondness, but George Godwin was right. They were too frail.

They unlocked the heavy door, clutching their bounty, and I made my way past George's locked room. Henry's door was open and he looked up from his pile of papers, grabbing his jacket from behind his chair, following me along the ill-lit corridor to the old kitchen with its pointed brick arches and central Tudor rose. A line of trestle tables stretched along the middle of the room, long benches down either side. Lamps were burning against the curved stone walls, the soldiers playing cards round a guttering candle. They stopped when they saw me, rising stiffly from their chairs to make me welcome.

'Miss Martha, we thought you weren't comin'.' They

took my baskets, heaving them on to the trestle table, lifting the cloths with a smile. Almost at once, the remaining two bottles vanished from sight. 'I'll get Mr Trevelyan. Oh, ye're there, sir! John, bring up the prisoners.'

I thought I might retch from the stench. The air was thick and choking, no breeze blowing through the bars of the high window above. Smoke from the guards' pipes hung in the air, making it impossible to breathe. Buckets of water stood in a row beside an alcove and I knew that must be the latrine. As bad as the tannery, as bad as anything I had ever smelled, yet I had to act as if it were familiar, as if I had done this twice a week for the last three weeks.

Two guards began lifting up a central hatch and I could see slatted wooden steps leading down to a dimly lit cellar. Rooms branched to both sides, hammocks hanging from the ceiling. Men were stretching, rolling off their hammocks, their haunted eyes looking up through the hatch – eyes like caged animals – and bile rose in my throat. They began fastening their boots, making their way up the wooden steps, and shivers of disgust ran down my back. My cheeks burned with shame, tears stinging my eyes, and I turned to stop myself from crying. No one should be kept like this. No one. It was immoral and cruel. It was against a man's dignity – against humanity.

Henry Trevelyan was beside me, watching me as the men gathered round. Some swilled their faces in the water from the buckets, running their wet hands through their hair. Others shuffled towards the table, scraping back the bench to sit down, their shoulders hunched.

'How could you treat them like this?' I hissed.

'I don't like it either, but it's the best I can do. They can wash and they've access to the best medical care. They've plenty to eat and I see to it that they have fresh air daily. Their conditions are as good as I can make them.' He lifted back the cloths of the baskets, placing the contents on the table in front of him. He reached for his pocket knife, cutting round the wax seals. 'I need to check there's nothing in these pots – they may try to smuggle in knives, or a compass.'

The men sat glaring from under bushy brows. They were dark skinned, swarthy, dressed in an assortment of charity clothes. Their hair looked lank, but brushed, tied behind their necks or swept back from their faces. Most of them were bearded, a handful of youths among men mostly in their forties. Burly sailors who longed to be back at sea, the eighteen prisoners who had dug a tunnel out of Kergilliack in the hope of escape.

Henry finished examining one pot of jam, replacing the cork lid before opening the second. A tall, stooped man with heavy tattoos on his forearms smiled and bowed. 'Zank you, Mees Martha,' he said, beginning to distribute the food equally between the eighteen pewter plates the guards had laid out. Henry flicked through the blank pages of the notebook, searching the quill, holding the glass ink jar up to the candle.

'Have there been any fights, or incidences? Have you any complaints or requests? Monsieur Grimmald?' Henry asked.

'*Non*. Everything *fine*.' He nodded, bowing once again as he left to take his place at the table.

'They've already had their supper. They spend an hour playing cards or doing their marquetry and then they go below.' My heart was crying, yet his voice held the same dislike. 'It looks awful but this is humane and civilized compared to what our men can expect. I don't randomly choose to behead someone – nor do I beat them, nor lock them in cramped conditions without food and water for a week. Prison is punishment enough; constant fear of torture and death is inhumane. We must maintain our humanity at all costs. Never stoop to cruelty.'

He turned the basket over, checking the base. 'Sir Alex is doing everything in his power to build clean, efficient prisons to ensure the men have access to fresh air and exercise, but in the meantime, hulks and cellars are needed to take the load off our overcrowded gaols – and cramped cellars like this one.'

Handing me a basket, his voice dropped. 'Monsieur Grimmald will make a note of who puts what in your basket and then you usually say a prayer with them and leave. I'll tell them you've a sore throat. Perhaps you should sit by the door.'

They made short work of the food, licking the jam from their fingers. Monsieur Grimmald washed out the empty pot and put it in his pocket, smiling at his new acquisition; a pottery jar with the outline of a snow goose painted on it – the perfect receptacle for his new quill. A prisoner stepped forward, holding up a delicately crafted straw hat.

'This is very fine indeed,' Henry said, trying it on. 'Will you make one for me – only a little bigger?' He smiled. '*Un peu plus grand, pour moi, s'il vous plaît, monsieur?*'

With the collected work in the basket, Henry stood beside me. 'Miss Selwyn has a sore throat…I think she should go …perhaps one of you might read the prayer?' The looks of concern turned to rumbles of disquiet, the men shaking their heads, obviously wishing me well, and I held my handkerchief to my nose, following Henry through the door. The key turned in the lock behind us and he put his hand on my arm, ushering me along the corridor. 'Are you all right? They thought you were her – they all did. You did well.' He stopped to pick up his coat and hat. 'I'll just let Captain Fenshaw know I'm going.'

He knocked on George Godwin's door. 'Who is it?'

'It's Henry, Captain Fenshaw.' The lock turned, the door opening a fraction, barred by a heavy chain. Through the narrow gap, I saw George Godwin's desk piled high with papers. 'I'm leaving for an hour or two – it's all quiet.'

The heavy door remained jammed against its chain, Captain Fenshaw's red sleeve just visible through the gap. 'Very well, I'll check in an hour.' The door shut, the key turned, and Henry pulled on his coachman's coat with the heavy capes, the familiar well-oiled hat pulled low to hide his face. 'We won't walk together. You go first – I'll be right behind you. The ferry leaves from Fish Quay – do you know where that is?'

I nodded.

'Good. You'll need money – the fare's no more than a penny, though he'll ask for two.' He reached into his pocket, rattling some coins. 'Take this. I'll get into the same boat but we won't talk.'

Chapter Thirty-one

Ships lined the quay, the lanterns hanging from their decks casting shadows in the rigging above me. Sheltered from the wind, the sea lay silent, glinting like black glass beneath the half-moon. Stars filled the night sky, the smell of distant woodsmoke; across the water, the notes of a lone fiddle echoed from the frigate moored along Greenbank.

The taverns spewed out sailors too drunk to stand, a fight taking place on the quayside, and I walked quickly along the cobbles, searching the gaps between the hulls for signs of the ferry. The church clock struck eleven and I turned to see Henry only fifty yards behind me. A group of people were standing in the glow of an oil lamp, shadows flickering across their hats and faces, and through the half-light I saw a flight of steps and heard the splash of oars.

I took my place in silence, nodding to the ferryman who held out his hand to help me into the heavy rowing boat. A few nods, a few smiles, but most of my fellow travellers looked exhausted, as if another day's work had taken its toll.

Henry slipped to my side, sitting next to me, sombre and silent like the rest of them, and I held up my penny without saying a word. Some of the women clutched heavy bundles, others held empty baskets; all of them looked drawn and tight-lipped. The men hunched forward, their foreheads resting in their hands as the ferryman slipped his rope, gliding us out into the black sea.

Lights shone in the windows of the newly built terraces, the new streetlamps lighting the carriages waiting in lines outside the grander houses. Lamps were burning against the Fox warehouse, watchmen with chained dogs patrolling the quayside, and I pulled my hood further over my bonnet, staring up at the name of the adjacent ship – *Guillemot*, the lugger that would take me back to Truro.

There must have been ten naval ships in port; huge ships of the line, their black hulls merging with the black water, their gold stripes catching the light from the lantern hanging from our prow. The lights of Flushing harbour were growing nearer, the slipway fast approaching, and I could see Henry stiffen. His collar was raised, his hat pulled low over his face, fine stubble shadowing his chin. He looked strained, nervous, yet it was excitement I was feeling, not fear. I had the whistle clasped in my fist, and I knew Henry had brought handcuffs. No doubt his pistol was concealed beneath the layers of his coachman's capes.

The Ferry Inn stood just yards from the slipway, light shining through the small lattice windows, and I knew to go straight through the door without looking round. Tobacco smoke stung my eyes, the heat like a furnace. I made my way past the boisterous men, searching for a table by the back door. A place was laid, a wine glass standing ready, and I sat down at the end of the bench, my baskets on the table in front of me. A number of men turned to stare and I searched their faces but it was too dark to see if anyone fitted the description.

Henry stood against the taproom bar, nodding to the man beside him. The landlord was red-faced and bald-headed, drying a pewter tankard with a cloth, turning the tap on the barrel. The men who had stared at my arrival turned back to their ale and I settled against the hard wooden bench, trying to stop my heart from hammering. A woman in a tight bodice and large mobcap saw me and smiled. She made her way towards me, holding aloft a plate and jug of wine.

'Pie an' wine fer ye, my love,' she said, wiping her brow with the cloth hanging from her apron. ''Tis that hot in here, but he likes it like that fer they drink more. Yer friend left a message – said he'd be along soon. Ye just sit tight an' enjoy that rabbit.' She smiled and turned and I stared down at the huge crust of pie with carrots and cabbage spilling from the plate.

Henry must have ordered food. He made his way round the tables, sitting nearest the back door. His hat and coat made him merge with the crowd but even so, he looked out of place. He was sitting slumped forward, his arms on the table, his elbows wide, but there was no hiding his manners. No hiding the charm with which he thanked the landlord's wife, the elegant way he unfolded his napkin, the shy nod to his fellow diners as he began his meal and I looked away.

I glanced back. He seemed somehow vulnerable, a rather charming man doing the wrong job.

Any other circumstances — any other time or place — and I would have enjoyed his company. I would have enjoyed dining with him, enjoyed discussing his choice of poetry, asked him what he had done in America, how his mother was…which of my plays he had liked the most. I pushed my plate away untouched. He was my brother's gaoler, yet no man drew me so completely. It was as if I became alive in his presence. The touch of his hand on my cheek making my heart beat faster.

Sweat trickled down my back, the tight wig making my hair itch. I wanted to take off my cloak but no woman would sit in a tavern in a prudish grey gown with stiff white collar and cuffs and I pulled the cloak tighter. Henry had finished his meal and was stretching back against the hard bench, cradling his jar of ale in both hands. He was staring straight ahead as if too tired to talk, yet the moment the man took my baskets, he would clasp him in handcuffs.

The tavern slowly emptied, only a number of men left scattered among the tables. Thin curls of smoke coiled from the guttering candles, the room growing darker. Two men had fallen asleep on their folded arms, two others staring moodily into their empty pint pots. Martha Selwyn had said the man could keep her waiting for hours; it must only have been an hour, yet it seemed so much longer. I glanced at Henry and caught my breath. He was staring at me so intently, the ferocity in his eyes making my heart jolt. I had never been looked at like that before. It felt like pain. Like my body was on fire.

'Had all ye want, my love?' The landlady was frowning at my full plate.

'Yes, thank you. It was lovely but I've very little appetite. Do you…that is…did he say *when* he was coming?'

'Don't ye worry, my love – he'll be here.' She smiled, picking up my plate. 'Course ye're not hungry. Ye just sit tight – he'll come.'

Behind the bar, the large oak clock struck twelve and two more men shuffled to their feet. Henry's ale remained untouched, the sudden drumming of his fingers making my stomach tighten. I caught his glance and ice chilled my heart. He looked furious. He walked abruptly to the landlady who was wiping tables by the window. She shook her head at his question but he reached into his pocket and put a coin on the table. She drew him to the window and at her words he turned, frowning back at me through the dim light.

'It's a hoax,' he snapped, grabbing the baskets. 'The landlady's never seen you before…no woman ever sits here. A man came in earlier and paid for your meal – he said you were eloping and told her to feed you well. We've been tricked.'

'Why bring us all the way here?'

He was clearly shaken. 'Why make us wait? Why such an elaborate hoax?'

A crowd was gathering outside the door – the sound of shouting. The landlady looked up, peering through the window. 'Jesu, will ye look at that!'

Henry grabbed my hand and we ran to the door. High on the promontory a fire was blazing, huge orange flames lighting the night sky. Loud booms blasted across the harbour, bright streaks of light shooting above the castle. Church bells began tolling and Henry's grip tightened. 'Quick – the ferry's leaving.'

The smell of cordite grew stronger. The ferry scraped along the quayside and we leapt from the side, joining the crowd rushing up to the castle. Ahead of us, torches bobbed along the path, a long snake of people carrying buckets up the hill. Some were sailors but most were townsfolk, their coats thrown over their nightclothes, their boots hastily tied.

I had to stop, gripping the stitch in my side. 'I'm so sorry.'

'No, it's all right – catch your breath.'

Shouts passed down the hill: ''Tis the munitions gone up – the whole bloody lot.'

'Not an invasion – they've blown the munitions.'

My bonnet was slipping and I pulled it off, catching the fury in Henry's eyes. There was no need for words. They had set this up. Whoever they were, we had fallen headlong into their trap.

The gatehouse bridge was blocked with people crushing forward and Henry shouted, 'Make way – officer coming through. Make way – officer-in-charge coming through.' A soldier I had not seen before was directing men to form a chain. Sweat dripped from his face, black smears streaking across his cheeks. 'We've used up the water tanks – there's only the moat left.'

'How much has gone up?'

Another man stepped forward. 'The store's gone – there's

no savin' it.' He was stripped to the waist, his chest glistening. He began coughing violently, hardly able to speak. 'The straw must've caught and set the munitions off behind…Bloody idiots not stacking it properly – they had it under canvas… with the powder right behind.' He coughed again. 'For Christ sake – keep everyone the other side.'

Henry shouted to a man behind him, 'Keep everyone the other side of the bridge – there could be more explosions.' He pointed to a tall, burly man. 'You – don't let anyone across the bridge – direct everyone to the *right* away from the buildings. There's water in the moat to the *right*.' He pointed to another man. 'You – stop anyone entering the gates – we've enough men now, we just need water. Form the chain to the right.' He turned back. 'Can anything be saved?'

The man with the smeared cheeks shook his head. 'The barrack's gone – 'twas old an' rotten…went up like tinder.'

'Have all the munitions blown?'

'What was in the barrels – the rest's safe underground. Who stacks straw next to gunpowder? Idiots, the bloody lot!'

Through the arch, we could see flames licking the charred remnants of the brick building, the tarpaulins and straw burned to cinders. 'Where's Captain Fenshaw?'

'No sign of him. No sign of any of them – there's only half the men here that should be…to the right, sir – no women. Best get the women home. No bloody sign of him.'

Henry turned and I caught the panic in his eyes. 'Where's Private Mallory?'

I felt sick with fear, running through the side door of the gatehouse, almost too scared to look. A single candle burned on the desk, Private Mallory slumped awkwardly in his chair. His lips looked blue in the half-light. 'Henry – he's having a seizure – help me get him to the floor.' Henry put his hands beneath his arms and we lifted him down. 'He's blue – he's not breathing – put him on his side.'

He was a dead weight as we rolled him over, and we stood willing him to breathe. He took a sudden gulp of air and the duskiness left his face. He breathed again, a heavy snore.

'Stay with him, Angelica – I'll get someone to go for Luke.'

I cradled Private Mallory's head in my hands, trying to rouse him. 'Wake up, Mr Mallory. Wake up.' I lifted the lid of one of his eyes and my heart froze: a fixed black pupil stared vacantly back at me.

Henry stood at the door. 'We're in luck – Luke's already here. I've sent him a message to come as soon as he can.' He stopped. A wine goblet lay upturned on the floor, the empty bottle lying on the desk, and his mouth hardened. He rushed to the adjacent door and pushed it open. 'Angelica – there are more in here.'

Three guards lay slumped across the table, their empty wine glasses lying where they had fallen, and I ran to help him as he lifted them to the ground. 'They're breathing – but only just.' We worked fast; none of them was rousable, each staring back at us with fixed black pupils. 'The wine must have been bad...I gave them bad wine.'

Henry's eyes froze mine. 'The wine wasn't bad – it was drugged. Who else had it?'

I could hardly breathe. 'The prison guards – all of them.'

Chapter Thirty-two

Smoke caught my eyes as we raced across the field. The inner gate was deserted, an ominous silence confirming our fear. The portcullis was open, the door gaping wide. A man lay slumped on the ground and I ran towards him, recognizing his white hair at once.

'Private Evans, wake up.'

He lay awkwardly, a dark patch glistening on the ground beside him, and I screamed in terror.

Blood was seeping through his uniform, his glazed eyes staring up at me, and I fell to my knees, cradling him in my arms. His head lolled backwards and I laid him softly to the ground. Henry crouched beside me.

'A knife in his back – the coward's way to kill.' His voice caught. 'What have I done? Dear God, what have I done?'

Tears streamed down my cheeks, my chest so tight, I could hardly breathe. Private Evans' astonished eyes were staring at me, blood oozing from the corner of his mouth. He looked so fragile, his white hair soft against my shaking hands. Taking out my handkerchief, I closed his eyes, laying it across his face, terror now taking the place of fear. I would have to walk down those steps. Walk into my brother's cell. Henry's hand was firm on my shoulder. 'Stay here. I'll go below. You stay here – I'll come back…'

'No – I need to come.' There was blood on my hands, blood on my cloak. 'I must go to Edgar…' The words caught in my throat and I ran, spiralling down the steps, dizzy with fear. The heavily barred door lay open, two guards slumped beside it. Henry ran his hands over their jackets. 'No wounds – they're breathing but only just.' In the dim light, their lips looked purple, their breathing rasping.

'Loosen their collars.' Their tongues were swollen, blocking their breathing. 'Get them on their sides – they're going to choke.' It seemed to help, their terrible rasping turning to deep breaths. Two empty goblets lay on the ground next to them.

'I should have thought – why didn't I think?'

More laboured breathing filled the corridor and we ran to the inner gate, knowing what we would find. The gate stood wide open, two more guards slumped awkwardly against the wall. 'Get them flat.'

We turned them quickly, freeing their collars, my eyes searching the corridor. The door to George's room was shut but Henry's door was wide open, the eerie silence making my heart pound. Henry walked ahead of me, holding up a lantern, the shadows flickering across the damp walls. At once we saw the empty cells. 'Both gone…Where's Captain Fenshaw?'

317

A terrible groan echoed through the stillness; a hoarse intake of breath, the sound of clattering, and we ran through the open door to the Tudor kitchen with its pointed arches. Three guards were slumped over the table, their arms dangling by their sides, the hunched figure of Captain Fenshaw staring vacantly back at us. He was dazed, trying to raise himself, spittle oozing from his mouth, thick vomit coating his jacket.

'Here, let us help you.' Henry reached forward as Captain Fenshaw fell heavily to the floor. 'Captain Fenshaw, wake up.' He shook him vigorously, 'Wake up…'

Deep snores resonated round the room and Henry felt in Captain Fenshaw's jacket, bringing out a long chain with no keys attached. The central hatch was open, the slatted wooden steps leading down to empty hammocks. My fear was turning to panic. 'Where's Edgar? Why isn't he here?'

Henry stripped off his coat, his white shirt catching the candlelight. He picked up the fallen goblet, smelling the contents. 'Prisoners are never given alcohol.'

'Then why's he gone?' Fear made me feel faint, the blood rushing from my head. 'Why free him? They could have just left him.'

'They've taken the guards' muskets, Angelica – they probably forced him to go with them.' He looked up, the kindness in his eyes making my tears flow.

'He's not part of this – Henry, you must believe that.'

'I don't know what to believe. One certain death, and who knows if the others will live. Private Evans must have been awake – that's why they killed him.'

My heart ripped inside me, the pain almost unbearable; the dear, sweet man contentedly sipping his whiskey, watching the sun go down. 'He didn't have any wine – he said whiskey was better for his joints.'

'We'll find them, Angelica. We'll find the prisoners. We'll find the man who killed Private Evans.' He held up the empty chain. 'But why take Captain Fenshaw's keys – the gates were wide open and the fire distraction enough to prevent them from being seen?'

'Would they risk that if they could use a tunnel? Half of them are dark-skinned – they don't speak English. They'd stand out as different.' My heart hammered. I knew what he was about to say.

'Someone *inside* the castle must be behind this. Hardly anyone knows about the tunnel. There are only two keys: Captain Fenshaw's and mine. Martha must have been looking for the entrance the day I arrested her.'

I felt sick with fear. 'Henry – what if Edgar saw who it was? What if they took him because...because...they couldn't leave him...?' I covered my face with my hands.

He came to my side and for a moment I thought he would put his arm round my shoulder. He seemed to hesitate, his voice soft. 'If they were going to kill him, they'd have done it here – stabbed him like Private Evans. Either he's one of them or they're using him in some way.'

'He's *not* one of them, Henry. Edgar's innocent – we have to find him.'

'We'll find them – but they've got muskets and they won't hesitate to use them.' He rushed to his desk, grabbing a piece of paper, dipping his pen in the ink. 'I'll enlist Major Basset's help – and I need a naval commander.'

My courage was returning. 'Admiral Penrose is in port... HMS *Circe* is anchored opposite Greenbank – if he's not there, he'll be at their lodgings...I heard Mrs Penrose say it was somewhere near Mary's. Direct them to Mary. She'll know.'

He reached for another piece of paper, writing neatly despite his urgency. 'I'll send letters to both places. The fact they've used the tunnel narrows the search. Someone will have seen them. They'll have had a rowing boat waiting but they won't risk rowing to France – they'll be hiding along the coast. My guess is they've headed for the harbour. The plan's so well executed I believe there'll be a ship waiting and ready to sail.' He sealed the letters, the wax still dripping. He looked up in sudden horror. 'George! Angelica, we've forgotten George! Quick.'

The door was locked and Henry peered through the tiny grille. 'George...George – are you in there?' He banged loudly. 'I can't see through the grille, something's in the way.'

In the dim light, deep gouges pitted the door frame, fragments of jagged splinters where the wood had been split. 'They've battered the lock – look, they've tried to force the door.'

'The door's impossible to force. They had the key but thank God George always keeps his key on the inside – with his key in place no one can open it from the other side.' He peered through the grille again. 'It's barred from within and he'll have the chain across…it seems he's got it barricaded – there's a lamp burning but no sound.'

'He could be drugged.'

'Captain Fenshaw was with him – he must have taken the wine in.' He banged on the door again, stopping to put his ear against the grille.

'No wait – if George has barricaded himself in he must have known he was in danger. He must have done it *after* Captain Fenshaw left.'

'Of course.' Henry banged on the door again, shouting against the grille. 'George, it's Henry. You're quite safe. Look through the grille and you'll see it's me.' The faintest scraping could be heard and Henry whispered, 'Don't let him see you.'

I slipped to one side, watching from the shadows as something glinted in the dim light – the barrel of a pistol shook against the grille. George was sobbing, his voice unrecognizable. 'I'll shoot. Don't think I won't shoot. I'll shoot the lot of you. I'll…I'll—' The sobs grew louder, his petrified crying wrenching my heart.

Henry's voice was soft yet firm. 'You're safe, George – you've done well, very well. Put your barricade back exactly as it was and stay vigilant. They've gone but they might come back. I'll send someone to stand guard outside but *don't* open the door until you see Major Basset's men. Can you manage that?' The petrified sobs grew louder, the pistol shaking more violently. 'Another hour at the most, George – be brave a bit longer.'

He turned. 'We need to hurry.' He started running down

the corridor and I followed on his heels. At the foot of the steps he stopped. 'Do you have the whistle?' I nodded, reaching in my cloak, handing it to him. 'I'll find someone to take these letters. Luke will see to the men.'

We spiralled up the steps and into the night air. Across the field men were standing in groups, directing the last of the buckets to the glowing embers in the courtyard. Henry held up his pocket watch. 'Two o'clock. The tide turns in two hours. We'll need a list of all the ships in the harbour. If they've reached a ship, they'll be hiding below deck waiting to catch the tide.'

He blew the whistle, long sharp blasts piercing my ears, and as men came running, I knelt against the still body of Private Evans, knowing I must search his jacket. There was a tiny movement, the faintest mewing, and I pulled Lily from his inside pocket. She was matted with congealed blood, cold and barely moving, and I cradled her in my hands, slipping her into the deep pocket of my cloak. I would take her home. I would love her, cherish her, give her everything Private Evans would have wanted: a warm fire, a soft bed, a plate brimming with Molly's fine cooking. Lily Evans would forever remind me of this dear man who had showed everyone such kindness.

Chapter Thirty-three

Falmouth Harbour
Sunday 14th August 1796, 3:00 a.m.

The freshening breeze blew against my cheek, the half-moon glinting on the black sea. A grey haze lit the sky to the east and I breathed the heavy scent of gorse, the thyme and camomile crushing beneath my feet.

'If they're rowing round to the harbour, I think they're most likely to pull in somewhere right below us and continue on foot. My guess is they'll swap to a smaller boat and row out to an anchored ship.'

The stars were bright, the black outlines of the cliffs silhouetted against the night sky. 'Mightn't that take too long? Wouldn't rowing a boat back and forth to an anchored ship draw too much attention? Wouldn't it be safer to make their way to a ship moored alongside a quay? Most of the lamps on the quayside have gone out – and it's still dark enough for them to go unseen.'

For all his bookish looks, Henry was agile and strong, running without losing breath, his movements quick and lithe. He wore no hat, his chin poised in the air, as if he were trying to hear above the sound of the waves.

'Wait here,' he whispered, striding to a gate, vaulting it with ease, standing dangerously close to the cliff's edge, and I climbed the gate behind him, standing by his side. He smiled, pointing through the half-light to a huge rock jutting out to the sea.

'Perhaps you're right. There are too many rocks until that point but I remember seeing a small stretch of shingle. I think it's the only place they could pull in.'

I put my hand on his arm, peering down the cliff. I could hear the gentle splash of the waves, the rolling of the shingle. 'Why did they take Edgar with them? Henry, I'm scared – what if we find…? What if he's no longer useful to them and they…?'

He took my hand, leading me back to the gate, climbing it, holding up his arms to catch me as I jumped. His hands clasped my waist, strong and reassuring. 'We'll go to that stretch of sand – they may not be that far ahead of us.'

You who are so fearless. I had never felt such fear. I could hardly breathe; I thought I might be sick. He reached for my hand again.

'When he gets my note, Admiral Penrose will block the harbour – and I've asked Major Basset to split his men between the castle and the quays. If Edgar's with them, then you must brace yourself, but he may have run. He may have found his way out through the gatehouse.'

His grip was firm, leading me down the path. A brambled opening led from the right and we braved the thorns, cutting steeply down the hillside, skirting the boulders and hawthorns where the path disappeared. We were almost at sea level, a six-foot drop, and Henry jumped to the shingle, holding up his arms to catch me. A heavy rowing boat lay wedged against the rocks, eight oars still locked in place. A narrow strip of sand glistened with froth, indentations of heavy footprints slowly filling with water.

Henry searched the rowing boat. 'It must be theirs...he's not here,' and I fought my tears of relief. I had expected to find Edgar stabbed, to cradle him in my arms.

The sand was wet, sinking beneath our feet, and Henry's frown mirrored my fear. 'The tide's coming in. We're going to get trapped – quick...round here – over these rocks.'

The water was cold, well above my ankles, and I grabbed my skirts, lifting them high. Lily was safe in my pocket and I scrambled over the slimy kelp swaying around my feet. The rocks were jagged in parts, encrusted with limpets, the smell of dried seaweed mixing with the smell of rotting wood. A half-submerged tree lay across our path and Henry held out his hands, helping me over the smooth grey trunk.

A small shack stood on higher ground, the smell of burning charcoal, and Henry tested the branch of an over-hanging tree. 'The tide's coming in too fast – if I help you up, can you crawl to the end?' He cupped his hands and I tucked my skirts higher, my shoe held firmly in his grasp. I pushed off with a spring, reaching for the branch, clinging to it before hoisting myself up. It dipped but stayed firm and I caught my balance, inching my way slowly along. Henry waited for me to reach the trunk and jumped, catching the branch, dangling for a moment before wedging his arms and drawing up his legs.

'I somehow guessed you'd be able to climb trees,' he said as I skilfully negotiated my way to the ground. His eyes were warm, tender, full of approbation as he took my hand again.

A path led from the shack and we ran along the water's edge, reaching a slipway where rusting chains lay heaped in coils. Through the darkness we saw a hunched figure of a man and I cried out with joy. I could not see the colour of his jacket but I knew it would be green. His hair was tousled, his mass of black curls falling across his face, and sudden panic gripped me. Edgar seemed to be convulsing, his hands held rigidly in front of him.

'Stay back – leave me alone.' His glare was angry, the anguish in his voice echoing across the water. 'Stay back, Henry – for Christ sake stay back.' He began sobbing violently, his eyes blazing. 'Go away! Go away, you wicked, wicked woman. Haven't you done enough?'

'No, Edgar – it's me…it's Angelica. I'm wearing a wig …I'm helping Henry.' He was shaking violently, running his hands through his hair. 'Edgar, you're safe. You're safe. It's just me and Henry – no one's going to harm you.' The curls on his forehead were damp with sweat and even in the darkness I saw the unnatural flush to his cheeks. He was breathing heavily, as if he had been running. 'Edgar – are you hurt? Did you drink the wine?' He looked up and the torment in his eyes made me catch my breath. He looked haunted, petrified, a dribble of saliva pooling at the side of his mouth.

'Christ, Angelica. You've no idea the agony I'm in,' he

moaned, clutching his stomach. I dropped to my knees. Tears were rolling down his cheeks and I put my hands over his. He snatched them away. 'Don't. Don't. For Christ sake, go away. Leave me alone.'

I watched his shaking shoulders, fear ripping through me. 'What are you holding in your hands? Edgar, answer me. What is it you don't want us to see?'

He pulled himself away, standing up, making a run for the path that would lead him to the harbour, but Henry was too fast, grabbing him round the waist, hauling him back to stand in front of me.

'Answer your sister, Edgar.'

Held in such a grasp, Edgar's shoulders slumped. He opened his clenched fist and a small glass vial glinted in the half-light. His fingers widened to an open palm and I could see the cork was still firm, the contents undrunk.

'Give that to me,' I shouted.

He snatched his hand closed again, clutching it against his chest, and Henry let him go.

'Who gave you that, Edgar?'

Edgar's hands were shaking. 'The woman in the prison. She opened the door to my cell and put it straight into my hand. She said if I went with them I'd live, but if I stayed, I'd be killed.' He cried out, a terrible, plaintive howl, his face twisting in agony, his cheeks flushing deeper. 'It's the worst pain you can imagine – like rats gnawing my stomach…the craving's so deep – so, so, deep. It's consuming me. I can smell it…I can taste it…it's in my hand and I need it so badly.'

'No. You don't need it. Give it to me – Edgar, give it to

327

me. *Now.*' I grabbed his arm, pulling his hands towards me. I would bite, I would scratch. I would get it and destroy this terrible poison that was destroying my brother. 'Edgar – I mean it. Give it to me – *this instant.*'

I felt my arms gripped, Henry pulling me forcefully away. 'Stand back, Angelica. This is Edgar's choice. It's his life – it has to be his decision.' He swung me round, my head against his shoulder. To see my brother like that; I wanted to shake him, hit him, force him to hand it over, but Henry held me tight, the tears flowing down my cheeks. Hurt, fear, disappointment, this would never go away; this terrible addiction would keep my brother in its grip. Henry's voice was as firm as his arms.

'The choice is yours, Edgar. Either you take it or you throw it into the sea.'

'Henry! Take it from him.' I tried to break free but Henry held me tighter.

'No, Angelica. It's Edgar's decision. From now on, he'll face this dilemma every day of his life – every day he'll have to choose whether to give in or to fight.' His grip tightened, his voice softening. 'And each time he throws the vial away will make the next time easier. It's the only way.'

The strength of his arms, the strength of his voice; I could feel my courage return and I nodded, standing firmly by his side. Edgar stared at the vial in his open palm and I had never wished so fervently. *Finders keepers*, the stone with the hole I had picked up from the beach: I had threaded it with ribbon and was wishing on it now, wishing and praying that my brother would choose life.

His cry pierced my ears. His hand drew back, his body stumbling forward as he flung the vial far out to sea and I ran to hold him but he pushed me off, straightening himself with stiff lips.

Henry stepped forward holding out his handcuffs. 'Will you walk by my side of your own free will, Edgar, or must I cuff you?'

Edgar seemed to be growing stronger, his shoulders straightening, his chin held higher. 'Of my own free will. Find her, Henry. Find that woman and bring her to justice.'

'I intend to, Edgar. Did you recognize anyone? Who was with them? Who led the prisoners through the tunnel? Was it one of the guards?'

'No one led us.' He ran his hands through his hair; they were still shaking but his voice was stronger. 'The woman unlocked my cell – the prisoners were already halfway down the corridor...They had the guards' muskets and I thought they were going to kill me. I didn't see a guard – nor anyone else. The woman led us to a turret – there was a deep stair-well and a gate. The guards were asleep. The woman was ahead of us. She waited for us all to go through then she locked the gate behind us.'

'*Locked* it behind you?'

'There was no going back, Henry – we had to go on. There was no light – the tunnel was treacherous...it was wet and several slipped and fell – one quite badly. Some caught themselves on a sharp rock but we reached the sea and a boat was waiting on the sand – two boats, in fact, but there were only oars in one.'

'Are you sure there wasn't a guard leading you? How did they know which way to go?'

'No guard, Henry – I can assure you, but they knew to row to the left. My French is adequate enough to understand most of what they said. They knew a ship was waiting for them – they were to leave on the tide.'

'Which ship? What's the name of the ship?'

'No ship was named. I heard no name.'

'Edgar, think hard – try to remember.'

'They didn't mention a name – I'm sure of that – but they seemed to know which ship to board.'

Henry replaced the cuffs in his pocket. 'Don't think for one moment I don't understand the enormity of what you've just done, Edgar.' He smiled. 'But just for the record, I believe even if we hadn't chanced upon you, you'd have taken the same action. Stay by my side *at all times* – you're still my prisoner but you now have the chance to turn King's evidence. If you run, you'll be caught and I'll not be able to defend you.'

'I won't run, Henry. I want that woman caught. She's evil. I saw her for who she really was – I'm sure she was the woman in the den. They set me up that night and they expect to frame me for this escape. I'll stay right beside you, I won't run.'

Henry turned as loud barking echoed across the harbour. 'They're using the dogs.'

We started running towards the harbour and Edgar held out his hand, taking mine. 'Angelica?' He stopped, pulling me back, bending over to recover his breath. 'I hardly know you, do I?'

330

I smiled. I hardly knew myself. All I knew was that he was safe and Henry had said he could turn King's evidence. My heart was leaping; I felt like skipping, jumping. Henry believed Edgar was innocent; he was no longer his gaoler, more like his friend.

'Don't tell Luke or Mary,' I said, pulling him to run again, 'and never, ever tell Father.'

Chapter Thirty-four

The riggings jangled in the freshening wind, the hulls rising and falling, the waves getting stronger. The ships beached against the inner harbour were almost afloat, those against the outer quays preparing to leave. Sailors stood stretching and yawning, glancing to the east at the first pink streaks of dawn. A brazier was burning on the slipway of the Ship Inn, the smell of grilled herrings drifting across the harbour. Behind us, the church clock chimed the half-hour.

'There must be forty ships at least…some of them are ready to leave.' Upriver, the sleek black hull of the frigate HMS *Circe* remained anchored, lights dancing on her deck. 'They're getting ready to sail. We're in luck – the wind's shifting.' Henry put the whistle to his lips, piercing the air, catching the attention of the sailors standing by the brazier. 'No ship's to leave,' he shouted, running along the slipway. He pointed to the astonished men. 'You and you – go to Fish Quay – you, go to Greenbank – you, go to Custom House Quay. No ship's to leave. The French prisoners have escaped and they've got muskets — I don't want anyone shot. No one's to try an arrest, is that clear? Tell everyone we're looking for a woman with brown hair and a grey dress.' He pointed to the last two men. 'You and you — go down this quay and tell each ship no one's to leave. I want everyone below or sitting on deck with their hands on their heads. No heroics. No one must get killed. If they try to escape, the navy will follow and fire.'

An echoing whistle sounded behind Custom House; the dogs' barking was loud and vicious, making people turn, and a man called from the inn: 'You need the warning bell. I'll get that rung.'

Henry nodded, shouting to a man leaning against the bulwark of a lugger. 'Pass it ship to ship. Every ship's to be searched. No ship can leave until I say so. Major Basset will start on the other quay. Get lanterns lit — I need light. If the prisoners are sighted, raise the alarm.' His shirt gleamed in the early light. He was tall, commanding, issuing clear instructions, the men jumping to his orders. Word was spreading, shouted from deck to deck as they lay three abreast against the quay.

'Angelica, take off the cloak — and your wig. Where's the bonnet?'

'I don't know. It must have fallen off — perhaps when I jumped?' My hands were trembling. I fitted the exact description of the woman Henry had given them. They would see blood on my cloak and I would be arrested, held by Major Basset's men. They might shoot me if I ran. The wig was tight, gripping my head, and I pulled it off, shaking my hair free. It felt wonderful to be unconstrained and I turned to the cooling breeze, tossing my squashed ringlets to bring them back to life. I looked round. Henry was staring at me, the shadows from the brazier accentuating his high cheek bones and fine structure of his chin, and I stared back, our eyes locking. His gaze was fierce, devouring, and I caught my breath.

A faint mewing brought me to my senses and I slipped off the cloak, reaching in the pocket to press Lily to my lips. She smelled of blood and my stomach sickened. Henry turned away. 'Keep her hidden. Hurry – get aboard *Guillemot* before anyone sees you. I'll search her first so you can leave on time.' He sounded brusque, authoritative. 'I'm sorry you've no escort this time, but the wind's picking up and the tide's fast so you'll make good time. You should be in Truro for twelve, possibly nearer ten. If you don't want to travel alone...'

I matched his sudden brusqueness, the searing pain abating. 'I'm quite happy to travel alone. Just find the man who killed Private Evans – find him and bring him to justice.' Edgar was by my side and I reached up to kiss him. 'I wasn't here tonight, Edgar. I was in Truro – no one must ever know. Promise me you'll not tell Luke or Mary.'

He shook the black curls from his forehead, running his hands over his brow. 'I promise, Angelica. Your secret's safe.' He kissed my hand. 'I don't deserve you...what you've done for me...the fact you'd risk so much...Angelica, I know you think me weak and idle. You think I've let you down and I'm spoiling your chances of a good marriage. But I won't. I promise I won't. I won't shame you. Lord Entworth will not find me lacking as a brother.'

Henry's face stiffened; his mouth tightened. He sounded formal, stony. 'If it's all right by you, Miss Lilly, I'll walk you to the boat. Thank you for your help. I'm grateful, very grateful – I'm sorry for putting you in such danger. Believe me, your safety is paramount. Forgive the liberty I took. I too will never tell anyone you were here. Your secret will remain safe with me – always.'

Seagulls were screeching above us in the cold morning air, the ships' timbers creaking, pulling against the heavy ropes tying them to the quayside. I did not want to leave. I wanted to watch the prisoners caught and marched back to the castle. I wanted to be a witness, tell everyone the truth. I wanted my brother to be freed. Most of all, most terribly, terribly of all, I wanted to stay in the company of Henry Trevelyan.

Word was spreading, men sitting with their hands on their heads watching us from the decks above. We were walking slowly, Henry staring up at each ship. The gangplank was in place, the master of *Guillemot* glowering down at us.

Henry bowed stiffly. 'A safe journey.' He turned to the master. 'Every ship's to be searched – I'll search yours first so as not to delay you.'

The man was huge, his tattooed muscles flexing as he coiled his heavy rope. 'There's no bloody Frenchies on my ship. I'd have had the whole bloody lot of them in the water as soon as look at them.'

'They've got muskets – but I believe you would!'

I walked up the gangplank, breathing in the smell of tar and fish. Crates were stacked neatly against the bulwarks, two members of the crew nodding from beneath their bent arms, and I stared back across the rows of ships, searching the faces of the men. Someone was hiding the prisoners – one of these ships, or one anchored off the quay. I wanted to see Private Evans' killer arrested, handcuffed and brought to justice. Henry went below, the captain shaking his head and scowling, and I breathed in the smell of the fresh fish. The rigging jangled above me, the wind whistling, catching my hair, blowing its salty freshness against my cheek.

Henry raced up the hatch two steps at a time, pausing before descending the plank. He looked strained, no trace of a smile, and I looked away, trying to ease my scalded heart. He seemed suddenly so distant, almost hostile, not a friend at all.

'You'll be away first. That way, no harm can come to you. Thank you for your help, I'm very grateful.' His voice was terse, as if wanting me long gone.

A small lugger was on the outside of a group of three, her hull barely protruding past the others, but I caught the sudden glimpse of white paint against the black hull. Not a name but a bird painted on the side – a white snow goose with her wings outstretched – and the hairs on my arms rose. I had seen that exact goose before.

Henry was at the end of the quay talking to Edgar and I thrust Lily at a sailor, scrambling over the rail, running down the gangplank. 'Henry...Edgar...' They turned and I whispered, 'A ship's moored at the end of the quay with a snow goose painted on her hull. A snow goose...'

'Like the one on the jam pot?' Henry's eyes burned mine. 'That's got to be the ship.' He put out his arms, grabbing me by the waist, swinging me round, and I found myself laughing, squealing like one of the nephews as my hair swung loose. His arms were strong, his shirt open at the neck, rolled to his elbows and I thought my heart would burst. In that instant, I knew I loved him – loved his intellect, his strength; I loved his shyness, his manners, his bookish looks. The way he ate, the way he smiled. The small dimple on his left cheek, the way his eyes crinkled when he laughed. I wanted him to put me down and hold me to him.

He put me down. 'Forgive me.' He bowed formally, holding his whistle to his lips, the sound shrill, urgent and compelling, drawing the whole harbour's attention. 'Edgar…bring Major Basset's men to this quay. Miss Lilly, please return to the ship – get to safety. Stay below deck.'

His shout rang across the harbour. 'Everyone below deck – everyone.'

I hurried down the quayside, forcing back my disappointment. He had been so abrupt, so formal, yet what did I expect? He was doing his duty   his *duty*, nothing more.

I sat wedged against a barrel, hugging my knees, watching the curve of the river as we negotiated the bend round Trenwyn House. Egrets watched us from the lower branches, the beehives visible in the orchard beyond. Sheep were grazing, cattle drinking by the water's edge. The early sun glinted on the house, turning the façade a golden red; smoke was rising from the kitchen chimney, a cockerel crowing, and into my mind came the soft glow of moonlight, the smell of verbena and the scent of roses.

The path had been glinting, tears stinging my eyes. He had spoken softly, sadness in his voice. *The pain of enchantment lingers for ever...I will only ever love one woman — I'll survive without her love, I may even grow prosperous, but she has my heart and I'll not marry anyone else.*

I was Angelica Lilly, used to getting what I wanted. Angelica Lilly, spoilt daughter of an exceptionally wealthy man. I could snap my fingers and people would come running. I could do anything I wanted, have anything I wanted. Anything and everything — except Henry Trevelyan; he made that very clear.

He must have paid well for my passage. A bucket of hot water warmed my feet, a home-spun woollen blanket wrapped around my shoulders. Lily and I had shared a grilled herring, a jug of small beer, an apple and a pear, and I hugged my knees closer, the rhythmical swaying of the ship making me close my eyes.

They had let the ships go, one by one, until only three remained. We had been the first to go and I had watched each ship hoist her sails and leave. HMS *Circe* had her gun ports open, Admiral Penrose standing on deck with his telescope to his eye, yet there had been no cannon fire, just a mass of white and red sails catching the last of the tide, passing Black Rock and out to the English Channel or turning north to drift upriver with the incoming tide.

My tiredness was overwhelming, the gentle rhythm lulling me to sleep. Lily was clean and dry; I would tell Molly and Kitty everything — Grace too, but not Father, nor Amelia nor Lady Clarissa. I pulled the blanket round me like a hood and settled to sleep. The crew knew me as Miss Penrow and there were no other passengers to recognize me. Henry had thought of everything.

The boy in the window, the youth watching my school plays. I remembered him now. I had almost bumped into him that day. He had seemed clumsy and awkward, painfully shy. He had not been wearing his glasses but I remember he was holding them in his hand. Perhaps he had been cleaning them. All that time, Mrs Penhaligan had been looking after me, understanding my heartache; well, my heartache had returned, burning me with its severity.

I loved his seriousness, his flashes of humour – the way he teased me that first night in the garden. He was right, I had felt enchantment – the enchantment of being myself. I had been myself with him right from the start – the real me, no need for a mask, saying what I wanted to say, not biting my lip, scared I might do or say the wrong thing. Our conversation on the ship had left me wanting more – I was almost envious of Edgar, certainly envious of Mary and Luke. I wanted to discuss poetry and philosophy, argue about trade policy long into the night.

I had no idea the pain of longing could hurt so much. I kept my eyes shut, my heart racing. We were in a room, a slight sea breeze blowing the flimsy curtain. Dawn was breaking, the first pink streaks lighting the night sky. His head was resting on his hand, his eyes burning mine. He was smiling and I was smiling back: smiling and smiling. I was the woman in the poem, the lover in his arms.

Chapter Thirty-five

Trenwyn House
Sunday 14th August 1796, 2:00 p.m.

A sudden jolt woke me. I must have fallen asleep because we were already at the gatehouse, swinging left down the long drive to Trenwyn House. I smoothed my gown, checking my bonnet in the reflection of the window. Bethany was with the driver and I was grateful I had slept without being seen. The fields were baking under the heat of the sun, the sky intensely blue and cloudless; a group of cattle stared up at me from under the branches of the spreading oaks and I felt so happy to be back.

It was like coming home, yet how different I felt – a world of difference between this journey and the heady exuberance of my first journey with Amelia. Everything had changed. I had changed. I had been so shallow, seeing everything as a prank – a spoilt child, not the woman I was now.

I heard their shouts before I saw them. The driver pulled hard on the reins and we rumbled to a stop. Young William had Charles in a wheelbarrow, Henry running behind them with a homemade bow. Both had leather pouches brimming with stick arrows, both holding up their bows, ready to shoot.

'*The Procurer* says you're to come with us,' shouted William as Charles tipped out of the wheelbarrow. 'We're to take you to our den. But you mustn't look. Promise you won't look?'

They did not blindfold me but marched me through the cow dung to a coppice of newly planted trees. A tarpaulin hung from ropes suspended from the trunks, woodsmoke drifting from the embers of a stone-ringed fire. Two men stood quickly in greeting, Amelia and Charity smiling broadly.

'You're back – thank goodness for that. We've missed you.' Amelia put down her bow. 'You remember Frederick, don't you? And this is our new guest, Capitaine Pierre de la Croix.'

Of course I remembered Frederick; every girl in school remembered Frederick Carew. We were all in love with him and with good reason too. His youthful good looks may have had us all reaching for our fans, but age had certainly added to his bearing. He was tall, sunburned; even more handsome as he held his son in his arms, the boy's blond hair and blue eyes mirroring his father's.

Captain Pierre de la Croix stood stiffly to attention, his dark hair falling forward as he bowed. He was not in uniform but wore the clothes of an English country squire, his face browned by the sun, etched heavily with lines. He must have been in his late forties, his hair greying, held loosely in place with a black bow at his neck. He had kind eyes, a scar on his cheek, a long nose and bushy black eyebrows. 'My deelight is mine to meet you,' he said, bowing again, his eyes full of bewilderment.

He glanced down and I knew I must join them sitting cross-legged round the fire. Amelia reached for her bow, handing me the curved hazel branch with twine encircling both ends and drew a forked stick from her pouch. 'You've come at just the right time. Here, your job is to keep marauders off.'

I smiled at Pierre de la Croix as his eyes widened. 'Who's *The Procurer?*' I asked.

Frederick looked shocked. 'Never ask that, Miss Lilly – never seek to know. *The Procurer* summons and we obey. Those are the rules.'

Charity was looking lovely in a peach gown, a circlet of flowers framing her blonde hair. 'How was Truro – did you resolve the *boudoir* fabric?'

'Yes…it's all sorted. I've put a stop to it.'

Amelia reached into a large wicker basket. 'Thank goodness for that,' she said, bringing out a bowl and lifting the cloth. She smelled the contents with obvious delight. 'Perfect. Pass the sticks, Frederick. I'm ready.'

Frederick must have scraped the sticks with a knife, stripping each of their bark and pointing them like the arrows. He began handing them to her, one by one, and Captain de la Croix's face fell. Amelia was shaping a soft substance round the tip of each twig. 'I've never seen such *hideous* material,' she said as she handed us each a stick.

Frederick took his, expertly twisting it above the embers of the fire to show us what to do. The green sap hissed, the white goo setting solid as the scent of burned sugar filled the air. 'What is it?' I asked.

'Mallow root – those marsh mallows growing by the lake.

I boil the roots and pulp them, then strain them and let them dry. Then I whip them up with sugar and egg white…quite stiff because they mustn't be too runny…but sometimes I have to add a little water – wait Capitaine de la Croix…it's too hot. You need to let it cool.'

His bewilderment was clearly turning to panic. 'It ees to eat?'

'Indeed it is to eat,' replied Amelia with her most enchanting smile. 'Here, boys, I've done you two each.'

I did not know the French for *radical, free-thinking children brought up in nature* so I just shrugged and smiled in what I hope looked like encouragement. Frederick licked his fingers and reached for his bow. He positioned an arrow, drawing it tightly back. 'Stay very still…over your shoulders… marauders coming. At least ten of them…don't move.' He shot his arrow and behind me I heard the stampede of cattle.

Amelia reached for her bow. 'I've got the others covered. Oh, look – is that Father coming back?' A horse was thundering along the turnpike, a cloud of dust billowing behind it. 'He's been in Falmouth. Oh goodness, Angelica, you won't have heard the news, will you? There was a terrific fire last night…we saw the flames from here. It was on the promontory – it looked like the castle…but not the keep. We think it must have been those old buildings by the gatehouse. Frederick woke because he thought he heard cannon fire – he thought it was an invasion but it was relatively short-lived. Father and William went first thing this morning to see what happened.'

Frederick threw a bucket of sand over the dying fire. 'Father shouldn't gallop at his age. It's dangerous. I thought Mamma forbade it.'

'She does,' replied Amelia. 'You take William, I'll take Charles. Captain de la Croix, would you mind carrying Young Henry?'

He looked relieved, putting down the blackened offering as if given a reprieve. 'My pleasure, Miss Carew – on my back like a horse?' He laughed, obviously trying to get into the spirit of things.

Amelia's smile was bewitching. 'No – on your shoulders, Captain de la Croix, if you wouldn't mind – Henry prefers giraffes.'

Lord Carew summoned us all to the drawing room. Lady Clarissa looked up, catching her reflection in the gilt mirror. She rearranged the two roses in her hair and smiled. 'It can't be that serious if he has time to check Acorn first. That piglet has doubled in size.'

The scent of roses drifted through the open windows, the river sparkling blue in the sun. The children were playing with Jethro on the lawn and I breathed deep for courage. Edgar's identity could not remain hidden for much longer: sooner or later it would come to light. Frederick and Captain de la Croix were standing by the mantelpiece, Charity and Amelia sitting on the chaises longues. 'Here's Papa now.'

Lord Carew had removed his jacket and wig, his trusted red felt hat back in place. He drew out his handkerchief and wiped his forehead, his face more florid than ever. 'A sorry business, I'm afraid. Your compatriots made another dash for freedom last night, Captain de la Croix.'

Frederick swung round. 'Never! Were they captured? Tell me they didn't escape?'

'No they didn't escape. They were captured. A sorry business all round.' He nodded at Captain de la Croix. 'Sir – I appreciate this is hard for you, please sit if you wish. You are our guest and nothing will alter that. This changes nothing – except perhaps that you're safer here than anywhere else at this moment.'

Frederick nodded, indicating a chair to Captain de la Croix who shook his head. 'That fire was part of it, Father? Who caught them? How far did they get?'

'I regret to say they reached the harbour. They were on board a ship waiting to leave.' He shook his head. 'They're claiming complete innocence…they say they knew *nothing* prior to the escape. They said the first thing they knew was when a guard opened the central hatch and handed them weapons.' He shrugged his shoulders. 'They're denying everything – especially the murders.'

'The *murders?*' I whispered.

'I'm afraid so, Miss Lilly. The guards had been drugged – that's how the prisoners made their escape, but one guard was found knifed in the back and I regret to say is dead – but the others seem to be recovering – though some are still having difficulty seeing. I must say Dr Bohenna is a highly proficient man. Knew what to do straight away. '

Amelia sat forward. 'Drugged with what, Papa?'

'I don't know — it was in the wine. Some woman brought it in baskets earlier that night and *gave* it to the guards.'

'*Gave* it? Surely someone must have thought that odd? You don't just walk into a castle and *give* wine to guards…?'

'Precisely, Frederick — that's what they're investigating now. Henry Trevelyan's being questioned. His story doesn't add up.'

'Henry Trevelyan? Don't I know that name?' Lady Clarissa smiled but I had already seen her eyes sharpen. 'Angelica, my dear, wasn't that the name of the coachman who played such excellent cricket?'

I knew not to stutter but my throat was constricting, my heart hammering. 'Yes, I believe it was.'

'It turns out the man wasn't a coachman after all. Strange thing is, he's one of Alex's Foundation Boys — Alex had left him in charge of the prisoners, his one job to keep them from escaping.'

'Poor man — his one job…how very unfortunate. I rather liked him.'

Frederick was pacing the floor, swinging round as if wishing to be in the action. 'Poor man indeed! What was he doing drinking wine, letting them walk free? They reached the harbour, for goodness' sake. No one saw them leave the castle and they reached a ship? It's inconceivable…it's sheer incompetence. Who stopped them?'

'I believe it was Major Basset. He got wind of it — I'm told there was an informer. Another prisoner was being held and he led them straight to the ship. The whole thing's a sorry mess. Three men dead.'

'*Three?*' My heart thumped so fast, I could hardly breathe. '*Three* men murdered?'

'I'm afraid so, my dear. It's a terrible business – the ship's master and first mate knifed as they slept. No one knows their names, nor who owns the ship, but the prisoners swear they didn't do it and they're sticking to their story – all of them. They're adamant they killed no one and knew nothing about the ship. It's a complete shambles. Major Basset wants them all transferred to Lord Falmouth's jurisdiction and says they'll swing for this. Mark my words, they're as good as dead.'

Lady Clarissa took the roses from her hair. 'My dear, you'll have to put a stop to that. They might be innocent. They may be telling the truth.'

'They say a jam pot in the woman's basket had a snow goose etched on it and apparently the same snow goose was painted on a ship in the harbour. The woman's only instruction to them was to head to the nearest quay and board before it got light. They say when they boarded the ship they found the two crewmen dead.'

'How terrible.'

'Stabbed like the guard. Probably the same knife. They'd drunk the wine so they must have been sitting ducks.'

'And we're to believe that?'

'No one knows what to believe. Someone alerted Admiral Penrose and he had his ship positioned, ready to fire, but the whole thing's a complete shambles. They're sailors, yes – but a bunch of French speakers getting a ship ready to sail from a crowded harbour with at least a dozen of His Majesty's best naval commands at hand? They'd never have got away without a crew. They'd have needed the master to sail them out while they stayed below. I'm sorry, Captain de la Croix, would you like Frederick to say all this again in French? I believe you understand English well enough…but do you need a bit of clarification?'

Captain de la Croix nodded and Frederick began answering his questions, seeking facts from Lord Carew, and I fought the nausea rising inside me: *Henry's story did not add up*. They were discussing him again and I reached for my fan. Charity was already using hers, so I hoped my heightened colour did not look amiss.

'Henry Trevelyan *didn't* drink the wine but he allowed it in – without a thought of stopping it. Worst of all, he was on some wild-goose chase – I'm sorry…but that's rather appropriate, wouldn't you say? There's a rumour circulating that he's behind the whole thing. Nothing adds up. He leaves the castle at the exact time everything's about to happen, takes his lady friend who was *dressed* as a Methodist and spends the evening dining with her in an inn in Flushing.'

'The man must be a fool. Has he been arrested?'

'Course he's a fool – a damned fool. But there's nothing to incriminate him. Not yet, at least. He's being questioned – he's not to leave the castle. Major Basset's left his men in control. William's there now – arranging for a competent garrison to take charge. The Falmouth volunteers aren't ready so he needs to send to Helston and Truro. Damned man's acting like some strutting peacock. Can't abide him. Pompous idiot.'

'Henry Trevelyan?'

'No, my dear, no – Major Basset. The odious man stood expecting me to apologize. Apologize, for God's sake! The man was tipped off. He was fast asleep yet he takes all the credit. Damned bitter pill to swallow.'

'Because he stopped the prisoners from escaping?'

'No, my dear – because George Godwin was proved right.'

Lady Clarissa's hands flew to her mouth. 'I'd forgotten all about George. How is he? Oh, that poor boy – he warned us.'

Lord Carew's heavy white brows sliced his forehead. 'That's the bitter pill, my dear. Turns out our George was quite the hero, certainly the last man standing! The captain had doubled the guard and was in the room with George. They both had wine but George was working and hardly sipped his. He noticed Captain Fenshaw dozing off but apparently that was quite normal. Anyway, someone banged on the door, yelling for the captain to come quick, and George saw him stumble. Asked him if he was all right and the captain said he was just sleepy.'

'He didn't think it odd?'

'Why would he? The man works all hours – but when Captain Fenshaw opened the door he fell over the bodies of the guards and shouted back to bar the door. George locked it pretty damned quick and barred it and I believe moved every piece of furniture against the door as a barricade.'

'Oh the poor, dear man.' Lady Clarissa was clearly horrified. 'And we dismissed his fears...almost lightly.'

Charity had been listening silently. 'Poor George, he must

have been completely petrified. But that was very clear thinking of him.'

'Yes — very clear, decisive thinking in the heat of battle. Splendid, really. Says he's never been so scared. Says he… well, never mind what he said, suffice to say he was terrified and feared for his life. They tried to force the door — he could hear them hacking at the lock. You can tell the poor boy's still terrified. He's jumping at his own shadow. Quite honestly, I wouldn't be surprised if he barricaded himself back in his room and stayed there until the wagons arrive. His only thought is to get that prize money to safety.'

'That would do him no good at all. I hope you told him to come here and rest.'

'I did, my dear. He says he'd like to come — and if you ask me, he needs to come. The poor boy's exhausted.'

Captain de la Croix was trying to follow the conversation, his heavy black eyebrows rising and falling, his frown deepening. At the sudden lull in the conversation he straightened.

'Lady Clarissa…Lord Carew…I am wishing to stay but my place is in the castle. I must go these men to be with.' He turned to Frederick, continuing in urgent French.

Frederick nodded when he finished. 'I'm sure you all understood what Captain de la Croix has just said — but in case you didn't catch it all, he thanks us profusely for our hospitality but believes his place should be with the prisoners in the castle. His official parole starts in Bodmin next week and rather than stay here, he asks to be taken back to Falmouth. And I believe he should go. The prisoners are from merchant ships — they've little or no English. This is their

350

second attempt at escape and he believes they need a senior officer of the French navy to speak for them.'

Lord Carew nodded. 'Indeed, Captain de la Croix, I salute your decision.'

Lady Clarissa picked up a leather-bound book from the table, opening it where the ribbon separated the pages. She found what she was looking for and smiled. 'The tide's lowest at six. Enjoy the day until then – you can leave on the rising tide. I believe your uniform will be pressed by then, Captain de la Croix.'

I hardly heard her; Henry had been as good as arrested. They would be questioning him this very minute.

Chapter Thirty-six

Trenwyn House
Monday 15th August 1796, 6:00 a.m.

I could not sleep; the night sky had been alive with stars, Moses attending his beehives, the owls hooting across the lawn. I had spent the night staring across the river to the distant castle, going over the escape in my mind.

Whoever ordered the ship must have ordered the meal in the inn. The same person must have brought the wine, organized the straw, drugged and murdered the master and his mate. He had started the fire, found Private Evans alive and killed him. He had gone down the steps, taken the keys from the sleeping guard, unlocked the central hatch and set the prisoners free. He had knocked on George's room because Captain Fenshaw was in there and he needed the keys to Henry's room and the tunnel.

'Yer never awake an' ready to be dressed, Miss Lilly?' I had not heard Bethany come into the room.

'I think some fresh air will do me good.'

She stood beside me. 'Are ye listening to the birds? They sing lovely this time of the mornin'. 'Tis a cryin' shame

Lieutenant Carew had to go back. He loves the garden in the mornin' – always out first thing.' She wrapped my silk gown round my shoulders. 'Ye're cold, Miss Lilly. I saw ye at the window an' I knew ye'd be cold. River air's damp – ye need take care.'

'Thank you, Bethany. Perhaps I'll get changed. Is that hot water?'

'I've brought it up specially. Here, let me fill the bowl.'

Martha Selwyn must have been going to bring in the drugged wine that night but she had been arrested so there had to be a change of plans. She needed to get Henry away from the castle and had sounded so plausible, making us both believe her. It was a clever ploy, so simple – just a case of being handed the basket by a boy. Such an obvious trap, yet we had walked straight into it. But that was *after* her arrest.

I stared at the steam rising from the china basin. The only way they could have set the new plan in motion was if her accomplice had visited her in the castle *after* Henry had left for Truro. Someone went there.

''Twas lovely havin' Lieutenant Carew here. He loves that child – 'twas a pleasure to watch them…and Mrs Carew looking so happy. Will ye wear yer silk or yer cotton today, Miss Lilly?'

'Perhaps my silk – no, my cotton. I'll look in on Persephone.'

I washed my face, my hands shaking. What if the man was *already* there? What if it was one of the guards? That's why they had freed Edgar – because they knew he could identify the killer – because they knew he would take the opium. My heart jolted. What if they had laced the opium with poison?

'Miss Lilly, ye don't look well. Sit here. Shall I help ye back to bed?'

'No, I'm fine. Just sudden giddiness – it's passing.'

Edgar would have seen them or heard them talking. He would be able to identify them. Yet Edgar had said nothing.

'Ye look that pale, Miss Lilly. Ye don't look yerself. Would ye like these ribbons threaded through yer hair? I'll pin these curls back and twist the ribbon round here. There that looks lovely – would ye like some chalk fer those shadows under yer eyes? Perhaps a dab of rouge? Only Lady Clarissa won't like ye looking so pale. She'll have ye on spinach an' eggs five times a day! Honest, I'm not joking.'

I shook my head, paling even more at the thought of eggs. 'How's Acorn?' I managed to ask.

'That fat little rascal? Ye'd never know he was the runt. Honest to God, that little piglet's found his way into everyone's heart. There isn't one person that don't slip him something. Even Lady Clarissa sneaks him the odd apple. Acorn indeed! He'll be bigger than an oak soon enough. He's assured himself of a happy life – he'll be used fer breeding, ye mark my words! Oh, sorry, Miss Lilly, I was fergettin' myself – but he's in fer a happy life, I can tell ye.'

I walked quickly through the kitchen, snipping off some grapes with the delicate silver scissors, cradling them in my hands as I made my way down the path towards the pigsty. I hardly dared look at the post where Henry had hung his jacket; that leap of my heart, that tightening of my stomach that had been impossible to ignore. I must have fallen in love with him when I saw him reading his book in the coach house…or was it when he looked up in the courtyard of the inn, or when we talked in the moonlight? Or was it when I watched him play cricket, or that very first glance when I thought I knew him?

Persephone grunted in greeting and I balanced the grapes on the bricks, picking up the forked stick to scratch her back. She was on her side, ten fat piglets squealing round her. Or was it that last drop to the beach when he had held out his arms? The way he spoke to me as an equal? I had always felt my true self with him – no aping social veneer, no following protocol, no having to do or say the right thing.

'And how's my beauty this morning?' Lord Carew leaned against the sty next to me. 'I'm sorry, I didn't mean to startle you, Miss Lilly.' He wore a rough sack cloth over his nightshirt, a strong piece of twine holding everything in place. On his feet, red jewels glinted on a pair of pointed Turkish slippers, on his head, his trusted red felt hat pulled low over his ears. 'I've brought some grapes for you, my dear. Oh, I see you have some already.' He leaned over the sty, feeding Persephone one grape at a time. 'You're up very early, Miss Lilly. I couldn't sleep either. Damned business all round.'

I had never been alone with Lord Carew and seeing him in his pointed Turkish slippers tore my heart. I had never seen Father in slippers or nightclothes. 'The prisoners' escape?'

'Well, there is that, my dear, but no – my concerns are with my land. We're behind with the harrowing. The ground's sodden, the soil's too heavy, and the wretched harrow's stuck tight. The more the oxen try to pull it out the worse they sink and the worse the quagmire becomes.' He leaned over, scratching Persephone's floppy black ears. 'That's what's keeping me awake.'

'Charity explained you rotate your fields – could you leave them fallow?'

'Too many, my dear…there's plenty already left fallow. We've spread the dung and lime and those fields can certainly be left but we need to pin-fallow the wheat stubble – or what passes as wheat – because it's rotting on the stalks. We can't harvest it and we can't leave it. Most pressingly, we need to harrow the lower fields because until we do we can't sow the new barley. Couch grass is a tough old bugger – it proliferates without repeated summer ploughing and if we don't remove the roots it'll choke next year's wheat. Without harrowing, we'll just plough back the roots and we'll get a crop of healthy couch grass.'

'And next year's harvest mustn't fail.'

'A good harvest next year is imperative – if we get the weather.' His sigh was heartfelt. 'Shall I feed Persephone your grapes too – best to feed her, not the little uns? There, that's your lot.' He turned, smiling. 'I tell you what, Miss Lilly, if we join ranks and attack on two flanks, do you think we could persuade Cook to do us some ham and buttered eggs? You look half starved, my dear.' He held out his arm and I rested my hand on the sleeve of his silk nightshirt. 'Truth is, my dear, I won't sleep until the harvest's in and we've salvaged what we can.'

Amelia ran along the grass by the beach, her bonnet and curls dancing as she swung round. 'What a beautiful day, finally, we have the sun back.' She shielded her eyes with her hand, staring across the sparkling blue water. 'That must be Mr Maddox now. Yes, look, they're taking down the sails – I can see him.' She seemed so happy and I tried to smile. William had not yet returned from Falmouth and I was desperate for news.

The high tide rippled against the shingle, clumps of flowers spreading along the stones and growing between the rocks. Amelia stooped to pick some, laughing back at me. 'These must have blown over the wall – look, they're doing really well. They're self-sown – they've made a bid for freedom.' She began picking a handful, laughing as she handed me them. 'You know what these are, don't you? They're *Angelica*. I never really thought about it before – how silly of me.'

I stared at the delicate white flower heads. 'This is Angelica?' I was fourteen again, inconsolable with grief; no flowers to throw into the dripping black hole that would engulf Mamma for ever; Father, fighting the wind with his umbrella, Edgar, pale under his huge coat and sodden hat. 'I never knew this was called Angelica. Molly called it Lady's Lace.'

'Well, there's a host of names, some I've never heard of…' A wet hand in a soaking sleeve reaching out to give me his rain-drenched posy. I could hardly hear her. 'I usually dry the roots but you can use the seed heads and the fruit. It's used for heartburn and loss of appetite. It's a very good tonic – sometimes it's used for arthritis and I believe it strengthens the heart. There's even talk it helps in childbirth. It has a funny sweet taste but it's not unpleasant. And it's pretty, don't you think?'

She stopped, her voice dropping. 'Are you all right, Angelica? Only you don't seem yourself these days. You've grown so pale and Mother's worried – we're all worried. You're hardly eating – are you homesick? Do you want to return home?'

'No, definitely not. I love it here. I want to be here.'

The boat was gliding towards the jetty and we ran to catch the ropes. Daniel Maddox was standing at the prow, his wide-brimmed hat flopping over his forehead. He was wearing what looked like a new green waistcoat, a cream linen shirt and a smart red neck chief. He stood smiling shyly at Amelia as she expertly caught the rope.

The boatman stepped ashore and took it from her. 'Thank you, Miss. There, I've got her. Steady she goes.' Another two men stepped ashore with ropes and we walked back down the jetty, watching them unload the last of the glass boxes.

Daniel Maddox began fussing over them like a mother hen. 'Thank you – over there. They're very precious. They're mainly glass...if you wouldn't mind...it's just that they've been especially made and...well, they're very expensive. If the glass breaks they'll be no use.' He took off his hat, running his hand through his hair. 'If you can take them one at a time, I can store them in the hothouse. Thank you... thank you most kindly. I appreciate your help. Steady as you go.'

He walked in front of them, stopping at the wall where

we were sitting. 'Good afternoon, Miss Carew, Miss Lilly; a beautiful day.' His eyes plummeted to his newly polished boots.

Amelia smiled. 'Indeed it is, Mr Maddox. Are those the last of your boxes?'

'They are. I only hope they survive. I'm to pack them tight with straw...Nail planks over the glass to keep them tight. I've got the nails and the planks and I'm to do that once I've filled them with soil.' He wrung his hands. 'I don't think I've ever been so nervous about anything. Mr Fraser is very particular – I need to get this right.'

Amelia slipped from the wall. 'I'm sure you've done everything you can, Mr Maddox. He couldn't have picked a better man for the job – you've an exciting adventure ahead of you.' She looked at the solid oak box with the glass lid. 'They look splendid – very sturdy. What happens when the plants grow more than two feet?'

'Then we'll prop the lids open. We won't disturb the roots as there'll be enough soil to sustain a year's growth – we just need to get the plants established under glass, then we'll gradually open the vents and introduce them to different temperatures.'

'They're very clever,' I said. 'Indeed, I almost envy you your journey.'

He swallowed, pulling at his new neck chef. 'Thank you. Yet the nearer it comes to leaving, Miss Lilly, the more reluctant I am to go. I love this garden...it's...well...suffice to say it's going to be hard to leave.' He hurried up the path, my heart following him. The poor man had tears in his eyes. He turned at the entrance to the walled garden, reaching into his pocket. 'Oh, Miss Lilly, I nearly forgot. Mrs Fox gave me this letter for you.'

'Thank you.' I ran to him, drawing a deep breath, slipping my finger beneath the seal, smoothing the letter against my lap. Her writing looked hurried: no formalities or pleasantries. Just a few scribbled lines and I thought I might faint.

My dearest Angelica,

The ship used by the prisoners is insured through us. The owner is Mr Edward Banks in Penryn. Robert wrote to him directly and we have just received his reply. I must warn you — the ship was commissioned and paid for by Mr Edgar Lilly for the week commencing the 10th.

Written in haste,

Your friend,
Elizabeth

Someone was calling, Bethany running down the lawn holding her skirt high. She doubled over, catching her breath. 'Mr Carew's back and Lady Clarissa wants ye both to come.'

Chapter Thirty-seven

They were in the drawing room; Amelia's brother, William, standing with his back to the mantelpiece, Lord Carew by the open window. Lady Clarissa rose from her chair and just one look at her face made my heart plummet.

'Come in, my dear. Shut the door.' She held my hand tightly, drawing me next to her on the chaise longue. Amelia grabbed my other hand and we sat in a rigid row, staring back at William Carew, eldest son, William and Henry's father, the next Lord Carew.

His glance was awkward, his raised brows slicing across his forehead just like his father's. 'There's no way of dressing this up, Miss Lilly, I'm afraid you must prepare yourself for a shock...I've just returned from Falmouth...Your brother – believe me, this is very difficult...' He was stouter than Frederick and not so blond, with the Carew good looks and the bearing of a farmer. His cheeks were rounder than his father's but he had his same ruddy complexion and hearty manner. His hair was worn short, his riding boots covered in dust. He glanced at his mother.

'Angelica, you must be brave, my love. Your brother is in Falmouth. He is held prisoner at the castle under suspicion of helping the French prisoners to escape – he—'

'I know...' I whispered.

'You know? Oh, Angelica! You *know* your brother's being held in Pendennis Castle and you didn't think to tell us? How do you know?'

'Mrs Bohenna told me when we were in Falmouth.' My hands were trembling, my heart hammering. 'I wanted to tell you...I so, so wanted to tell you but I didn't dare – Henry Trevelyan arrested him...' I stopped. I needed to be careful. 'I wrote to Father straight away, telling him what had happened and urging him to hurry...and I've been waiting... hoping, desperately praying he'd come. I was petrified of the scandal...petrified of shaming you...shaming my family. I thought if Father could only get here, he'd sort it out – get Edgar freed...' Tears rolled down my cheeks.

Amelia loosened my hand and reached for her handkerchief. 'Oh Angelica – of course you were frightened, but you really should have told us.'

'I just prayed and hoped no one would find out. Edgar wasn't being held under his own name – he was being held as Mr Ellis so I thought there was a chance it could all be resolved and no one would ever know...I thought if Father came quickly he would resolve it...that it was all a prank... some silly, foolish prank...and Edgar would be freed. Just a misunderstanding – something that could be resolved and no one need ever know.'

William Carew shook his head; he had kind eyes but his

face remained stern. His voice was soft but firm. 'It's more than a misunderstanding, Miss Lilly.'

I held out my letter. 'I know, I've just this minute received this letter from Mrs Fox. I don't understand it – it can't have been Edgar.'

Lord Carew left the window, pulling up a chair to read my letter. He handed it to Lady Clarissa and leaned forward, clearly shocked. 'The ship was commissioned by Mr Lilly? When was this?'

'The negotiations were done by post – the payment arrived the day after Mr Lilly's arrest but was dated the day *of* his arrest. I've just been with Mr Banks, the owner. The ship was required for two weeks and was paid for upfront. The master went straight to Falmouth to await instructions – he believed the cargo was to be lime. Mr Banks vehemently denies knowing or suspecting it would be used as an escape vessel. I've read the contract letter. It was signed by Edgar Lilly.'

The room was spinning. 'It couldn't have been my brother. We have our *own* ships...' Even as I said it, I knew how lame it sounded.

'Anyone could have signed that letter – it means nothing.' The strength in Amelia's voice gave me courage. 'Why was he arrested? What for?'

'Well, there you have it. Henry Trevelyan's resolutely refusing to tell us anything. He won't let anyone near your brother. He's not prepared to say a single word. States categorically it's a matter for the Transport Board and the *Transport Board alone*...says he's under no one's jurisdiction except Admiral Sir Alexander Pendarvis' and insists he'll speak only to him *when he returns*. No one can verify the signature on the letter. He's refusing point-blank to answer any of Major Basset's questions – or show him any paperwork. The man will say nothing. He's refusing anyone access to Mr Lilly. No one can talk to him until Sir Alex returns.'

'That's outrageous! The man's a bloody fool. Alex has been sent for?'

'Yes, Lord Falmouth's sent three expresses – all to different locations – but there's more: the man's clearly implicated. You're right, he is a fool. He's not been arrested, *yet*, but he's confined to the castle. Major Basset's taken command from Captain Fenshaw and set up headquarters in the gatehouse.'

Lady Clarissa's eyebrows shot up. 'Henry Trevelyan is implicated?'

'No question about it – he allowed in the wine, took himself conveniently off across the river *where he had previously ordered a meal*.'

'Oh no!'

William nodded. 'Yes, Father. He sent a boy to order a meal and paid for it in full, just like the ship. But there's more – much more. There was a lady with him and the description fits the exact description of the woman who brought the wine in the baskets. A Miss Martha Selwyn who's now missing – her wig and bloodstained cloak were found on the quay.'

'Bloodstained?'

'I'm afraid so, Mother. The woman was clearly the murderer – or helped him, at least.'

Amelia reached for her fan. 'Mary Bohenna told you when we were in Falmouth? Before the escape?'

The room was spinning. I was going to faint. I could hardly breathe. Nausea churned my stomach. 'Yes…Luke recognized Edgar when he was looking after the other prisoners,' I managed to whisper.

'And that's another man who's not saying anything! He's not implicated, of course, but Dr Bohenna's claiming physician's *confidentiality*. He won't say a word other than to confirm he's been attending the prisoners. It's all very well this silence, but they'll have to speak in the end. Come the trial, they'll need to speak out loud and clear.'

Lord Carew returned to the window, staring across the lawns to the distant castle. 'Why kill the ship's master and mate? That's what I don't understand. *Someone* – and I mean that most emphatically for there's no guilt until proven – *someone* went to a lot of trouble to free the prisoners, yet if we're to believe the prisoners, the two men were dead *before* they reached the ship. Why?'

'There's evidence they were drugged with the same wine. The prisoners were expected to sail the ship.'

'Out of a crowded harbour and in full view of naval vessels? It doesn't make sense. Unless they caught wind of the plan and refused the commission?'

Amelia's eyes sharpened. 'Or they recognized the man who brought them the wine and he had to go back and kill them or else they could identify him on their return.'

William looked up. 'That's a very good point, Mel.' His voice softened. 'Miss Lilly – it's unthinkable your brother would hire the ship in his own name – Major Basset believes he may well have been set up as a target of malice. Have you any thought who might wish your brother harm? Are we looking at a simple case of extortion – a way of getting money from your father?'

I shrugged my shoulders. 'He must have been set up...' I wanted to scream with the pain. Henry Trevelyan was protecting us and I needed to make that clear. I needed to speak up, tell them he was a good and kind man. That he was honourable. That he was fiercely loyal, doing his duty to Sir Alexander. That he would be exonerated, that he was far from implicated.

I had to tell them that I was the woman in the cloak. That I had lied to them all.

'Angelica, my love, did you hear me? I'm asking about Sir Jacob Boswell. None of us liked him – where is he now, with his friend held prisoner in the castle?'

'I don't know. I've had no contact with him – only when he came here...'

'Could he be part of this? I only ask because it has to be asked. If his plans are for his mother to marry your father, then might it be convenient for the son to be implicated?' She paused, shaking her head. 'No, that doesn't make sense, does it?'

Amelia stared at her mother. 'You wouldn't release someone if the first thing they could do is follow the prisoners and raise the alarm.'

'That's what I was thinking.'

'But what if something went wrong? What if they meant to kill him too?'

I put my hand to my mouth and ran through the open window, bending over to retch on the grass. I was shivering, shaking, shards of ice piercing my heart – the opium *had* been laced. He was meant to take it. He was meant to be found dead.

Amelia handed me the steaming cup and I breathed in the smell of lemon. 'Drink this,' she said, untucking the eider-down next to me and slipping between the silk sheets. 'It's mainly lemon with a touch of brandy and a pinch of valerian to help you sleep. I'm staying with you tonight. Mother says you're to have spinach and eggs between meals tomorrow and plenty of ale. And she's ordered roast beef for supper for you to get your strength back.'

I sipped the proffered brew, knowing there was more than just a touch of brandy in it. Amelia had drawn the curtains tightly shut and the room lay in darkness. 'Now sleep, please. Close your eyes and go to sleep.'

The icy fingers still clutched my heart – Edgar was meant to take that opium; he was meant to die. Who knew about his addiction? Who knew?

Footsteps shuffled along the hall, a door creaked open. 'We must sleep now – close your eyes and try.' Amelia adjusted her pillow, moulding it to a better shape. 'And just in case you're too scared to tell us, Mother says a lot of people take opium…and before I forget, Mother says we're to wear our best silk tomorrow…you're to wear your diamond pin and those sapphires that match your eyes. Father says when you're under attack you must go on the offensive.'

Chapter Thirty-eight

Trenwyn House
Tuesday 16th August 1796, 2:00 p.m.

No flag flew from the flagpole and the garden seemed uncannily quiet. The spinach and buttered eggs lay uncomfortably in my stomach. I had finished my plate under their watchful eyes and my diamond pin was glinting, my best silk gown feeling restrictive and tight. Lady Clarissa had insisted we fill every vase in the house with flowers and had tidied away all trace of the treehouse she was building with Jethro; yet no one had called, only Daniel Maddox walking swiftly across the lawn.

We sat straight-backed under the spreading oak, smiling as he held out a letter. 'So, you are to depart *before* the cricket match, Mr Maddox? We cannot have that.'

Daniel Maddox wrung his hat in his hands. 'I'm afraid it's beyond my control. The ship leaves from Plymouth but they've a number of provisions to pick up from Falmouth so they're sending a boat to collect me and my boxes...I'm so sorry, I'd have loved to watch the match.'

Lady Clarissa smiled. 'I did not mean you to *watch*, Mr Maddox. I rather hoped you might *play*.'

He looked shyly down again, the hat gripped tighter. 'I can't...I never seemed to get the way of cricket...I'm not... well, I think I'd let you all down.' He looked up with sudden resolution. 'Of course I'll play...but if the boat comes in the morning, I'll have to catch the tide.' He reread the letter. 'It says the morning of August the eighteenth...but if they haven't come, then I'd be proud to walk out with Lord Carew and I'll do my very best.'

Lady Clarissa cast her eyes down the comprehensive list of instructions he had crammed on to three pages. 'I believe you have thought of everything, Mr Maddox. We shall follow these instructions to the very last detail. Thank you for this — and thank you for *all* the work you have done for us. You must come back and visit us — to see the fruits of your labour. You have an open invitation to visit any time and if we can be of further assistance to you, then you need only ask.'

He seemed suddenly overwhelmed, looking down, nodding, crushing his hat as he backed away. 'Thank you...you're very kind. And the cereus...? You'll have the cereus in the house? Only it doesn't like draughts...'

Amelia smiled from beneath her bonnet with its mass of yellow silk flowers. 'I will treasure your cereus, Mr Maddox. I promise it will come to no harm.'

He backed further away, smiling painfully, turning to hurry across the lawn. He hardly saw Jethro, or if he did he was too upset to stop.

'Ah, Jethro, is everything in hand for the match?' Lady

Clarissa beckoned him nearer. He held a rolled-up newspaper in one hand, patting it against his open palm like a bat.

'Ready as we'll ever be, my lady – though we'll be fielding more boys than men this year. And we've no twelfth man unless Young William can play – but it's not about the winning, is it? It's about the playing.' He batted the newspaper against his palm again, his smile belying the frustration in his eyes.

'What's Trelawney's side like? You must have sent spies?'

'They're down to nine men and two youths – but they're good. They've got neither Mr James nor Mr Ewan because they're still at sea, but they've got a new groom and he's got a powerful bowl. Bats well, too – he's the one we've got to watch.'

Amelia shrugged her elegant shoulders. 'I don't see why we can't play. I caught Frederick out the other day and I made thirty runs – and Angelica can play just as well. You need to change the terms of engagement, Jethro – it should read the annual cricket match between the men *and women* of our neighbouring estates. Add those two words and you'd field a complete team.'

Jethro smiled, slapping the newspaper harder. 'One day, perhaps, Miss Carew.' He looked back across the lawn to the house. 'I believe I've missed Lord Carew…I thought to show him this.' He unrolled the creased newspaper. ''Tis only a day old but this caught my attention – 'tis an advertisement for a single-wheel plough…here, it looks flimsy, mind, like it should be fer pressing gowns but if ye read what it says, they claim they're using them in France and they work well in wet pastures.'

He smoothed the paper on the table, pointing to an advertisement he had ringed in black ink. 'See, here. They're pulled by *horses*, not oxen. Big horses, mind – not the mares in the stables – big strong shire horses...and they're lighter in construction so they don't sink so deep...says they harrow as well as they plough.'

Lady Clarissa smiled. 'So it does – well, well. I shall show this to Lord Carew the moment I see him. It says there are two for sale...shipped from France. They were taken as a prize, I presume?'

'I believe so, my lady.' He bowed to leave. 'Miss Carew, before I forget, I must warn ye there's a hornets' nest in yer garden. I'll see it destroyed, but t'would be best to keep Master William and Henry away from yer garden fer now.'

Amelia smiled, knowing if it were up to Jethro those two words would have been already added to the challenge, but the winning estate always issued the terms of engagement and the Carews had not won for three years.

Lady Clarissa glanced back at the newspaper, leaning forward as another advertisement caught her eye. 'The Trebarthon Estate is up for sale, how splendid – about time too.' She looked up and I caught the sparkle in her eye. 'Your father needs a country estate, my love.'

The buttered eggs churned in my stomach. 'Doesn't that depend on...well...wouldn't it be...what about Lady Boswell? She already has a large estate.'

'Which is entailed.'

Amelia leaned forward, clapping her hands. 'Trebarthon would be perfect. Angelica, your father *has* to buy it. You can see the roof from our roof so you'd be able to see our flag – I'd be able to signal you...But what about Frederick, Mother? We had it down for Frederick.'

Lady Clarissa shook her head. 'Frederick can't afford it yet. In ten years, perhaps, but no...this would be perfect for Mr Lilly. It's on the river and an easy journey to Truro. I've often told Mr Lilly he needs a country estate.'

Her face fell and she closed the paper but it was too late; I had seen the large letters screaming from the page: *Two to hang, three for transportation. Lord Entworth insists, 'Let this be a lesson to those intent on riot and disorder. There must be a return to proper obedience. We must rid our town of this scourge.'*

We could hear a carriage pull round the circular drive; the door opened and footsteps crunched the gravel. Lady Clarissa sat rigid. 'Straight backs, girls...chins up. I thought Lord Entworth would grace us with his presence. He is here and I was wrong about him. He is not a man – he is a monster.'

I breathed deeply, trying to fight my nausea; that he could hang men who were starving – men whose only crime was to want to feed their families. I hated him, hated what he stood for: hated his power, his lack of compassion. I sat staring down the vast sweeping lawn, trying to stop the thumping in my chest but a cry of pleasure made me turn round. Lady Clarissa was smiling. 'Mr Lilly – by all that's wonderful.'

Father was hurrying across the lawn. He looked flustered, his travelling coat creased, his hair uncharacteristically dishevelled, yet it was the look in his eyes that jolted my heart. He looked flushed, frightened, completely distraught, and I ran to him, holding out my arms, embraced by him for the first time in more years than I could remember. He held me tightly, holding back his tears. 'My dearest child… my dearest, dearest child.'

He seemed to recover, standing suddenly stiffly but I kept hold of his hand.

'I was so worried you wouldn't get my letter…I've been hoping and praying…'

He looked older, tired, his cheeks drawn, shadows under his eyes. 'I came as quickly as I could. The express kept missing me – following in my wake – but he caught up with me in Bristol. I've been travelling through the night. How is Edgar? Has he been released? You do understand, don't you, that if this gets out it will ruin every chance you have of a good marriage – that boy will be the ruin of us?'

I let go of his hand, standing firmly, my chin in the air. '*That boy* is vulnerable and lost,' I said softly. 'He's been pushed too far. *That boy* has done everything he can to please you, but it's never been enough. You knew he hated Oxford – he should never have gone. He wanted to join *you* in your business. He wanted to work in the foundry, learn things the way *you* learned them.'

I had never spoken to Father like this but I wanted to speak the truth not artifice – our family always saying one thing and thinking another. All my life I had been acting, striving to be the child Mamma wanted me to be, the daughter Father wanted me to be. Edgar, too – both of us walking the tightrope between trade and society. Well, I did not want that any more. I wanted us to be who we were and proud of it.

His eyes hardened. 'I did what I believed was right, Angelica.'

My heart fell; the same clamping of the jaw, the same tightening of the mouth, but I was not to be dismissed. Any other time I would have acquiesced, bitten my tongue, but not now. Now I would speak from my heart.

'I know it was you who paid for Luke to study medicine and so does Mrs Bohenna. I was angry with you because I thought you kept a fancy woman – but I was wrong. I often look at your account books; I have done since I was fourteen. I often give money to charities on your behalf.'

He looked up, holding my gaze. 'I know – I thought to say something, even change the lock, but I knew you'd somehow persist. I had enough grateful letters to know something was afoot.'

I was thrown by the affection in his voice. 'There were several payments I couldn't place – random payments to different towns all over England. Now I think about it, I believe you've been helping Theo and Kitty Gilmore as well – I believe you've been subsidising their theatre company.'

He cleared his throat, his voice gruff. 'These last few years have seen them pay their way. I'd rather not talk about it. They must never know.'

My extraordinary prosperous father always holding back, afraid to show his feelings: my heart jolted – it was as if I was seeing him for the first time. What I had always taken as sobriety suddenly had meaning. He wore the dark clothes and pointed hat that Mr Fox always wore, the same white collar and cuffs. Never any outward sign of wealth, never intricately embroidered waistcoats, but exactly the same sober clothes, a simple gold watch his only adornment. I thought my heart would burst. 'Father, how well do you know Mr and Mrs Robert Fox from Falmouth?'

He stood smiling shyly back at me. 'Quite well, my dear – more so of late.'

I had been so blind. 'Are you...? Father, do you belong to the *Society of Friends*?' All this time it had been staring me in the face and yet I never realized it.

'No, my dear,' he hesitated as if the words were being wrung from him, 'not yet, at least...though, one day, I believe I might very well think to join them.'

'Why not now?'

His voice grew stronger. 'Because of a promise I made your mother. Non-conformists are on the edge of society – they rarely marry into the aristocracy: neither are they permitted to go to Oxford, nor can they be Members of Parliament...' He swung round. Another carriage had drawn up outside the front door and urgent footsteps were crossing the gravel. His eyes sharpened when he saw who it was. 'Does Lord Entworth know about Edgar?'

My heart had started to pound. 'I'm afraid everyone knows – Father, it's far worse than you think.'

Chapter Thirty-nine

Lord Carew summoned us all to the library. Lady Clarissa and Amelia were sitting either side of me at the table, Father at one end of the marble fireplace, Lord Entworth at the other. Lord Carew stood at the window watching George Godwin dismount on the drive outside.

'Well, here's the man himself – he's the one to ask.' He pulled up the sash. 'We're in the library, George. Please come in.' His grey wig looked strangely formal, his well-cut jacket trapping his broad shoulders. 'All I know about the man is that he arrived on that first corn ship. His name's Henry Trevelyan. First time we saw him was when he was acting as a coachman.' He shut the window.

Lord Entworth's frown deepened. 'I've found out all I need to know. The man's clearly implicated. He's one of Sir Alexander Pendarvis' *Foundation Boys*...comes from a very dubious family...the grandfather was an embezzler, imprisoned for bankruptcy.' He glanced towards me and I felt my cheeks redden. That quickening of my heart had always been fear; he stood commanding the room yet his smile was gentle, his eyes softening as he caught my glance.

'I'm sorry, Miss Lilly, I know how hard this is for you, but everything points to your brother being framed. Someone has played their cards very skilfully. The wine was bought in your brother's name and so was the straw.'

Father paled. 'That's impossible. Who knew he was being held?'

'No one – except Henry Trevelyan. He was the only person who knew his true identity. Your son's name was kept even from the guards – he was entered in the books as Mr Ellis. Not even Captain Fenshaw knew – except...' He paused, his voice hardening. 'Dr Luke Bohenna is a family friend, I believe, Mr Lilly?'

'He is.'

'And would have recognized him straight away?'

'He would.'

'He's claiming his physician's right to remain silent – Henry Trevelyan *and* Dr Bohenna are both resolutely refusing to say anything and lawfully that is their right, but Major Basset questioned Captain Fenshaw under threat of court martial and he told him everything. Henry Trevelyan's clearly implicated. He'd been acting as your son's coachman and the arrest was made under very dubious circumstances. The man's not to be trusted. Several eyewitnesses have come forward saying they saw him that night in the company of a woman.'

Lord Carew nodded. 'He was in Flushing with a woman answering the exact description of the woman who supplied the wine. Her bloodstained cloak was later found on the quayside near the ship but she remains missing.'

Father reached for a chair and sat quickly down. His cheeks were grey, shadows beneath his eyes. 'Why hide Edgar's identity? What does he want?'

The room was spinning, the scent from the large vase of lilies almost overwhelming: it was so hot yet Lord Entworth insisted all the windows remain shut against listening ears. I needed to breathe, stop my terrible dizziness. Henry was trying to protect Edgar, not entrap him. Lady Clarissa pressed her fan into my hand but remained straight-backed and I knew to do the same. They needed to know he was protecting Edgar – that he loved Mamma and was protecting her son – yet I could not speak in front of them all. I would wait until I was alone with Father and tell him everything.

Lady Clarissa coughed. 'Lord Entworth, I believe you said Henry Trevelyan was seen on the quayside several days before the escape?'

'Several times – and by a number of witnesses – it's absolutely certain, irrefutable, that the master of *Snow Goose* recognized Henry Trevelyan. There's no exact time of death – no one had seen the two men for some time. Some believe they'd been dead all day, maybe longer. Henry Trevelyan had to kill them because they could name him. They died, because he went on board to drink with them, but they recognized him. We're looking at a callous killer here, Lady Clarissa, a ruthless man who'll stop at nothing.'

Lady Clarissa's eyebrows rose in a perfect arch. 'And what of Mr Lilly's friend Sir Jacob Boswell? Has anything been heard or seen of him since the arrest? They were together in Falmouth, yet I believe he left the morning after Edgar was imprisoned. How do we account for that, I wonder?'

Father looked surprised. 'Sir Jacob came to find me, Lady Clarissa. It was *he* who alerted me. In fact, if he hadn't detained me, the express might never have caught up with me. I'd have been—' He stopped. He must have been about to say *aboard ship*. He cleared his throat. 'I'd have been delayed several more days.'

'He alerted you? Well, that at least is in his favour.'

'He has returned to Oxford. I believe I have been mistaken in both the son and the mother.'

The door opened and Lady Clarissa's frown turned to a welcoming smile. 'Do come in, George. You already know Lord Entworth...but this is Mr Silas Lilly, Miss Lilly's father. This is my cousin's son, Mr George Godwin.'

George Godwin bowed deeply. 'A pleasure, Lord Entworth...Mr Lilly.' His round cheeks were more than usually flushed, his forehead glistening. Despite his cheerful nod, he looked tired, his hair lank and unwashed, a child-like vulnerability in his brave smile. 'I hope I don't intrude, Lady Clarissa...only Lord Carew said to drop by. I thought to accompany the wagons all the way to Truro but when I saw your gatehouse, I...Well, to be honest I thought a walk round your pleasant gardens would do me a power of good.'

'Indeed it will. After what you've been through, I hope you'll at least stay the night?'

'I would dearly love to, Lady Clarissa, but I must get back to Falmouth. I've another two consignments to send tomorrow.' He lowered his voice, despite the shut windows. 'Major Basset has allowed me a number of his best men and we're to use wagons lent to us from the post office. The first contingent has left but there are two more to follow and I shall not sleep until they're securely packed and on their way.'

Lord Carew smiled, his white brows slicing his forehead. 'You've done well, George.'

'Thank you, sir.' George's already flushed cheeks turned crimson. 'The remaining prize money is sealed in a vault, but...well, when I think of what *might* have happened.' He drew out his handkerchief, wiping his brow.

'It's over. You must not torture yourself.'

'I'm using Russell's wagons for transport. They're a reputable firm and have never been robbed, but all the same, we're not taking any chances. I've packed the caskets deep into the straw and we've provided the drivers with horse pistols and blunderbuss. There's a guard of soldiers marching with them – one on either side...two at the rear. They'll not be stopped.'

'Lord Entworth was just saying – before you arrived – that you've shown great courage.'

George Godwin stared down at his feet. 'Thank you, sir.'

'Tell us everything you know about Henry Trevelyan, Mr Godwin. I believe your room is next to his in the castle. What manner of a man do you find him?'

'I'd say an extremely pleasant man, Lord Entworth...very courteous and well-liked by everyone. He's firm, but I'd say fair. He never raises his voice or speaks rudely. He's intelligent...'

'Where did he come from?'

'From the States of America...from New York. He arrived on that first grain ship. I believe he works for a shipping company. But I know he's originally from Truro. He hardly talks about his past but he knows Sir Alexander Pendarvis because he was one of his...'

'*Charity boys* – yes, we know.' Lord Entworth stared at him from across the room. 'What else can you tell us, apart from the fact he cohorts with women of very dubious morals?'

George ran his hand through his hair again and I could see it was trembling. 'I...can't tell you anything more except I like him and believe him to be honourable. I can't account for why he went missing for so long, nor why he left the castle at such an inappropriate time. He won't speak about it. He says he's waiting for Sir Alexander Pendarvis to return. The prisoners are held under the jurisdiction of the Royal Navy Transport Board and he's refusing to hand them over.'

'I'm fully aware of that.' A look of anger flashed across Lord Entworth's eyes and Lady Clarissa rose.

'We must get you into the garden, George. In fact, may I invite you *all* on to the terrace for some refreshments? It is far too stuffy in here. I will ask Cook to serve us some of her iced-cream or perhaps you would like some rather delicious raspberry sorbet? Mr Lilly, you will stay and take tea with us?'

Father's smile looked forced. 'Thank you, Lady Clarissa, another time. I must go to my son.' He bowed. 'But may I ask for a word *alone* with Lord Entworth?'

He looked older, half the man he had been when he left for Swansea, and my heart burned; dearest Father, I could see it so clearly. He must have sat on her bed, clasping her hand. He must have pressed her hot palm to his lips, his tears splashing his cheeks; his adored wife burning up with fever, her throat too swollen to speak. He would have swabbed her brow with his handkerchief, watching her close her eyes for the last time. Somehow, he would have found the words to comfort her, promising her everything she had ever wanted – her son would grow up to be a gentleman, her daughter would marry a lord. He would have held her beautiful body in his arms and kissed her burning lips. The gypsy's prophecy would come true. He loved her. He would always love her.

Amelia rose, elegantly smoothing the creases from her silk gown. 'Mr Lilly, please don't go until I've given you some honey for Edgar. We must send him some eggs as well. And some fruit. I'll go and get a basket.'

They left the room and Father saw me hesitate. '*Alone*, if you don't mind, Angelica. Lord Entworth and I have matters to discuss. Wait for me on the terrace, if you wouldn't mind, my dear.'

I swallowed hard. Dismissed as usual, sent away when it was my future they were about to discuss. Lord Entworth must have seen me bite my lip and came forward, putting his hand on my arm. He pulled me gently towards him, shutting the door, turning his back on Father as he bent to whisper. His words were soft, his eyes full of pain. 'Miss Lilly...I wish you'd come to me. I wish I'd been your first port of call – you've been suffering such heartbreak and I could have comforted you.'

He swallowed, reaching for my hand, bringing it to his

lips. 'I will do *everything* in my power to free your brother and get him exonerated – that is my solemn promise.' He turned my hand over, his lips brushing my palm and I fought the panic flooding through me. He was too close, taking such liberty. Father had turned his back to us and was looking out of the window, yet he must have seen him kiss my hand.

I stood rigid, his lips pressing against my palm, his voice dropping so I could hardly hear him. 'Though it might not be as easy as I would like...a lot of people are saying that your brother is *clearly* guilty – that he set everything up to make it *look* like he's been framed.' I tried to pull my hand away but his grip tightened. 'A number of people have come forward to tell me they've seen him with a whore who bears an uncanny resemblance to the woman in the prison.' He kissed my palm, slowly, deliberately, his tongue tracing a circle, travelling up my wrist. 'He's been seen several times in an inn in Malpas and in a certain opium den in Falmouth...and I believe he was seen abducting a whore outside the theatre in Truro, but that's hardly surprising considering his appalling behaviour during the play...'

I could not breathe. I wanted to snatch my hand away but his hand held mine. Father must see our reflection in the glass; he must be witness to his terrible liberty, but he did not turn round. He must only see two lovers – a man comforting the woman he loved. He could not hear the threat in his voice nor feel the power of his hold. 'There are as many witnesses *against* your brother as there are against Henry Trevelyan,' he whispered in what must look like adoration. 'Like the theft of a certain necklace and Lady Clarissa's silver dish, which went missing the night they were both here…I'm sure you must realize that either man could have those thefts pinned on him.'

He put his finger beneath my chin, forcing me to look up. 'Captain Fenshaw told me he signed for them when your brother was arrested. And there was the pistol, too, wasn't there? Now, they *could* belong to your brother or they *could* belong to Henry Trevelyan…it just depends which witnesses we find to swear in court…*my* court, let me remind you, Angelica, where *I* will be the judge.'

I thought I would be sick. My heart was hammering so fast, fear making it hard to breathe. Father had moved to the other side of the room and was now intent on studying the books. He must be delighted by our obvious intimacy and I tried to breathe, shutting my eyes as Lord Entworth towered over me. 'You know how to save your brother, don't you, my little love?' He kissed my palm again, vile, reptile kisses that sent shivers down my spine.

It would be his court, his paid witnesses, his judgement; he would rush this case through just like he had with the rioters. Either my brother or Henry Trevelyan would be arrested and put on trial. One of them would be committed to hang long before Sir Alex Pendarvis returned. Sedition and treason could be tried at any time – no waiting for the assizes. The blood was rushing from my head, I needed to breathe. He smiled a lover's soft smile, bringing my hand once more to his lips. 'Go now, dearest girl. Run along and enjoy the iced-cream and raspberry sorbet. Leave your father and me to talk.'

Chapter Forty

The door closed behind me and I leaned against it, trying to control my dizziness. He was too powerful to stop. He could implicate either Edgar or Henry – one or the other would be accused. The charge a treasonable offence – conspiring to free French prisoners. One would hang, one would go free. I hardly saw Amelia waiting by the drawing-room door. She came hurrying forward and grabbed my elbow, pressing her forefinger against her lips. She drew me across the hall to a small cupboard and looked round, checking no one was looking. She opened the tall, painted door and pulled me inside.

The cupboard was long and thin, lined with shelves on one side and hooks on the other, and I knew instantly why we were there. Enamel buckets stood in a neat row, an assortment of mops and brushes. Most shelves were stacked with jars of polish and candles but a couple were piled high with oddly shaped driftwood, a selection of peg dolls and a stone jar full of charcoal. A bench ran down one side and she shuffled me along it.

'It's *The Procurer's Cupboard*,' she whispered as my eyes adjusted to the semi darkness. Above us, a small row of grilles let in pinholes of light. 'Frederick and I used to play in here as children. The boys use it too – the *Procurer* summons us here on rainy days.'

The cupboard seemed to stretch the whole length of the hall. She indicated for me to shift along the bench and turned round, running her hands along the bricks behind her. 'The fireplace is just behind here.' She began twisting something in the bricks, gently pulling out a cork. 'Mother doesn't know about this, though she does know about the cupboard. Frederick wasn't always the golden, blue-eyed hero he is today. He was very naughty as a boy – he used a skewer to drill some loose mortar and made this hole.'

She turned round, kneeling on the bench. 'It's too high up the fireplace to be able to see anything, but you can hear well enough what's being said. Once Frederick took the cork out and the cupboard filled with smoke – we thought we'd be found out but, luckily, we weren't. We used to listen when Father had important meetings, but mostly we just heard Father snoring in his chair.'

There were voices coming from the other side of the bricks. Father and Lord Entworth must have returned to the fireplace and were just the other side of the hole. Amelia shuffled back along the bench. 'I'll keep *cave*. When it's clear, I'll come and get you. Don't make a sound. You won't hear everything, but you'll probably make out enough of what's being said.' She looked through the crack of the door, checking the hall was empty. 'That's how I found out they were sending me to boarding school — pre-warned is pre-armed, as Father says.'

I took off my bonnet and placed my ear firmly against the hole. They must have been standing right in front of the fireplace.

'There's something I didn't say before.' It was Father speaking. 'The name Henry Trevelyan is very familiar to me. His grandfather went by the same name...he worked for me...or rather he worked for a shipping firm I bought. The company was in trouble, about to go bankrupt...and they asked if I could buy their ships from them and I did. I took a good hard look at their accounts and it soon became apparent why they were losing money — a clever, systematic fraud was in place and I could see at once who the perpetrator must be. Mr Henry Trevelyan was accused of fraud and charged. He was told to refund every penny or be gaoled for bankruptcy. To this day, I would defend my accusation, though no money was ever traced to him.'

'Sounds perfectly reasonable to accuse the man...So, what you're saying is that Henry Trevelyan is this man's grandson and very likely intent on revenge? No doubt he's as profligate and untrustworthy as his father and grandfather before him.'

'Only the grandfather was accused of the fraud — I believe his son was an honourable, hardworking man who worked for the same company. He died just days after clearing the old man's debts. He paid everything back, but he borrowed heavily – I believe he mortgaged everything. His untimely death left the family in great penury.'

'And with a perfectly sound motive for the son to return and seek revenge – how better to avenge yourself on the man who ruined your family than have him watch his son hung for theft and treason? The man's clearly both intelligent and dangerous.'

'I believe I must engage the services of Mr Matthew Reith, Lord Entworth. His is the foremost legal brain in Cornwall. If the man's guilty, then Matthew Reith will prove it beyond reasonable doubt. I can't have people think I have a personal vendetta against the family.'

There was a pause, a long silence, followed by the sound of a snuffbox snapping. 'Get Mr Reith involved and your son will surely hang. Mr Reith and Sir Alex Pendarvis have always had a close association, and believe me, neither are men you want to cross. The evidence against your son is far greater than that against Henry Trevelyan. Your son is a wanton, unprincipled imbiber of opium who frequents the worst brothels and stinking dens used only by the lowest vermin of our society.'

'That's a terrible accusation. I ask you to—'

'It's the truth, Mr Lilly. I've had my men watch your son – and they will be compelling witnesses who'll testify under oath they've seen your son crawling from gutter to gutter. Your *son* is a depraved, profligate disgrace – sent down from Oxford for claiming another man's work as his own. If it wasn't for your charming daughter and her obvious delight at the prospect of being the next Lady Entworth, I would back swiftly away like any sensible person. But we have a deal, have we not? And a gentleman honours the deals he makes, even if he wasn't born a gentleman, and his son's a profligate disgrace.'

There was another pause, a long draw of snuff. 'Get Matthew Reith involved and I'll be powerless to help. Your son will hang and any hope of a good marriage for your daughter will be lost. Act now and Henry Trevelyan will be up before my bench and the matter resolved with no hint of scandal to yourself. Your son's indiscretions will be silenced.'

'Lord Entworth...I must protest. You're forcing me into a very difficult position. The man must have a just and honest trial.'

'Who? Henry Trevelyan or your son?'

'Both, of course.'

'Allow another court and another judge anywhere near the case and your son will hang, do I make myself clear? The evidence against him is stacking up as we speak. Mr Lilly... I admit to being disappointed and not a little disgusted. To align myself with your family is going against all sound judgement.'

'Lord Entworth, it was you who came to me.'

'That was before...now I see things differently. We agreed a fifteen per cent discount on all my smelting costs, but in view of the change of circumstances, I fear I must change that to twenty per cent. Times are hard and profits are falling and I need a clear advantage over my competitors for both tin and copper. I want twenty per cent discount on *all* my smelting deals and a twenty per cent stake in your shipping business…and no charge for the use of your ships.'

'Lord Entworth, I must protest…You ask too much.'

'Too much to save your family from ruin? I believe a twenty per cent reduction for both shipping and smelting costs is a fair deal – your son's life and your daughter's advantageous marriage at very little inconvenience to yourself?'

'I'm sorry—'

'You may well be sorry – very sorry – if you refuse my terms. Your daughter's dowry of twenty thousand will remain as we agreed but I require a further annual income of *two thousand a year*, which I will put by for the benefit of your grandsons – and all this must be signed for, and agreed, on the day I propose to your daughter – which will be here, at Lady Clarissa's birthday party. Though I believe we have a tedious cricket match to sit through first.'

'Lord Entworth, your terms are too demanding.'

'My *terms* are simple. And as for my part, I promise I will love and honour your daughter. I will cherish her to my dying breath – I'll give her everything she wants. She'll lead the life she deserves…she'll grace the highest society, which is where her beauty belongs. My *terms*, as you rather vulgarly put it, are to save your family from disgrace – my *terms* will grant you everything your wife wished. Her portrait can hang in Carrick Hall, if it must, and I'll even teach my son to revere his actress grandmother.'

There was sudden iron in Father's voice. 'That portrait will not leave my house. And it will be *me* who teaches my grandson to revere his Irish grandmother.'

In the frosty silence I heard the door open. Their voices were faint, difficult to hear. 'Understand...tired...rather over wrought...sharp words between us must be forgotten...sake of...children's future...only important ones. Their happiness...must take my leave.'

I pulled away from the tiny hole, doubling over in pain. They were standing in the hall and had been joined by Lady Clarissa. She was thanking Lord Entworth for coming, sending Amelia to try to find me. Father was telling her he must leave straight away; he needed to see Edgar as soon as possible. I could hardly breathe but sat hugging my knees, fighting the fear ripping through me. Nothing made sense, only that Father was being blackmailed.

The pain was so severe, I wanted to cry. Henry Trevelyan must have sat staring at me through the window of his hovel with such loathing. He must have hated me, detested everything about me. Perhaps he still did. Perhaps he had used me, framing me just like he had framed Edgar. I could be traced helping my brother – the ship's crew back to Truro had seen me without my wig. They had brought fish for the kitten, seen the blood on her, brought water to help me wash it off.

Lady Clarissa was sending a maid to find me but Father's voice grew urgent. 'I must leave, now...I have to see Edgar.'

'Of course, I will tell her you were in a hurry. I'm afraid you'll find Falmouth very crowded at the moment and you may find difficulty obtaining a room. You'd be most welcome to stay with my son Frederick and his wife and child...at number four, Dunstanville Terrace. Do tell them I sent you.'

'Thank you, Lady Clarissa — you're very kind. But I believe I'll call on Mrs Bohenna, first. I've not seen her for a long while...'

There were more pleasantries and I heard her say, 'They must be in the shrubbery...she'll be so sorry to miss you. But do come back, please, Mr Lilly, come back any time... come for the cricket match.'

I breathed in the aroma of damp mops, the sweet perfume of the beeswax polish. Henry Trevelyan had never seemed malicious or unkind. He had never looked at me with hostility or cunning — never with resentment or revenge. Yet the more I thought about it, the more the hurt deepened. He had always remained distant, almost critical — making sure I knew he loved another. The pain felt like treachery, sharp stabbing thrusts ripping open my heart. What if I had been right all along not to trust him? What if the woman he loved was the woman in the prison? The woman who had trapped Edgar in the opium den?

I could hardly breathe. He alone knew Edgar took opium. At the water's edge, he had held me back, telling me it had to be Edgar's choice. But what if he wanted him to swallow the vial? What if he expected him to take it?

Exit Stage

Chapter Forty-one

The tiny door opened. 'They've gone. I told George I've left my parasol on the terrace. Are you all right, only you don't look very well?' Amelia shut the cupboard quickly behind me, hurrying me across the hall. 'What did Lord Entworth say? No...don't say anything, George is coming.'

George's hurried footsteps stopped. 'Oh, I'm sorry, do I intrude?'

I turned my back on his beaming smile, adjusting my bonnet in the large gilt mirror. 'A slight headache...well, to be honest, quite a bad headache, but I'm fine now.'

He held up Amelia's parasol like a trophy. 'It was next to the urn and I knew you'd be looking all over for it. You must have left it there and forgotten...' His face flushed with pleasure as he held it up. 'Now, I'll have the very great honour of escorting *both* of you round the garden. Shall we go down to the shrubbery...or maybe the rose garden?'

The heat of the day had passed, a gentle breeze now cooling my cheeks. It was the height of the tide, the blue water sparkling against the wooded banks, and I breathed in the rose-scented air, wanting to cry. Father had seemed so alone.

'I must say, this is a very welcome breath of fresh air. The air in the castle is so damp – almost unbreathable. It's not the best place for me but it's the best place for my vault. To be honest, I'm not sure Captain Melvill will allow me to stay where I am when he takes over command. His arrival has been hurried forward and not a moment too soon. The Fencibles are volunteers and not trained for artillery – the place is a shambles, even Major Basset's Dragoons won't stable their horses there.'

We walked by his side through the shrubbery, his conversation aimed mainly to Amelia whose large bonnet shielded her face from his view, her basket held rigidly between them. She stopped, lifting a flowering shrub for closer inspection. 'How are the guards? How's Captain Fenshaw? I hope he's recovering. Does Dr Bohenna know what was in the wine? What symptoms did they have?'

'Tiredness for a start – I should've been alerted when Captain Fenshaw grew drowsy. He shouted back at me to lock the door but he collapsed on the other side and I didn't know what to do. I'll be honest and tell you I was absolutely terrified. I was shaking, petrified...I could hear him shouting to me to barricade myself in and I did so at once. I'd barely sipped my wine – I was going to, mind. Captain Fenshaw brought it in to pass the evening but I was too busy at the time. I was going to enjoy it later. As it happened, it's a good job I only sipped it.'

'Did it taste sour, or different?'

'Not at all, it tasted very good. It was a Portuguese wine – a good one at that.'

'Did anyone vomit, did they convulse?'

'Captain Fenshaw was very sick. Dr Bohenna believes it was laudanum poisoning. There's plenty about – the sailors bring it with them from China and sell it to make money. A number of dens are springing up. Men go there to smoke it but I believe they sell it as a tincture.'

Amelia glanced anxiously at me and I looked down. 'Drowsiness, followed by delirium and extreme pallidness of countenance...sighing, followed by deep, snorting breathing...cold sweats and apoplexy?'

'Yes, I believe so. You're very knowledgeable, Amelia.'

'And the prisoners – was Dr Bohenna called to any of them?'

'I believe one had a nasty laceration, but otherwise they were unhurt. They continue to deny all involvement in the plan. According to Captain de la Croix, someone simply let them free so naturally, they took the opportunity to run but, now I remember – I think one of the prisoners is suffering from excessive heart beats.' He seemed suddenly shy. 'Captain de la Croix has become the prisoners' spokesman and I've seen quite a lot of Lieutenant Carew over the last day – your brother is a very impressive man.'

'Thank you.'

'He's considered quite a hero. Did you know the crew of Captain de la Croix's ship had terrible dysentery and Admiral Penrose and your brother insisted they should be put ashore in Guadeloupe and only take Captain de la Croix as prisoner?'

'Yes, he told me. It was a very honourable thing to do, though I believe the Admiralty are looking into the case.' Her voice faltered. 'But leaving behind men who were dying and yet had a chance to live seems a very straightforward choice to me. They would have all died on the journey back.'

We walked on in silence, a blackbird singing loudly on the arch above the wrought-iron gate. Amelia's herbs spilled over the brick paths, the sound of bees filling the air. Moses was weeding the herbs on his knees and rose stiffly as we approached, bowing and smiling his wonky smile, his gardener's smock covered in dry soil.

'Moses, do you have some honey in a sealed jar I can give to Edgar?' I mimed bees in the air, holding out my hands as if holding a honey pot and he seemed to understand.

Amelia turned to George. 'You will take it to Edgar, won't you, George? Only Mr Lilly left in such a hurry.'

George Godwin beamed with pleasure. 'Of course…I'll take anything you like. As it happens, they've clamped down on allowing anything into the castle. Major Basset's set up a guard at the gatehouse – no one's to enter or leave…absolutely no prison visitors and nothing for the guards. Even I'm being searched and all correspondence read.'

'That's a bit like shutting the stable door after the horse has bolted, don't you think?'

'He believes they may bolt again…but you're right, we're all still so nervous. The castle is very exposed.'

I looked up from watching the bees on the lavender. 'Who

unlocked the prisoners and let them out, Mr Godwin? They must have seen who it was.'

'It was the woman Henry Trevelyan arrested and imprisoned. She let them out and led them away, but that's all I know. Henry Trevelyan is insisting that the prisoners say nothing until Sir Alex comes back and they get proper representation. Nothing's to be said...but I know a guard was seen crossing the inner field towards the keep. Most of them were running *towards* the fire, but this one was seen running *away* from it, towards the prisoners.'

Amelia blanched. 'They think it was one of the guards?'

'They don't know for certain. I hear very little even though I'm in the midst of it. I stay behind my locked door most of the time.'

We walked down the centre path, stopping for a moment at the marble birdbath brimming full of water. 'Can you take some digitalis for me, George? Only Dr Bohenna might need some for the man with the excessive heart beats.' She stooped down, picking a handful of dandelion. 'And some of this? The diuretic properties alone might help...Oh my goodness...!' She stepped back as a huge hornet flew at her. 'Take care.'

George Godwin was by her side and cried out in pain, clasping his hand quickly to his throat. 'Ow...oh, my God... the pain!' He pulled back his hand and I saw a huge, red lump at the crease of his jaw.

Amelia lifted his chin. 'That looks very painful – quick, go with Moses...get lemon balm or witch hazel...I know he's got vinegar in his shed.'

George fell to his knees, clasping his neck, shouting loudly, 'No, not vinegar. Get mud…mud for a poultice.'

'Does that work better?'

'Yes…quick…it's the only thing that works. I react very badly to stings…they seem to spread…I'm sorry…I don't mean to shout…but the pain is terrible. Quite the worst I've ever had.'

I stood rigid, my heart thumping. *Not vinegar. Get mud…mud for a poultice*. I had heard those exact words before, shouted with the same urgency, the polite veneer of a polished accent slipping in the grip of pain. Those exact words, shouted from a room of debauchery; an open door with a woman swaying from it, a woman in a gaping bodice, bumping into us, leaning over the staircase with her goblet of red wine. I breathed deeply, turning to hide my shock.

'There's some mud where Moses was weeding…and there's water in the birdbath.'

George Godwin had been in that room with Lottie Lorrelli; George Godwin had been at the Heron Inn. He would have seen Edgar in the throes of addiction, he knew he took opium. He would have known he was the perfect target – a man he could manipulate and frame. The insider was not a guard, but George Godwin. He was in league with the woman, *he* had helped the prisoners escape. I stood staring down at the disturbed earth, watching Moses dig up some mud and mix it with water to form a stiff paste. George Godwin's office was the room next door to Henry's – it was he who had visited her when Henry left for Truro. He knew exactly who had the keys to which part of the castle. He did not drink his wine because he knew it to be drugged.

He was sitting on a bench now, Amelia and Moses applying the poultice. He was smiling, back to being his sweet, anxious self. He had fooled everyone. He had planned the whole thing. His acting may be perfect, but so would mine have to be. I knew just what to do, my concern so genuine, my eyes soft and caring, offering him my handkerchief to wipe his brow. He was smiling back at me, so very grateful, such an honourable young man who would never venture into brothels or take bribes to help prisoners escape.

I could not believe how blue the sky looked, how beautiful the herbs, how happy I could feel. I wanted to smile and laugh, jump for sheer joy, but I must remain looking concerned, offer George Godwin my arm to help him back to the house. Henry and Edgar were not implicated, both were innocent.

'Mr Godwin, allow me. Has the poultice helped? Is the pain easing?'

We were walking across the lawn, both of us by his side. He might rest a while, but he would soon be leaving I had to warn Henry but what could I do? My mind was racing, time was running short. George Godwin was already shaking off his mishap, assuring Lady Clarissa that the pain was easing.

She stood in her gardening gown and heavy men's boots, her hands deep inside thick leather gloves. 'Jethro will see to it as soon as it gets dark. He'll smoke them first then set fire to the nest. You must stay the night.' She smiled. 'You can help build the treehouse if you like. Jethro's just gone for the ladder.'

George Godwin smiled. 'Another time, Lady Clarissa. I

fear I must get back. The pain has passed...though I'm reluctant to leave. It's such a beautiful day and...'

I left them talking, rushing quickly to the open door of the drawing room. Lady Clarissa's desk was in the corner, her writing paper and utensils left neatly in a silver tray and I glanced at them, knowing I could not use them without her consent. Behind me, Lord Carew stood in his red felt hat and corduroy jacket. He held a fishing rod in one hand, a large chunk of bread and jam in the other. He wiped his mouth with the back of his hand, swallowing as he spoke.

'Plenty of paper on my desk in the library, Angelica my dear. Help yourself. I take it you want to write to your brother? Use what you like.'

I rushed to his desk, yet what could I write? The paper trembled in my hand and I laid it on the leather top, taking his pen, dipping it in the ink. George Godwin would read my letter long before the guards opened it – that was just his excuse to explain the open seal. He would read every word, telling Edgar it had been read by the guards at the gate. I would have to write the bare minimum, yet somehow warn Henry. But what could I write?

Dearest Edgar,

Never doubt that I love you and know you are innocent of all charges.

Take heart that the real perpetrator will be soon discovered. Keep well, dear brother.

Tell your gaoler, Henry Trevelyan, that justice will prevail.

Your loving sister, Angelica

402

I could hear George Godwin in the hall outside. He was saying farewell to Lord Carew, assuring him he was well enough to travel. His horse was saddled and held by a groom on the gravel outside. I folded the letter in three, folding it twice again. I needed to hurry, but how to warn Henry? He needed to know about George, but also that Lord Entworth was about to arrest him — if he had not done so already.

George Godwin was standing by his horse, Lord Carew pointing towards the window, no doubt telling him to wait for my letter. Henry would read it, he read all correspondence sent to the prisoners, so I smoothed out the page again, dipping the nib into the silver inkwell to add at the bottom.

PS You must come as soon as you can. The garden is magical at night; I fear Puck is watching me — the interference of woodland sprites can cause great mischief.

It was all I could think to do. I folded the letter again, doubling over the sides, tucking them in, pressing it against my heart. Please come, Henry. Please come. The clock on the fireplace struck five. Please, please come.

Chapter Forty-two

Trenwyn House
Wednesday 17th August 1796, 1:00 a.m.

If he came, it would be by boat; he would row up river with the rising tide. A quick glance in Lady Clarissa's small leather-bound book had shown me the height of the tide would be two in the morning. Low tide had been at half past ten and his journey could take two hours, maybe more. If he came at all, it would be one o'clock at the earliest. I knew the river so well; I had studied it from the ship and watched it from the shore. He would not use the jetty as that could be seen from the house; he would leave his rowing boat tied to a branch along the shore and wait for me on the shingle below the walled garden.

I drew my cloak about me, staring out of my window. Moses was in the orchard, tending his beehives. I could see his large bee-keeper's hat and cloak moving beneath the apple trees. He had seen me in the garden before at night, even seen me talking to Henry, and would not raise the alarm. The moon shone above the castle, the stars full of brilliance, lighting the night sky. The clock behind me struck one: it was time to leave.

Lord Carew had taken the precaution of having his live-stock and stores guarded and his nightwatchmen would be patrolling the stables and grain store round the back of the house. I knew to slip from the terrace and run straight to the shrubbery; if anyone saw me I would tell them I was hoping to see the cereus bloom. It may not be a full moon, but I could plead ignorance and hope they thought me too enthu-siastic to remember.

The window opened as I had carefully practised and I slipped into the cool night air, the scent of lilies flooding the terrace with their heavy perfume. The owls were hooting, a slight rustle in the leaves, the path glinting as if strewn with tiny diamonds. I walked quickly down to the wrought-iron door leading to the walled garden. I would go through the garden to the shingle beach; there, I would wait for Henry – *if* he came.

He had to come. My mind was whirling: George Godwin must have done it for the money, but his business was begin-ning to do well. If I accused him, no one would believe me. I would expose myself to the worst possible gossip and my name would be ruined – Father would be ridiculed; George Godwin would deny everything and everyone would think it a desperate ploy to save my brother – even save myself.

It would not be long before they traced me to the castle; someone would identify me as the woman on the quayside – the blood on the kitten, the wig and cloak found near the ship. They would question the crew of *Guillemot* who had seen me without my wig. They would identify me, swear in court they had sailed me back to Truro. If my testimony rested only on *hearing* George Godwin and not *seeing* him, I would be laughed out of court.

A rabbit stood at the gate and I knew not to trip over the wires Daniel Maddox had put in place to catch them. Bells would ring to alert everyone, so I picked up my skirts, slipping silently past the birdbath that stood ghostly white in the pale moonlight. The herbs shone in long silver rows, the scent of lavender rising as my skirt brushed the flowers spilling over the path. A movement caught my eye, the cloaked figure of Moses crossing the lower garden, passing swiftly in front of the entrance to the hothouse. He had a heavy basket in his hand and I wondered if I should follow him. It would be nice to have his company as it could be a long wait. What if Lord Entworth had already arrested him? Henry could protect his prisoners but he would be powerless against an arrest of treason.

I heard a sudden grunting, a shuffling and a thud, and ran quickly down the path, drawing back behind the twisting boughs of a wisteria shrub. A man was on the ground, Moses towering above him, kicking him viciously. The man was cowering, whimpering, trying to roll away, but Moses was kicking harder, his heavy leather boots slamming into the man with incredible ferocity. Bile rose in my throat. I had to stop him.

The kicking ceased and Moses looked round, his hands resting on his hips, and I drew deeper into the shadows. The man was too upright, his movements too assured. It was not Moses doing the kicking, but Moses lying grunting and sobbing on the path. The man stood towering over him like some avenging daemon, the light catching his cloak, his huge bee-keeper's hat with its heavy veil, hiding his face, and I crouched lower as he glanced in my direction. He reached down, hooking his hands under Moses arms, dragging him across the brick path to the door of the little painted shed.

The green door looked grey in the half-light and I watched the man fling it open and drag Moses inside, my stomach sickening as I heard further, brutal kicking. I was too terrified to move. The man was coming out, stripping off his cloak, throwing it back into the shed on top of Moses' prostrate body. He looked round, pulling off his hat, and I caught a glimpse of tousled hair and the furious eyes of Daniel Maddox.

He looked evil, no trace of the gentle man who had filled my heart with such compassion. His mouth was tight, furious, his movements swift, as if he had done this all before. With an angry twist he locked the door of the hut and put the key in his jacket pocket, and I stood trying to breathe. I had never felt so scared and crouched lower, watching him through the twisted branches. My cloak was dark green velvet, my hood pulled low over my hair and I froze as he turned once more in my direction.

It was as if he knew he was being watched. Moonlight lit the branches on either side of me but I was in shadow, pressed as far against the wall as I could go. The earth was damp, leaf mould crumbling on my trembling hands. A branch caught my cloak; he must have heard something as he stopped at the birdbath, the moon striking his boots, outlining his heavy basket. I thought he would turn back and come towards me but he walked swiftly down the row of herbs to his hothouse.

I was too terrified to stay, too terrified to leave. I needed to go to Moses but I was too petrified to move. I stood rooted to the spot, knowing Moses would be in pain and I had to go to him, but the door was locked and there was no window.

Poor, poor Moses. My heart jolted in sudden realization – this was not the first time he had been kicked so cruelly. Daniel Maddox must have done this to him before, perhaps many times. His painful walk was as a result of kicking, not rheumatism. It was suddenly so clear – Moses was terrified of Daniel Maddox. That was why he had become such a recluse. Moses had run away when Luke wanted to examine him because Luke would have seen the bruises inflicted on him by such an evil brute. I tried to stop myself from shaking: poor, dear Moses, alone and undefended, at the mercy of such a bully; protecting his beautiful garden from an evil, vicious man, enduring everything out of love for Amelia. She must be told – everyone must be told.

Daniel Maddox was in his hothouse; I could see him moving among the benches of plants. If I reached the birdbath without him seeing me, I could make a dash for the gate that led to the river, but even as I contemplated going, I knew it was probably futile. Henry might never come; my note had been too vague, he might not have understood it and I would spend the rest of the night fearing Daniel Maddox might find me. He had sensed someone was there, he had searched the shadows; that long, penetrating look had been more than just caution. He knew someone was watching and he would come back. He would find me hiding and know I had seen him.

I stared through the wisteria, searching the hothouse. Daniel Maddox was out of sight, bending down, emptying his basket, and I saw my chance. I would keep to the path along the wall where it was the darkest and go back to the shrubbery to wait by the terrace. I would have to leave Moses for the moment. This had obviously happened before but it would never happen again. I would go straight back and tell Amelia. Lady Carew would dismiss Daniel Maddox and summon Luke. Moses would have the best care but I had to leave him now – I could not risk confronting a man like that on my own. I was strong, but he would overpower me too easily.

I was nearly at the gate, making no sound. Suddenly, I tripped and a bell shattered the silence. My hands grazed the bricks and I tried to sit up but a shadow crossed my path, muddy boots on the path beside me. I looked up. His hair was dishevelled, his eyes piercing mine.

'Not a rabbit, but Miss Lilly, how very surprising.' He laughed to cover the threat in his voice, but there was no hiding the cruelty in his eyes. 'How very pleasant to have your company. Are you alone?' He looked over my shoulder to the shadows beyond.

'I am…I couldn't sleep…it's such a beautiful night after such a warm day…the garden smells divine. I hope you don't mind, but I came to see if the cereus might bloom.'

'It's not a full moon.'

'Does it really need to be a full moon? Surely it's bright enough?'

He was standing so close, his hand reaching down for my elbow, helping me up, but he did not let go. His grip tightened as he began drawing me to the hothouse. 'Come and see for yourself. I'm delighted you've come. I'm busy getting everything packed and ready – there's so much to do if I'm to leave everything neat and tidy. Now you're here, you can see for yourself that the cereus lies dormant. Won't you join me for a drink?'

His grip was too firm, his voice unkind. 'No – I must go back...I shouldn't have come. I've been very silly...what will they think if they find out I've been out at night?'

'What indeed?' His voice had turned vicious, a further tightening of his hand as he drew me into the hothouse. The humid air caught my throat, the overwhelming scent of the flowers making it hard to breathe.

'A farewell drink, Miss Lilly. Will you join me and wish me well?' He shut the hothouse door, turning the key, placing it in his pocket. 'Forgive me, a mere precaution. These plant boxes are very valuable – as are the orchids. Turn my back and thieves could steal the lot.'

He was no longer pretending to be charming; he was watching me, a terrifying glint in his eyes. He knew I had seen him. His plant boxes were protected by planks and nailed firmly down with only one remaining open, the heavy basket on the floor in front of it. 'Will you have cider... or mead...or will you share a bottle of wine?' He reached down to the bottom shelf and I thought I would faint. I could

410

hardly breathe, the humid air, the heady perfume stifling me, making me dizzy. The wine bottle looked familiar.

Not this bottle, not tonight, but that first night when I had surprised him. He had bent down in just the same way – but the cork was already pulled from the bottle and no glass lay ready. An uncorked bottle and no glass – he told me he was drinking alone but he had not been drinking.

He was watching me, the lines round his mouth tightening. Gone was any pretence of being shy or grateful: no smile, no lies about unrequited love, no pulling at my heart strings. We were past that. Just the calculating stare of a vicious man and I stifled my scream as my terror grew. He knew George Godwin. The thought was terrifying. He knew George Godwin. They were both from Devon – only this afternoon I had seen them nod to each other in polite greeting. I fought my dizziness, trying to smile. 'A glass of wine would be lovely.'

'Then wine it shall be. I hate to drink alone. We can toast my departure and the wonderful opportunity that awaits me.'

I could see it so clearly. Mr Maddox had been bending over his potting table at the far end with a bottle of wine open beside him. The bottle was the exact same shape; he had opened it but was not going to drink it. I could hardly stand for the fear sweeping through me. He had been filling the bottle with laudanum.

He was the other man – the ruthless killer who had stabbed the boatmen and Private Evans to death. He had the eyes of a killer, I could see that now. They were devouring me, cold, calculating eyes making my blood turn to ice. He had been testing how much laudanum to put in the bottles – trying out the doses. Those days when Moses was asleep all day – had he been made to drink the wine to see what dose was needed?

He was coming closer, his eyes glinting in the moonlight – the man who had just locked me in his hothouse was the very man who had opened the prison gates and freed the woman. He was the one who had given the boy the baskets and started the fire. He handed me the wine and I gripped the stem.

'You're shaking, Miss Lilly.'

Was that what killers looked like when they were about to kill again? He had seen me hiding in the shadows. The wine would be drugged, I would be found tomorrow washed up along the river.

I could not hide my trembling. The wine rippled in the glass and I bent to sip it, turning round, pretending to swallow. This would be the most difficult role I had ever played. 'This wine is lovely, thank you.'

His eyes followed me as I walked between his newly commissioned plant troughs. All except one had been sealed with planks and nailed tightly shut. There was straw on the ground, spilling out of a sack. It was him I had watched tend the beehives, not Moses. The bee-keeper's hat and cloak were to keep his identity hidden, but why tend the beehives?

'Does anyone know you're here?'

'Amelia knows. She was too tired to come…' He was planning what to do with me. I could scream all I liked but no one would hear. He would overpower me with those huge gardener's hands. He would stifle me, drag me to the water's

412

edge and force my head into the shallow water. The shingle would leave no prints and the tide would wash away all trace of my struggle.

He saw me glance at the heavy basket and his voice sliced the air. 'What are you really doing here, Miss Lilly? You're not a fool – you know the cereus only blooms in the full moon. Amelia doesn't know you're here, does she? No one knows you're here except me…not even Moses knows you're here.'

He must be hiding something in the beehives; hiding it there and transferring it to his boxes. Something had been niggling me; something I had forgotten but I remembered it now. Moses had drawn two bee-keeper's hats. Amelia had thought it meant he needed another one, but he must have been trying to warn her that another man was attending his bees.

I turned my back, tipping my wine quickly into a large flowerpot, pretending to drink, but he caught the reflection in the window and his heavy boots stomped behind me. He grabbed my elbow, clamping it tight.

'Not drinking your wine? Why's that?' He forced me round but I could not look at him. He had killer's hands, a killer's clamped mouth. 'What are you *really* doing here, Miss Lilly?' His laugh was cruel, his grip bruising my arm. 'You look scared…are you scared, Miss Lilly? Is there a reason why you can't look me in the eye?'

Chapter Forty-three

Through the glass, I saw a shadow cross the birdbath, a momentary disturbance in the otherwise silent garden, and sudden hope flashed through me. I shook my elbow free, edging my way round the plants, the profusion of orchids blocking my view. There was a gap between two of the pots and I leaned over the bench, peering through the stems to search the moonlit garden. Daniel Maddox came straight to my side, standing squarely behind me.

I knew to sound angry. 'Mr Maddox,' I said, matching his tight mouth and clipped tone, 'I believe you know very well why I'm here. If it's money you're after then you can have it – I'll give you more than adequate funds for your silence.'

I could see his surprise in the sudden stiffening of his shoulders and my courage strengthened. 'You know very well I've come to meet my lover, so we might as well talk freely – he's the man I love, *not* the man I'm intended to marry. He's out there waiting for me but if this gets out the scandal will ruin me. I can pay well. I'm a very wealthy woman. I don't have sufficient money with me in Trenwyn but I can get the money into your account as soon as I return to Truro – all I ask for is your *absolute* silence.' He made no movement, his jacket almost touching my cloak. 'No one knows I'm here because no one must *ever* know. Mr Maddox…name your price but promise me your silence.'

'He's out there?'

'You know he is.' My hands were trembling; if I gripped the stem of the glass any tighter, it would shatter.

He leaned forward, peering through the glass. 'I can see him – he's behind the wisteria. How long's he been there?'

'He's just arrived. I've been waiting for him in the shrubbery – Mr Maddox, does twenty pounds seem reasonable?' I sounded angry but my knees felt weak. I could hardly walk yet he must not see my terror. I brushed past him, making for the door and he followed close behind, reaching for the key, holding it in his hand.

'*Thirty pounds*, Miss Lilly, and I hope we part amicably. Your good opinion is important to me…maybe an offer of work should I ever require it?'

I stared back into those black eyes. 'Lord Entworth will give you full employment the moment you return. I can assure you of a *very* generous salary and anything else you might require.'

He stared across the garden. A dark figure was standing in the moonlight, his hat pulled low over his face. No glasses glinted back at me but my heart leapt, thumping wildly in my chest. Daniel Maddox was still not letting me out. 'And thirty pounds will enter my account?'

'You'll get everything – and more.' He put the key in the door, turning it swiftly. 'Now, lock it behind me,' I said, pulling my hood over my hair.

I knew he would not. He would follow me, watch me: we both knew I had seen too much. Henry must stay in the shadows; I would run to the gate and down to the river, that way he would not be recognized. I could hear Henry's footsteps crunching the shingle behind me and I ran for my life along the water's edge, taking shelter in the overhanging trees. I swung round.

'Henry, we're in great danger – don't let him see your face. I told him you were my lover – that's the only reason he let me go.'

He drew me to him. 'You're trembling. Let me hold you.'

I leaned against his chest, taking refuge in his strong arms. 'He's the killer…he and George Godwin. The two of them…that night in the inn…I heard George shout out for a poultice and he shouted the same today…he knew Edgar… he framed him…I saw Daniel Maddox kicking Moses…he's been hiding stuff in the beehives…he's evil. He had the same wine bottle…I think they drugged Moses so they knew how much to use…'

He held me tightly, my hood had slipped and his lips brushed my hair. 'He's watching us now. I can see him in the bushes.'

Tears of relief splashed down my cheeks, my hands shaking against his jacket. 'I'm so glad you came – I didn't know if you would. He was going kill me…he was honestly going to kill me.'

His arms tightened. 'No one will harm you. You're safe, now...I've brought my pistol and I'll use it if he comes anywhere near us. But you'll have to say that all again. Take a deep breath, talk only when you're ready.'

'He mustn't know it's you, Henry.'

'He won't. My hat's too large and I've taken off my glasses.' His lips brushed my hair again. 'Daniel Maddox and George Godwin...but why? Just for money? What are we missing?'

'He's hiding something in the beehives. He's transferring it to the plant boxes and sealing it with nails. It's not earth. There was no earth in the boxes – just straw.'

His arms were as strong as I knew they would be, his chest as hard, his lips resting against my hair. 'I'm afraid we need to make this look real,' he whispered.

My heart jolted. 'Real?'

'A lover would hold you more tightly...I'm sorry...may I?' He drew me closer. 'What would they be hiding? Why free the French prisoners?' He was freshly shaven, his jacket and hat dark in the moonlight. He smelled of soap, of recent exertion, and I clung to him, my cheek resting against his chest. I could hear his heart thumping. 'This is very awkward, Miss Lilly, but I'm going to have to pretend to kiss you... he'll know you're lying if we don't look like real lovers.'

He bent slowly forward, his finger gently lifting my chin. His lips were a fraction from my own, hovering, almost brushing mine but not quite. Not quite. The moon was dancing over the river, the owls hooting from the trees above, and I closed my eyes, wanting, desperately wanting, to feel his lips press against mine. He pulled away. 'I'm so sorry...'

'No, it had to be done.'

'He's still watching. I suggest we sit against that trunk and you can tell me everything.' He undid his jacket, his white shirt catching the moonlight, and we knelt down, the waves lapping the water beside us. A fallen trunk lay along the water's edge and he laid out his jacket, his face almost unfamiliar without his glasses. He had fine bones, a strong chin, but it was the kindness in his eyes that had always drawn me. They held compassion – strength and kindness, no sign of arrogance. Yet that night in the shrubbery they had sparkled with mischief.

The shingle smelled of fresh seaweed and damp stones, the scent of manure drifting from the meadow alongside us. 'I nearly didn't get your message. George Godwin gave it straight to Edgar. I was leaving but Edgar called me back. He said he couldn't make sense of it and thought I should see it. I read it and grabbed the pistol – I knew straight away you wanted me to come.'

'Maddox is evil, Henry. I saw real hatred in his eyes. He's a callous killer. Pretending to be so deferential and in love with Amelia but he hates us all. He's been terrorizing Moses.'

His arms tightened, his lips brushing my hair. 'You're safe now, Angelica. I won't let him anywhere near you.' I wanted him to kiss me. Wanted it so badly, willing him to lean that little bit closer. Just that little bit nearer. 'Was Moses badly harmed? Should we go to him?'

'He's locked in his hut. I saw him lying on the floor.'

'I think we'll have to leave him. The man's a killer. He knows when to kill and when to harm. He won't risk Moses being found dead just before he leaves. A man like that knows just how much pain he can inflict without arousing suspicion. Moses will stagger from that hut in the morning like every other morning, but I promise you, Daniel Maddox will swing for what he's done.'

His grip tightened and I knew I belonged in those strong arms. I loved Henry Trevelyan so completely. I loved his strength, I loved his gentleness. I loved the way his eyes creased into laughter lines, the way the side of his mouth curled into a smile. I loved his short hair, his straight nose, his strange mixture of humour and seriousness. I loved his poems, the way he talked of trade policies. I loved his man-ners...I loved everything about him.

'I've been trying to understand why Martha Selwyn locked the tunnel behind the prisoners,' he whispered. 'I couldn't understand why she didn't go with them but it makes sense now. She went back to George Godwin.'

He leaned against the trunk, pulling me gently next to him, his arm keeping its tight hold. 'A bit closer perhaps, Miss Lilly...real lovers would lie entwined but we might just get away with sitting side by side...I think that should do it...perhaps I ought to play with your hair?'

'Yes...if it's...necessary.'

He curled a ringlet round his finger, bringing it to his lips, and a terrible ache coursed through me, such acute longing. He was so close, my body on fire. I wanted him to reach forward, his lips to brush mine. He stopped, the curl left dangling against my cheek. His voice was urgent, still a whisper. 'How can we have been so blind? It's obvious – she went back to *help* George…to steal…what would it be – gold, money, jewellery? The caskets are weighed – only the *weight* is checked.'

'You mean the escape wasn't real – or at least it was real, but planned as some sort of cover?'

'Yes – an elaborate way to hide all trace…as prize agent, George is responsible for the safe handling of everything his clients bring him – ships, cargoes, money, gold. His job is to record everything and ensure the prizes are transported safely up to London. Ships remain where they dock, cargoes are sold locally, but any gold or coins or jewels are weighed by the casket. His job is to record them, but the valuation and costing is done in London.'

'But he's opened them?'

'He must have…the caskets are sealed with chains and the keys travel separately. The weights are recorded when they're received into port and when they're transported to London. *No one* is allowed to open the caskets.'

'But he has.'

'Yes…somehow, he's opened one – or some. But the gold would be heavy. He needed to drag it away from the castle so he needed the guards to be asleep and he needed a diversion. The escape was the perfect cover. All it took was a sail upriver and Daniel Maddox hid what they stole where no one would think to look. They probably replaced the weight with shingle.' He looked across the glistening beach. 'I think we should lie back again. I wonder if you should play with the buttons on my shirt?'

He nestled me against him, his arm tightening round my

shoulders. 'Obviously just pretend to – he won't see details, just the outline.' The top button of his shirt was undone and I rolled the second button in my fingers. I could feel the strength of his muscles, his chest rising and falling beneath my hand. He closed his eyes, leaning back against the rough trunk. I could feel fine hair beneath my hand. I wanted to trail my fingers over his chest, trace the contours of neck, his cheek, the outline of his lips.

'The master and mate of *Snow Goose* must have recognized Daniel Maddox,' I whispered. 'He was often on the quayside. He must have taken them the wine but they recognized him from his boxes – so he went back to kill them. There's too much at stake, Henry. Daniel Maddox has killed three men – he'll kill us too.'

He opened his eyes, his voice firm. 'He'll not risk coming near us – I'll shoot him if he approaches – that will wake everyone.' He reached into his bag, drawing out the pistol I had seen glinting on the road back to Truro and laid it beside him on the stones. 'He'll be expecting me to be armed. A man does not row upriver to trespass in the garden of his lover without some means of defence.'

Henry had always seen me as myself, never any pretence, but as I watched him place the pistol by his side and settle back, my heart was breaking. Father had been the ruin of his family. He must hate me – no wonder he still called me Miss Lilly.

'Does anyone else know about George?' he asked.

I stopped playing with his button. 'No one else knows, only us. Daniel Maddox leaves the day after tomorrow. He's told everyone he's got employment as a plant collector but those letters must all be lies. He'll just sail away with the gold – George Godwin will probably go with him.'

The pungent aroma of tobacco smoke drifted across the bay. 'I'll go straight to Admiral Penrose and ask him to take command. He's kicking his heels round Falmouth and he'll be delighted to step in.' His arm tightened, his lips brushing my hair. 'Daniel Maddox is still watching, Miss Lilly. I might have to pretend to kiss you again.' He curled the abandoned ringlet in his finger. 'Perhaps I should undo this ribbon?'

I could barely speak, the pain so wretched, I wanted to cry. 'You must hate me, Mr Trevelyan,' I whispered. 'My father was the cause of your family's ruin. You must have watched me through the window with such loathing.'

Chapter Forty-four

A sudden breeze rippled the water, blowing against our cheeks. The leaves shimmered on the trees, the shingle glistening as the tide retreated. 'The tide's turned,' he said, pulling his arm from round me and sitting upright. 'That wind's from the south – blowing straight upriver. It'll make my row back slightly bouncy. I'll watch you safely across the lawn – then I'll row straight to Admiral Penrose.' He glanced across the curve of the bay. 'Daniel Maddox won't follow me – not if there's gold in his plant troughs.'

He sounded distant, different, nothing like the man who had teased me about ladders and windows, who had argued with me about trade policy and shipping.

'Do you hate us very much?' I repeated.

His voice softened, his whisper catching his throat. 'I don't hate you, Miss Lilly...far, far from it.'

'I know nothing about you...yet you know so much about me. You've always kept so silent...we've talked, but you've never given me a sense of how you feel. You keep everything so close – you give nothing away. It's like you're roped up, bound by silence – as if you stifle what you really want to say and I understand why now.'

He stared at the glistening water. 'I've never looked at you with loathing – never, ever loathing. I looked at you with shame, Angelica – not shame that we were poor, that we were starving, that I had no shoes, that my shirtsleeves never reached my wrists or that my trousers had darns, but because my grandfather stole from your father and yet your mother still sought us out for her charity.'

'But there was never any proof…your grandfather was *accused* of the theft, but you said he always claimed his innocence.'

'He did…always claim his innocence.' He tapped his joined fingers against his mouth as if in prayer. 'He told everyone he was innocent…except me – to *me* he told the truth – not exactly the truth…not straight out…but enough for me to know he stole the money. He just didn't expect to get caught.'

Blood rushed to my cheeks. 'Why tell you? Why burden you with knowledge like that? That was cruel…he should never have told you. Does anyone else know?'

He shook his head, a slight smile on his lips. 'You rush to my defence? Thank you. I was angry too – mainly because I bore the secret alone.' His smile vanished. 'Like you, I never wanted to burden my mother or sisters with the shame. They believed in him. They loved him. I was eight and my father was working day and night to clear his debts. We had moved from our home to save money. My mother was taking in washing.

She had a small child and was expecting another. We lived on bread alone but my father was proud and hard working. He believed his father was innocent and was determined to clear the debt. He was going to restore our good name if it killed him – and it did. It took two long and hard years but the money was recouped and my grandfather would be free the moment the last farthing was paid.'

A pink haze lit the sky to the east, the first light of dawn. There was pain deep in his voice. 'I was a child of eight – I loved my grandfather, we'd been inseparable from my birth – I followed him everywhere...he taught me to read and write – how to make long columns of figures add up. I never thought him dishonourable or a thief, but the last time I visited him, I saw a side to him I'd never seen before.'

He picked up a shell, turning it between his fingers. 'Bodmin debtors' gaol is a foul place. I watched him deteriorate despite all the food we could afford, the oranges and lemons smuggled in to keep his lips from cracking. It was a cramped, stinking place where men were sent to rot. I used to vomit when I left. I hated going but I wanted to visit him – I loved him so much and wanted him home. I wanted everything back to how it had been, but that day...that day I knew my dream would never come true. We both knew he was dying. A purulent cough wracked his chest; he had lost too much weight – he was bone thin and unkempt. He stank and had lost most of his teeth...and I knew if we got him home, it would only be to die.'

His voice dropped. 'That day I had gone by myself and he grabbed my arm with his bony fingers, forcing me to look at

him. *Your father's heart is weak*, he told me. *He's an ill man —
he'll not be there for you…he's never going to provide for you, but
I've seen to your future. Use it well. Make it count. Take care of your
mother and sisters.'*

'He stole the money for *you*?'

'I didn't know what he meant – not at the time – all I knew
was that he was confessing to the theft…so you must understand, I wasn't looking at you with hatred, Angelica. I could
hardly hold my head up for shame, not only knowing that my
grandfather was an embezzler, but the terrible knowledge
that he'd done it for me.'

'Your poor father – working so hard to clear his debt. He
died because of it…?'

'He died – but not because of it. It just brought his death
forward. Father was never strong – he'd long been battling a
weak heart. I often saw him clutch his chest – he used to go
blue round his mouth. He had angry red veins on his cheeks
and was getting increasingly breathless by the day. He'd turn
away from Mother so she wouldn't see him but I saw him.
I used to lie awake thinking he wouldn't be there in the
morning. Mother begged him not to work so hard but he
was determined that our family debt must be cleared and our
name restored.'

'You were eight – your grandfather should *never* have
burdened you with his dying confession.'

'That's what I thought…and why it was so hard for me to
accept your mother's baskets. She showed us true compassion, Angelica – and Sir Alexander showed us true charity.
Without their example, I'd not be the man I am today. Your

426

mother's alms and Sir Alex's bursary made me a very different person. I'd never have gone to Truro Grammar School, and I certainly would never have gone to Oxford.' He smiled again. There was love in his eyes — love for Mamma. 'Their kindness and generosity was the making of me.'

'You went to Oxford?'

He shrugged, his smile slightly rueful. 'My grandfather taught me well. Sir Alex found I had rather a good head for figures — only *my* columns added up correctly.'

I loved his smile, the slight rise to his eyebrow. 'And your mother married again — to Reverend Penhaligan. I liked him very much — though his sermons went on too long. Your mother was so kind to me. She used to leave me gingerbread on my pillow…'

His eyes held such tenderness and searing heat burned my chest. 'I know. I helped her fill the little gauze bags. I watched all your plays, Angelica — the first when you were fifteen…the second when you were sixteen.' His voice broke and he coughed to clear his throat. 'The last play was when you were seventeen. I was twenty-one and had just left Oxford. We met on the lawn. I'd taken off my glasses because I thought you'd think me too bookish…but I was so clumsy and bumped into you. You won't remember — but I remember it so clearly.'

'I do remember,' I whispered. I felt safe in his arms. I wanted him to hold me again, draw me to him, let me rest my head against his shoulders but he sat staring at the retreating tide. Islands of seaweed were forming on the sand, the smell of decaying mud; from the orchard beyond, a cockerel crowed.

He cleared his throat and his voice hardened. 'That was two weeks before I got a letter. The signature was hastily written, almost illegible – it asked me to meet a man on the quayside. No one was to come with me – I was to be alone and I was to burn the letter once I'd read it. It didn't come as a shock – I'd been half-expecting it and I burned the letter, knowing this was something to do with my grandfather. An old man was waiting for me on the quay, his white hair blowing in the wind. He knew exactly who I was and though I'd never seen him before, he looked strangely familiar. He introduced himself to me as Josiah Trevelyan – my grandfather's brother.

'He had a stout stick in one hand, a leather case in his other. He was sunburned, with a long white beard and side whiskers, a stiff gait, gnarled fingers, but he looked robust and in good health. We went to the tavern and he spread papers out in front of me. The money had bought two ships – one for me, one for him. Both ships had been damaged but they had been well insured and he had replaced them. The two new ships were profitable, both doing well.

'One set of papers was in my name, the other was in his. My grandfather had stipulated that until my twenty-first birthday any profit would go to his brother, after that, the profits of my ship would come to me – as would the ship itself.'

He threw down the shell and picked up a smooth round stone. 'She was behind us on the quay – a beautiful two-masted lugger, complete with crew. She was called *Dolphin* and until the last six months had been trading from New York. I was twenty-one years old and I was being handed a bank draft of fifty pounds and a profitable ship with the crew loading her with your father's ore.'

'*Father's* ore? I remember her…she was part of the Welsh fleet. She was a beautiful ship—'

'And in pristine condition, yet I could hardly look at her. She seemed tainted. I'd worked so hard to rid myself from the stigma of embezzlement and there I was – staring at my grandfather's ill-gotten gains.' He glanced up at my silence.

'You refused her?' I whispered.

'Yes, I refused her. I refused her and I refused his bank draft. I wanted nothing to do with either and I told him in no uncertain terms. But the old man was expecting that – I had a month to decide. It was in the document I held in my hand – an agreement they'd both signed. I had every right to refuse the ship and his brother would keep it, but I must wait a month before making my decision.

'I walked away…or rather, I stormed away. I was angry, very angry – furious to have the past come back to haunt me. It felt like the devil tempting me…but the ship's accounts had been spread out before me – the harbour dues, the price charged for docking and unloading, and though I had hardly glanced at them I saw at once where profit could be made. A ship's company needed to own their own dock.'

'Father knows that – to his cost. That's why he's building a smelter in Porthcarrow and why he's interested in—' I stopped.

'In transferring his smelters to South Wales where he'll most probably build an iron works…maybe branch into building iron bridges or iron barges – if I guess correctly.'

He smiled and my heart burned like fire. I loved this man. I adored him. 'You didn't just walk away, did you?' I whispered.

'I thought I had. For a week I lay awake at night – the next week I took to walking in the moonlight. The next week, I walked by day. I walked everywhere, following the rivers and creeks, getting lost, wading knee deep in water – then I realized what it was I was doing. I wasn't deliberating whether to take the ship or not, I was searching for the perfect stretch of river where the creeks could be dredged and sluices built. A tidal reservoir could be constructed and wharfs built – then I went to your father.'

'*You went to Father?*'

His voice hardened. 'It was naive of me, certainly. I went thinking I could restore our name. I wasn't going to take the ship – instead, I had a plan that would wipe the slate clean. In Oxford, I'd shaken off all sense of stigma but on my return to Truro, I saw the veiled look in people's eyes and knew they had long memories. The debt had been repaid and my grandfather had served his punishment – he had even died because of it – but it wasn't enough for those with long memories. Sir Alex had offered me a secure post with the Transport Board but I didn't take it. I wanted to make amends, prove to your father that the name Trevelyan was honourable and could be trusted.'

A knot twisted my stomach. 'What did he say?'

'Your father laughed me out of his office. Well, not laughed, so much as *shouted* me out. No, I'll be honest – he all but threw me out.'

The knot twisted further. 'Father never shouts — he rarely shows anger — you must have said something terrible.'

'I did. But I also asked for employment — to wipe the slate clean and restore people's trust in my name. I told him with a small investment he could make huge savings on his shipping. Land was available — leases were being sold for long stretches of the riverbank and I suggested he bought as much land as he could. I told him to dredge the creek and build sluices...I offered to manage a new wharf for him. I had thought of everything — I had the exact calculations, even the name of a reputable dredging company that would do the work. I laid the costings in front of him, detailing my plans, but he was resolute. He wanted nothing more to do with me. Nothing. I was to leave and never come back — our business was at an end.'

Anger flamed my cheeks. 'No one should bear the sins of their fathers. He was wrong not to give you a chance. I'm so sorry...What did you do?'

'I went straight back to Josiah Trevelyan and collected up the papers of the *Dolphin*. I deposited the fifty pounds into a new bank account and went to Falmouth to mortgage the ship through Robert Fox. The next day, I bought the land and the next week I sailed to New York on my own — if mortgaged — ship.'

'Good. I'd have done exactly the same...*if* I was a man. Only I would have started on the dredging.'

He smiled, his hand reaching for mine. 'I did. I engaged the dredging company before I left. They had my detailed plans but they had equally good ideas of their own so I left it to them. I could not stay in Truro and I was glad to be travelling. I arrived in New York in the middle of a yellow fever epidemic and the port was in disarray. The whole town was in chaos and I soon realized why my grandfather's two ships had been doing so well. Only *British* ships could trade with British colonies and I took every opportunity I could. I soon expanded. A new stock market had just been established and I sold shares in my company and invested in more ships. I sold the *Dolphin* and gave the money to the wives and children of men lost to the fever. My investment in Truro was beginning to show a profit and that helped finance more investments.'

'The wharf in Truro is yours...?'

His voice dropped. 'Yes, and it pays very handsomely – especially with your Father's Welsh fleet being so busy.'

'I thought it belonged to the Tregellan Line.'

He smiled, that slight curl to the corner of his mouth. 'My mother's maiden name – one day, I'll change it. I'm sorry... do you mind me holding your hand...?'

'No...we must make it look real.'

He turned my hand over, stretching out my palm. 'That day – I went to your father with the intention of telling him everything. I was going to ask his advice but I made a terrible mistake. I angered him. He asked after my mother and I told him where she lived...and that I'd seen you in your plays... that you were...that I was—' He stopped, his lips brushing softly against my palm. 'Angelica...you once told me that I should tell the woman I love that I loved her. That I adore her...that she is the only woman I could ever love...that she has stolen my heart so utterly...so completely...that I could never love anyone else…and that she would never know unless I spoke of my true feelings—'

He stopped, suddenly lifting his lips from my hand. 'How do you know your father had my grandfather arrested? You didn't know before.'

My hand burned from his touch. 'Father told Lord Entworth – they were both here earlier this afternoon. They thought someone might be trying to frame Edgar and a possible motive might be hatred for our family – Father told Lord Entworth all about your grandfather and Lord Entworth said he would have you arrested. I was going to tell you…'

His face went stony, his mouth tight. 'Ah yes, Lord Entworth. For a moment there, I had forgotten Lord Entworth.'

'He said he'd summon any number of witnesses. Lord Entworth's a very powerful man. He said it would be *his* court and he didn't have to wait until Sir Alex got back because he said the charge would be treason. He said his word was law…'

Henry reached for his bag, his voice turning cold. 'Yes, and how very convenient it is for him.'

'Father didn't know what to think – but it doesn't matter…they'll soon know the truth. But Henry, you have to take care…I was worried you might not come because I was frightened Lord Entworth might have already arrested you.'

His voice was clipped, back to being roped-up. 'It's very kind of you to warn me, Miss Lilly. I'll go straight to Admiral Penrose and not return to the castle. My ship leaves for New York at the end of the week and I shall be on it.'

My heart ripped in sudden pain. 'You can't go. Henry, you can't just leave.'

His voice was resolute, his mouth tight. 'I have to...I can't stay.'

A glorious pink glowed across the early sky; the cockerel's crowing gaining strength, echoing across the stillness. Song birds were waking in the hedge behind us, cattle ambling to the water's edge, lowing softly, nudging each other as they stooped to drink. The sand was glistening, the wind blowing against my cheeks and I forced back my tears. He was angry. No, he was resolute. He was leaving, going back to her. He had plucked up the courage to tell her he loved her and I turned away, forcing back the tears that welled in my eyes. I could hardly breathe, my heart shattering into a thousand pieces. I loved him. I loved him so completely and he was leaving me. This wonderful, clever, kind and compassionate man was leaving me.

A streak of white caught my attention and I looked up. Bethany was running down the lawn, her apron billowing in the wind around her. Her hands clasped her mobcap as she disappeared momentarily behind the branches of a magnolia bush. 'Bethany's coming.' I turned round. Henry had put the pistol in his bag and I got to my feet, watching him grab his jacket and run for cover. I forced back my tears. Bethany was on the gravel, bending over to recover her breath.

'There ye are, Miss Lilly – ye're such an early bird. Soon as I saw yer window wide open, I knew ye'd be out here. Ye're watching the sunrise. It's a pink sky...means it won't last. The weather's turning, an' what with Lady Clarissa's birthday coming up…and the cricket match—' She stopped, looking up at me. 'Miss Lilly, ye're crying. Dear love, ye're crying.'

Yes, I was crying; salty tears rolling down my cheeks. I felt so empty, my heart ripping in two. *The pain of enchantment lingers for ever*. He was leaving me. He would return to New York and would never know I loved him. *You can't rely on woodland sprites and fairies – a woman can't just guess*. I had to tell him I loved him. How else would he know? I turned to the bushes lining the shingle, pleading through my tears: 'Cricket…the cricket match…we need every player we can get – *everyone* who plays cricket. Please come. Please, please come.'

Bethany took my arm, leading me gently across the shingle. 'Come with me, my love. Come back to bed – only ye seem very over wrought. Here, let me help ye. I'll bring ye some nice warm milk…only…we know about yer brother, an' we're that worried about ye. Come, let's get ye back to bed.'

I froze like a statue. *I will only ever love one woman*. Could it be me? Could it be? Tears rolled down my cheeks and I spun round, shouting for all I was worth. 'I hate Lord Entworth, I hate him…hate him. I'll never marry him. Never…'

Bethany looked petrified. 'No, my love…course not… no one will make ye marry him – least not Lady Clarissa… come with me…come, my love…let's get ye back to bed. Perhaps Miss Amelia can give ye something…come…that's it, my love…come this way.'

Chapter Forty-five

Trenwyn House
Wednesday 17th August 1796, 9:30 p.m.

They kept me in bed all day and I was glad of it, swallowing the buttered eggs as best I could. Lady Clarissa had brought them up to my room herself, balancing the silver tray on my bed, watching me eat every mouthful as she updated me on her birthday preparations. They had filled my room with flowers, Amelia running up and down the stairs to bring me books and snippets of stolen frangipane and caraway cake, and freshly squeezed lemon juice, and a bowl of raspberry sorbet. By afternoon, they had allowed me to sit by the window and I had witnessed the flags being hung in long lines across the terrace and listened to the hammering of nails as the tent took shape.

I had stared down the newly cut lawn to the dazzling blue water of Carrick Roads, my longing so great my whole body ached. Henry Trevelyan was missing. Major Basset had mobilized his Dragoons and the Fencibles were searching every ship. He would be found. Frederick had been given leave of absence for his mother's birthday and I watched him standing on the terrace with his arm around Charity. A makeshift stage had been erected, a bower decked with flowers. There was to be a concert, Charity and Amelia would sing and I would recite sonnets.

The roasting pit had been dug and was already fired. The barrels were in place. Lord Carew had chosen his finest claret and Cook was being given a wide berth by everyone. Bethany had finished sewing her dress and Persephone's ribbons lay ready by her sty. Horace had been washed and was rolling in the newly cut grass and long lines of lanterns now decorated the shrubbery.

Amelia stood by my bed in her silk nightgown, smiling her sweet smile, and I caught the aroma of hot honey and lemon. 'Just the *tiniest* pinch of valerian,' she whispered. 'You need to sleep.' Her tincture was bitter, despite the honey, but I swallowed it in one and she took the cup from me, crossing to the windows to close the shutters. She pulled back my eiderdown and rearranged her pillow, leaning over to blow out the candle.

In the darkness, I whispered, 'Is Daniel Maddox leaving tomorrow?'

'Yes,' she whispered back. 'And I won't be sorry to see him go. He's to leave with the morning tide. A ship's coming to take him to Plymouth.'

'How was Moses today?'

'Busy cutting lavender – he's been like Mother's shadow for most of the day. He's hardly left her side but he's limping again. I've written to Dr Bohenna and asked him to come.'

'He'd like that,' I whispered, as the valerian took hold.

Chapter Forty-six

Trenwyn House
Thursday 18th August 1796, 10:00 a.m.

I would not go down, but sat watching Daniel Maddox from the terrace instead. I had seen the ship arrive and I stood staring in icy dread as they loaded his troughs carefully on to the deck. Lady Clarissa had arranged a line of honour and I watched him walk down the row of gardeners, nodding and accepting their good wishes, and my heart thumped with fear. What if Henry had been arrested? What if he had not had the chance to alert anyone? What if I was just letting this murdering thief go free?

Lord Carew and Lady Clarissa were waving from the jetty, their grandsons dancing with flags. Amelia handed Mr Maddox a basket and he was bowing, his hat clasped in his hand. He would have tears in his eyes, his parting words wracked with such pain. Moses was watching him too.

The sounds of last-minute panic were giving way to giggles and excitement. The heavy palm trees were in position, Cook was happy with the ice from the icehouse, and the maids had unravelled the knots in the maypole. The long trestle table

438

lay ready for the refreshments and already I could smell meat roasting in the pit.

Frederick and Charity were walking arm in arm below me on the lawn. He was in full naval uniform, his white sash shining in the bright sunshine, his gold buttons glinting. Charity was wearing her peach organza with matching roses in her hair. Their voices drifted on the breeze. 'We can only do what we can do, but it doesn't bode well. It'll be good to see Major Trelawney, though – I gather he's to umpire.'

'Can Amelia umpire? The rules don't stipulate the umpires have to be men.'

He kissed her gloved hand. 'You're absolutely right. I'll suggest that to Jethro.'

The ship had slipped her mooring, the crew hoisting her sails. A perfect summer's day, and fear clamped my heart. Bethany came to my side. 'Shall I get you into your gown now, Miss Lilly? Only, then I can see to Miss Amelia.'

Lord Entworth stood tall and commanding, watching me from across the terrace. I was wearing my best gown – my cream organza with lace frothing at my sleeves. My parasol was also Belgium lace, threaded with blue silk; there were blue silk ribbons on my bonnet with a mass of pink and cream silk flowers cascading down one side. My gloves were made of fine gauze, my satin shoes also blue, tied with white satin laces and decorated with mother-of-pearl buttons. The next Lady Entworth had obviously passed muster because his smile had broadened when he saw me. Now he was frowning.

Elizabeth Fox nodded at my whispered question. 'Yes – the Tregellan Line is gaining quite a reputation. We handle a lot of their shipments...' She looked over her shoulder, drawing me away. 'And it's always the same...a tenth of the cargo must go to charity – though he'll have to stop that getting quite so known. The owner of the ship is contesting Lord Entworth's sentence of hanging and deportation of the *so-called* rioters – he's absolutely determined to get their convictions over-ruled. We're drawing up a petition and taking it to the highest court. Matthew Reith says he'll take the case. There were *not* fifty people – and it was *not* a riot.' She stopped, swallowing hard. 'Though of course, we don't know who *he* is...'

'Yes you do,' I whispered. 'He's Henry Trevelyan – the man everyone's looking for.'

'Oh...is he?' She was a terrible liar, but then she probably never lied.

There was just the right amount of breeze blowing off the river to flutter the huge blue flag flying from the rooftop, but not enough to ruffle the feathers on the guests' headdresses. Elizabeth's white bonnet glowed in the sun.

'Is he safe, Elizabeth?' I whispered.

She smiled, bringing out her fan, tapping my arm. 'I don't know *who* or *what* you mean. We have recently learned, however, that if you leave the doors of an empty warehouse open, no one thinks to look inside.'

William and Frederick were dressed in their cricket clothes and were busy checking the boundaries, Major Trelawney walking stiffly by their sides. They were nodding in agreement but Amelia was shaking her head, pointing five yards further out. The groundsman moved the flags to her obvious satisfaction and the posts were knocked in again.

'I don't think the match is going to last very long,' I whispered. 'Does Mr Fox play?'

Elizabeth shook her head. 'I'm afraid not. They've already asked him.'

He was safe. He was in the warehouse, watching them search his ship. He would wait until the last moment and slip across the quayside to board the vessel as she was leaving. My emptiness felt like pain – the pain in his poems. The agony of being separated from the person you loved – the second point of a pair of compasses, bending towards the one you loved, never, ever, letting go.

Captain Pierre de la Croix was resplendent in his newly laundered French uniform, as Young William held Henry and Charles firmly by the hand. 'Are you coming, Miss Angel? Oh, sorry…that's what the servants call you…so sorry.'

'Coming where?'

'To see who that is.'

A ship was hauling down her sails, inching closer to the jetty. There were men on board, a woman's beautiful bonnet fluttering with its familiar ribbons, and tears sprang to my eyes. They were coming – my family was coming. I could see Father's black jacket and pointed hat, Edgar's mass of unruly curls. Luke Bohenna was standing ready to throw the rope and Mary was laughing, clapping her hands as the boat pulled alongside. I picked up my skirts and hurled myself across the terrace.

The path sparkled as I tore down the shrubbery, racing through the rose garden, stopping only to open the gate of the walled garden. I could hear them crunching the shingle and I threw my arms round Edgar, unable to speak. Tears splashed my cheeks as I clasped him to me.

'Steady on, Angelica. A man can't take this sort of emotion.' But he was smiling, and so was Father. He was undoing the buttons of his jacket, handing it to Mary, rolling up his sleeves as was Luke Bohenna behind him.

All of them, stripping off their jackets, their shirts catching the sun. 'We're here to play cricket,' said Father. 'I hope we're not too late.'

Edgar strode ahead, turning back to call to me, 'I hope those tears aren't because we've already lost.'

'No...no...you're just in time. They're just about to start. Lady Clarissa will be so pleased to see you.'

I watched them striding up the path, bumping into Young William and his two charges. I saw my family, reaching down, swinging the boys up on to their shoulders, walking to the terrace, each one of them a giraffe, and I turned to the wall, gripping my fists to my mouth. I needed time to compose myself, I needed time to breathe, to hide the disappointment ripping through me.

There was a crunch on the shingle, footsteps crossing the beach, and I wiped away my tears, afraid to be seen like this. Someone was coming into the walled garden and I turned round ready to don my mask, but caught my breath. Henry was holding out a posy of Angelica flowers and I ran to him, throwing my arms round him – the same wet hand in a soaking sleeve, reaching out to give me his rain-drenched posy, only today it was glorious sunshine and I could see his face. The face I loved.

'It's only ever been you,' he whispered.

'*Angelica* – you knew the flowers were *Angelica*?'

'I thought we might be too late for the funeral but I wanted your mother to take Angelica flowers with her. I admired your mother so much. I believe she knew all along my grand-father was guilty yet she gave us alms. She wasn't going to let a child bear the sins of his father.'

I lifted the flowers to inhale their scent. 'What did you say to Father – that day you went to him? What did you say that made him so angry?'

He held me tightly, drawing me to him as if he would never let me go. 'I didn't say anything – at first. But he must have sensed something in the way I spoke about you. He wheedled it out of me…and before I knew it, I was telling him how much I loved you – and that I wanted to marry you.'

Those words, those wonderful words, said with such love. 'And he threw you out?'

His arms tightened. 'Yes – really *very* forcibly. He told me I didn't stand a chance. You were engaged to a lord and were soon to join the peerage and that if I did really love you, I'd leave you alone and never pester him or you again.'

'He was lying…'

'He was protecting you, and quite rightly, too. I had nothing to offer – no name, no money, no way of giving you what you deserved. Anyone could see you were destined to shine and I understood exactly what he meant. I had nothing to offer, nothing at all.'

I belonged in those strong arms. How I belonged. 'Why did you come back, now, after so long?'

'I wasn't going to come back – not until I had rid myself of the longing. I was angry and hurt, furious that your father hadn't even given me the time of day. I was afraid to come back and explain where my ship had come from. I thought it would add to my already dubious reputation, but there I was in a new land with a fast ship. I had been given the chance to make good and I worked night and day to make it happen. I saw opportunities and I took them, driven by your father's taunts. Once I'd sold the ship, I felt differently. I had more than given back what I had been given but I still couldn't bring myself to tell Mother the source of the money I sent back for my sisters.'

'I'd have done just the same. I'd have taken the ship – the money had all been paid back. The punishment had been served.'

He held my hand to his lips, kissing it softly through my fine gauze gloves. 'I love the way you jump to my defence – just like you jumped to Edgar's. Watching you plead was the hardest thing I've ever had to do.' He kissed my hand again. 'Then, one day I got a letter from my mother – one glorious spring morning and I knew...or least, I hoped...I so fervently hoped I'd been given a second chance. I arranged a shipment of wheat and I stood on that deck praying I wasn't too late. Mother said you had sent her a shawl, that you weren't married, and that you were called Miss Angel by the people of Truro. Angelica, I couldn't get here fast enough, but when I did, I realized I was too late. You were engaged – your father had found you your lord.'

'I was never engaged to him – he's waiting to ask me now. I don't know who sought who, but it's a purely a financial arrangement on his part. He wants discounts on every smelting deal and money off his shipping costs.'

He smiled that rueful smile, the corners of his mouth lifting just a fraction. 'I think that's because his shipping costs are rather expensive,' he said, kissing my palm again.

'Double them, Henry.'

'I have done.' Across the garden we could see Moses dressed in his best clothes, opening the top vents of the glasshouse. 'By the way, Admiral Penrose has rather a lot of plant troughs cluttering his deck – and three very shame-faced passengers.'

'Three? George Godwin and Lottie Lorrelli?'

'Fortunately, George Godwin suspected nothing. Daniel Maddox's ship briefly docked at Falmouth and George Godwin was seen to step aboard. Either he was going to see the gold safely deposited or he was leaving with Maddox – though I rather think someone like George Godwin would stay and find some other way to steal.'

'Lottie Lorrelli was with him?'

Henry nodded. 'Dressed as a man. Admiral Penrose followed them out of the harbour and HMS *Circe* opened her gun ports – and there's not a lot you can do if one of His Majesty's finest frigates opens her gun ports and signals you to stop.'

The first sound of leather on willow; a round of applause. Henry held out his arm and we started walking back through the herb garden with the lavender spilling over the path, under the wrought-iron arch with the scent of honey-suckle, passing through Charity's rose garden with its heady perfume, stopping where we had stopped what seemed like a lifetime ago.

'Have you told your mother about the *Dolphin*?'

He nodded. 'And I've told your father. He listened very attentively this time – he even said he'd have done the same.' He smiled and I thought my heart would burst. 'Then he asked if there was some way I might reduce his harbour fees.'

I burst out laughing. 'He didn't! I hope you said no!'

'I said I'd *think* about it and I'd let him know.' He laughed and drew me to him, putting his finger under my chin, lifting it gently, and I looked into the glasses I loved so well. His eyes held mischief as I knew they would.

'You must know we're in great danger, Angelica.'

'Are we?' I whispered, every nerve tingling, every bone in my body weakening.

'The interference of woodland sprites can cause great mis-chief. They make their potions strong because they expect them to work. They like total enchantment, no half meas-ures.' His voice was soft, his eyes burning. 'Puck might be watching, Oberon and Titania fighting over you this very minute. I think I had better kiss you, Angelica...and I think I need to make it look real.'

Epilogue

Truro Theatre, High Cross, Truro

December 20th 1796

Dearest Angelica and Molly,

The performance starts at 7:30 p.m. Come round the back for 6:30. — Theo will be waiting.

Yours in anticipation,

Kitty Gilmore

20, High Street, Falmouth

December 21st 1796

Dear Lady Clarissa,

It gives me the greatest pleasure to accept your kind invitation to join you at the theatre on Saturday, and afterwards for a reception at Town House.

Yours sincerely,

Luke Bohenna

Perren Place, Pydar Street, Truro
December 22nd 1796

Dearest Lady Clarissa,

You are extremely kind, but my husband is insistent we pay for the new glasshouse. Do you think encasing it in wire might work this time? I look forward to seeing you on Saturday.

With warmest regards,
Mary Lilly

Trenwyn House, Trenwyn
December 23rd 1796

Dear Mrs Penhaligan,

I will not hear otherwise — in view of this snow, you must allow us to collect you tomorrow. My coach will arrive at six o'clock.

Yours in friendship,
Clarissa Carew

My planning had gone so smoothly. The whole family together for Christmas: Lady Clarissa would ensure Amelia and Luke spent the evening together and Mary had promised me Father would never know how much this new greenhouse cost.

The Love Poems of John Donne lay open in my hands and already I had them by heart; every line on every page, just like my dearest husband. A fire was blazing, the room warm despite the snow covering the streets outside. Henry took the book from me, blowing out the candle. His arms were warm, the pillow soft; moonlight streaming through the window.

Firelight flickered round the room, red shadows dancing across the ceiling. A loud purr rang from the bottom of the bed and tiny feet jumped on to the eiderdown, turning round in circles. I threw back the covers, and reached for my shawl.

'It's such a beautiful night, Henry. The moon's so bright and it's glinting on the snow...come and see.'

Henry shook his head, smiling as he followed me to the window. 'She's just where you left her, my love,' he whispered as we gazed down to the quayside. Our new ship, *Jane O'Leary*, shimmered in the moonlight and my heart leapt with joy.

'Mamma would be so proud,' I whispered as his arms closed round me.

The End

Acknowledgements

This is my fourth novel and I'd like to extend another, huge, thank you to my agent, Teresa Chris, and my editor, Sara O'Keeffe, and her talented team at Atlantic Books. Without them all, my books would not be the books they are. Thank you to my family and my friends, and especially my husband, Damian, who must sometimes wonder which century I am in.

A big thank you for reading my book; to my readers who write me such lovely messages, and to the book-blogging community who give of their time so generously. I do not include references in my books, but the history and inspiration behind my characters can be found on my website. www.nicolapryce.co.uk. Do follow me on Facebook if you would like to keep in touch. Nicola Pryce—Author.